MW00576186

AN INTRIGUE OF WITCHES

AN INTRIGUE OF WITCHES

Esme Addison

**SEVERN
HOUSE**

First world edition published in Great Britain and the USA in 2024
by Severn House, an imprint of Canongate Books Ltd,
14 High Street, Edinburgh EH1 1TE.

severnhouse.com

British Library Cataloguing-in-Publication Data
A CIP catalogue record for this title is available from the British Library.

ISBN-13: 978-1-4483-1261-0 (cased)
ISBN-13: 978-1-4483-1262-7 (e-book)

All Severn House titles are printed on acid-free paper.

Typeset by Palimpsest Book Production Ltd.,
Falkirk, Stirlingshire, Scotland.
Printed and bound in Great Britain by
TJ Books, Padstow, Cornwall.

Praise for Esme Addison

About the author

Esme Addison is the Amazon bestselling author of the Enchanted Bay mysteries, the first of which was nominated for an Agatha Award, and the brand-new Secret Society mysteries.

Esme lives in Raleigh, NC with her family and is a member of Sisters In Crime, International Thriller Writers, Mystery Writers of America and Crime Writers of Color. When she's not writing, you can find her reading, traveling, and indulging her love of history at museums and historical sites.

Twitter: @EsmeAddison
Facebook / Instagram / YouTube: @EsmeAddisonAuthor
esmeaddison.com

To my mother and father for their unconditional love and support.

To my children, thanks for not complaining that I spend too much time on my laptop writing.

To my dad, thank you for always filling our home with books. Thank you for always telling me I was a writer. For encouraging me to write and as a teenager to set a goal of becoming a published novelist. It's because of you that I grew up to be one.

I'm grateful you were able to see the cover of this book before you passed in November 2023 but sad that you will never be able to read it. All of our fun talks about history, fantasy, science fiction and conspiracies went into this story.

So dad . . . this one is for you.

The sceptre shall not depart from Judah, nor a lawgiver from between his feet, until Shiloh come; and unto him shall the gathering of the people be.

Genesis 49:10
King James Bible

ONE

My mentor watched me, her dark brown eyes apologetic. 'I've told them, no need to have security walk you out, but you do need to leave today. I'm sorry, Sidney.'

The door closed with a soft click, and I was left staring at the wall.

What did Dr Philippi mean? She'd said I'd been placed on furlough because of budget constraints. I took in a breath, trying to understand. The walls of my office seemed to shrink; the certificates of achievement, my diplomas, the books on the shelves all blurred to watercolor around me, a Monet of disappointment.

At the last department meeting, we'd been told our museum had a surplus of funding. But now they could barely make ends meet and I had to go? Like, right now?

I rose from my desk chair, ignoring the cardboard box the woman who'd guided my career since I'd been accepted into my doctoral program had so helpfully left for me. I went to my window and stared at the magnificent skyline of whitewashed Neoclassical buildings, my gaze finally landing on the Egyptian obelisk from the George Washington Monument.

I couldn't understand it. I'd just been the Smithsonian's darling, appearing on talk shows making American history look cool – their words not mine – and consulting for the History Channel on the latest Early American archaeological discoveries.

And then I'd traveled to western North Carolina, discovered what could only be described as an ancient Egyptian relic in a Native American mound . . . and basically been sacked for my trouble? I should never have shared my find with the lead archaeologist, who'd apparently gone running to his bosses the moment the relic left my hands. That's what this was about. Not budget cuts.

I'd expected a promotion. Senior Historical Consultant to the National Museum of American History sounded nice. More travel, more consulting in the field. A few podcasts and talk shows . . . But instead, I'd been forced to sign a non-disclosure agreement about what I'd found, been relegated to my desk for months, and now *this*.

My gaze went to the piece of paper on my desk. I was *regretfully required to take unpaid leave*? I reached for the paper, crumpled it into my fist and tossed it into the nearby trashcan.

Fine. They wanted me to leave after *Glamour* magazine just last year had called me the coolest historian in America? I yanked my desk drawer open and began grabbing pens and pencils. No problem. I could clean out my desk and be gone by end of business.

I'd almost filled up my box of belongings when I heard a soft knock. Frowning, I stalked to the door, wondering what other news my boss had to share, and jerked it open.

No one was there.

I stared into the empty hallway, my anger momentarily abated, then stepped out of my office and looked up and down the hallway. Empty.

I was just about to step back into my office when I looked down. To the right of my black pumps was a large, square envelope on the floor. My name was written across the front in beautiful calligraphy, reminiscent of old letters I'd seen in many an archive.

Calmer now, I picked up the envelope, turning it over in my hands. It was sealed with a glob of red wax into which the stamp of some sort of bird was imprinted. An owl, or a peregrine perhaps? I trailed my finger over the wax, charmed. *How antiquarian.*

Closing the door behind me, I returned to my desk, found a letter opener and ripped the envelope open. I read the text once, then flipped it over, looking for a name. There wasn't one. Strange.

I glanced at my box of belongings, then returned to the invitation. Someone was inviting me to visit Robbinsville, North Carolina, the location of my college. And they wanted me to find *something* for them. No mention of what that might be.

So much secrecy. What was it all about? And should I go? I had no idea who was inviting me and no clue what I was supposed to be finding.

I picked up the last item on my desk, a calendar, and chuckled, a quote from one of my favorite movies coming to mind. *It was Friday. I didn't have a job. I had nothing to do . . .* And every reason to accept this invitation. My gaze returned to the card. One million reasons, to be precise.

I picked up my box, gazed around my office – no, not my office, for the walls were bare, desk clean. No sign that it had ever belonged to me. And I headed for the door wondering how soon I could get a flight to North Carolina.

I'd gone to college in Robbinsville . . . and I knew someone there.

My grandmother.

And she was due a visit.

I breathed in the scent of honeysuckle as I stood on the porch of my grandmother's home, tiny butterflies fluttering in my stomach, wondering if I was doing the right thing.

Three days ago, I'd been in DC, hair in a bun, dressed professionally and feeling like I owned the world. But after packing my bags and closing up my townhouse, I was in North Carolina, and July was as hot and steamy as I remembered it.

My grandmother's home was a large farm home built in the early 1800s with a wide wraparound porch, white wood paneling and angular green roofs snuggled in the middle of a patch of green, a small portion of a twelve-acre farm. But her plot of land, where she lived, grew her kitchen garden and had chickens strutting around was two acres, fenced in with a pretty white picket fence. Beyond that was a large red barn and several fenced-in pastures that used to house both cows and horses.

My grandmother had been so welcoming when I'd called asking if I could come for a visit.

It felt good to be home.

Robbinsville wasn't actually *my* home. I'd grown up in Northern Virginia, but this place, this small town thirty minutes north west of New Bern, and lying along the Neuse River had always felt comforting to me.

My heart thumped against my chest, when I heard the muffled sound of feet coming towards the door. And then it swung open. My grandmother, a slight woman with wavy white hair pulled back into a tidy bun at the nape of her neck, pursed her lips, deepening the fine lines around her mouth.

A light-skinned black woman, her face was covered in freckles, as was mine. We also shared red hair, or we did until her hair had turned a coppery-brown while I was in college, before going the snowy white it was now. Achromotrichia, unfortunately, was the fate of all natural redheads. Hair follicles stopped producing the required pigment so that the hair simply lacked color.

I supposed that would be my fate too, unless I decided to dye my hair. At thirty years of age, I hoped I had plenty of time to deal with the loss of a hair color that had been both a blessing and a curse.

She planted her hands on her hips. 'Well, I will be.' Her mossy green eyes lit up and she opened the screen door. 'Come give your grammy a hug, darling.'

I stepped out of the humid southern heat and into the icy cold air of my grandmother Fiona's house, wrapping her in. It looked and smelled exactly the same. Of lemon-scented wood polish, moth-balls and lavender. I gave her a tight hug, careful not to crush her or the glasses that hung around her neck on a chain. Despite how strong I knew her to be, she felt so frail beneath her elegant white blouse and grey slacks.

As we hugged, I looked around the large living room. It looked exactly the same as I remembered. An eclectic mishmash of antique and modern furniture were arranged casually around a wood coffee table strewn with large glossy books, a decades-old *Ebony* magazine featuring my parents, glamorous and glittering in tux and gown, held up as an example of black excellency. An old *Newsweek* introducing the latest crop of US Representatives touted as the next big thing in politics, and a more recent copy of the local newspaper congratulating my father on becoming Speaker of the US House of Representatives.

I waited for my grandmother to break our embrace, and her gaze followed my own, which had landed on the periodicals, a visual timeline of the end of our family as I'd always known it. Prior to my father's political career we'd been a normal family. Dad was a lawyer, Mom worked in the news. Sure they'd been busy, but they'd been able to make time for us. That all changed when my mother became a national news anchor and my father, the voice of the American people.

My grandmother watched me, a hint of sadness on her lips. 'He loves you, you know.'

Yes, I knew he loved me. That was never in doubt. My father was a wonderful man. Loving. Supportive. He'd just ceased to be present in my life after he'd gone into politics. With his eye eventually on running for president, America was his top priority.

I tore my eyes from the covers, blinking away the memories, thoughts I hadn't lingered on in years. Returned to the present. To Robbinsville. To my grandmother.

She appraised me from head to toe, taking in my kinky-coily red curls barely contained by hair gel, leave-in conditioner and its ponytail holder. 'You know, I had a dream you'd come to visit me. I'd even prepared the guest room before you called.' She reached out and pushed a tendril of hair springing towards my face.

'I forgot about your dreams.' My grandmother had always said she saw things in her dreams that sometimes came true. I'm not sure anyone ever paid it any mind. But in this instance, she'd been correct. 'It's good,' I joked. 'You had plenty of time to prepare, right?'

She laughed with me. 'That I did. How was your flight?'

'Uneventful,' I said with a grateful sigh. If only my life flowed as easy as my trip down south from DC.

As if she read my mind, she shook her head. 'No more of those bad thoughts. You've left them behind, remember? It's why you're here.'

I forgot how I couldn't hide anything from her. I thrust thoughts of the drama at work from my mind, and swallowed the lump in my throat.

'Hmmm,' my grandmother said, as if she were considering whether to believe me or not. But then she gently pushed me towards the stairs. 'Take a shower, change and we'll have some refreshment. I made your favorite treat.'

I turned to the kitchen sniffing the air. 'You made your sweet potato bread pudding?'

She arched an eyebrow. 'I did.'

I crossed the room and gave her another careful hug. 'You're the best, Grams.' Her sweet potato bread was full of cinnamon, sugar and butter. And it was so good. So comforting, and just what I needed right now. I breathed in her familiar scent of lavender. 'I've missed you so much.'

'Me too, my sweet Sidney, me too. Now, go and freshen up.'

I picked up the several suitcases and valises I'd brought with me, and walked up the flight of stairs. The same end tables from my youth were on the second-floor landing filled with fresh flowers. A whimsical fairy door made of bark was attached to a corner of the wall, decorated with flowers and a little doorknob, giving the appearance that if you just pulled on the door, entryway to another world would appear.

I couldn't help but smile. My grams always had a love for plants, flowers and trees. And I assume that included the fairies that supposedly lived therein.

My gaze went upwards, to the large family portraits that lined the walls. There was a photograph of my parents on their wedding day, and I stepped forward to look at my mother. Despite my big, frizzy mane of red hair and freckles inherited from my paternal grandmother, I had my mother's brown eyes, nose and mouth. Most people said I looked like her, a black woman with thick, naturally curly hair that bounced around her shoulders and perfectly symmetrical features that added up to beautiful in any culture. But we couldn't have been more unalike.

There were also individual photographs of me and my sister, who took after my mother with her brunette coloring, taken at our debutante balls in frilly white princess gowns. My sister, excited to be dressed up, her dark brown eyes bright, her grin large. And me looking stiff and unhappy, probably feeling the stare of my mother on me urging me from the sidelines to look perfect. I stepped away from the photograph and the memories. Not today, Sidney. Not today.

I passed several closed doors and found the last on the right, the guestroom that had always been mine when we visited, and pushed open the door. The large white canopy bed that had made me feel like the heroine in a fairytale was still there, surrounded by a set of white pine furniture, a frothy pink comforter set with matching pillows.

Smiling, I twirled around the room, finally moving to the dresser. On top of it, just as I remembered, was an exquisitely crafted writing box, which I imagined was as old as the house. My fingers trailed the oiled wood, the intricate grooves that looped into pretty floral patterns, and I opened the box. It was meant to hold writing paper, journals and whatever else a writer might need, but it was still empty.

I'd always been intrigued by the pretty wooden box. What secrets did the box contain, the inquisitive little girl I used to be would wonder, making up great stories of circumstance and mystery during my summers spent here.

The box was an antique, museum worthy and a family heirloom. My grandmother liked to say it must've belonged to a spy who needed to hide papers. I never did discover its secrets, but perhaps that was why I'd gone on to become a historian, so I could discover secrets from the past.

Speaking of secrets . . . I glanced at my purse which I'd tossed onto the bed, its contents spilling out. The invitation was covered with my ring of house keys, a Fenty lip gloss and a small pot of cocoa butter. *How and when would I be contacted?*

After a shower and change of clothes, I felt wonderfully relaxed and floated down the hall for some of my grandmother's sweet potato bread – and a conversation I wasn't sure I was ready to have.

When our bellies were full and I couldn't eat another bite, my grandmother pushed her plate away and I knew the interrogation would begin in earnest.

She raised an eyebrow as she looked at me. 'Well, how long do you plan on staying?'

'Is there a limit?' I hedged. I could feel anxiety tightening my chest.

'Of course not, you can stay forever if you like.'

'That's probably too long,' I said with a quick smile, then gazed out of the window behind her. 'I just need a break.' I was careful to look away from my grandmother lest she discern I was telling a lie. When I was younger, I'd felt like she could practically read my thoughts.

'I thought I might stay a few weeks . . .' Hesitantly, I met her eyes. Would that be enough time to recover from being placed on furlough? Enough time to possibly find some *thing* for *somebody* . . .? Unless it was all a cruel joke or prank, in which case I'd just have a nice visit with my grandmother. Long overdue as it was.

'Well, I'm glad you're here. Sounds like just what the doctor ordered.' She leaned forward and patted me on my knee. 'I'm going to take good care of you. You just relax and write or read . . . whatever you want.'

'Thanks, Grams. I already feel better being here. And I'm so sorry it's been so long.'

She stood, plate in hand. 'Nonsense, my girl. I'll just . . .'

I stood too, taking the plates from her. 'I'll do the dishes.'

My grandmother handed me her coffee cup for washing. 'Your old bicycle's out back. Why don't you ride into town and get me a few things when you're done?' She pulled something out of her pants pocket and handed it to me. It was a handwritten grocery list and money neatly folded and clasped with a paperclip.

I thought of my old ten-speed bicycle, orange with a white basket on the front. How had that old thing not rusted into a heap of metal?

'I'm happy to go, Grams, but I've got money.' I handed her the bills back with a smile.

She pushed my hand back, also smiling. 'I'm planning a special dinner tonight. You remember where the general store is, yes?'

I looked at the list and smiled.

One whole chicken.

A bushel of collard greens.

A pound of carrots.

Some things never changed.

TWO

I pedaled down the long dirt driveway of my grandmother's home and turned onto Meadow Lane, the road dotted with large homes on even larger plots of land.

The air was redolent with wild blackberries and scuppernongs. Kudzu climbed up the trees on either side of me, flies and mosquitos buzzed around and the wind whipping past me was warm and wet. There was no traffic coming towards me or behind me, and I marveled at how freeing it felt to ride a bicycle alone on the road.

Robbinsville represented a lovely time in my life, particularly my undergraduate days when I'd attended Robbins College, twenty miles south of town. I'd been able to indulge my love of American history by working part-time in a living museum, where historical interpreters, experts on the character they represented or the era in which they lived, dressed in period costume, acted out the daily life of colonial North Carolina for museum patrons, at the same time educating them. It was like Colonial Williamsburg, but smaller, more intimate. As a history student, it had been the perfect job. And I'd been able to visit my grandmother whenever I wanted, which had been often.

Hard to believe that nine years had passed without me returning to visit my grandmother. I was suddenly filled with shame, realizing that the periodic phone calls, Facetimes, cards, Christmas and birthday gifts had not been nearly enough. But there was nothing I could do about it now, except to make up for the past. I'd spend as much time with her as possible while I was on furlough.

I turned off Meadow Lane and onto Main Street, the road that bisected the historic downtown district of Robbinsville. It was only one street of shops, three blocks long of Federal-style red brick buildings lined up on either side, but it was a tourist draw for the town. Visitors toured the colonial village, and then they walked up and down Main Street for a bite to eat, a refreshing libation, something to read and gift shopping.

I pedaled slowly as more cars filled the road and pedestrians crossed the street. Finally, I coasted onto the sidewalk, and parked the bike alongside the wall of a bookstore. The front window was filled with fiction and non-fiction about colonial and early American history, and I was happy to see they still focused on local lore. I was tempted to go inside and buy a few books, but I honestly wasn't sure I had the budget for it. I wasn't exactly poverty-stricken but I was in the process of paying off my debts.

That's why I'd been so disappointed about the furlough. I wasn't getting paid and, like most people, I had bills to pay. I should've rented in a less expensive neighborhood and had three roommates, but at my age and career juncture . . . Well, the truth is my parents are very successful and very, very wealthy. And people always think I am too.

Not true.

My parents were of the mind that their kids should earn their money and not live off their inheritance. After paying for my undergrad and doctorate, I'd been cut off financially, which would've been fine if I could've found work right away.

But, while living in one of the most expensive cities in the country, it had taken me two years to find a full-time job, because in DC everyone is qualified and everyone knows someone. I knew people too, but unlike many of the friends I'd gone to school with, I hadn't wanted my parents' help finding a job. And I'd suffered for it. After a string of freelance consulting gigs, I'd procured a low-paying research position – which helped, but not much.

I'd asked my parents for loans to help me but all I got was a compassionate smile, a 'no' and 'you'll thank us for this later'. I was still waiting for the gratitude to kick in. I'd applied for credit cards then, and maxed them out paying rent, buying groceries and keeping up appearances with the required wardrobe, bags and shoes – because looking good in DC was a necessity.

I tried to understand it but knowing my parents were millionaires but loath to give me a few thousand dollars to make life more bearable stung. Having been employed by the Smithsonian for the last two years, I'd almost paid off most of my debt, but just needed a bit more money and I'd be free and clear.

And that's the real reason why I'm in Robbinsville. If I can find whatever this treasure is for whomever it is that invited me?

I get one million dollars.

I looked up and down Main Street, taking in the tourists window shopping. I hadn't brought a bike lock, but Robbinsville wasn't the kind of place where people locked up anything, so I felt comfortable leaving the old bike unsecured on the sidewalk. But I wouldn't have dared tried this in DC even in the posh area I'd rented in, was still paying rent on.

I passed the bookstore and saw that the coffee shop that used to be located right next door had apparently been sold. The large glass windows were blacked out and there was a key code pad on the door which looked heavy and dark. A discreet sign hung above the door: QLabs. A cute sixties-style emoji of a robot, all square and smiley-faced served as a mascot.

I had to admit, a tech company on this street seemed out of place, but progress was progress and the more business brought to the town the better.

I kept walking, studying everyone that passed, wondering if he or she were the person who'd contacted me. And then I stopped at the Josiah Willoughby Museum. It was a narrow space filled with the belongings of one of Robbinsville's most famous former residents. Always intrigued by his story, I opened the door and stepped inside. Josiah Willoughby had been one of the very few freemen of color in Robbinsville during the colonial era, having come from a wealthy family known for their excellent cabinet making and furniture crafting.

This museum had in fact been his shop. The walls were brick and the floor spit-shined hardwood. The cool air smacked against my face, a welcome respite from the moist heat of the day. I was the only person in the museum. The faint sounds of classical music softened the silence, and the room smelled of a lemon wood oil.

On the walls were framed oil paintings of Josiah. In the most striking one, he must've been in his fifties or sixties. His face was lined and his curly black hair had grayed, but his dark brown eyes were bright and his grin, almost a smirk, lit up the painting. He sat at a desk with books stacked up neatly behind him.

If I recalled his story correctly, he'd learned cabinet and furniture making from his father who had a steady business of wealthy clients throughout North and South Carolina. In his free time, he'd taught himself to play the piano, often playing Schubert and Beethoven while he visualized his next piece of furniture.

He had surpassed his father's craftsmanship, creating works that governors and presidents had sought after. Even today his furniture was displayed in museums or purchased in private sales for hundreds of thousands of dollars.

I walked down an aisle reading the placards alongside some of his best works. A cabinet. A bureau. A secretary. A framed piece of sheet music, yellowed with age; it was Beethoven's Moonlight Sonata, which flowed from the speakers above, with notes for a chaise longue penciled in the margins.

His status as a freedman, during a time when people of color were discriminated against, wasn't the most interesting fact about Josiah Willoughby. Nor was the fact that several of his pieces of furniture were in the White House, the Smithsonian and several European embassies. No, what interested me was the work he did in the American Revolution. He'd reportedly been a much in demand cryptographer.

I paused to look at the next exhibit.

'Fascinating, isn't it?'

I jumped at the voice and turned around. A black man with a bronzed complexion, dreamy features, and golden-honey-colored eyes that sloped downwards at the corners, grinned at me. His curly dark hair was cut close. He was about six-two with broad shoulders and an athletic build. Maybe in his early thirties? And he was terribly handsome.

'Sorry,' he said. 'Didn't mean to startle you.'

I bit my bottom lip and could feel my forehead wrinkling. Where had he been all this time? I almost laughed – hiding behind a cabinet? 'Were you here the entire time?'

'No.' He chuckled, pushing his hands into the pockets of his khaki pants. 'I was in the back office taking a call. Saw you on our security monitor.' He moved towards the exhibit I'd stopped in front of and pointed to the descriptive text. 'My great-great-great-great-grandfather . . . the cabinet-making spy,' he chuckled.

I looked at him anew. 'You're a Willoughby?'

'At your service.' He doffed an imaginary hat.

'I didn't realize this museum was family-run. We have a Willoughby – rather my grandmother does,' I said.

His eyebrows lifted. 'Oh? Which piece?'

I frowned. 'I'm not sure . . . My grandmother has only ever called it the Willoughby writing box.'

'You have the writing box?' He chuckled. 'I've been searching for that piece for years.'

'Really? Why? I believe it was a gift . . .' I paused, trying to remember the story behind the heirloom. 'Actually, I'm not sure how my grandmother found it.'

'I was beginning to think one of those secret agent types at the Smithsonian had swooped in and taken it.' A dimple appeared. 'No matter. Mystery solved. Who is your grandmother?'

'Fiona Taylor. She lives off of—'

He crossed his arms over his chest, eyes narrowing as he inspected my hair and face. 'Mrs Taylor is your grandmother?'

'You know her?'

'I do.' He nodded. 'She's asked me to look at her car once or twice.'

'A museum curator *and* a mechanic?' I teased, feeling like a teenager.

'Not exactly, but I am good with my hands . . .'

I cocked an eyebrow. *Oh . . .*

'Well, at least I know where the writing box has been all this time. Safe and sound in your grandmother's house. That case is very special. It has a floral design ingrained on the sides, right?'

'Yes. A lotus. It's beautiful.'

'It was designed for a daughter.' He paused, his eyes searching mine thoughtfully.

Heat rushed to my cheek, and I looked away – saved by the bell. My cell phone chimed, and I retrieved it from the small tote criss-crossing my waist. It was a text from my grandmother. She wanted me to pick up a bottle of wine. Change of plans: company was coming.

'I have to run, but it was nice meeting you . . .?'

'Gabriel Willoughby.' He extended his hand, which I shook. 'Gabe to my friends.'

'And I'm Sidney Taylor. Nice to meet you.'

'Perhaps I'll see you around?'

I smiled despite myself. 'Perhaps.'

I could feel the heat of his stare on my back as I floated out of the museum on the languid ebb of the Moonlight Sonata.

When I came downstairs for dinner, freshly showered and changed into a yellow sundress and sandals, I heard a man's voice. The aromatic scents of fried chicken and the sweet herbaceousness of boiling collards curled in the air around me and led me to the formal dining room, which was now lit with low, warm light from the candelabra hanging over the long, rectangular table.

My grandmother, pretty in a simple dress, turned when I entered the room.

'Grandmother,' I said, rather formally in front of the guest. He was a short, stocky but fit man in his early fifties with matinee idol thick black hair. His wide shoulders stretched the fabric of his jacket. When he turned to smile at me, I saw gleaming white teeth framed by a thick mustache and neat beard. His brown eyes were warm.

I knew him, I realized.

'Sidney, you remember Abner Robbins, don't you?'

'Abner,' I said, warmly. 'How are you? It's been years.' Abner was the president and owner of the Robbins Early American Living History Museum & Village and a member of *the* Robbins family.

'Sidney, you're lovely as ever.' He came towards me and clasped my hand with his own. Close to, he smelled of wood and leather. 'It's so nice to see you after all this time. Your grandmother has been telling me about all you've done since you graduated from Robbins College and left your part-time job at the village.'

I blushed. 'That was a long time ago,' I said, a smile tugging at my lips. Based on his clothing choices, he was still as eccentric as ever. In a nod to his passion for history, he wore a dark blue three-piece suit tailored with meticulous detail, boasting rich mustard gold fabrics and an intricate brocade pattern. His waistcoat, adorned with elegant dark gold buttons, glistened in the light. A pristine white ruffled cravat encircled his neck, cascading down his chest in a river of delicate folds. His longish hair was pulled back into a low ponytail with a strap of dark blue ribbon.

I wasn't sure I'd ever actually seen him in contemporary clothing. At the museum, with almost all staff in period clothing, it seemed normal, but off the village grounds here in my grandmother's house it was quite strange. But, I thought with a suppressed giggle, Abner had always been a bit strange himself.

'And you're very accomplished, Dr Taylor. I've seen you on a few talk shows.'

I tried not to blush. 'Sidney is fine. And yes, I became the museum's go-to person for public appearances though being in front of the camera was not my thing. Very stressful, though I was assured the camera –' I made air quotes – 'loved my face.'

'Like your mother.'

'Yes, like my mother.' In high school, she liked to remind me, her nickname had been Black Barbie because she was so pretty. And a cheerleader. And the homecoming queen.

He grinned. 'How is she by the way?'

'Still anchoring the news and loving the limelight.' My tone was a bit brusque, and he took the hint to keep it moving.

'Well, you should be quite proud of yourself. Your grandmother certainly is.'

I looked at my grandmother. What was she up to? Why the fancy dinner? Why the guest? But she only smiled at me.

'I bet you miss rooting around in old places looking for artifacts.'

Artifacts. I threw him a quizzical look, but his expression remained the same. I looked at my grandmother who looked equally enigmatic.

'Pour yourself a glass of wine. Dinner's just about ready.'

After I'd refreshed myself with a lemony Sauvignon Blanc full of grass and pear notes and more small talk, we sat at the elegantly appointed table.

Abner sipped from his glass of mineral water with lime, observing me. When we made eye contact, he smiled. 'Sidney, how long do you plan on staying in Robbinsville?'

'I'm not sure.' I reached for a bottle of hot sauce and began sprinkling it over my greens.

'Well, what will you do when you leave? Are you returning to Washington, DC?'

The bottle of hot sauce froze in my hand. His questions were causing the muscles across my chest to tighten. I didn't want to explain my furlough. Who knew when I'd be back, if I'd even *be* back. I attempted a cheerful expression. 'Why do you ask?'

He exchanged amused glances with my grandmother, and I shoved several more bites of greens into my mouth.

'Honey,' my grandmother began, 'Abner has a proposition for you. Something that will help you keep your mind off . . . things.'

Great. She obviously knew something was up. I looked at Abner, suddenly embarrassed by my annoyance with his questions. I hoped my irritation hadn't been evident.

He grinned at me. 'We'd love to have you have back at the museum, Sidney.'

Momentarily stunned, I set my fork down. 'In what capacity?' I looked from him to my grandmother and back to Abner. 'I haven't been there in—'

'Years.' My grandmother answered for me and then stood. 'I'm going to check on the apple pie.'

I watched her leave before turning back to Abner. 'You'd want me to be . . . a historical interpreter?' I tried to imagine myself returning to my previous role of an indentured servant selling produce at the village market, teaching history to tourists. I'd loved every minute of it, but I couldn't see myself being in that role now.

'Interpreter?' he repeated with a laugh. 'No, unless you want to?' He speared a sliver of honeyed carrot with his fork. 'I need your help. Considering your success with finding or rather identifying lost artifacts . . . You found an Egyptian artifact in a mound in the western part of the state, yes?'

I laughed to hide my confusion. 'That has been kept very quiet.'

'I know. But I donate a lot of money to the Smithsonian. At my level of donation they tell me about interesting finds. Things that may not be publicly announced for twenty or fifty years?' He lifted an eyebrow. 'Or maybe never.'

'Maybe never is right.' There was a growing pool of archaeological evidence that ancient Egyptians had been in North and South America, but the mainstream museums weren't sure how to position that information in the current historical narrative. For now, you'd have to go to YouTube to find amateur historians discussing it.

'So, you want me to find . . . an artifact?' *Wait.* I lowered my voice. '*You* invited me here?'

He cocked his head, as if he were deciding how to respond. He glanced towards the kitchen, as if he wondered if my grandmother could hear him. 'Yes. I sent the invitation. And you're here. You've accepted? Or are you just visiting your grandmother?'

'Let's just say both. I'm dying to hear more. What can you tell me? And why the secrecy?'

'Something is hidden. And I want it found.'

'What's hidden? Who hid it?' My questions tumbled out. 'And are you truly prepared to pay me a million dollars if I find it?'

He shook his head like he was admonishing a cheeky toddler. 'Not so fast.' He laughed. 'But I'm glad you're interested. I thought you might be when I did a little digging and found out you weren't receiving the appreciation you deserved at work.' His expression was grim. 'A victim of budget cuts. You? Their media darling.'

I blinked. 'How do you know about that?'

He leaned back against his chair, ignoring my question. 'I'm hoping you'll stay. I could use someone of your caliber. Your talents and special skills will be valued here.'

I didn't know how to respond. I wasn't quite ready to give up on my dream of making it big in DC and in the museum world. My hope was to find the artifact, collect my money, pay off my debts and return to DC in a blaze of triumph. I was determined to show my supervisors I deserved more respect and a permanent position. 'We'll see.'

'You didn't say no,' he observed. 'It's a start. Now, finding the artifact is of the utmost urgency. We need it, now more than ever.'

There was an edge to his voice that quieted my inner snark. Who was *we*? His family, the museum's board of directors? 'What can you tell me about the artifact?'

'It begins with a conspiracy of very powerful men. Of course, you know about Josiah Willoughby's work in the American Revolution?'

I nodded, thinking of Gabe. 'I stopped by his museum today.'

'Not only a highly sought-after craftsman for the rich and powerful, Josiah was also a skilled cryptographer who encoded letters and hid documents for Presidents and leaders in the Patriot movement. Josiah overheard women talking . . .'

He lowered his voice, as if someone might be lurking in the shadows. 'Women who worked in the household of men, the kind of men who ran governments . . . and plotted. He discovered a conspiracy to overthrow the newly founded American government, just as we were rebuilding from the war with England. He relayed the information to the most powerful man he knew: President James Madison, who was also a customer.'

I leaned forward, my stomach flipping with excitement. 'Madison,' I repeated. Beads of sweat moistened my hairline. 'Really?' He couldn't possibly know I'd written my graduate thesis on President James Madison and consulted on several archaeological digs at his property in Montpelier, in the mountains of Virginia.

'You're a noted Madison scholar, yes?'

Or perhaps he did. 'It's been a while since I've done any work related to him, but earlier on in my career? Absolutely. And he would've trusted Madison . . . I know from my own research that he was a strong supporter of the union, and that he worried – no, obsessed would be more accurate – about spies and conspiracies to undermine the country.'

'He had every right to worry. But these women also knew of an artifact, something apparently with the power to stop these men.'

'Wait . . . What are we talking here?' I laughed. 'Magical beans? The Holy Grail?' I suddenly felt like I was the butt of a joke. 'This all sounds a bit far-fetched, you have to know that.' *Please don't tell me I came all the way down here thinking I was going to get paid to find a real archaeological treasure . . .* I leaned back in my chair and crossed my arms.

'I see you think I'm . . . what? Pulling your leg? I promise you, this is all very real. Granted, I don't know what I'm looking for, but I do know how to find it. Rather, I know how *you* can find it.' He pressed his lips together. 'Josiah and Madison corresponded on the matter, and a secret plan was hatched to be implemented when Madison visited Robbinsville. He stayed in what's now the museum with my ancestor, Elias as host.'

'What's in the letter?'

'Josiah asked Madison to write a letter that appeared to only discuss ordinary topics, but in reality held clues to the location of the artifact. Elias then placed the letter in our library's Madison collection, which is overseen by our librarian, Daphne De Costa, to be revealed at the right time.'

'And that time is . . . now? Why?'

'Men like Josiah and Madison were forward-thinking.' His dark brows dipped into lines of concern. 'They knew there was a threat that would simmer and fester for as long as it took. And we were to wait before we revealed our hand . . .'

I frowned at his words. What could he possibly be referring to?

His expression cleared, and he leaned forward, gently grasping both of my hands. 'You're to read the letter and decode the clues that Josiah hid in plain sight. Every clue leads to another. And once you've decoded the entire letter, you'll find the artifact.'

THREE

'Even if this is true, and I'm not saying I believe you . . . How is this imagined *plot* relevant now? Two hundred years is a long time ago. And the republic is as sound as ever.'

His eyebrows raised. 'Is it?' He gave me a rueful grin. 'Something may still be brewing. Now. Here. In our time.'

I couldn't hide the skepticism on my face.

'Doesn't the world feel like it's being steered in the wrong direction? Like one minute, the world was normal and in a blink of an eye we're in a science fiction movie?'

I knew what he was referring to. It was in all the media reports. But it couldn't possibly be related. The current administration was pushing for a future where we all worked and played in a virtual reality. It didn't seem real, and yet all the news was talking about was how we'd moved straight from the Information Age to the Quantum Age, with the dawn of AI and VR.

I was fine with the Information Age, for the record, but I didn't feel so strongly that I needed or wanted to do something about it. But perhaps I just didn't believe all things the news reporters – including my mother – were discussing were truly going to happen.

'You can't be on board with what the current administration is trying to do,' Abner said. 'The president is trying to usher in a new era, one of AI, digital currency and virtual reality.' He laughed. 'And it's not even the president. You know that, right? He's a puppet. It's the people behind him pulling the strings. They're the problem.'

I sighed. Whomever *they* were. 'Yes, it's hard not to hear talk in DC,' I admitted. 'But he's very nice,' I hedged. President Edward J. Williamson seemed like a good person with sincere intentions. I'd met him twice at Smithsonian functions.

Despite his affinity for being photographed in jeans, a plaid shirt and posing with an ax and a stack of logs – his family had made their fortune in the logging industry – he seemed obsessed with ushering America into a new era where everything and everyone was online, going so far as to create new legislation in his first two years in office urging both business and citizens to spend more time in the virtual space.

A segment of the population loved his ideas, but many did not and thought lobbyists and donations from tech giants were behind it all. In fact, thanks to the media's focus on the subject, they were integral in the growing divide in America with two groups forming. Those who wanted to live in virtual reality and those that did not.

It was a weird time, honestly.

'He's trying to destroy life as we know it!' Abner said. When I hesitated, he frowned. 'Come on. The Digital Reality Access Act he's trying to push through Congress? That's reasonable to you?'

'Of course not. I'm concerned . . . I suppose I assumed someone would do something about it.' The vice president had been very vocal about his opposition to the act though nothing had come of it yet. And, I supposed, a modern-day conspiracy to destroy the republic wasn't unthinkable. As a historian, I knew that better than anyone. The Burr Conspiracy? The Nullification Crisis? The Business Plot? Some people favor the long game . . .

I sighed. Repeated myself. 'Yes, I'm concerned.'

'Thirty years ago, a young woman, a student named Marta De Verona published the Foundational Acts for Digital Reality Integration as her thesis paper. She later shared it publicly as a think piece on where she thought our society as a whole should be by the year 2050. It included ten pieces of legislation that need to be on the books before governments could begin a full-on virtual reality integration. We're still over two decades and some change away from their deadline, but they're making serious headway. De Verona doesn't just have a doctorate in quantum physics, she's also completed a Masters of Public Administration in Public Planning and Policy.'

'She's a famous person, Abner. Lauded in DC circles. I know her bio.'

'But she clearly has prepared herself to restructure our society. Did you know she was born in Robbinsville?'

'No, I've never heard that.'

'It's not widely known. She was born here but moved away at a young age. Not something I'm proud of, I can tell you that much.'

'This is all fascinating, but respectfully . . .' Respectfully, because I didn't want to annoy the man who might hand me a check for a million dollars. 'I know most people consider De Verona to be a highly intelligent but eccentric personality like Elon Musk or Steve Jobs. Interesting but harmless in the grand scheme of things.' Why were we even talking about this? It wasn't getting me any closer to understanding how I could find this artifact.

'Not harmless. Twenty years ago, she moved to Columbia, married a coffee plantation billionaire, and then established an institute, presenting her ideas to thought leaders, politicians and corporate CEO. The organization flew under the radar for a while, until ten years ago when she moved her headquarters to Washington DC after the death of her husband.

'She rebranded as the Global Virtualization Conference, an annual meeting of the most important and influential people on the planet discussing their dystopian sci-fi version of the future. The GVC received a designation as an international body like the UN five years ago. Marta might have stepped down from chairing the conference recently, but we know where she is today. How much power she has. Those ten Foundational Acts for Digital Reality Integration she wrote about as a college student . . .?'

'Marta De Verona and her ten acts are all over the news,' I agreed. 'President Williamson followed England, New Zealand, Australia and China in creating cabinet positions on integrating virtual reality into our societies at a federal level. He's just being competitive though.' I studied Abner's look of incredulity. 'No?'

'No. Absolutely not. All these countries are blindly following her game plan for the future. I've read all of her books on the coming virtual reality revolution. Many times. Took notes.' He leaned forward, his face flushing. 'Committed parts to memory. Her books are instructional guides, and these countries are just falling into line. I mean, when we're doing the same thing as China somebody should be concerned.'

'I'll admit I'm not as well-read as you obviously are on Marta and what she's been up to for the past decade or so. My view of her has generally been one of admiration. She's a woman making waves. She's super-smart and carving a path for herself in a new industry. When I hear her name, I know she's on the forefront of new ideas and technologies . . . that's about it.'

'Did you hear she's predicting the development of a new religion

centered around an AI? There's a company right now working on
a software program that replicates religion for the masses.'

My chest tightened. I missed a lot not watching the news and
participating in social media. 'I didn't hear that.'

He smirked. 'She's a major shareholder.'

'OK, I get it. She's evil incarnate and she wants to use virtual
reality to control mankind.' He frowned at my tone, but I couldn't
help myself. 'I think I saw this on the Science Fiction Channel.'

'Be that as it may, that is exactly what she wants to do.'

Neither of us spoke. He wore his frustration like a red cape, and
I couldn't hide my skepticism.

'You may think this is some sort of joke, but I'm doing my part.
I have a museum that reminds people – or should remind people
– of how and why America was founded. We offer classes for patrons
to learn heirloom skills: blacksmithing, leather-making, broom-
making, candle and soap-making, canning and the like. These skills
should not die out, you know?'

'I know.' Then I laughed. 'I just read a study that said teenagers
rather play a game about baking cakes than actually making them.'

He rubbed his temples and sighed. 'That's exactly the fight I'm
fighting. Trying to keep people grounded on planet Earth, not
plugged into a matrix where they play life like a game with in-app
purchases that make the fat cats richer.'

Any minute now and Abner, who was probably richer than both
my parents combined, would be talking about The Man and how
he was holding him down. I suppressed a giggle. Sometimes Abner
was so . . . extra. Could I actually take a man wearing a perfectly
tied cravat seriously?

'And this artifact that you can't tell me about?'

Sweat was dripping down his cheeks. He pulled out a monogrammed handkerchief and mopped his face. 'Will stop her. It will
stop them all.'

FOUR

shifted uneasily in my seat.

He was as serious as a heart attack. I needed to respect that. I wasn't laughing, but I also wasn't quite drinking the Kool-Aid. 'This sounds suspiciously like a conspiracy theory. You sure you haven't been spending too much time on YouTube and TikTok?'

He didn't even crack a smile.

Yeah . . .

Despite the early American wardrobe and impassioned pleas to return to a simpler time, Abner was well respected in the community, and a longtime friend of my grandmother, but . . . was he sending me on a wild goose chase? 'You think this is how the government will be overthrown? By VR? *This* is what Josiah Willoughby was worried about?'

'It's already happening, isn't it? We have a shadow government and a bobblehead for a president. It can only get worse.' Sweat was springing up on his face again.

I held up my hand. 'I think you should calm down. You're getting worked up.' There was no way a man from the 1800s had foreseen a VR revolution. And I had zero confidence that Abner was onto anything legitimate. But there was a million dollars on the line . . . I glanced towards the kitchen, wondering if my grandmother had put him up to this. I was just about to ask when the look on his face stopped me.

'You can't tell anyone what you're actually doing.' He gave me an ominous look. 'No one.'

'Sorry?'

'At the museum, you'll have to be there for . . . another reason while you're conducting your search.'

'What about Gabe Willoughby? I just met him, and he's a descendant of—'

'No, not even him,' he warned.

I leaned forward. 'Why?'

'It's complicated and a long story, much of which you don't need to find the artifact. You mustn't trust anyone. You need to be aware that others may be trying to find the artifact . . .' He paused. 'And they may take extreme measures to reach it first.'

Seriously? There were other people that believed this story? A weird feeling danced in my belly. 'I have to fight people for the money?'

'No, not exactly . . .' He inclined his head. 'However, there may be some who try to stop you from finding it. Stop anyone from finding it. It's why the artifact has been hidden for so long.'

'Excuse me?' A nervous chuckle floated between us.

But he only nodded, face growing even more somber by the minute. 'But that's only if word gets out about the search to the wrong people. So . . . it would be better for everyone involved if you conduct your work in secret.' His look was almost apologetic. 'It's for your own good.'

'So, I'm to be at the museum with . . . a cover?'

'Yes, I suppose so.'

'And what do I say when a museum employee asks me why I'm wandering about the grounds with a shovel?' I jested, but still . . .

He chuckled. 'Not to worry. I've thought of that. What you need is just enough work to look busy but still allow you to search for the artifact.' He gave me a meaningful look. 'I thought you might provide cover for one of my staff on maternity leave. You'd be in a supervisorial role that would include managing our team of inter- preters. You used to be one. You'll be in charge of hiring and sched- uling the interpreters work shifts, supervising their per- formance and overseeing their training.' He shrugged. 'Sasha's been out for two months and scheduled to return in two weeks.' He cleared his throat. 'And you've got fourteen days to find the artifact.'

Two weeks to find an artifact? *Sure. No problem.* Adrenaline was already coursing through my body.

I tried to imagine returning to the museum, not as a college student but as a member of the staff. 'Has it changed much? The village?'

Abner laughed. 'Of course not. It's a museum. We live in the past.' The right side of his mouth quirked upwards. 'I'm pleased you accepted my offer. I wasn't confident you would. I know you come from money, so money couldn't be a motivation for you, and yet I thought a million dollars might pique your interest.' His gaze softened on me. 'I've followed your career ever since you graduated.'

'Why?'

He shrugged. 'You're a Robbinsvillian. Daughter of our most famous son, a US representative. Unlike Marta De Verona, I'm proud of you. Many of us are.'

My cheeks warmed. 'I haven't done anything special. That's my parents.'

He gave me a hopeful look. 'So, you want to come by in the morning and take a look?'

'Of course.'

'There's just one more thing.' He paused. 'The clues in the letter may take you on something of a . . .' He paused, trying to find the word. 'Treasure hunt.'

'What do you mean?'

'The clues to the artifact were hidden by Josiah Willoughby in the same way he hid military and government secrets during the war. Strange locks. Hidden compartments. Odd symbols, special devices . . . Nothing you can't handle, right?'

'Abner, I'm a historian. Yes, I've been on many an archaeological dig and I do love a good puzzle, but I'm not sure I'm up to decoding anything Josiah Willoughby encoded.'

'If I recall correctly, weren't you the president of the Robbins College Escape Room club?'

'How do you even know that?' I scoffed. 'That was so long ago . . .' But yes, I'd taken over as president my sophomore year and managed the group for the rest of my time at school. Even taken us to the national competition twice, though we'd never brought home a championship.

'I think you'll find you're more than qualified. It's why I sent you the invitation. You're uniquely qualified for this job.'

'Why didn't your ancestor, Elias, leave the location of the artifact for prosperity? For you?'

'Three can keep a secret if two are—'

'Dead,' I finished for him. 'I'm aware of the Benjamin Franklin quote.'

'Then you'll understand why Josiah didn't share the location of the artifact he hid with Madison or Elias.'

I chewed on that for a minute, wondering if Josiah had left information for Gabe. 'May I see the letter?'

'Of course. It's in the museum's library. You'll go there first thing Monday morning.'

I nodded, my excitement growing. 'Do you have any Josiah

Willoughby furniture at the museum? If so, maybe he hid the artifact inside.'

Abner tipped his head modestly. 'We do have a few pieces. He was a respected friend of my great-great-great-grandfather's and one of his most loyal customers. But we've examined every piece of furniture we own that was crafted by him. Nothing. I assure you, it all begins with the letter in the library. It is your roadmap to the artifact.'

Josiah had been a genius. Alongside his woodwork, Josiah created complex puzzles and devices in which secret messages of all kinds were hidden. And he'd hidden clues to an artifact?

I couldn't wait to get started.

FIVE

A fter dinner, coffee and lemon sorbet on the screened-in porch, Abner stepped outside to take a phone call and I cornered my grandmother.

'Did you have anything to do with Abner's invitation?'

'I only mentioned to him that the last time I spoke to my beautiful, intelligent and very talented granddaughter on the phone, she said how underappreciated and undervalued she felt at work. He came up with the idea all by himself.'

I narrowed my eyes as I studied her. She knew about the treasure hunt? 'The idea to . . .'

'Work at the museum, of course. Temporarily.' She patted my arm. 'You need to spend time with your family. Reconnect with who you are.'

OK, so she didn't know . . .

Abner returned with apologies. 'My social media manager. Trying to nip a potential PR crisis in the bud.'

'Oh?' I grinned. 'A social media war brewing with Colonial Williamsburg?'

He chuckled. 'I wish.' His lips twisted into a frown. 'No, there's a YouTuber, an expert on King James the first, and his work *Daemonologie*, who's constantly posting nonsense videos about how a hanging we had here hundreds of years ago is related to King James' obsession with finding all the witches in Scotland.'

King James was outside of my area of study, but I was familiar with the treatise the king had written before he interestingly enough ordained his version of the Bible. In *Daemonologie*, the king shared his views on witchcraft, demons, and the supernatural in his kingdom.

I'd taken a class in undergrad, in which we looked at King James' work and how it had impacted views of witches in colonial and early America. It had been significant, fueling the prevailing belief in witchcraft and the devil's influence, and leading to a heightened fear of witches.

I'd been horrified to read how this fear contributed to the persecution and execution of numerous women accused of witchcraft, as authorities saw them as threats to society. The ideas presented in *Daemonologie* were used to justify these witch hunts and provided a theological basis for the persecution of those believed to be involved in occult practices. Many people knew about the King James version of the Bible, but not so much *Daemonologie*.

'It's YouTube. Maybe no one will take him seriously.'

'Yes, but he's also a professor of British history and a bestselling author. So, I'm pretty sure someone is taking him seriously.'

'What's the name of his book?' I said, suddenly curious, an idea forming.

'I don't have it committed to memory,' he said somewhat peevishly. 'But I can look the ill-mannered buffoon up.' He was on his phone searching. 'Ahh, here we go: *Witchcraft and Belief Systems in Colonial America*.'

I laughed. 'Pretty sure that's the book I read in college. I had a class with a visiting professor. Professor . . . Chapp? No – Sharp.'

Abner's face twisted like he smelled sour milk. 'Yes, that's his name. Well, you'll see him around town then. I've yet to see him with my own eyes, but reportedly he's continuing his research and generally being a nuisance.'

'*Is* there a connection to Robbinsville?'

'Absolutely not. And that's the problem. He just makes up garbage to share with his fans. And now I hear he's looking for time portals and signs of fairies on the property or something like that.'

'Fairies?' my grandmother asked, an amused look on her face.

Abner threw up his hands. 'What are you going to do?'

My grandmother chuckled. 'I've only heard good things about fairies.'

Abner shrugged, then bowed courtly towards my grandmother and then looked at me. 'I hope to see you at the village Monday morning? Say around ten?'

'Yes, I'll be there with bells on,' I assured him.

SIX

The next day, a warm and sunny, lazy Sunday, was spent with my grandmother.

I got reacquainted with her farm. The flowers, the gardens, the berry bushes. Rediscovered the fairy gardens my grandmother had always hidden in her flower plots. I think I'd found all of them.

And then we were in the kitchen. I watched my grandmother batter fried chicken, but I didn't partake because I don't eat meat. I helped her bake biscuits, snapped green beans that were roasted with rosemary from the garden along with freshly picked potatoes, and gathered lettuce, tomato, cucumber and basil for a simple salad.

We ended the day with glasses of sweet sun tea on the porch, with me watching my grandmother embroider sunflowers on a handkerchief.

With all that fresh air and sunshine, I slept like a baby.

Monday morning, bright and early after a hearty breakfast, I dressed in capris, a seafoam green shell of silk and tied my hair back into a messy-on-purpose bun, since I'd be riding my old bike into town.

My grandmother was waiting for me by the front door when I headed out. She gave me a kiss on the cheek.

'Thanks, Grams. I'll be back soon.' I hopped on my bike, waving to a farmhand leading a beautiful chestnut brown mare to the stables, and pedaled down the driveway.

After I'd rode past Main Street, I turned right onto Robbins Way, the long stretch of road that led to the Robbins House, a large sprawling brick home with black shutters and roof. White columns decorated the wide sweeping porch, and a white balcony festooned the second floor.

The home was enclosed by a wrought-iron and brick wall. The

grounds were perfectly manicured, crisscrossed with brick laid walk-
ways, large shade-giving oak trees and rose gardens. The home
included a museum on the first and second floor, and the administrative offices of the property and the charitable foundation that ran
the museum plus a ballroom for special events.

I wiped drips of sweat already forming on my forehead in the
moist morning air, thick as molasses and hot as Nashville hot sauce.

A modern parking lot, with restrooms and a café were on the
property directly to the house's left and I found a spot for my bike
there, before walking into the house. The museum had just opened,
and the parking lot was already half full, I noted. I opened the door.
The greeter, an older woman in period dress with an infectious grin
welcomed me holding a tray of water filled with peppermint.

'Welcome to Robbins House,' she said, with a drawl and a slight
curtsy. 'I'm Zadie. Please have some refreshment.'

I took a cold glass from her and sipped. It was ice cold and so
refreshing. 'Thank you.'

'Is this your first visit?' Zadie was probably a few years older
than me with a walnut-brown complexion and enquiring brown eyes
framed by thick dark eyebrows and an infectious grin.

'No, I've been here many, many times. But thank you. I'll just
wander around a bit.'

When I was last here, the character of Zadie – a real servant that
worked in the home during post-colonial times – had been played
by another woman, but she'd worn the same costume: a bright
yellow dress decorated in purple paisleys with a high neck, white
trim and full billowing sleeves. She wore a yellow head wrap to
match. Frizzy tendrils of dark hair escaped the wrap and framed
her angular face.

Each character had a story, a history that stayed the same, but
the re-enactor was interchangeable.

'I just wanted to introduce myself,' she said now. 'My real name
is Reba. Reba Jeffries. It's a pleasure to meet you.' She reached for
my hand and held it tightly.

A feeling of warmth ran up my spine, and I immediately felt
comfortable with her. I knew in that instance she and I could be
good friends.

'I know who you are. I've seen you on *American History Today*,'
she said.

'That's right.' I grinned, pleased that she knew.

'I teach American history at the community college part-time, and we watch the show as part of our curriculum.' She leaned in and lowered her voice. 'It's always nice to see one of our own doing well.' She winked and elbowed me like we shared a secret.

I returned her smile. 'I'll be in charge of schedules, and generally managing the interpreters, so if you need anything just let me know.'

'Since you're so good at finding lost things, maybe you can solve a mystery for me,' she asked.

Did she know about the missing artifact? 'What would that be?' I asked.

'The case of the missing painting.' She chuckled. 'I want somebody in this big ol' house to explain to me how they got every member of the Robbins family on the walls here, except the main man himself.'

'Elias?'

'Yeah. It's a real mystery. Ain't it?'

I nodded, recalling that when I'd worked here we often had to field questions on what Elias may have looked like. 'It is that. Yes . . . If I stumble upon it, you'll be the first to know.'

I moved out of the foyer and into the formal sitting room directly to the left. It was filled with requisite period furniture crafted of mahogany. Blue Persian rugs decorated with peacocks covered the floor, and paintings of pastoral scenes lined the walls.

I dipped inside the gift shop directly to the right of the foyer, in one of several formal sitting rooms, and began wandering through the items. I was hoping to find a candle or a jar of preserves to send my sister, Aislin, when I heard an ear-splitting squeal behind me.

'Sidney, is that you?' This was said with the deepest of Southern accents.

I turned around and regarded an attractive young woman with long, pale, blonde hair and blue eyes. She wore a sundress and high-heeled sandals and had a pair of mirrored sunglasses in her hand. 'Sidney Taylor, as I live and breathe – it *is* you!'

Her voice rose even louder if that was possible, and several visitors to the museum turned to look at us curiously. And while I felt like I *should* know her, I couldn't exactly place the face.

She crossed the few yards between us and wrapped her arms tightly around me. Her scent of very sweet fruit and hints of vanilla enveloped me. 'It's *me*, Bessie Montgomery.' She pulled back and looked at me with wide expectant eyes.

Bessie Montgomery? As in my best friend from undergrad? But

Bessie Montgomery had short, curly, brown hair, was sixty pounds overweight, and wore both glasses *and* braces.

I gently peeled her arms off my shoulders. 'You look nothing like the Bessie I remember,' I said, unsure of what to say next. Because even her voice and personality were different. Bessie from college was quiet, a little meek, really.

But she only squealed again. 'Right? So, I got Lasik, and I got my braces taken off, teeth bleached.' She presented me with a wide perfect grin. 'And I've been getting Japanese straightening for the last seven years.' She tossed her hair over her shoulders, and I was gifted with the scent of apples and pears. 'And I bleached my hair.' She teased out a strand and showed it to me. 'Moonlight Blonde, it's called. Isn't it gorge?'

I stared at her, trying to find the mousy introverted girl that I'd lived with and studied with and worried about boys with. Whoever this girl was, it appeared she'd eaten the old Bessie and swallowed her whole. 'You're literally a brand-new person.'

'Exactly.' She stabbed the air with a gelled, French-manicured finger. 'You have no idea how hard I've worked to be somebody totally different.'

A rush of memories washed over me. We'd met at freshmen orientation and immediately felt like kindred spirits. She'd been sweet, sincere but with low self-esteem. 'But I liked the old you.'

'Did you?' She shrugged. 'Well, you were the only one, then. So, I haven't heard from you in years. What happened? I thought we were going to stay in contact? I was supposed to come see you in DC, remember?'

I did remember. I'd planned to call her to come visit me when I was settled in, but when I arrived . . . Honestly, I didn't think she'd like DC. She was too quiet, frightened of her own shadow, introverted. But I couldn't tell her that; instead, I said, 'I know. I'm sorry about that. I lost touch with a lot of people after I moved.' Which was true. I'd made all new friends once I got there. 'It's a crazy place. Kind of overwhelming.'

'It's fine. I get it. I'm *so* kidding.' Her hands covered her heart. 'We went through so much, remember?'

Yes, I did remember. Unrequited loves, difficult professors, playing wingman at college parties, the village. We'd both worked at the museum together. Pretended to churn butter and make candles together for the visitors. That made me smile.

'So, are you still living in Robbinsville? What do you do?' I asked.

'Oh. I have the best job.'

I stared at her, wondering at her level of enthusiasm.

'I work here – at the museum.'

'That's great. So, are you married? Have kids?'

She wrinkled her nose. 'No and no. I'm still having fun, enjoying the new me. Not trying to get tied down. Not for a while.'

'Well, wow. It's been amazing running into you. I'll be at my grandmother's only for a few weeks, and I'll be pretty busy, but maybe I'll see you around?'

'Pish posh. We can get coffee. Every day if we want.'

'Speaking of which, what happened to the coffee shop on Main?'

'It was purchased by one of those companies that received a virtual reality initiative grant from the government. You heard about them?'

I shook my head. 'Seriously? VR has reached small-town North Carolina?'

Bess laughed. 'I know, an odd mix with all of our early American history.' She brought out her cell phone again. 'Let's exchange numbers. I don't want to lose you again.' She made a pouty face. 'Let's get together soon. OK? We can be besties again.'

For the few weeks that I was going to be here? 'Sure.'

'Oh, and it's just Bess now. Not Bessie.'

We exchanged numbers. I thought of Bessie, the old Bessie I'd known in college. It was remarkable how much she'd changed. Including her name.

I left the gift shop and wandered around the rest of the first floor, visiting the formal dining room, the study, and another larger sitting room with a shiny black grand piano. I was trailing my fingers across the back of the piano, when I heard my name called again.

Abner was standing in the entrance of the room, dressed in charcoal gray breeches, black tights, light blue dress shirt, black overcoat with large gold buttons and a navy-blue cravat.

This guy lived and breathed history.

'There you are. Come with me.' He offered his arm in a courtly manner. 'Let me show you to your office. And then you can take your meeting with Daphne.' He gave me a pointed look. 'In the library.'

After a brief tour of the museum's administrative wing, breakroom, bathroom and conference room, and a brief meet and greet with the men and women I'd be supervising, Abner led me to my office, a spacious room with a large window overlooking the gardens. The room was furnished with a large ash-grey desk, comfortable green leather chair, and walls lined with bookshelves filled with books, artworks and the previous owner's photographs. In the corner was a table with two chairs for work sessions. The walls were filled with watercolors of the grounds.

It would do.

I stored my things into a locked cabinet, logged into my computer for the first time and made sure my passwords worked. I checked the clock on the wall. Time to go.

The library was a short cobblestoned walk from the main house. It was another charming former brick cottage, one story with black shutters and roof with brick stairs leading to a landing with a bright green door.

Icy refrigerated air hit me immediately when I walked inside, along with the comforting smell of old books and lemon-fresh cleaning supplies. The carpet was thick and muffled our steps as a library assistant led me past the circulation desk, several conference rooms and finally to a room marked Special Collections.

A petite bespectacled woman waited for us inside the large room lined with bookshelves and filled with glass display cabinets, her arms wrapped tightly around her chest as if she were freezing. Her caramel blonde curls were pulled back into a low ponytail, and she wore a long navy-blue skirt, white blouse and a soft olive-colored cardigan. Her name tag identified her as Daphne De Costa, *Librarian*.

She thanked the assistant and greeted me. 'It's so nice to finally and formally meet you. I've heard so much about you from Abner.'

I shook her hand. Her bones were tiny and her palms soft and wet. I wiped my hands on my capris and told her I was happy to meet her as well. Although, I have to say, she had a quality about her, a genteelness, a slowness of movement I found . . . interesting. And she had an accent I couldn't quite place, like she'd grown up with the Amish or maybe the Quakers?

As I moved around the room, I felt a tickle of anticipation in the pit of my stomach. Perhaps I could solve the mystery of the letter.

I trailed my fingers across the books in front of me, a collection of obscure titles in ancient scripts. 'So, what can you tell me about the James Madison collection?'

'Being a historian yourself, you probably know most of his papers are at the University of Virginia Library. But what is not generally known is that he visited New Bern in April of 1819 and apparently took a small detour to Robbinsville and had dinner with some prominent families, the Robbins included.'

I looked around, my gaze falling on a framed painting on the wall. It showed a woman in a blue satin dress holding a dangling necklace in her hand. I leaned forward to get a better look at the gold pendant. If I wasn't mistaken, it was a hieroglyph.

'That's a painting by John Hesselius,' Daphne said.

'Yes, I recognized his English Baroque style. The narrowness of the head and features.' I pointed to the woman's face. 'And the pendant? I know Egyptian iconography was popular during that era . . .'

'It's the symbol for scribe. She must've had an affection for writing or reading. Or perhaps she was a collector of books and paper –' her lips twitched – 'like me.'

I turned away from the painting, properly focused on the task at hand. 'So, Madison was here? On the estate.'

Her hazel eyes lit up. 'Most definitely. He stayed in the main house for one night before leaving for New Bern. There was a fancy dinner, then a dance in the ballroom. He was friends with the patriarch of the Robbins family, Elias. I believe they were of like-minded political affiliations.'

'And President Madison gave him the letter for safekeeping?'

'Yes, and it's been in our library for generations. Abner says you're going to find . . .' She lowered her voice. 'The artifact?'

'I'm certainly going to try.'

'Would you like to see it? The framed letter?' Her eyes focused on something behind me, and she strode across the room and gently lifted a picture frame off the wall.

I held the frame in my hand reverently. 'Thank you, Daphne.' I sank into a nearby chair.

'OK, well . . .' She fidgeted. 'I'll be in my office if you need me.' She gave me a nervous smile and left.

When she was gone, I began reading the letter.

April 10, 1819

Dearest Dolley,

I have only a few moments to share my thoughts with you as I journey to Georgetown and onward. I have stopped in New Bern to discuss mercantile efforts and review the current military fortifications. Elias Robbins, his wife Susannah and their family have provided wonderful hospitality for me and my travel companions.

Our dinner was most complimentary. Peanut soup, the creamiest I've ever had, a dandelion salad to cleanse the palette, then ham, crab cakes and oysters with corn pudding and sautéed celery. A delightful apple tart for dessert. I would love for our cook to make the pie.

Their home is stately and their lands handsome, though not as expansive as our own beloved Montpelier.

I visited Elias' library. Of which he is most prideful. And rightly so. Took prayer in the family chapel and spoke at length with a friend on the subject of moral philosophy. I even gifted his daughter with a trinket.

You will be delighted to know I have procured the services of a local craftsman of some repute, a colored gentleman by the name of Willoughby. He is the handiest man I know, and we spoke at length, and I suspect I left him with good thoughts and cheer. I've commissioned him to build you a new pie safe. Cook will be most delighted. It shall be ready and arrive home by the next full moon.

I hope my letter reaches you soon. I wish you well and safe keeping until I return from my trip. Be of good cheer, for Elias and his wife send you their regards and blessings.

Until I see you again, I shall think of you often. Keep the hearth burning for me. And remember, you alone hold the key to my heart.

Yours Affectionately,
James

This was the start of my treasure hunt? I re-read it again, shaking my head. On the face of it, there was nothing here. If there were clues hidden on this page . . . I read it a third time. The only thing that stood out to me at first was the reference to Josiah. Clearly, he had made a pie safe for Dolley. But what else? I retrieved my pad and pen from my purse and made a list:

1. I had only a few hours to walk the grounds, but I visited the library
2. Took prayer in the family chapel
3. Spoke with a friend – Who is he referring to?
4. Significance of the trinket? Who is the daughter?
5. Possible hiding locations: Georgetown? New Bern?

There was also a little doodle on the bottom of the page, almost as an afterthought. It was a bird, probably an owl.

But more importantly, where was Dolley's pie safe? Maybe the artifact was hidden inside it all this time. Perhaps Daphne would know? And what of the chapel? I returned the frame to the wall, grabbed my belongings and found Daphne in her office.

A historical interpreter dressed as a preacher was just leaving. He smiled politely at me as we passed.

Daphne's full pink lips moved into a smile. 'Did you find anything?'

I glanced over my shoulder at the man who'd just left. 'Sorry, did I interrupt something?'

She shook her head. 'Oh no. Matty was just asking a question about a book.'

'I have a few questions of my own.'

She pushed her glasses up her nose. 'What would you like to know?'

'Where's the pie safe Josiah built for Dolley Madison?'

'No one knows. It's not here or it would be on the museum's inventory.'

I glanced at my list again. 'Abner said the grounds had been searched. I'm assuming he means the library and the chapel?'

'Yes, many times. Every nook, cranny and hidey-hole, and most recently by me personally. I'm afraid if it were hidden on the property, we'd have it by now.'

Something tugged in my gut, though. I scanned the library searching, searching for something. 'Are there any stories that connect Madison to the library?'

'Well,' she said, eyes narrowed in concentration. 'As you know he was a voracious reader and collector of books. In fact, he donated several books to Elias when he saw his collection lacked legal texts and botanical studies.'

'He had them sent after he returned to Virginia?'

'Yes, and he commissioned Josiah Willoughby to build the bookshelves. Josiah himself oversaw the books being moved into the library and placed on the shelves. The Specials Collection room isn't the original library though. Abner decided to convert the summer kitchen into a freestanding library to hold book events that wouldn't compete with the exhibits in the original library – the keeping room in the main house.'

I nodded, knowing the keeping room, a large open-plan space in old colonial homes had multiple uses as a gathering space for socializing, reading and eating. Had anyone checked the original library, then?

I thanked her for her time. Abner wanted an update immediately after my appointment with Daphne. Unfortunately, I didn't have much to share. But perhaps after I searched the keeping room, I'd know more.

When I stepped onto the library porch and back into the heat, my phone vibrated with an incoming text. I retrieved my phone from my purse and swiped at the screen. I read the message once, blinked several times as my eyes adjusted to the brightness of the early morning sun and read it again.

I know why you're really here.

My heart tripped over itself as I stared at the screen in disbelief. Breath caught in my throat. I tried to swallow as my mind raced. The number was blocked, and I quickly looked up, inanely wondering if I could see the texter. People were milling about everywhere, singles, couples, families, groups . . . many people were on their phones, but no one carried the telltale look of a prankster – not that this was a prank . . . was it?

I began typing.

Who is this?

And then stared at the screen for several moments. There was no response, and I got the feeling there wouldn't be one. Sighing, I glanced around one more time, shoved the phone into my purse and descended the stairs.

*   *   *

I entered the main house through the back doors that lead to the ballroom, went down a long hall lined with handcrafted wood panels. A grand chandelier filled with candles emitting a warm gold light hovered ahead, and a Persian rug ran down the length of the hallway. Portraits of family members depicted in heavy, rich oil paints stared down at me as I walked by. Almost all portraits of the family were represented, except for Elias'. Supposedly the only portrait of him had been destroyed as it sat in an artist's cottage that was flooded during a bad storm. But one painting in particular stood out. It was about three feet tall and featured the lady of the house, Susannah Robbins: She had a fair complexion with a tinge of soft yellow undertone, dark brown eyes and thick, wavy, chestnut hair pulled to one side with a beautiful hair comb decorated with blue peacock feathers.

She wore a dark gold gown that revealed a deep cleavage, a tiny waist and a full skirt. She reclined indulgently on a chaise of rich red fabric and held a purple fan in one hand. She was lovely and must've been a beacon of love and light in the village. I could see why Elias created a garden for her. She looked like a flower herself.

The place where Elias' framed painting should've hung beside his wife was bare, with the outline of a large frame still on the wall. The placard beside the empty space stated that Elias Robbins died in a mining accident, soon after his wife drowned when their boat capsized on troubled seas. The house went to a distant cousin and their descendants.

I passed the kitchen, the entryway to the house servant quarters, the study and salon before reaching the keeping room. It was a long, wide room filled with large windows that allowed for gorgeous sunlight to stream through.

There were a few patrons in the area, stopping to read placards and exhibit signage. I stood in the middle of the room, wondering where to start first. I went to the first bookshelf as if I was casually reading the spines of the books. I ran my fingers along the wood, not sure what I was looking for. It was mahogany. Dark, rich and shined to a luster. I glanced up at the security cameras discreetly blinking red in the corners of the ceiling.

I completed my search of the first shelf of books without any result. There was a brick wall between the next bookshelf, and I stared at the bricks. They were solid, perfectly crafted by some bricklayer hundreds of years before. I went to the next bookshelf, pausing to visually inspect the craftsmanship. Nothing. Surely, Josiah wouldn't have hidden something in the actual bookshelf, would he? It seemed too obvious.

So, I continued to look around, hoping the last visitors would leave me alone in the room. I stopped in front of the fireplace, admiring the exquisite mantle above it. I stepped to the side, read the placard describing it, and stifled a gasp.

Josiah had created the mantle and fireplace surround.

I walked from end to end visually inspecting the mahogany piece. It was covered in flowers carved in bas relief around the corners of the mantle. I retrieved my phone from my purse and found the photo of the letter. *I visited Elias' library. Of which he is most prideful. And rightly so.*

The first direction was to go to the library. The original library. I felt the word *prideful* was a clue. My gaze strayed to the large mirror over the mantle. It was about two feet high and across. A massive thing in a dark gold frame with spires like a sun. Looking into a mirror could be considered prideful.

I looked at the glass, noting the last of the stragglers were gone. Good. I stared into the mirror – *And rightly so* – and looked to my right. There was nothing there but carved flowers. According to the placard, they were woodland phlox, a five-petaled flower, and blue-eyed grass, a six-petaled flower. Both flowers were indigenous to Louisiana and grown in the Robbins garden. Apparently, Elias requested that Josiah carve only the flowers in his garden onto the mantle. It was beautiful, but nothing stood out to me.

I looked at my reflection again. Perhaps he meant my reflection's right, which would actually be *my* left. To the left of the mirror but above the mantle was a trio of carved wooden flowers, different in appearance from the others. I leaned forward to inspect the petals of one, when I heard the rustle of skirts behind me.

Reba, the interpreter I'd met as the character Zadie earlier, appeared at my side in period dress. 'You noticed too, huh?'

'Yes. The craftsmanship is unbelievable.'

She looked confused for a moment, then nodded. 'Right. It is beautiful. But it never made sense to me that Josiah Willoughby would make such a mistake.'

I turned to her, intrigued by her tone. 'What kind of mistake?'

She laughed. 'Sorry, I learned about this from my grandfather . . . He was a gardener here long time ago. I probably shouldn't

say anything. Especially with you being my new boss. I'm sure
Mr Robbins wouldn't like me saying anything to contradict the
exhibit.'

'Now you've got to tell me.' I leaned in conspiratorially. 'I won't
say a word.'

She pointed to the carved flowers on the left. 'It's simple. Those
flowers are daisies. But this mantle was only supposed to be decorated with flowers from his Susannah Garden.'

'His Susannah Garden,' I repeated, remembering the story. 'He
created a garden for his wife full of flowers from the area she was
born in. New Orleans.'

'Right. So those right there –' she pointed to a row of exquisitely
carved daisies – 'are European.'

I looked at the row of daisies decorating the mantle. 'You're
right, it is an interesting mistake for a man like Josiah Willoughby
to make.'

'I better get going.' She glanced at the six-foot-tall grandfather
clock in the corner of the room. 'Almost time for my shift to be
over.'

'Thanks, Reba.' I watched her leave in the mirror, then my gaze
fell to the offending flowers. The daisies. Also known as narcissus,
the god so taken with his reflection in the pond, he was turned into
a flower. The fruits of his prideful behavior.

Josiah was thoughtful and meticulous. He didn't make mistakes.
This was purposeful. I touched each flower. There were a trio of
carvings. The first, the second . . . the third. The last one moved
slightly. I pushed it again. It wobbled. I grasped it and it turned in
my fingers. Once. But I could tell it would keep turning, so I
continued the revolution. I turned it until it clicked. Then a second
time. Another click. And then a third.

At the third click in place, there was a creaking sound and the
wooden surround pivoted inward, leaving the fireplace in place and
a space for someone to walk through.

I looked over my shoulder quickly before stepping inside. It
was dark and musty smelling. I took another step, felt something
springy under the floorboard release and the entrance closed behind
me.

I was in complete darkness.

SEVEN

I ran back to the door, but it closed just as I reached it with a quiet snick.

I stared into the darkness, not believing what had just happened. I pressed my hands against the wall and could not find a seam to pry open or any device that would open the door. I was literally in an escape room.

I took a deep breath and tried to focus. Okay, I could do this. I'd done these for fun numerous times. Timed and in competition with other teams. This was just another fun escape room.

First things first. Call for help. And then I'd figure out how to escape the room. I turned on my phone and groaned when I saw it was on twenty-five percent. I tried to dial anyone, Abner, Bess. Then noticed I had no bars. I looked around at the thick walls and ceiling. No service.

I turned on my phone's flashlight, and saw that candles in walled sconces were placed strategically around the room. In front of me was a wooden table, simple but exquisitely made. My hands went out feeling various objects. My fingers stilled on a small metal object. It was a tinderbox, a small container that held flammable materials used to start a fire. I quickly struck the flint against the steel, creating sparks and lighting a piece of tinder. With shaking fingers, I ran to the candles and lit them, illuminating the room with a dull glow, and shut off my phone to preserve battery.

In the room was a large wooden chest with a padlock on it. I went back to the table and ran my fingers along it again, but could find no key. I touched something else, however, and held it up to the light. It was an hourglass, and somehow when I entered the room the sand had begun to run. What would happen when it ran out? Would I run out of air? Would something heavy fall from the ceiling and knock me unconscious? Or maybe I didn't want to know.

It was clear to me that I had less than sixty minutes to figure out how to get out of this room.

As my eyes adjusted to the dim amber light of the candles, I saw that they were quick burning. Perhaps the candles would burn down to nothing in sixty minutes. My cell phone probably before that.

There was a painting on the wall. It looked like market day, with townspeople at their stalls selling fresh bread, fish from the Neuse and Trent rivers, handcrafted house goods, ribbons and more. Under the painting was something like an abacus, with four wooden rods and round marbles on notches. I quickly shined my phone at it and saw that the marbles moved up and down the rods. I picked up the frame and gently shook it. There was something metallic inside. Maybe a key to the trunk?

Back to the frame. Five marbles. Four rods, each with ten notches. If I moved the marbles to their correct order, hopefully the box would open. But what *was* the correct order? I hadn't noticed the first time in the dim lighting, but above each rod was a symbol.

A triangle above the first rod. A circle above the second. OK, I could do this.

I went to the painting and stared at it, scanning my phone across each inch of paint. As I stared at the images, I realized I recognized the style of painting. It looked very much like Joshua Johnson, considered the first painter of color in America.

I needed to look for triangles. And I saw one. A triangle hidden in the folds of a woman's skirt. And then I spied a triangle in the pattern of a horse's spot. Then another and another. Overall, I counted seven. I moved the first marble to the seventh notch.

I did the same for circles. And found seven again. Wondering if I'd counted right, I went back to the painting, but my number seemed to be correct. I moved the notch.

A square above the third . . . I went back to the painting. And found three. I put the marble in the third notch.

I went to the last rod. There was no symbol. My chest clenched. No symbol. Josiah was trying to make this difficult. I went back to the painting, searching for symbols. What could it be? He was using very simple shapes. So maybe a rectangle?

I glanced at the hourglass. I'd already spent at least a quarter of my time. But I couldn't find any rectangles. Not a one. Josiah was a furniture maker, so he'd have a technical mind. Be good at math. So maybe those first symbols had just been his attempt at child's play.

I searched for more advanced shapes. At first, I thought I saw several rhombuses. Two. I moved the marble to the second notch and tried to twist the top portion of the frame. It didn't budge. I went back to the painting. I saw one parallelogram. I moved the marble and tried to move the compartment. It didn't budge.

Sweat had formed on my forehead, and I swiped at it, drying my hands on my pants.

My phone was on seventeen percent. I turned it off to save battery and relied on the candlelight, which hurt my ability to see clearly but it had to be done.

And then I saw it. A hexagram. One in a carriage wheel. One on the wing of a bird and one in the pattern of brick on a sidewalk. I moved the marble to three and turned the compartment. It moved slightly. I twisted harder and it opened.

Like I thought. There was a key inside. I plucked it out and held it to the light. It was small and rusty with a circular design on the end. Inside was also a scrap of paper slid into a small glass tube and stopped with a cork. I opened the tube and read the paper.

The key to heaven.

I ran to the trunk and inserted the key. It pushed in with some resistance, but it fit. I shone my light into the trunk. Inside was a flute, and a wooden device I recognized as a wheel cypher, a device Thomas Jefferson had created. It consisted of multiple concentric rotating disks with letters of the alphabet engraved on them. A central knob allows participants to rotate the disks to create different letter combinations, encoding and decoding messages. I knew from history that usually there were two cyphers, and as long as each user had the string of letters to roll the tumblers too, the secret message could be found.

There were twelve rows of letters going in a horizontal direction, meaning I had to figure out a string of twelve letters in order to find the secret message. I looked around the room. Where would Josiah hide twelve letters? I went back to the trunk, running my fingers along the bottom and felt something the light had been too dim to illuminate: a book wrapped in parchment paper and sealed with wax.

I tore the paper off, revealing an old copy of Benjamin Banneker's *Almanac*. I stood by a candle and flipped through the pages, noting that passages had been underlined, sketches drawn in the margins and certain words circled. Blobs of quill ink splattered a few pages. The effect was chaotic, and I could see no discernable pattern or string of twelve letters to use on the wheel cypher.

I flipped through the pages again, as sweat pooled on my forehead and began to drip into my eyes. It wasn't just that it was hot in the room. I was concerned that my phone would die. And nervous about what would happen when the sand ran out . . . what would happen if I didn't figure this out in time.

I wiped my eyes and stared at the pages, willing the letters to make themselves evident to me. Eventually, a pattern did reveal itself to me. On every page that had a little sketch – a kite, a key, a bell, a candle, an eye – there was a passage underlined. And each passage had an ink blob – perhaps accidentally on purpose allowed to splatter on the page to the right of the sentence. I counted. There were twelve ink splatters. And underneath each ink splatter was a letter.

I began to input each letter into the cylinder. And then I rolled it around to see if a sentence appeared out of the jumble of letters. I could see it.

Beauty is in the eye of the beholder.

I wiped the sweat rolling down my cheeks. What did it mean? Where did I go from here?

Panicking, I turned on my phone and shone the light on the walls. My phone was now at ten percent.

I looked at everything in the room. Twice. I thought of each word in the sentence and tried to find an object it referred to. I finally stopped on 'beholder'. Holder. Was it referring to something being held? I searched again, stopping to look at the sconces. They held the candles which were quickly melting.

I was probably reaching, but the sconces held beeswax candles. Bees. Bee holder? Josiah wanted me to look at the candles? There were six, two on each wall evenly spaced apart which gave the room a nice warm orange glow. Perfect for a cozy evening with a cup of tea and a book. Not ideal for trying to solve puzzles created by a master cryptographer.

I looked at each candle, finally picking them each up, careful not to burn my fingers, and inspecting all sides. To my surprise, I saw a letter was carved on the bottom of each and stained with a blue color, perhaps indigo. The first candle had the letter 'F'. I moved to the next candle. The letter 'G'. I crossed the room. That candle had the letter 'A'. Then 'D'. The next wall was 'C' and 'G', again. The last wall held candles with the letters 'B' and 'D'.

But no letter 'I'. And I thought I'd been onto something. Then I remembered . . . There were little drawings in the almanac. I went back to the book and found the page with the drawing of an eye on it. Various words were underlined across the page. When read

together it said: Play. The. Flute. To. Open. The. Door. I stared at
the words.

Play the flute to open the door?

I'd studied the recorder in elementary school. I'd taken pride in
learning how to play 'Mary Had A Little Lamb' and 'Hot Cross
Buns'. So much so, that I'd asked my father to get me flute lessons
which I took until middle school when I opted to switch to ballet
and hip-hop dance.

I could play the flute. But what were the notes?

I looked around the room, remembering the letters on the candle.
Of course. F. G. A. D. C. G. B. D. I'd play them clockwise first.
And if that didn't work, counter. I looked at my phone.

Three percent battery left.

I scrambled for the flute in the trunk. My fingers feeling thick and
clumsy. I played the notes, forgetting a few at first in my hurry. I
took a breath, slowed down and played clockwise. Nothing happened.

I tried again, this time counterclockwise. There was a creaking
sound . . . and the door opened.

Fresh air flooded the room, and I almost swooned with relief. I
grabbed the book and ran out of the room.

When I appeared on the other side, a family of four stared at me.

'Where'd you come from?' the mother asked with a startled
expression.

I pointed to the wall behind me, but it had already closed.

The father frowned at his wife, grabbed his kids and scurried
from the room.

EIGHT

'**A** secret room?' Abner asked again.

I nodded, still recovering from the experience. The dark
room, the lack of air, and the feeling of panic that had
overtaken me. But also the exhilaration of figuring out Josiah's
puzzles. Abner wasn't making this up. The letter was real. It had
hidden clues. Clues that lead to something.

I was in his office, sitting in a chair across from his desk. The
door was firmly closed.

'What did you find?' he asked.

After I explained everything I'd seen, I told him I'd keep the Benjamin Banneker almanac under lock and key in my office. It must be worth a fortune.

'My instincts were right to invite you to my treasure hunt,' Abner said with pleasure. His desk phone rang, and he took the call, gesturing for me to wait. A moment later, he was off the phone, anger shadowing his features.

'Everything OK?'

'If it's not the YouTuber, it's the government. You know how President Williamson created the Digital Reality Integration Administration, currently run by Marta De Verona?'

I nodded. Seemingly innocuous and benign, it had been created to help foster a culture shift to virtual reality environments. Like the Space Force, it was initially seen as a joke. But the news conferences, sharing updates, the latest advancements and the reason we should move away from what De Verona had coined as IRL Culture – in real life culture – made it less funny.

'It's bad enough there's a DRIA-funded company on our historic Main Street. Now they've got these AI robocalls, reminding me as the museum admin to create a VR version of the museum for the millions of tourists who travel – or who will be traveling in the virtual environment.' He grunted. 'It's literally the opposite of what the museum stands for.'

'At least the vice president is against the VR pivot. As far as I can tell, he's the only person in the administration against it.'

'And God bless him,' Abner said. 'The president and DRIA are doing everything they can to make his life difficult. Vetoing his bills. I've even heard they've cut back on his speaking engagements just to be spiteful.'

I'd wondered why I hadn't seen much of the vice president, a quiet studious man from Montana who worked hard for farmers and blue-collar workers. 'You know VR sets were introduced years back, and they didn't really take off. Even if the companies now have government backing, we're too smart to be coerced into living our life like it's a video game. Maybe try not to worry so much and it will blow over.'

He exhaled angrily. 'If only it were that simple.'

I shrugged. 'Who cares if a few people plug in to the matrix?'

'I do. You have no idea where this could end. Try reading De Verona's books. She's evil.'

'What if it's the anti-social psychopaths in our society that need to stay home and away from people? It could be a good thing.'

'Trust me it's not. As a major landowner in this town, I'm feeling the pressure. And if I'm feeling that way in small-town Robbinsville, imagine what the mayors of big cities like New York City and Los Angeles are feeling? I'm not going to let it happen in my town. Not on my watch.' Abner seemed very protective of the town. But rightly so. His family's museum *was* the town. 'Our social media director, Bess, is creating a strategy to counter all this.'

'I know Bess. Bess Montgomery,' I said with a smile. 'We were friends. Worked here at the same time. Did you know?'

'Not sure I did, no. But nice for you to have a friend here, right?'

I nodded. 'VR aside, I feel like you're leaving out something important. Why are other people looking for this artifact?' I thought of the anonymous text I received. 'Or trying to stop me from finding it?'

Lowering his voice, he glanced at the closed office door and said, 'What I tell you must stay between us, do you understand?' His dark gaze seared through me, and I nodded, indicated for him to continue. 'It was a weird time. First there was the comet of 1811 that appeared in March and was evident with the naked eye for over two hundred days. Then the massive Missouri earthquakes in December, felt hundreds of miles away and causing trees to crash, riverbanks to melt . . .' He shook his head. 'Then President Madison began the war of 1812 in February. He thought they were signs, signs that he should do something about intelligence he received by loyalists. He put out the word that if anyone saw or heard something, they should share it with him. And when Josiah heard something . . . that's exactly what he did. What Josiah discovered was just the tip of the iceberg. Once Madison and others looked into what Josiah heard, they discovered a small group of politicians in the nation's capital working against American interests.'

'And you believe this same group exists today?'

He nodded. 'Bigger and stronger than ever. And, they're the ones behind this push to change our society to a *Black Mirror* episode that never ends.'

'How is that even possible?'

He shook his head like I couldn't possibly understand.

'This is the wildest goose chase I've ever been on,' I finally said.

'And the biggest golden egg at the finish line.' He side-eyed me. 'If you're motivated by that kind of thing.'

'I am. I actually want to save our country too, *if* it needs saving.'

'One day you'll see I'm right, Sidney. The people in charge of the American government are not for Americans.'

NINE

fter I left Abner's office, I was crossing the grounds and on my now recharged phone googling the DRIA's latest news when I heard my name called.

'Interesting reading?'

I stopped in midstride and saw Gabe Willoughby grinning at me. A Willoughby. Did he have any idea what his ancestor had created at the house?

His hands were shoved deep into the pockets of his khaki pants. And his denim shirtsleeves were rolled up to show his muscular arms. 'Hi,' I said, my voice lifting in surprise.

He held up a cup of iced coffee. 'Saw you leaving the main house as I was leaving the coffee shop, and thought I'd say hello.'

My throat inexplicably tightened. I swallowed. 'Hello.'

Dimples appeared on both cheeks. 'I had business here too,' he added. His voice was deeper than I remembered.

'Museum business?'

'Sure. I'm part of Abner's small coalition against the DRIA initiative for museums. We had a meeting on Zoom with other museum directors around the country.'

'I see.' Our eyes locked, and I felt a tug of interest that went both ways. But there was no way I could be distracted by a hand-some tall drink of water when I had so much to do – so much to find.

'Maybe we can go together sometime, get a bite to eat . . .'

'Sure, that would be nice.' I flashed him a teasing look. 'We can talk about the secret room Josiah built.'

'Secret room?'

I know what I'd promised Abner, but I needed to discuss Josiah Willoughby with a Willoughby. I just wouldn't give the proper context. So, I told him about the fireplace surround, the daisy and the challenges.

Gabe looked pensive for a moment. 'I'm sure the lack of air was not Josiah's doing. He wasn't sadistic.'

'I didn't think it was. Probably just poor ventilation.'

'But you figured it out. That's amazing. How did you find it, if you don't mind me asking?'

'I was just inspecting the exhibits when the door opened, and I walked in. Next thing I knew, I was in a race against time to get the door back open.' I laughed, hoping it all sounded plausible.

'I wish I could've been there with you.'

Good. He bought it. I smiled. 'Really?'

'Yes. Really. To see Josiah's puzzles up close . . . Next time you're off on an adventure, call me.' He handed me his business card. 'I'd love to be there to help you.'

'I'll remember that.'

He went off in the opposite direction, and I tried not to think about the way his scent of sandalwood and orange had preoccupied me. Or the fact that he was a descendant of *the* Josiah Willoughby. I mean, how amazing was that?

I took the scenic route back to my office, past the broom-maker holding court with all manners of brooms. I stopped for a moment to watch a young woman in period dress churning butter.

Someone beside me nudged my arm. 'Almost makes you miss simpler times, am I right?'

I looked to my right and did a double take. It was the YouTuber vexing Abner, my former college professor. 'Professor Sharp?'

His grin widened. 'I thought that was you. I could never forget all of that red hair or your sharp intellect.' He extended his hand. 'Sidney Taylor, yes?'

'You got it. And great memory. How long has it been? Five or six years or so?'

'Yes, I'm currently on a sabbatical to write my next book.'

'I heard about that. Interesting that your research brings you back to me in little ol' Robbinsville.' I waited for him to elaborate. He didn't.

'Actually, our paths have crossed once before,' he said. 'I attended a seminar you gave at the Smithsonian, on the Native American artifacts you found in western North Carolina.'

'You should've said hello.' I remembered the presentation clearly.

I'd been all prepared to talk about the interesting Ancient Egyptian tablet I'd found too, but after I'd shared my notes with my supervisor, I'd been called into a meeting and told I could not mention it.

'You were busy. Well done, by the way.'

'Thank you. And now you're a YouTuber,' I prodded, hoping he'd explain his presence in town without me overtly asking.

'That, I am. Two hundred thousand followers and counting.'

'That's amazing. Congrats.'

He dipped his head, humbly. 'I just share the truth, and grateful there are people interested in learning.'

'Well, it's great to run into you, Professor.'

He extended his hand. 'You're no longer my student. My friends call me Llew.'

I shook it. 'OK, Llew.' I plucked the lanyard from my chest and held it up. 'I work at the museum now.' I eyed the man, taking in his lanky frame, wide dark-glass frames and thinning brown hair. 'Does Abner know you're here?'

He read my name and titles on the ID card with inquisitive hazel eyes. 'Of course, you know the museum's illustrious owner.'

'I do. And I know he's not a fan of your work.'

'That's because he's a stubborn jackass.'

I took a step away from the man, repelled by his bitter tone.

He noticed and chuckled uncomfortably. 'I'm sorry.' He held up his hands. 'I'm harmless, I promise you. It's just . . . Abner and I came to be friends when I first met him five years ago. He welcomed me, actually, brought me in, introduced me to the staff, gave me a VIP tour . . .' He shrugged.

'So what happened?'

'I told him I wanted to write a book about something I'd discovered here. He wanted to review the manuscript before I sent it to my publisher, which I allowed. He read it, and immediately had an attorney fire off a cease and desist. We fought over it, verbally – of course. I decided not to publish the book . . . but we haven't been friendly since.'

'What happened to the book?'

'On a virtual shelf collecting virtual dust. Maybe one day I'll be able to publish it.'

'Why not just play nice, and maybe Abner will agree to an edited version?'

He grimaced. 'I tried. A year or so back, I extended an olive leaf to Abner. Asked him would he work with me to come up with a version he was comfortable with. He rejected me outright and unilaterally . . . so I created a YouTube channel to discuss all the things he didn't want me to write in the book.'

I didn't want to say I found the move particularly vindictive, but I think it must've shown on my face.

Lew shrugged. 'Hey, I warned him.'

I reached for my phone, opened my YouTube app and searched for his channel. He leaned close to read my phone.

I glanced up from the screen after reviewing his most popular videos. 'Ghosts. Witches. Time travel portals . . . Fairies . . . You've certainly strayed from your academic roots,' I asked, my tone teasing.

He shrugged.

'And now you're writing a new book?'

'My agent already made the deal on proposal; advance check's been cashed. It's happening.'

'Why not mermaids while you're at it?'

He laughed. 'That's a whole other book. But I have found proof of paranormal activity in this region.'

'Is this where the fairies come in?'

He chuckled. 'Not fairies. Fairy doors.'

'Like the cute little doors you can make or buy at craft stores?'

'No, I'm referring to the common term used to describe the scientific phenomenon of time-dilated magnetic nexus. It's based on Einstein's study of special relativity.'

I shook my head. 'Pretty sure I have no idea what you're talking about.'

He rocked back on his heels, considering me for a moment. 'A fairy door is a magical place where one can slip inside, et voila, they're in a different place.'

'I was a kid once. I get that part.'

'As if the fairies just pulled you along on a wave of fairy dust.'

'And where are these . . . fairy doors supposed to be?'

He shrugged. 'That's the million-dollar question. One I hope to discover.' He scanned the area. 'Fairytales would have us believe they're found in nature. Inside large trees, maybe a thicket of brush . . .'

I followed his gaze. 'Don't think there's any magical forests around here. But I'll check out your channel.'

'I'd love to talk with you about my work.' He handed me a card.

'I'm staying in town for a couple more weeks to wrap up my latest research.'

I inspected the card, flipping it over to read both sides. 'Thanks. I'll give you a call. Hey, how do the witches figure into this idea?'

'Oh, they guard the fairy doors.'

'Not fairies? I'm confused.' I grinned.

He laughed. 'Me too. And that's what I'm trying to figure out. What's fairytale and what's fact.'

When he left, I looked across the grounds to the small brick church and started walking towards it. The next clue in the letter was the church. Perhaps something there would lead me closer to the artifact.

While I walked to the church, I did a quick internet search for Professor Llew Sharp. I was surprised to find several blogs mocking his research and categorizing him as a respected academic turned pseudo-science researcher. Even his Wikipedia page described him in negative terms.

When I approached the church stairs, I held up my phone and looked around cautiously before I entered. No one had seen me going in, though, and I hadn't seen anyone watching. First, I went to the temperature-controlled display cases holding the Robbins' family Bibles. They went back to the 1700s and had been lovingly restored. Next, I went to the pews, dragging my hands over the wood, checked behind the choral books in the shelves behind the pews and finally went to the pulpit.

The pulpit was several feet above the church floor and it gave me a better view of the church. Nothing stood out. Disappointed, I stepped down and was heading to the exit when I heard a throat being cleared. I jumped at the noise.

'Seeking something, my child?' said a voice.

I searched the room, my heart still beating wildly. A short stocky man in his early forties with soft round features, brown hair that lay oily against his scalp and round spectacles stood behind me. Matted blond curls formed a short beard that almost hid a weak chin. He was dressed in the garb of an early American-era preacher, heavy black robes with a white scarf gathered at his throat.

I relaxed. It was the interpreter who worked here. 'Where did you come from?' I laughed self-consciously. 'I thought I was alone.'

He pointed to a door in the floor. 'You're not the first person I've scared in that way. There's a cellar under the church, we use it for extra storage of artifacts, but sometimes I go down there,' he chuckled, 'to sleep.' He stifled a yawn. 'I am only a man.'

'Your secret is safe with me,' I said, returning his smile. 'May I see it?' I gave him my card. 'I'm working on a special research project here and hoping to see many of the artifacts not currently on display.'

He pocketed my card. 'I do enjoy a good mystery. I'd love to be your tour guide.' He led me down to the cellar by a rickety staircase that was so old I wondered if it was safe.

When we reached the ground floor, the cold dampness of the room covered me. 'Is there a light?' I asked, hoping it would remove the creepy crawly feeling I had.

'Of course.' And then there was a click, and a bare bulb shone a small beam, illuminating dust-covered pieces of furniture and shelves of knick-knacks.

I glanced at him over my shoulder and caught him staring . . . at my hair.

'How interesting. You don't see many women of color with that shade. Titian red, is it?'

For just a second the hair rose on the back of my neck. But then I relaxed. The color of my hair caused all sorts of reactions. Men were mostly aroused by it, even if they didn't understand that they were. It was a weird thing that I'd mostly become accustomed to, the oddness of being a black woman with a mane of big, bushy, frizzy red hair. For some, I supposed it was like seeing a unicorn. But when I looked in the mirror, all I saw was a black woman like my mother with afro-curly hair that just happened to be red.

'Yes, just like Queen Elizabeth's.'

'And Mary Queen Of Scots,' he pointed out. He blinked, and a silly smile appeared. 'Sorry about that. It's just such an enchanting color.'

'Right,' I said, probably too quickly, but ready to move on. I waved a hand around the room. 'What is all of this?'

'Previous items on display, artifacts that have never been on display but will be, and items that have never been on display and never will be.' He winked at me. 'Guess we're like the Smithsonian in that way.'

I said nothing.

'That was a joke,' he offered. 'I alternate between them and the Vatican. Usually gets a laugh.' He cleared his throat. 'You've heard the stories, how the Vatican supposedly hid artifacts that support a different view of history?'

I raised an eyebrow, and he grimaced. Then I smiled. 'I'm just messing with you. Of course, I've heard the conspiracy stories. The Smithsonian basement is supposed to hold proof of advanced ancient civilizations, but I've never seen it.'

His eyes widened. 'You checked?'

Laughing, I turned, inspecting the room. 'Have you seen everything down here?'

'Pretty much. Like most of the interpreters, I have a day job, but playing the part-time pastor here has been my hobby for the last five years. I took over when my father who previously had the role passed away. Not much I don't know about in this church.' He grinned. 'My great-great-grandfather was the real preacher here back in the day. Matthias Toliver. So, I'm just keeping it in the family, so to speak.'

'I'll have to take you to lunch sometime and hear some stories.'

'Oh, I've got plenty. That's for sure. I'm also called Matthias by the way. But everyone just calls me Matty.'

I remembered him now. I'd seen him in Daphne's office when I first arrived.

He studied me for a moment. 'What are you looking for specifically?' he asked.

I looked down at the ring of keys jingling on his waist. 'A key.'

'Can you be more specific?'

'The key to heaven?' I offered, wondering if even that small bit would clarify.

He turned and looked at me with amusement. 'That's the name of a famous sermon my ancestor gave.'

Not an actual key? 'Is it written down? Is there a copy here?'

'Of course. The very first copy with notes from Matthias himself.'

He went to a locked cabinet, patting the large chain of keys on his waist, found the one he needed and opened the door. The book was leather-encased, and small, the size of a large man's palm.

He offered me a pair of vinyl gloves, and I took the book, turning the pages with great care. A line jumped out at me from the sermon. *Beauty is in the eye of the beholder.* That couldn't be a coincidence. But where did this clue lead? 'A woman who eyes her beauty and sees naught is a beauty truly to behold,' I read aloud.

Matty nodded. 'He was referring to Elias' wife, Susannah. She'd made much ado about a beautiful mirror she'd received from Paris. A woman stole it and was put to death for it, and he spoke in his sermon about the piety and humbleness of women and how that was prized over actual beauty.'

I frowned. Did the clue lead to this woman? Or the mirror? Was the mirror the artifact? 'What was her name? The thief?'

'Izzy or Isla something.' He waved a hand dismissively. 'But it wasn't just about her. There were several women in the community at that time he thought were . . . a little uppity.'

'Do you have any boxes with keyholes in the collection?' I asked, on a whim.

'Of course,' he said. He picked his way to the back of the room and busied himself compiling several items from the shelves.

I studied the assortment of decorative wooden cases he'd collected: music boxes, jewelry boxes and small wooden chests. There were nine in all. I gestured to the items. 'May I inspect them?'

'Of course,' he said with an expansive wave of your arm. 'Take your time. I'm just happy someone is paying attention to these treasures. They're beautiful, the lot of them. All with a story to tell. Unfortunately, the museum only has so much space.'

And then my breath caught in my throat as I approached the last locked box.

'This was Susannah's toilet box. Originally, her mirror inlaid with pearl and decorated with embossed flowers was kept here. The one that caused all the ruckus.'

'It's beautiful.' It was about the size of my two palms set side by side. Crafted of polished wood and encrusted with red and clear stones with an amber sheen, stylized engravings of bulls in full stride decorated the sides. They were almost Egyptian in their depiction. As I moved the box around, the clear stones sparkled gold.

'The story goes that President Madison gave the case and mirror to Elias when he made his famous visit, and Elias in turn gifted it to Susannah. Thomas Jefferson brought over the set from France. When he was ambassador.'

Madison. That couldn't be a coincidence. He and Jefferson were the best of friends and neighbors. There'd been Jefferson's wheel cypher and now a gift from him. Was he also involved in this puzzle?

I couldn't take my eyes off the jeweled box. 'Why is it kept in the church and not in the house? It's beautiful and it was given by a president. I would think it would be a featured piece.'

'You would think,' he agreed. 'All we know is that in Elias' will he specifically asked that the jewelry box be kept with the church effects and never put on display.'

I gestured towards the box. 'May I?'

Nodding he handed it to me. I turned it over, inspecting it from all angles. I undid the clasp and opened the box. It was lined with a dark purple silk, but it looked like pieces I'd seen before, where the lining could be safely removed as the material was held in place by several hidden hooks. I was beginning to gently lift the lining up, when the preacher grabbed my arm.

'What are you doing?'

'I . . .' I saw the look of horror on his face and realized he thought I was destroying a priceless heirloom. I showed him the way the fabric was designed to be removed, and the tension in his face disappeared.

'A private compartment?' he puzzled.

Nodding, I continued to peel the material back and we both saw the lock in the fake bottom of the box. 'I think this is it – what I'm looking for. Would you mind if I took this with me? I promise to take excellent care of it. And I'll bring it back, as soon as I'm done with my . . . project.'

He frowned, his lips pursed to object.

'Abner has given me carte blanche,' I reminded him with a gentle smile.

He swallowed slowly, then nodded, a grin on his soft, round face. 'I know where you work. I'm sure you'll take proper care of it.'

'Thank you.' I watched with excitement as he wrapped up the box and handed it to me.

'Good luck . . . with your project.' His smiled widened, but something about his expression seemed off to me. For the first time, I wondered if I could trust him. The pastor garb had lured me into a false sense of security. He wasn't a real man of God; he was only acting like one.

I hadn't told him everything, but I hadn't been completely discreet either. An itchy feeling crawled across my neck, and I turned to scan the room once more. Took in the crowded area filled with antiques. The shadow-filled corners, the mothball smell of the room, and the cobwebs in the corners.

'Was there something more?' he asked, coming to stand close to me. He glanced at his watch, as if I was taking up too much time.

And I took the hint. Jeweled, antique toilet box in hand, I offered another thanks and hurried away from the church.

The last clue had brought me to the case, which I'd placed on my desk for further inspection. The interior was decorated with . . . cows? I wondered as I inspected the drawings. As I first thought, they were engraved in the Old Kingdom Egyptian style. The angle. The horns . . . it reminded me of the drawings I'd seen at the temple ruins for the goddess Hathor. She was known to be the consort of the sky god Horus and the sun god Ra. She also represented their earthly representatives, the Pharaohs.

I closed my eyes recalling the images of the goddess I'd seen in Dendera, Egypt. Hathor represented feminine beauty, so it wasn't far-fetched that an imaginative craftsman inspired by Egypt would adorn a jewel box with a goddess of beauty – but it was rare.

I ran my hand along the true bottom and felt a panel move. There had to be something I was missing. I pushed it again and it depressed, lifting slightly. Inside was a velvet panel with a circular indentation. A coin with the goddess Hathor lay inside . . . In all my time as a historian I couldn't recall seeing . . .

My eyes flew open as a memory came to me. Something I'd seen at the Smithsonian in their colonial American exhibit. It was an ornate hair comb made of wood with an intricately carved design . . . of a cow. The same cow?

I opened my laptop and quickly sent an email to Professor Philippi. She'd been with me when I'd seen the comb. If anyone remembered the significance of it, it would be her.

I hit send and my phone chimed with an incoming text. I checked the screen and saw it was another anonymous text.

I know why you're here.

I scanned my office, wondering if there were cameras installed. I could feel my face flush with anger as my fingers flew over the keyboard.

Who are you? Don't be a coward. Tell me who you are.
Wouldn't you like to know?

My response was immediate. *You think this is a game?*

I stared at the screen, waiting.

It's all fun and games until someone dies.

I swallowed hard, wondering if that was a joke. And then I shoved my phone into a drawer and slammed it shut.

A knock sounded at my door, and I jumped halfway out of my chair. I took a few deep breaths and stared at the door. *Was it him?* And then the knob turned. I watched it for a moment, listened as it rattled. *Someone was trying to get in.* I plucked the coin off the desk and slid it into a pocket in my purse. I'd locked the door because I wasn't completely sure I wanted anyone to know I had the box.

'Sidney, you in there?' I heard Bess call through the door and I exhaled loudly in relief, sagging against my chair.

I jumped up, opened a cabinet drawer, placed the box inside, locked the cabinet and pocketed the key. The cabinet made a bit of noise when I opened and closed it, but the lock was sound. I went to my office door and swung it open, hoping my expression looked normal – not like I'd just been texting with a psycho.

'Hey, come on in,' I said with a bright smile.

She looked behind me into my office with curiosity. 'Everything OK in here?'

'Yeah. I was on the phone and wanted some privacy.' I led her into my office and sat down.

'What's up?' she asked.

I swallowed hard, wondering what I could say. 'My mother.' I made a face. That would be a good cover for my discomfort at lying. Bess knew how contentious our relationship was.

She nodded with understanding. 'Things still awkward between you?'

'Always.' That at least was the truth. I waved my hand in the air. 'But enough about my mother. Did you need something?'

'I was looking for you earlier. One of the janitors said they saw you go into the church?'

I simply nodded in response. I'd forgotten how gossipy small towns and the museum itself was.

'OK, well . . . I just stopped by because . . . well, I'm glad you're here. I've missed you, missed having a good friend. I want to hear all about . . . your entire life since you left here.'

I felt like a heel. An actual horrible bad person. 'I'm glad you stopped by,' I said, as I stood. I held out my arms to her and she stood too, stepping into my embrace. 'I've been a bad friend. Forgive me?' Every moment we'd shared in college came back like it was yesterday.

'Of course,' she said, her voice muffled against my shoulder. Then she pulled back, her eyes shining with happiness. 'We'll take up where we left off. I can't wait to hear everything. I bet you've lived a fascinating life while I stayed here in boring ol' Robbinsville.'

'Why don't we meet for coffee tomorrow and have a chat.'

A mischievous grin lit up her face. 'I have a better idea.'

TEN

B ess had convinced me to meet her at The Patriot, the dive bar we used to frequent as college students with fake IDs. The bar was even more divier than I remembered.

We sat in a corner booth sharing a bowl of tortilla chips and guacamole. I'd ordered a frothy, pink, wild berry sour beer brewed locally while Bess sipped a glass of white wine.

'I can't believe we spent so many Friday nights here.'

'It was the only place that pretended to believe our oops-we-left-our-drivers'-licenses-at-home story.'

'You'd think they would've renovated in the last decade.' I laughed. 'At least purchased new tables.' I drank some of my beer, and then mentioned Professor Sharp to her. 'I read his bio. Apparently, he began his career at the Smithsonian before turning to teaching. I don't think I knew that.'

'That guy . . .' She groaned and sighed. 'If Abner could get away with murder.'

'Is it that bad?'

'Abner is very particular about the museum's image. He's afraid Llew's research into Robbinsville's witch trials will attract the wrong type of attention.'

'Don't forget the fairy doors,' I added with a mischievous grin.

She burst out laughing. 'I know, right? Such fanciful stories. Oh, to be a fairy.' She gazed dreamily into the distance for a moment. 'To skip or dance into a magical cave and come out . . . oh, I don't know, on the beach. Wouldn't that be lovely?'

'Sounds a bit like teleportation, actually. Beam me up, Scotty?'

'Oh you.' She waved a hand. 'Don't take the romanticism from the idea with boring science fiction.'

'I guess I just don't understand the story.' I looked down at my drink. 'Or maybe I've had one too many already?' I giggled, and she joined me. 'I mean, Llew said there were witches, *not* fairies. So, are there fairies?'

'I have no idea. My grandmother used to put me to sleep with stories about fairies in the Susannah Garden, but . . . it's just talk, you know? Still, I'm happy to imagine Tinkerbell tossing glitter around.' She laughed.

'I'm not sure why Abner doesn't play those stories up. There's a big market for the weird, strange and creepy. It could bring in a whole new demographic,' I pointed out. 'A haunted Robbinsville tour?'

'Don't you think I've tried?' She ate a chip. 'I told him exactly that, but he wants the museum to be a place of wholesome, family-friendly tourism. The colonial Williamsburg of North Carolina. The Disney of American history. He won't even create exhibits about the family's past with mining because a tunnel collapse killed Elias.'

'Was anyone else hurt besides Elias?'

'No. But that's my point. Most museums have these horrible histories with slaves but the Robbins mostly hired indentured servants from Scotland and Ireland to mine their quarry, though the house servants were a mix of paid, indentured and enslaved.'

'People drive miles just to see the quarries in New Bern, though. I think it would be a selling point. Especially if you allowed visitors to view a portion of the tunnels.'

Bess made a face. 'Definitely not. He practically turned red with anger when I tried to persuade him of the same.'

'I don't understand how he's kept it so private all this time.'

'I'll tell you. Any proof we have about the family's mining past is kept in a place only he knows about.'

'Really?' I laughed. 'How mysterious.'

'I only know because I came across old documents that had been filed in the wrong place showing the purchasing of mines back in the 1700s and asked about it. Wondered if I could post about them on social media. He practically threw a hissy fit, snatched the documents out of my hands and left the main house.'

'Presumably to his secret hiding place?' I laughed. 'Well, he's always been eccentric.'

'You don't know the half of it.' She rolled her eyes. 'He came back with biscuits from my favorite breakfast place downtown, so maybe he's got a stash on Main? Who knows. Now Abner's obsession is VR. He thinks that we're moving to a future where we're wholly dependent on the government who will be tracking our movements in VR and assessing with a social credit system like China does now. And if we don't act right, we lose food or the ability to buy clothes.

I for one think he's wrong. VR could be cool, and I can't wait to . . . oh, I don't know, go shopping in Paris while I'm in my house in my pajamas. But Abner is making it *not* fun because it's part of my job to use social media to make sure our one point two million followers understand the coming move to VR is the spawn of the devil.'

She grabbed a glass. 'I need a drink.' She took a sip. 'Maybe I should play a game. Every time Abner says virtual reality, I take a swig.' She laughed. 'I need to get one of those cute little flasks and put it in my purse.'

'Let's hope it doesn't come to that. I don't recall Abner being like this when we were in college.'

'He still dressed like a cast member from *Hamilton*,' Bess pointed out.

'Yeah, he did . . . But the rhetoric was different. Back then he was all, let's get people into the museum. History is fun! Now, he's like Hunger Games are upon us. Learn how to make your own soap now or perish with the unclean.'

Bess giggled. 'Maybe he just needs a girlfriend.'

'He's married to the museum. Isn't that what he used to say?'

'Still does.'

'I'm still interested in Llew,' I said. 'I wonder why Abner hates him so much?'

'Maybe he's afraid Llew, with all his research into conspiracies, knows about the Madison letter, and is afraid he'll post a video about it next. Have a bunch of people descend on the town looking for whatever the letter leads to.'

So, Bess knew about the letter too. I nodded slowly. OK. But she didn't know I was searching for the artifact. 'It's certainly a coincidence. Maybe Abner is afraid Llew will find it first.'

She laughed, almost choking on a chip, and shook her head.

I waited for her coughing to stop. 'What? You don't believe the letter has clues to something in it?'

'I think Abner believes it does and most people indulge him because, well, he's a Robbins.' She picked up her wine glass and swirled it around, and then her phone rang. Bess took the call with a finger stuck in one ear. A minute later she was off. 'Ugh.' She threw up her arms. 'Speak of the devil. Abner is pestering me about this new YouTube series he wants to create.' She exhaled loudly. 'He's tasked me with creating online tutorials for all the crafts the museum displays. Broom-making, blacksmithing, leatherworks, bread-baking, et cetera et cetera. And all before fall. It's too much, not to mention ridiculous. Teaching one person how to make his own leather belt is not going to change the world.'

'Enough talk about work. I thought you brought me here to let loose. Let's have some fun.'

She looked with longing at the small dance floor. 'You're right . . .' With the start of the music, the space had filled with patrons lining up to dance. 'Come on,' she urged. 'They're doing "Cotton Eyed Joe". You remember that, don't you?'

It was only with a little embarrassment that I could admit publicly, I could line dance with the best of them. But that's what happens when you go to college in a small southern town where the only entertainment is dive country bars or a colonial museum. And the museum closes at six p.m.

Bess stood. 'Let's go.'

I grabbed my mug and threw back the last of my beer. 'Just one dance,' I warned.

Famous last words. Five songs later, we were still going strong, and I was having fun. I hadn't line danced in years. I wondered if I'd need to pick up some cowboy boots for my stay in Robbins. It was happy hour, and Bess and I both had on our clothes from work. Classic pumps were not ideal for the 'Boot Scootin' Boogie'.

Another song started up and a cheer rose through the room. Something about having friends in low places.

The next morning, I felt good. A few drinks with a friend, a little dancing, two things I hadn't done in a while. Bess was right. It was just what I needed. I was humming a song I'd heard last night when I saw Daphne standing in the hallway with Matty.

He wore his historical preacher garb but carried a Star Trek lunch box in his right hand. An odd pairing.

Daphne's hands were wrapped in her cardigan which pulled the fabric tight around her waist. Her smile was pinched. 'Hi Sidney, how are you?' she said when she saw me, her voice high-pitched and unnatural.

She looked like she needed saving. 'I've been looking for you.' I gave her a meaningful glance. 'You're late for our meeting.' I gave Matty a quick grin. 'Sorry, am I interrupting something?'

'No, not at all.' His tone was good-natured, and I wasn't sure why Daphne looked so aggrieved.

He took a few steps backwards putting space between him and the librarian. 'I was just asking Daphne if she wanted to join me for lunch.' He held up his old-school kid's lunchbox. 'Grilled cheese and tomato soup in the garden? I thought it sounded like a good idea.'

Matty seemed harmless. Sweet even. But she linked her arm in mine; tugging at me, we began to move away from him. 'I'll see you around, Matty,' she called out as we rounded a corner. When we were out of sight, she removed her arm from mine.

'Thank you. I'm afraid Matty's always been a little sweet on me, and constantly putting me in a position to reject his advances.'

'Have you told Abner?'

'No, I don't want to cause any problems. And Matty's never done anything wrong, I just don't . . . I'm just not interested in him.'

'Would you like for me to talk to him?'

'Certainly not. No . . .' She smoothed down her sweater. 'I'd better get back to the library.' She took a deep breath and seemed to return to her normal composed self. 'How's your grandmother?'

'You know her?'

'I've seen her around.' A smile appeared on her face. 'Small towns, you know?'

'Right. She's doing well. I'll tell her you—'

'No.' She shook her head. 'No need to say anything. I was just asking after her. You look a lot like her, you know? Especially when her hair was red.'

'You knew her then?' I studied her, wondering at her age. She was maybe in her early forties . . .

'Not just the hair. The way you carry yourself. There's an elegance. A regal bearing. Your grandmother has it, and so do you.'

'Probably get that from my mother. She was a Miss USA, you know.'

Daphne laughed. 'Perhaps.'

After work, I came home, took a shower and put on a pair of shorts and a T-shirt.

My grandmother was in the backyard pulling up weeds. I sank to my knees beside her in the soft grass and began helping her.

She looked up at me under the brim of her large floppy hat. 'Nice day at the museum?'

'You could say that,' I began. 'It's nice to be back.' I closed my eyes, turned my face up to the early evening sun and let the heat sink into my skin. I knew I'd have more freckles on my face in the morning, but the sun just felt so good, so therapeutic.

We worked in silence for a moment and then I spoke. 'Grams, you've heard of a letter at the museum?'

She chuckled. 'Abner's letter?'

'Not a secret then?' Jesus. I felt like a fool. Why was I being so discreet?

She pulled off her floral print gardening gloves. 'Everyone's heard about the letter. The secret is that it does lead to a treasure.'

She rose, and I followed suit. 'How do you know?'

'I heard it from my mother. And she from hers. Not that anyone believes its real.'

We began walking back to the house. 'You never talk about your mother. Or grandmother. Why is that?'

'Because there's not much to say. You know I was adopted, and while my family took good care of me, my father was a strict, religious man and my mother – the woman who raised me – was . . . well, she was kind but keenly aware of our differences.' She closed her eyes for a moment. 'Some of the children teased me, said I was a changeling.'

A changeling was thought to be a fairy that had been left in place of a human baby. 'Why would they say that about you?'

'I don't know. Everyone knew I wasn't my parents' natural child. I guess they made up stories to fit why a black couple would have a baby that looked like me. Whatever the case, it always ended up the same. I was the daughter of a woman who gave me away.'

I stopped walking. I'd never heard her talk like this, her tone flat, shoulders slumped. The topic made her sad. 'I'm sorry, Grams, for bringing it up.'

I knew from photographs that she'd been raised by a dark-skinned couple who weren't able to have children. She, with her clearly ethnic features, but pale freckled skin and big, bushy mane of curly red hair, must've stood out like a sore thumb.

'They were good decent people, but my father always seemed concerned about my religious education, and my mother . . .' She paused, thinking for a moment. 'She seemed shy and hesitant around me.' She shrugged. 'But I'm just grateful I was adopted. Many children aren't. Or they were and they weren't treated well. I have no complaints.'

'What happened to them?'

'They were killed in a car accident when I was eighteen and just off to study at Howard University.'

My mouth fell open. 'How did it happen?'

'The police said their car drove off a bridge into a river and they drowned. There was a bad storm, and they probably couldn't see.'

'How horrible. Grams, I'm so sorry.'

'It's all right. It happened a very long time ago.' My grandmother paused on the porch and held the door open for me.

'And your biological parents?'

She averted her eyes. 'No clue.'

I'd upset my grandmother. I reached out to her. 'We don't have to talk about this . . .'

'Don't feel sorry for me, Sidney. I met your grandfather at Howard when I was a freshman. I wasn't alone for too long.' She almost smiled.

We headed for the kitchen and washed our hands. I gave her a sideways glance. Her family was my family. I didn't know about anyone but her and Granddad, and he'd passed away when I was little. I barely remembered him beyond a tall, dark, thin man who smelled like sweet tobacco and wore a fedora.

My grandmother sighed, feeling my gaze. 'All I know is that I appeared in the Susannah Garden, wrapped up in a blanket with a scrap of paper pinned to my clothes with my name on it.'

'Your mother named you Fiona.'

She nodded. 'A woman found me, I believe she was a teacher or maybe worked at the library in the community. And she found a family for me.'

'You had a good relationship with your parents?'

'My father doted on me in his own way, but my mother always seemed to be a bit afraid of me. My red hair, I think. She'd recite the Lord's Prayer whenever she styled my hair.'

I frowned, but she continued.

'I once overheard her saying she thought I'd been left in the garden by the fairies.'

'Fairies? Seriously?'

She nodded, a blush crossing her cheeks. 'Just a story. Mama was a superstitious woman. Not well educated as my father was, many weren't back then, but she was kind and nurturing.'

I could tell she didn't want to keep talking about her mother, so

I changed the subject. Back to the letter. 'Any idea why Abner's so interested in the letter?'

She dried her hands on a towel. 'Abner's been searching for the pot of gold at the end of his rainbow for a long time.' Her expression was shrewd when she turned to me. 'It's a bit of a mystery, isn't it? I know you like those.'

I rubbed some lavender lotion on my hands, then took the time to inhale the spicy floral scent in my cupped hands. 'This smells wonderful. I should learn your recipes, Grams.'

Her laugh was light. 'I wish I could say I was the one who created them, but they come from a book I received from the museum.'

'How so?'

'Daphne gave it to me many years ago.'

'She asked about you today, by the way. You know each other?'

My grandmother nodded. 'Not very well, but she's worked at the library for . . . at least twenty years.'

I made a face. Twenty years? Daphne didn't look old enough to have worked there that long . . .

'When I was a docent there,' my grandmother continued, 'we'd chat over coffee every now and then. Mostly about cooking or herbs. One day she told me about a book she'd found in the library archives and gifted it to me. It just happened to be on my birthday. Not that she could know that of course.'

'You were adopted. You knew your birthday?'

'Not really. It was the day I was found in the garden.' She shrugged. 'Anyway. It's an old leather journal with recipes for lotions and healing balms and teas.'

'I'd love to see it sometime.'

She shrugged again. 'Knock yourself out. It's falling apart but quite useful. It's in a drawer around here somewhere . . .' She glanced around the kitchen. 'The recipes I use the most I already know by heart, so it's been a while since I've looked at it. The writer put in little notes about life and love. Sweet things. I've found it quite useful over the years.'

I sat at the kitchen table while my grandmother poured water from a crystal pitcher filled with ice cubes and sprigs of fresh mint into glasses. She handed me one, then took the other and sat across from me.

'I've known Abner for a very long time, and he's always been

fascinated by the story of the letter filled with clues to something
special. I've heard every Robbins man before him has searched for
it and failed.'

I sipped the cold water, sighing appreciatively as it cooled me
down. 'Seems strange that no one has been able to find it.'

ELEVEN

The next morning, I returned to my office determined to find
this artifact. I sat at my desk with a cup of coffee.

I referred back to my notes taken from the letter from
President Madison to his wife Dolley Madison.

1. I had only a few hours to walk the grounds, but I visited
the library
2. Took prayer in the family chapel
3. Spoke with a friend – Who is he referring to?
4. Significance of the trinket? Who is the daughter?
5. Possible hiding locations: Georgetown? New Bern?

I'd sketched the little drawing of the owl, to the best of my ability
since artist was not a skill I could claim. To be honest, it looked
more like a snowman with cat ears and bat wings . . .

I'd already gone to the library and found the secret room. And
then I'd gone to the church, where I was sure the jeweled box and
its hidden coin was important. I hoped my old boss at the Smithsonian
could help me there. What next? I turned back to the letter.

. . . and spoke at length with a friend on the subject of moral
philosophy. I even gifted his daughter with a trinket.

I thought the unnamed friend was my next destination. Who out of
Madison's friends was known to discuss moral philosophy? It had
to be a known figure, he had to believe the reader of the letter would
know exactly who he was talking about.

I retrieved my phone and searched for 'James Madison' and
'moral philosophy', scrolled down the page and read: 'James

Madison studied at the College of New Jersey, now known as Princeton. While there, he was a student of John Witherspoon, also the sixth president of the university.'

I clicked on John Witherspoon's web page, discovering he'd published a series of lectures called 'On Moral Philosophy'.

It would seem I'd found my man, but where was he in April of 1819?

I referred back to the website I was reading and found a timeline of his life . . . Huh. He died in 1794. So whoever he was talking to on that trip, it hadn't been John Witherspoon.

I continued reading.

He'd had ten children, five of which survived to adulthood. James, a graduate of Princeton and a major in the army, John, who practiced medicine and lived in South Carolina, was lost at sea. Then there was David, the youngest son who practiced law. And lived in New Bern.

I inhaled sharply. That couldn't be a coincidence. The Witherspoon family had lived at Pembroke Plantation in New Bern. David had died in 1801, though, age fifty-one. I reread the sentence of the letter pertaining to the visit. *I even gifted his daughter with a trinket.* What was he saying here? He gave something to David's daughter. Did David have daughters?

No . . . no daughters, I discovered. He'd had one son, John Knox, who would've been twenty-eight years old at the time of the visit. I wondered if that line in the letter was subterfuge. Had he given the letter to his son? Or to a woman that was *like* a daughter to . . . whomever he was visiting.

I wondered where John Knox had been during the presidential visit.

I quickly searched online and found the answer. Hillsborough, NC. He'd been the pastor of a church there, and the principal of the connected school, Hillsborough Academy. Madison hadn't gone to Hillsborough on his visit to Robbinsville . . . but he could've gone to New Bern, which was only thirty miles away.

Were there any Witherspoon relatives still living in New Bern today? I called Daphne to see if she had any insight, and she told me about the New Bern Historical Society and suggested I make an inquiry there.

I made a quick call there and was told an archivist would follow up with me in a few days.

Fingers crossed.

A couple of hours later, and I'd almost finished up next week's staff schedule when there was a knock at my office door. 'Come in.'

The door opened, and Abner poked his head into the room. 'Got a minute?'

'Of course, have a seat.'

He decided to remain standing, his eyes roving around the office. 'I see you're getting comfortable.'

I hoped he hadn't come for an update on the search. Or for the schedule. 'I'm almost done with the schedule. With summer vacations, it's a little tricky to . . .' I paused, noticing how agitated he seemed. 'Everything OK?'

His gaze went unfocused for a moment, then he blinked. 'I'm afraid I might be in a bit of a pickle.'

My phone chimed with a text. I swiped the screen, my eyes on Abner. 'How so?'

'I've been summoned to DC.'

'For what purpose?' I looked down at my messages. It was another anonymous text.

Your kind isn't welcome around here. Leave while you still can.
I screwed up my face. *My kind? What was he referring to exactly? My race? My gender? I almost laughed, historians?*

Abner exhaled loudly, bringing my attention back to him. 'Not sure. Oh, it looks like an invitation to a dinner for this association of museum directors I'm in, but I'm afraid I may be called to task by the powers that be for not complying with the *suggestion* –' he made air quotes around the word – 'that I create a VR version of the museum and also encourage the other museums in town to do so.' He plucked a gold card off the desk and handed it to me.

I reluctantly set my phone down and read it. Gold-embossed script invited Abner plus one to a black-tie gala event in Acme, Virginia, a small but wealthy town outside of DC near Alexandria and Arlington. 'Doesn't seem threatening.'

'It wouldn't. They're offering a lot of free money to museums who jump on the virtual bandwagon.'

'Why is it so important to the DRIA that museums are in the VR?'

He laughed, then shook his head.

'What?' I prompted.

'You'll think I'm spouting conspiracies,' he warned.

I laughed. "Never stopped you before."

"George Orwell wrote, "Who controls the past controls the future. Who controls the present controls the past.""

I nodded, knowing he was referencing the novel 1984, and not liking what he was implying.

He leaned forward, face hard with conviction. "If they control all of the museums, they can change our history, rewrite it . . . do whatever they want.' He sighed. "I've turned them down three times. They'll want to know why.'

'And what will you tell them?'

He snorted. ""The devil took him to a very high mountain and showed him all the kingdoms of the world and their splendor. 'All this I will give you,' he said, 'if you will bow down and worship me'.""

'Right . . .'

His features pinched with exasperation, he huffed, 'I better get back to my office.'

After he left, I returned to my phone, itching to type a response to the threat. But first . . .

What do you mean by my kind? You're a racist? A misogynist? Just want to know what kind of idiot I'm dealing with.

An emoji of a devil appeared. Then . . .

You know what you are, you evil red-haired bitch.

I stared at the screen, truly confused by his response. He was a . . . a gingerist? Discrimination and hate directed to people with red hair was an actual thing, with some believing red-hair denoted all sorts of things, from Satan worship, criminal tendencies, mental illness, sexual promiscuity to practicing witchcraft, none of which applied to me.

What a weirdo.

I began typing.

I'm not afraid of you, and I'm not going anywhere.

I waited a moment, then saw the texter responding.

You've been warned.

I felt sick to my stomach and stared at the words for a long moment. What kind of sicko was I communicating with and to what end? I ran through everyone I'd met: Abner – not him because I'd received them in his presence; Daphne; Bess; Llew; Gabe. Then there were the re-enactors: Reba; Matty; and a few others I waved to in the halls. None of these people had a reason to warn me off.

The identity of the texter vexed me but I had to return to work. After sending staff schedules out, I'd received several emails requesting shift changes. So, I was revising the schedule and trying to make everyone happy when my email notification chimed. I clicked on the message. Professor Philippi had responded to my request for information.

After pleasantries, she wrote that she knew exactly which comb I referred to, and had even attached an image of the artifact. I stopped reading her email to look at the photo, anticipation growing in the pit of my stomach as the large file downloaded. And then it appeared. The engravings on the comb were an exact match for the Hathor coin and jewel box.

I knew it.

I went back to her email. She said several artifacts had been found over the years that shared the same cow imagery, sometimes with a woman's head and halo. Always on women's instruments of beauty, like hair accessories and makeup containers. The prevailing thought was that the imagery was of the Egyptian goddess Hathor and that there were a group of women who worshipped her, a religion as it were.

I stopped reading to think about her words. How extraordinary. Cult Egyptian goddess worship in colonial America? It didn't seem possible.

And the most interesting aspect of the theory, she went on to write, was that there's proof that the cult was made up of women from all races and social classes. She ended her message by suggesting I visit her in DC. There were more things she could share with me about the artifacts, but she'd rather not discuss them over email.

Return to DC? The idea did not appeal to me, but I did want to find out what else she knew. I opened up a browser to check for flights to Reagan Airport, then sent the professor a quick email, letting her know I'd see her tomorrow. She responded immediately and told me she looked forward to seeing me.

I returned my notepad and pencil to my purse and checked my watch. Four o'clock. I needed to see Abner, let him know I'd be going out of town and possibly get the museum to cover my most likely expensive last-minute flight to DC.

I found him in his office. He stared at me, fingers steepled under his chin. 'You're going to DC?'

I nodded. 'Tomorrow. I just need one day off. You won't even notice I'm gone.'

He laughed. 'No, it's not that. You can come and go as you please, of course. Especially if you're looking for the artifact . . . You are, aren't you?'

'Yes. I'm sure it's related.'

'The thing is . . .' He shifted in his seat. 'I need a date for the gala.'

I must've made a face because he hurried to correct himself.

'Not a date-date. It's just, it's a black-tie event and I don't want to show up alone. You work at the museum too; it could be a professional engagement. And perhaps you could back me up on my position not to create a VR environment for the museum?'

I pursed my lips as I thought. I certainly didn't think he was trying to come on to me. I was thirty, and he was in his late fifties, old enough to be my father. 'I suppose I could. I don't have a dress, but . . . who doesn't love a gala.'

He cleared his throat. 'Then it's settled. And we'll take my private jet.'

'You have a jet?'

'Technically it's owned by the non-profit that manages the museums,' he clarified. 'And we're going on official museum business.'

'It seems extravagant.'

'I'm a wealthy man.' He shrugged. 'It's not a big deal.'

'If you say so.'

TWELVE

The work day was officially over, and I headed to the coffee shop before I rode my bike home. At this hour in the day, most tour buses had left and the museum, which closed at six p.m., was low on customers. I liked the museum this way. Quiet with just the interpreters moving around the grounds. I imagined this is what it looked like hundreds of years ago.

Inside the coffee shop I saw Llew sitting at a table, typing on his laptop. I waved, then joined him after I received my order.

'I did some checking up on you,' he said. 'You're Speaker Taylor's daughter.'

'Not a secret. You didn't know when I was a student?'

He shook his head, picking up his glass to take a sip.

A whiff of spicy chai drifted my way. 'I'd love to hear more about the book Abner doesn't want you to publish.'

'You're interested?' I nodded, and he continued with a smile, 'In that case . . . The book's about a group of women accused of witchcraft. Their story's pretty interesting.'

'I'm intrigued.'

'Three women, all immigrants from Scotland, were targeted for prosecution by a local minister.'

'I heard it was about the theft of a mirror? Must've been some mirror.'

'Yes. And after doing some research, I discovered that same mirror was listed on an inventory of museum items.'

'I heard about it.' I told him about my visit to the basement and my chat with Matty Toliver. 'There was a notation that it was never to be exhibited.'

'I saw that too, and it got me wondering.'

'About?'

'How women could be accused of theft if the item was never taken.'

'You think the Robbinses don't want it shown because it would be proof the women didn't steal?'

'Something like that, yes.'

'But why would it matter two hundred years later?'

'Why indeed? That small little question started me on a very interesting path of research.' He chuckled. 'And when Abner became so angry when he found out I was researching it, I knew I was on-to something. My theory is the women were targeted because the minister believed them to be witches. I proposed to call the book *The Witches Of Robbinsville*.' He flared his hand dramatically.

'It's certainly sensational.'

'You remember what you learned in class? What started King James on his path to root out all the witches in the British Isles?'

'Vaguely. Something about a ship, and a woman who made a pact with the devil?'

He chuckled. 'Let me put on my professor's hat and refresh your memory. In the year 1590, King James and his wife Anne of Denmark were en route to Scotland when their journey was marred by a series of violent storms. These storms were so intense that they forced the royal couple to seek refuge in Norway. As you can imagine, this was a harrowing experience, and it left King James feeling quite unsettled and looking for answers.' He stopped to sip his tea.

'Upon his return to Scotland, rumors began to circulate that the storms had been caused by witchcraft. These whispers grew louder, and eventually, a group of individuals came forward, claiming to be witches who had participated in a sinister plot to conjure the storms and harm King James.

'The epicenter of these claims was the town of North Berwick, located along the Scottish coast. It was alleged that a coven of witches had gathered there, engaging in rituals that involved summoning demons, casting spells, and even attempting to create storms at sea. These practices were believed to be directed against King James and his voyage.

'Acting on the Scottish Witchcraft Act of 1563, the authorities swiftly conducted investigations, leading to the arrest and trial of several individuals accused of witchcraft in North Berwick. The trials were far from fair, and many of those accused were subjected to intense questioning, torture, and even coerced confessions. These events culminated in several individuals being executed for their alleged involvement in the supernatural conspiracy.'

'It's all coming back to me now. More than one hundred women were suspected as witches in North Berwick,' I said, finishing up the story. 'They were arrested, with many confessing under torture to having met with the devil in the church at night, and devoted themselves to doing evil, including poisoning the king and other members of his household, and attempting to sink the king's ship. Amazing the leader of a country was so involved with hunting down witches – or so-called witches. They weren't really, were they?'

'That's a great question. Are witches real? Is magic real?' He shrugged. 'During the sixteenth century magic was a concept that most people believed in, especially in Scotland. Even the ruler of the realm. Interesting sidenote. Do you know why the persecution of witches stopped?'

I shook my head.

'Religion. Religion started teaching that there was no such thing as magic. Hard stop.'

'After years of fearmongering about magic and sorcery?'

He nodded. 'They just decided it no longer existed, and laws were made stating you could no longer accuse anyone of witchcraft. But the thing is . . . if magic was real at one time, and most people just stopped believing in it . . .'

'It doesn't mean magic ceased to exist,' I finished trying not to show the skepticism I felt. 'Are you saying that you believe in . . .

well . . .?' I felt silly for just asking. 'This is all very interesting but what does this have to do with Robbinsville?'

'I'm getting there . . . Seven years later the Great Scottish Witch Hunt of 1597 began, with King James overseeing the proceedings. This was one of five massive nationwide hunts. King James seemed to be obsessed with killing witches. Women and some men afraid for their lives ran to England, Ireland and Wales, and others hopped on ships and found freedom in America.' He raised his eyebrows. 'Scots came to North Carolina in droves during the colonial period. You'll have heard of the *Seonaidh* disaster?'

I nodded, recalling the large ship carrying thousands of immigrants from Scotland to New Bern had been caught up in a bad storm, and capsized off the coast. Hundreds of Scots saved the lives of fellow shipmates who were drowning, and salvaged trunks, personal goods and other items. Many of them had settled in Robbinsville. 'So you think some of these Scottish witches were in Robbinsville?'

'Sure. Possibly arrived on the *Seonaidh*. Some preachers thought the crash was God's judgement. Like Toliver that preached here?' He shrugged. 'They were escaping the witch trials.'

'Would it be possible for me to read your book?' I asked. I knew it wasn't published, but I suspected he had a manuscript with him.

'Sure,' he said. 'I'd be interested to hear your thoughts. I'll email you the Word document.'

His phone chimed, and he checked the screen. Distracted, he tapped his watch. 'I've got to take my car rental back to the lot. Darndest thing. The brakes failed on my way out of town last night.'

'That must've been horrifying.'

'It was, but fortunately I was able to stop the car with a bale of hay. Taking taxis here on out though. I've enjoyed talking with you. Let's do this again real soon.'

I rose too. 'Yes. Absolutely.'

I watched him leave the coffee shop. But my mind was on the letter. What was I missing?

On my way back to my grandmother's house, I was lost in thought, going over the clues I'd discovered. I pedaled onto Main Street, which at this point was almost a ghost town. Everything shut down by eight o'clock.

I turned down Meadow Lane, and heard an engine behind me. I moved closer to the side. It revved again, and I looked over my shoulder, saw a large black pickup truck with blacked-out windows riding very close to me. I glanced forward. I was already on the white line, I couldn't move any further off the road. I raised my arm and waved him past me. But the engine only revved louder, the truck speeding towards me.

I pedaled faster, but I couldn't move over. The grassy area beside the road sloped down to a creek with a rocky bed. I looked over my shoulder, fear coursing through my body. What was wrong with this driver? There were no other cars on the road. He could easily pass me. And then it hit me. This was another warning from the texter. If I could get his license plate number, maybe I could trace his identity.

The truck was now riding right beside me. I glared at the darkened windows. 'Move!' I screamed at the anonymous driver. I waved him forward with a frantic arm, but he only pushed on the horn, the noise startling a pack of birds that suddenly took off from their perches. And then he swerved towards me, the side of his truck tapping me just enough to make me fall off.

I tumbled off the bike and down the slope.

THIRTEEN

I'm OK.

My first thought was of the texter. He'd made good on his promise.

My bike was a mangled mess, and the knees of my pants were shredded by rocks and bloodstained. My nails were broken in places and my palms were bruised and scraped. I'd probably be sore in the morning, but right now adrenaline had replaced fear and probably common sense. I scrambled up the side of the slope, hoping I could catch at least part of the license plate, but knowing that truck was long gone.

When I reached the top of the embankment, I was shocked to see the truck, only several yards ahead of me now parked on the side of the road, the hazard lights blinking. I ducked down, suddenly seized with fear. Why was he still here? To finish the job? To make sure I was dead? I grasped at the ground, found the largest rock I could and peeked over the edge of the embankment.

I couldn't make out the tags but could recognize the Virginia plates. The truck suddenly went into reverse and sped backwards in a perfect line. He was coming for me again. The truck slammed to a halt, kicking up a cloud of dust around it. The passenger side window slid down and something long and black appeared.

A rifle? He was going to shoot me?

Instinct kicked in, and I threw the baseball-sized rock in my hand as hard as I could at the truck. The sound of a bullet exploded in the air just as the rock made impact with the truck's back window. The bullet went wild, hitting a tree branch above me. And the window broke, shattering in a million pieces.

The driver swore, then I heard the engine rev and the truck sped off, wheels spinning in a cloud of dust.

Breathing a sigh of relief, I slid down the embankment and rested my head against the grass and dirt. I should've been frightened, but I was elated. This wouldn't be happening if I wasn't close.

I wasn't too far from my grandmother's home, so I made it there walking in a few minutes. I'd thought about pushing the bike with me, but it was such a mess, I doubted it could be saved. I'd notify the town garbage of its location for pickup. And I'd think about getting a rental later.

As I stepped onto the porch, I wondered if I could sneak in without my grandmother noticing. I didn't want to worry her. I used my key to open the door and closed it quietly behind me, crept up the stairs and made it to my room, when her bedroom door opened.

I turned my back to her, but she called to me anyway. 'Sidney, how was work, dear?'

'Fine, Grams. Just going to take a shower.'

Her laughter filled the hallway. 'Why are your pants so dirty, what have you . . .' And then she stopped, and I could feel her gaze on me. 'Sidney, what happened to you? Turn around.'

I slowly turned around, and she took in my disheveled appearance.

'What happened?' she repeated.

'I fell off my bike.' And I couldn't help it. My voice trembled and tears welled in my eyes, as the enormity of what happened dawned on me.

She crossed the hall and placed a hand on my shoulder. 'You fell?'

I nodded as a tear splashed down my cheek. 'But I'm fine. Just shaken, is all.'

She gazed at me for a moment. 'How did you fall off your bike?'

I shook my head, not wanting to acknowledge aloud what had happened, but also not wanting to lie. 'It was an accident . . . I think. A truck got a little too close . . .' A lump formed in my throat as her eyes grew wide.

'Someone ran you off the road?'

I quickly shook my head. 'I don't think so . . . I mean, I don't know what to think.'

She gave me a hug then pulled back to look me in the eye. 'Where does it hurt?'

I held up my palms. 'I fell, so my hands, my knees . . . But no broken bones. Just some scratches . . . I'll be fine.'

'Of course you will. But let's get you into a nice hot bath and I'll bring you some of my lavender tea and white willow bark salve for when you get out.'

'Grams, you don't have to do all of that. I'm fine. It was just a fall.'

'Nonsense. That's what grandmothers are for.' She planted a kiss on my cheek, concern burning in her eyes. 'You just go hop into your bath.'

'The bike is a mess. I'm sorry. I'll have to figure out how I'll get around town now.'

'Don't you worry about that.'

After a long bath, soaking in lavender oil, I braided up my hair, put on my softest pajamas and climbed into bed.

I was exhausted but the bath had helped. Llew's email with his manuscript had arrived, so I hoped reading would offer a distraction. I was a few chapters in when my grandmother softly knocked on the door, popped her head in and held up a mug of something warm.

'My lavender and spearmint blend. Guaranteed to calm the nerves.'

I gestured for her to come in. 'Thanks, Grams.'

She set the cup on my nightstand. Her gaze went to the screen of my laptop, then drifted to my face. 'A little light reading?'

I chuckled. 'Something like that.'

She left and I continued reading until I got drowsy. I'd just reached the names of the women who'd been accused of the theft of the mirror: Isla McIntosh, an indentured servant; Zadie Jeffries, a slave; and Bathsheba Montgomery, a paid servant.

* * *

When I woke up the next morning, I felt better. The bath last night helped, but the four ibuprofen I took after a breakfast of strong milky tea and a hunk of brown bread with butter and raspberry jam Grams canned herself, took the edge off my aching body.

Grams also left me a note to head to the garage, and a set of keys. I grabbed my backpack and went outside, heading down the porch stairs and around the side of the house to the barn that served as a garage. The doors were open, and Gabe walked out with a big grin on his face.

'Morning, Sidney. Just finished detailing her for you.'

'Gabe? What are you doing here?'

He laughed. 'Your grandmother didn't explain?'

'Um . . . no.' I was surprised but not unhappily so. Wearing a pair of tan shorts with a million pockets and straps on them, a white T-shirt with a few streaks of oil on it and hiking boots, he looked ruggedly handsome and not quite so polished and suave per his usual.

I decided I liked him both ways.

He gestured for me to follow him into the space, which was as clean as my grandmother's kitchen, and pointed to a two-door convertible in immaculate condition. It was the color of Cheerwine, a very dark burgundy with a metallic sheen. 'She's a beauty.'

I walked closer, dragging my fingertips across the side. It was a Jaguar Roadster. 'What year?'

'Sixty-seven.' He grinned. Proud as if he was the owner.

I peeked inside the passenger side window. All-leather interior. 'Where did it come from?'

'Your grandfather bought it for your grandmother as an anniversary present, I think. I work on cars, the older the better,' he finally explained. 'When I'm not at the museum, it's a hobby of mine. I like to find old things and restore them to their glory. Your grandmother knew that about me and asked me to check in on the car every now and then and make sure I kept it in order.'

So this was what he meant when he said he was good with his hands.

I walked around the car, taking in the smooth, feline curves of the vehicle. 'You've done a great job. It looks brand new.'

'I don't make furniture like Josiah, but I'm handy in my own way.' He smiled at me. 'And now she's yours.'

'To use while I'm here,' I corrected.

'No, Miss Fiona is at the DMV doing paperwork right now. She's giving it to you.'

'I can't accept this car,' I protested, wondering why my grandmother would give me such an extravagant gift.

'You must. She hasn't driven it in ten years. Besides,' he said, his expression quickly sobering, 'how will you get around town? I hear you had an accident?'

I nodded and told him where I'd left the bike.

'I'll pick it up. I have a truck. See if I can fix it.' He gestured towards the car. 'You have errands to run today? Take her for a spin.'

I gave him a lingering look. Something about him was very attractive to me. He was earnest and kind, laid-back but still very . . . masculine. A part of me wanted to get to know him . . . but I had to find the artifact. Time was running out and I didn't need a distraction. Not even one that looked like him.

My gaze went to the car. I needed to visit a boutique on Main and buy a dress for my DC trip later in the day. With my banged-up body, walking a few miles wasn't ideal.

'OK. I'll drive it, for now. But if you don't mind, please see about the bike, I rather liked pedaling around the town.'

'Of course.'

Later in the day, and after finding the perfect dress for a gala event, I heard the crunch of wheels on the dirt driveway. Abner had sent a car for me.

Abner was already on the plane, laptop in front of him, retro eighties earphones over his ears when I arrived. He nodded to me as I got settled but told me he'd be on a call the entire flight with other museum directors resisting the virtual reality initiative.

I held up a fist in solidarity. 'Fight the power.' And moved to my own seat.

When we arrived, we went our separate ways, arranging to meet later for the gala.

I arrived at the Smithsonian's National Museum of American History and was standing in the lobby when I heard my name called.

I turned around to see Professor Gwen Philippi coming towards me. She was a petite, mahogany-colored woman with a short, softly curved, fluffy Afro, large blocky red eyeglasses and rounded features.

Her eyes were large, made larger by the glasses and they gave her an aggressively inquisitive look. She wore a burgundy pants suit with black and burgundy two-toned heels.

The professor reached for me, and we hugged. 'Sidney, it's so wonderful to see you.' She pulled back to search my face. 'I hope there's no hard feelings?'

About being laid off, without warning . . . or cause? I faked a smile. 'Nope. We're good. I'm sure it was just business?'

Professor Philippi frowned. 'Well, I suppose . . .' She blinked, looking a little confused. 'I think you'll be pleased by what I've found for you.' She began walking and gestured for me to follow her, shooting me an interested look over her shoulder. 'How are things at the Robbins Museum?'

'It's interesting to be back as an adult.'

She led me to her office. 'I'm sure Abner is glad to have you back. He had to grease several proverbial palms to get you "laid off".' She made air quotes with her fingers.

On that table were an array of artifacts nestled on a thick velvet blanket. I wanted to study them, but her words distracted me. 'What do you mean? Abner was involved with me being placed on furlough?'

Her eyes widened behind her spectacles. 'You didn't know? I suppose it will all make sense by the end of our visit together.' Her smile was enigmatic, and she gestured for me to study the table.

Reluctantly, I slid on a pair of gloves laid out for me and went to the display. It was obviously a collection: women's beauty items, from brushes and combs, to containers for makeup. I turned to look at her. 'These pieces are beautiful. Where did you find them all?'

She stood beside me and slipped on her own pair of gloves. 'The Smithsonian has been compiling them ever since it was clear there was a connection between the items. The first piece –' she pointed to a six-inch comb crafted from bone and engraved with tiny images of Hathor – 'was found on an Alabama dig in the thirties. The second piece was found in the fifties in South Carolina. But it wasn't until the early seventies that researchers became interested in what the pieces could mean.'

I turned to look at her. 'And what do they mean?'

'What do they all have in common?'

I noted the solar disk, the all-seeing eye and horns on several of the items. 'The decorative elements. The goddess Hathor.'

'And what might be the link between an Egyptian goddess and

American history?' she asked, as if she were presiding over a class.

I couldn't tear my gaze from an exquisite cuff bracelet made from what looked like pure gold. 'That's the million-dollar question, isn't it?'

She chuckled. 'Surely, you have a theory or two?'

I considered the pieces. 'Possibly a secret society? Cow worshippers?' I guessed with a laugh.

'What of it?' she prompted, not laughing.

I paused, surprised at her response. 'I'm not sure. That's why I'm here . . .'

She cocked an eyebrow.

I squirmed, feeling like I was in front of the class giving all the wrong answers. 'Hathor was a symbol for the mother of the Pharaohs. I'm not sure how this relates to American history. The group is for women. Hathor was a mother of the Egyptian ruling class, of pharaohs. So, the group could've been for the mothers of the ruling class . . .' I stopped, feeling my eyes widen. 'In America . . .'

She nodded slowly. 'Keep going. Think conspiracy theories.'

Llew Sharp and his paranormal research YouTube channel and research into witches and fairy doors came to mind. Speaking of which, I asked her if she knew the professor, since he'd worked at the museum.

'His name sounds familiar, but not sure why . . .' She went to her computer and keyed in a few words. She read her screen. 'He was a member of the Special Projects Department back in the early 2000s. I remember now, we started around the same time.'

'And?'

She shrugged. 'And nothing. He was quiet. Kept to himself. I recall he was let go for some reason. Or maybe he just left. He was nice enough. Nosy, though.'

'Special Projects Department?'

'Research arm of the museum. I wouldn't know more than that.' She thought for a moment. 'He was sent out into the field a lot. Boring work is what I heard.'

I returned my focus to the artifacts. 'You said conspiracy theories . . . And you've implied this group is about bloodlines?'

She nodded. 'Royal bloodlines that traverse the continents. From Egypt to the rest of the African continent . . . to Europe and beyond . . .'

I thought of a conspiracy theory about all the presidents being related I'd heard of before, but besides that I was still stumped.

Dr Philippi leaned against her desk. 'Do you read the Bible?'

'Not particularly.' I was embarrassed to say I couldn't remember the last time I'd been to church. 'I'm not religious.'

'Perfect. Because this isn't about religion. This stems from two royal houses at war with each other. Their stories and histories just happened to be partially recorded in the Bible. It's in other books as well, like *The Histories* by Herodotus and *The Babylonian Chronicles* for starters.'

'What does that have to do with all this?' I waved my hand around the artifacts. 'And my search for an artifact . . .' My gaze fell to the symbols of Hathor. 'She was an ancient Egyptian goddess. These people that started the cult . . . they worshipped her because they were from areas where Hathor worship was common. So, Egypt. The Sinai Peninsula . . . And it's continued to this day?'

My mentor gazed at me, her expression solemn.

I tried again. 'What royal houses? Who are we talking about?'

'The House of David and the Babylonian King Nebuchadnezzar.'

'You mean Israel?'

She rose off her desk. 'No. The House of David is different from the House or Tribe or Kingdom of Judah. When we speak of the House of David – the Davidic line – we're referring to a specific royal family that descends from King Solomon and King David.' She stopped to toy with a small globe on her desk, her fingers trailing over the African continent. 'This is a family like the royal Windsor family in England. An ancient bloodline. Not a specific race or group of people.

'This is also about a princess. A young woman named Scota who was the daughter of King Zedekiah, the last king from the Davidic line. And when King Nebuchadnezzar sacked Zedekiah's court and killed all of his sons, Scota, the prophet Jeremiah, his scribe Baruch and her royal retinue escaped to first Spain and then the area that would become Scotland, where she established a country and kingdom with her husband.' She turned the globe to Scotland and tapped it with a long red nail.

'Legally, the Davidic line could continue through a female if no more sons were left and the princess married a prince from the tribe of Judah, which she did. I doubt King Nebuchadnezzar knew this or he wouldn't have allowed her to live.' Dr Philippi returned to the desk of artifacts and picked up a hair comb, showing me the lotus flower on it. 'The Daughters of Hathor were originally the handmaids and ladies-in-waiting of Scota, loyal to a fault and fiercely protective of the queen . . . and eventually her bloodline.'

I took the comb from her, touching the decorative flower petals. 'Protecting her from what?'

'A secret society founded in King Nebuchadnezzar's court, a group of Babylonians loyal to him and intent on destroying the dynasty established under King Solomon. A group of men and women who even today refuse to believe the prophecy. We call them The Opposition.'

'And the prophecy?'

Dr Philippi closed her eyes and began to recite. 'The sceptre shall not depart from Judah, nor a lawgiver from between his feet, until Shiloh come; and unto him shall the gathering of the people be.' She opened her eyes and looked at me. 'Descendants of Scota are supposed to be in positions of power. After hundreds of years of being oppressed and persecuted for their bloodline, they came to America as immigrants, indentured servants and sometimes slaves.'

'You realize this is secret knowledge that most people, most Americans have never heard of, or wouldn't believe if they did?'

'And yet they still fight.' Her fists curled at her side. 'Despite The Opposition's strategies to enslave and oppress so they forget who they are.'

I placed the comb down, not sure what to say. This artifact Abner wanted me to find came with a heavy legacy.

'You might be surprised to know Scota and her Scottish people were connected to the people now classified as African-Americans. You think the enslavement and oppression of the black and brown races was accidental?'

'No, of course not.' I followed her movements as she began to pace the room, wondering how her comment was related . . . I'd assumed Scota, who was Egyptian, and her husband, a Hebrew, possibly a Scythian, would have had descendants who were a mixture of the people found in the Middle Eastern region: a spectrum of colors from the lightest to the darkest of complexions. Where was she going with this?

She stopped in front of the display of artifacts found on plantations and black communities throughout the south. 'Much of the bloodline was hidden among the darker races: the Sephardic Jews in Spain and Portugal, the Huguenots in France, the Moors in North Africa and much of Europe . . . the Africans. During the eighth, ninth and tenth centuries, Scota's descendants married within these noble and royal lineages, during a time when brown and black people ruled much of the countries we now consider white in majority.' She narrowed her eyes. 'I bet you haven't heard this, have you?'

I shook my head. 'No, I have not.'

'That's because this goes against the established narrative we're all taught in school. We're not supposed to know this.'

'How do you know it?'

She chuckled but didn't answer. 'I'm not done with my history lesson, Sidney.'

That was about right. I felt like I needed to be taking notes. 'Then what happened? There are no more black and brown royal families, are there?'

'There are still many to be found in Africa. And there's the deposed Ethiopian royal family based in Northern Virginia. They, too, have an origin story founded in the Davidic line, with the Queen of Sheba having a child with King Solomon which began their imperial family . . . but that's another story for another day.'

My head was swimming as I tried to process and remember all that she was saying.

'Needless to say, the tides change, fortunes fell and society flip-flopped, with the suppressed now becoming the oppressors. Brown and black people outside of Africa were forced to the lowest of classes, and indentured servitude and lifelong enslavement became institutionalized. Slavery was about many things, but it was mostly about making sure that Scota's lineage – now equally spread among all the races, but especially the brown and black races – was forgotten. Broken. Destroyed.'

I selected a cooking bowl made of ceramic, decorated in lotus flowers and glazed with purple dye. Ran my finger over the rim of it, wondering who had prepared meals with it. A descendant of Scota's? A woman with royal blood?

'Think about how many powerful white men, leaders of cities, states and countries, had children with their black female slaves. You think that was just by chance?'

I shook my head, setting the bowl down.

'The temptation to own a woman of the bloodline was too much for many. And they wanted to create children with the lineage hidden in their slaves. Sometimes the motivation was sadistic, other times they selfishly wanted an heir with the Davidic bloodline. The quadroon balls? Arranged pairings between female descendants of Scota and the men of The Opposition.

'The mulatto class created during this time, the one that went on to own land and have wealth in cities like Charleston and New Orleans? They were half-Davidic, half-Opposition. With the right bloodline but doing the bidding of The Opposition.' She huffed in exasperation. 'What a mess. I'm sorry, talking about this always gets me riled up, but that's okay . . .' She went to a mini-fridge in the corner of her office and retrieved two green glass bottles of Perrier.

A silver tray with glasses sat on a table, and Dr Philippi poured the sparkling water into the glasses, handing me one. She took a moment to refresh herself. Then closed her eyes, sighing. She nodded. 'That's better. Okay, where were we?'

'The mulatto class of the south,' I offered.

'Right. Oftentimes women of color carried the royal bloodline. And whether they were servant, slave or courtesan, the Opposition that ruled wanted – no, needed the Davidic lineage for their own. Why do you think Queen Charlotte was sought for King George III all the way from Germany?'

I sipped my water. 'She was a Daughter of Hathor?'

She nodded. 'From a swarthy line of Portuguese royalty – they were rife with Moorish blood themselves, but supposedly the king's black mistress was described as a Moorish woman. See what I mean? The line of Scota ran through a woman of color . . . and King Alfonso III of Portugal desired her . . . genetics, shall we say? Just as the English court desired an infusion of her Davidic lineage to boost their own perceived power. They needed her ancient royal bloodline, which thanks to her fifteen children are spread throughout all of European royalty today. So even though it's just a drop, it's accurate to say the Davidic line is on the throne.

'I wouldn't be surprised if Megan Markle was a Daughter. It's been a long time since the British royal family brought in a woman of color. I'd wager the Scota bloodline is just about to run dry and they need Megan's genetic offerings for future generations. Of course, that appears to have gone haywire, but you never know with the elite. They've been known to play the long game, and it's always shrouded in smoke and mirrors.'

I stared at a beautiful hairbrush, decorated with lotus flowers. 'Perhaps her son or daughter will run for American president one day, and there'll be a descendant of Scota's in the White House.'

Dr Philippi laughed, but then a thought occurred to me. 'Is there a male component?'

'Yes,' she said approvingly. 'Just like there are Masons for men and Eastern Stars for the women, there's a group called the Sons of Horus. Their motto is *Omnia pro libertas*, which roughly translates to "All for liberty". Sometimes you'll see it in their books or on documents. We believe President James Madison knew members of this group.'

'But he wasn't a member?'

'Doubtful.'

'But this *is* related to Madison's . . .?'

'Letter?'

'Well . . .' I rolled my eyes. Then grinned. 'It's supposed to be a secret.'

She laughed. 'Everyone knows about the letter. Most just don't believe it leads to anything.'

Should I tell her? Could I? Something told me I could trust her. She seemed to know so much already . . . So, I shared with her all about the clues the letter had led to so far. I told her what Abner believed – that the letter led to an artifact that could bring down whomever is trying to destroy our country. 'If that is happening,' I clarified.

Gwen cocked her head. 'You *don't* think it's happening?'

'You *do*?' I bit my lip. 'I don't watch the news.' That was my go-to line in these situations, but it was starting to grow thin.

'Maybe you should start.' Her tone was sharp. 'Things are getting weird.'

'So Josiah and Madison had it right. Abner is right.'

She nodded, a look of concern in her eyes. 'You doubted?'

I ignored the look of disappointment on her face. I told her about the texts. The truck. 'I have no idea who it could be.'

She looked thoughtful for a moment. 'It could be a member of The Opposition.'

'In Robbinsville?' I mused, thinking the idea was ridiculous. I stared at her, trying to take it all in.

'You understand the importance of the group now?'

'Yes, I get it.'

'The Opposition has infiltrated governments, corporations, anything that can influence society.' She snorted. 'They're organized. And they are many.' She sighed. 'But we have to stay one step ahead of them. This push to go virtual? That's not just weird, it's anti-people. And it's part of their strategy to suppress the population. Not just descendants of Scota but all people. First they lower the overall population on the planet, and then they force those remaining to live in a perpetual virtual reality. Easily controlled and monetized.'

Jesus, it sounded so dour. I had so many questions I wanted to ask, but with the artifacts in front of me, I had to begin there. 'Tell me more about these.'

'We believe that the women, the Daughters of Hathor as they called themselves, used these items to identify themselves to others. The women passed down everyday objects like mirrors and combs and broaches to the first daughter in their family, along with membership in the society, the stories, the heritage and all that goes with it.'

'What does this group look like today?'

'An exclusive alumna of sorts, a network that provides for each other in whatever ways are necessary. Sometimes the Sons of Horus marry the Daughters to create something of a political dynasty.' She laughed. 'And the children of the Daughters, men and women go on to become governors, senators, representatives and such, all devoted to the cause. All True Patriots.'

'I'm guessing The Opposition has their own candidates in place.'

She frowned. 'When they rule, and they do . . . it's always stolen. They were never meant to rule. It's why they're so desperate for one drop from our bloodline, however they can get it.'

We were silent for a moment, the heaviness of the moment settling around us.

'Is it just politics?'

'No, and that's the thing. The Opposition recognizes the value of the bloodline. Many of the descendants are in sports and entertainment. The media. Even the corporate world. But only if they can make money off the descendant.'

I felt like everything I thought I knew about the world was wrong. Like the Earth had just tilted and everything was topsy-turvy. 'The Sons of Horus membership falls to the first son of the first son?' I asked.

She nodded.

'So these men and women . . . they're everywhere.'

She met my gaze, her eyes gleaming behind her lenses. '*We* are everywhere.'

I looked at her. 'You're a Daughter of Hathor?'

'Yes,' she said proudly. 'That's how this began for me. I found a beautiful old straightening comb in my great-great-grandmother's attic when I was a teenager. It compelled me to learn everything I could about history, get my doctorate, to work at the Smithsonian. And when I discovered another item had been found with similar markings, I spearheaded a program to find similar objects, research their history, understand the implications and eventually do my part. So far, we've found seventy-five artifacts across the United States and as far as Mexico and the Caribbean.'

'The historian in me finds this absolutely fascinating. And the women themselves? Do you know who they are? Is there a list?'

'Don't laugh. But there are scrolls.'

'What would a secret society be without their sacred scrolls?' I laughed, covering my mouth with a hand. 'Sorry.'

Amusement relaxed her face. 'It's okay to laugh . . . But yes, maintained by scribes, trained for the purpose. In contemporary times, they're often teachers, writers, librarians . . . historically as well, I suppose. They've been digitized with the originals hidden for safekeeping and the new names are added to the digitized version. Though we do have versions printed on gold sheet, hidden in caves in West Virginia just in case . . .'

I paused at that. Just in case what? But I didn't ask. There was already too much swimming around my head.

'As you can imagine, we protect that information with our lives. There's a bounty on the members, since any of us could give birth to the next leader for our cause. A True Patriot.'

'With so many members, how are the people selected to run . . . chosen?'

'We have something like a board of directors that make those decisions generations at a time.'

'So what's happening now . . .'

'Was predetermined by previous generations. Yes.'

'And they meet . . . where?'

'In different places under the guise of various groups. Small towns. Big cities . . . And we communicate in creative ways.'

'So why wasn't that history given to you, first daughter to first daughter?'

'I wondered the same thing.' She smiled ruefully. 'And for a long time I had no idea. And then one day, me being me, digging in old things, found her old diary. She'd rejected the legacy, her role in the sisterhood.'

'But why? It seems like such an honor.'

'She'd resisted the traditional roles of mother and wife. She never married, having had bad experiences with men. And she didn't want to bring children into the world.' She shrugged. 'Even if she had the bloodline of kings and presidents in her. So it died with her. Thank goodness, I found the comb. I don't have any children and I probably never will – medical reasons – but I've got a sister and she has girls, and I've already made provisions in my will for the legacy to continue.'

'That's amazing,' I breathed. 'This multi-racial secret organization of women created when people of color and whites were at odds with each other . . .'

'Some things are bigger than race, and even then they understood that an attack on America was an attack on everyone. I'm just glad that a subset of the population was able to come together in this way.'

'So now that I know all of this, now what?'

'We prepare.'

'Do the Sons of Horus have a symbol as well?'

Nodding, she retrieved her phone from her pocket and swiped a few times, then showed me the image of a regal looking bird. 'This. The Egyptian falcon.'

The drawing on the Madison letter came to me then. I'd thought it was an owl, but it looked like this . . . a falcon.

I thought of other leaders, presidents, governors. 'When's the last time one of your . . . members has been in office?'

A shadow crossed her face, but she laughed.

'What's so funny?'

She shook her head. 'Not so funny. It's just an inside joke. If a president was assassinated, he's probably one of ours. If we could wear T-shirts – Abraham Lincoln, Garfield, McKinley . . . Theodore Roosevelt and Reagan were unsuccessful assassination attempts, thank goodness.'

'What about the Kennedys?'

She shook her head again. 'They're one of those families I told you about, Sons of Horus and Daughters on both sides. The Opposition have killed or neutralized so many members of that family. That really frightened the Daughters. What woman wants to raise her children only to put them in harm's way? Many of the Daughters went off the grid. But you've seen what's happening in our world, yes? It's because we've been fearful. Hiding. It has to stop now.'

'Why are you telling me all of this? If this is such a secret . . .' I glanced at the artifacts then back to her.

She paused, lost in thought as if she was wrestling with a decision. 'There's something you need to see.'

She retrieved a small key that hung on a necklace around her neck, hidden under her blouse. She unlocked a cabinet in the corner of her office that revealed an identification screen. She placed her palm on it and a pane on her office floor opened up and a glass tube rose up. She pressed her thumb on the top and it opened.

'Seriously?'

She chuckled. 'So James Bond, right?' She reached for the scroll inside. 'I paid someone a lot of money to build this for me. The Smithsonian had some of the best security in the world, so why not hide our most precious document here.'

She went to her desk and lay the scroll down, unfurling it. It was yellowed and old, like a slightly newer version of the Constitution of the United States. Only, the scroll was covered in long lists of names five rows across.

Professor Philippi pushed her glasses up the bridge of her nose, leaned over the scroll, dragging her finger up and down and across the paper. 'Here we are . . .' She looked at me, her eyes bright. 'This is a list of the Daughters.'

I met her interested gaze, then followed it as she turned her head and tapped the scroll. Under the letter 'T', down twenty spots . . . was my name.

Sidney Grace Taylor.

FOURTEEN

'I don't understand.'

I stared at the page until my vision blurred. It was my name, my birthdate, and my city of birth.

'Oh, I think you do.' Professor Philippi stood, began rolling the scroll up. 'You're one of us.'

'There must be some sort of mistake.'

'Trust me, there's not. I wouldn't have shown you and told you everything I did, if your name was not on that list.'

I watched her tuck the scroll into its holder and complete the security procedures in reverse. When she was done she reached for my hands, her brown eyes soft with compassion.

'Why was there a little purple star beside my name?'

'Because. You're special.'

Somewhat numbly, I allowed her to take my hands.

'Welcome to the sisterhood. You are a Daughter of Hathor. Colloquially known as a Sister.'

'Thanks,' I mumbled. 'I think. Why don't I know about this? How am I a part of this? Does my mother know?' Questions tumbled over themselves until I thought I wasn't making sense.

'Sometimes, the knowledge is purposely withheld and other times it's just lost. But we knew, we've always known about you. Keeping an eye on you in school, as you worked. We have people.' She grinned.

'People like who?'

'Like me for one. It's no accident that I'm your mentor. I sought you out because I knew who you are.'

'But—'

'No buts. I wanted to get to know you. Help you. Guide you. It's been a pleasure.'

It wasn't a pleasure for me. I was feeling manipulated. 'Who else?' I demanded, beginning to feel angry. 'Who else has been watching me and not telling me really important things about my heritage?'

She placed a hand on my arm. 'Don't be like that. We're sisters. Family. We protect each other. We take care of our own. And you've been given knowledge as needed. Sometimes a Daughter can live her entire life without knowing, and sometimes they know from childhood. Each situation is different.'

'But—'

'Now that you know, I suspect you'll learn more.' She looked into my eyes, slight frown lines creasing her forehead. 'I think that's enough for now.'

I stood rooted at the spot, feeling both hot and cold. Invigorated and numb. So now I was a member of a secret club? A society of women who . . . what? And how would I be able to identify them?

'This is probably a silly question, but is there a secret handshake or code or anything I should use when I greet other . . . daughters? I mean, if this is so hush-hush there has to be a way to recognize each other, right?'

She laughed. 'The cow jumped over the moon.'

I blinked. 'Sorry?'

She laughed. 'You say, "The cow jumped over the moon". And if they are a true daughter of the goddess, she'll say, "And the dish ran away with the spoon".'

'Simple yet clever.'

'Isn't it just?' She patted my arm. 'And of course there's the symbology. It's usually around if you have eyes to see. In jewelry, lots of small discrete tattoos have sprouted up with the younger generations . . . and then there's cows. Sometimes the rural members like to use a Jersey cow – as collectibles in the house.'

While Professor Philippi put the Daughter of Hathor items away in a locked cabinet, I tried to wrap my head around everything I'd learned. I wasn't sure I could.

'You said this knowledge is handed down from mother to daughter, right?'

She nodded.

'I can't believe my mother never mentioned anything to me.'

The professor pressed her lips together like she wanted to say something but didn't.

'What?'

Gwen Philippi's voice was quiet. 'It's not your mother you need to speak to.' She paused. 'It's your grandmother.'

'My grandmother?' For a moment, a wave of something like vertigo swept over me and I swayed on my feet. I tried to breathe. I honestly did but I just couldn't catch a breath.

And Professor Philippi wouldn't stop talking. 'There's a reason why all of the presidents are related. There's a reason why royal families marry each other going back to the pharaohs. It's in the blood. It's our DNA. We're special. Meant to rule. Regardless of color or nationality.' She stepped forward. 'You're not just a Daughter of Hathor in name. You share Queen Scota's blood. Do you understand what I'm saying? The blood of pharaohs and kings flows through you.'

What the hell was going on? 'My grandmother has no idea who her mother was. She's adopted.' I stared at Dr Philippi. 'You know who her mother is?'

'That information is in the archives. But it's not our place to interfere with the way her life has unfolded.'

My head swam. 'I don't know what you expect from me.'

'We sisters are all of the bloodline, but that purple star? It means you're a direct descendant of Queen Scota herself, undiluted through her daughter's daughter's daughter . . . There is a special mitochondrial DNA marker for her kin. You have it.'

I grabbed my purse. 'I need some air.'

'Wait,' she said, reaching out for me. 'Now do you see why Abner needed you in Robbinsville? Now do you see why I agreed to let you go?'

Angry tears welled in my eyes. I'd been manipulated. Was still being manipulated. The world was blurry as I navigated the hallways and found the elevator. I could barely see. And maybe that was just perfect, because I didn't want to see at all.

FIFTEEN

The gala was held in the ballroom of a very old, very beautiful hotel. Many senior officials from the federal government, think tanks and non-profits were in attendance, as well as the head of every major history museum in the nation.

I arrived alone, to see that for once Abner was not dressed like a time traveler from the early American era and wore a black tux that was probably only ten years old. I'd found an off-the-shoulder olive green dress with a kick pleat that made me feel like a flamenco dancer. Smoky eyes. Nude lips. Hair wrestled into an updo, and the look accented with aquamarine jewelry, I felt like I fit in.

Abner was nervous, mopping his forehead with a handkerchief as he talked to other directors. Normally, I'd find his idiosyncratic use of a handkerchief charming, but right now I was fuming with him. I mean, he'd reached out to my place of employment, basically gotten me fired and then swooped in like a savior with his offer of money. What kind of Machiavellian move was that?

A severe looking woman stepped onto the stage and tapped the mike. She had milky white skin, dark eyes, and patent leather shiny jet-black hair cut into a short, spiky female punk rocker style from the eighties. She gestured for the harpist to stop playing with the flick of a long hand tipped with blood red nails, and the crowd hushed, even though the residual tinkling of glasses remained.

'Hello, everyone. My name is Dr Marta De Verona. I am the director of the Digital Reality Integration Administration.' Applause erupted across the room.

Abner made his way over to me. 'I knew it. It's a trap.'

'Like the one you set for me?' I threw back, my voice low.

He did a double take, his dark eyebrows dipping. 'What are you referring to?'

'Everything. The way you manipulated my time off of work. The job offer. You lured me to Robbinsville under false pretenses.'

He stared straight ahead, his Adam's apple moving slightly. 'Perhaps.'

He wasn't even going to deny it? 'Really?' I whispered. *'Perhaps?'*

'No. Definitely.' He shrugged. 'Guilty as charged. Sorry.'

'That's all you have to say?' I laughed at the incredulity of his response.

He shrugged. 'I get what I want. And I wanted you in Robbinsville. Needed you there actually. Professor Philippi explained?'

I clenched my jaw. Of all the condescending . . .

'Your place is in Robbinsville. Your intelligence and skillset wasn't being properly utilized at the Smithsonian. And you have to agree you're having fun, yes?'

I glared at him. *Seriously?*

'Your grandmother is happy to see you as well.'

There were no words . . . I couldn't even . . . And then the microphone squealed as Marta moved it. I stopped talking, crossed my arms and focused on the speaker.

'And I want to thank everyone here who's joined our voluntary initiative to create affordable accessible virtual reality environments for our country's most valuable cultural resource: museums.'

More applause.

'As you probably know all major universities are in the process of creating their own VRs, many of our nations amusement parks have joined the movement to create virtual entertainment and most movie theaters have virtual theaters in the works. It's an exciting time to be alive.' Her voice rose. 'Am I right?'

Abner leaned towards me, his lips to my ear. 'Eventually, you'll see everything I've done is in the best interest of you and your family. For all of us.'

Rolling my eyes, I stepped away from him.

'Along with the federal government and all educational institutions, getting our cultural institution in the virtual realm is a must for our initiative to proceed. For all of you who have joined the pledge to create affordable, accessible VR museums to bridge the poverty gap that disproportionately affects our country's minorities . . .' A banner unfurled behind her: **Digital Equity: Closing the Opportunity Gap with Virtual Integration**. 'I thank you. Tonight is simply about celebrating your vision and willingness to be a part of something amazing.'

Clapping filled the room and Abner looked about angrily. 'How can they all be sheep? They're directors of history for Pete's sake. Don't they know what's happening?'

'To their credit, I don't think anything like this has ever happened in history.'

Abner snorted.

'I think they know they're getting a lot of funding which could help them in many ways.'

'It doesn't matter. It's just money.'

'You have your own jet, Abner. Most museums struggle to keep the lights on.'

Abner looked like the idea had never occurred to him.

'Shortly, we'll have a special presentation on the latest advances in our administration. But first, a word from one of our most generous sponsors. I give you the CEO of VirchWorld, Anton Jax.'

Thunderous applause, as a short thin man in his early forties, wearing expensive jeans, leather thongs and a plain, fitted, white T-shirt approached the podium. 'Greetings everyone,' he said in his slow, methodical low voice. 'Thanks for coming out tonight. As you most know, VirchWorld's technology is the federal government's partner in creating our brave new world. Of course, there are a few other options out there . . .' He looked across the room. 'But they're not as good as ours.' Laughter followed his words. 'Just remember we offer a universal guarantee. Once you upload your VR to our servers, it will exist in perpetuity. If your museum were to burn down the virtual world version will remain untouched, pristine and lovely as ever.'

People in the crowd looked at each other, clearly impressed by his words.

'He was already a millionaire,' Abner whispered. 'This partnership with the government has made him a billionaire ten times over.'

'Now, I'd like to bring up Samuel Chang of the San Francisco Museum of History who is one of our early adapters. His museum has had a VR in place for eighteen months. Sam, come on up.' More clapping, and a man in his forties wearing a red, white and black plaid tuxedo with his hair slicked back joined Anton on the stage.

At least Abner wasn't the only eccentric in the bunch.

Samuel spent fifteen minutes talking about how they created the environment with Anton's team, how easy it was to set up, how much more they could sell tickets for and the uptick of visitors, in person and online.

'So, it's not what you think. Our museum is still filled with patrons. They can come to our VR room and use the headset, or they can log in from their home for the exact same experience. And we still have patrons visiting our PR or physical world.'

I looked at Abner. 'Still not impressed?'

'I'm scared. For our fellow Americans. They're sheep being led to the slaughter. Happily.'

Samuel looked across the crowd. 'Any questions?'

'What's the ratio of IRL to VR patrons?' someone asked.

'Right now? Sixty-forty. Most of our VR patrons are from out of the area, the state, the country. The trend we see is that patrons who can travel to the museum still do.'

Anton Jax stepped forward. 'We hope to see those numbers flip-flop, with locals opting for the VR option. Just stay home and plug in, right?'

Samuel half-frowned. 'Well, no, we want to keep those IRL numbers up, just double our capacity with VR patrons. Get those customers who could never afford a trip to the museum because they live in Ghana or Croatia, for example.'

Anton stepped up then, bumping Samuel out of the way. 'But let's say, for example, there was another great fire that destroyed San Francisco like it did in . . .' He looked at the museum director. 'When was it?'

Multiple people in the crowd shouted the year.

Anton laughed. 'Of course. I'm in a room full of historians.'

'Let's say a great fire swept through San Francisco like it did in 1906, destroyed the museum completely.'

Samuel frowned.

'Now, no one can visit the museum and all of those great works have been lost.' He paused for dramatic effect. 'Or have they?' He cackled a laugh. 'Of course not. Because it's all been uploaded to the server. In *perpetuity*. Throughout the universe.' He gave an exaggerated wink. 'And because Samuel is one of our early adapters, as an early signer to the pledge he worked directly with VirchWorld to create his environment. You guys, you can plug into the environment and pick the type of day you want to visit. Hot and sunny. Raining. Cold. It's that detailed. You can feel your hand press against the door to push it open. Smell the same air freshener the IRL museum used . . .' He looked at Samuel. 'Lilac Fields, right?'

Samuel's frown increased. 'Sure, but—'

'But nothing. My point is every single detail of the museum has been recreated with loving care and accuracy. It's literally better than the real thing. No waiting lines. Every user gets a customized tour in their language with their learning style matched to their IQ because we'll already have that information in our databases. We own so many marketing and financial and political and social databases, there's nothing we don't know about your patrons.

'We will customize, customize, customize. And the best part?' He paused again. 'They can touch museum pieces in the VR environment. We're making this so unbelievable that visiting IRL will be a subpar experience. Patrons will prefer the VR experience. And this is the real value added. You can stop staffing the IRL museum. Stop paying utilities thereby decreasing the resources used. Costs go down, the environment is a little cleaner.'

He stopped, panting from his own excitement.

'Jesus Christ,' Abner muttered. 'He's a maniac. You see that right? He's obsessed.'

I couldn't help but agree. There was definitely something off about this VR initiative, but what resonated with me was the stated goal to stop staffing the museums. Maybe I was just extra sensitive since my furlough but using VR to force people out of their jobs was a red flag.

What would happen to all the people who worked there? And there was something about the references to the museums being saved if they just so happened to burn down that struck me as more like a threat than a benefit . . .

And then a flash of color caught my eye. A short, curly, brownish-red Afro caught my attention. *Dad?* Across the room, a handsome man with light brown skin covered in freckles was making his way across the floor, shaking hands and stopping to speak to almost everyone.

Abner followed my gaze and smiled for the first time since we arrived. 'Your father's here.'

A moment later my father saw me and made a beeline. He approached me, arms outstretched. 'Sidney, I had no idea you'd be here.' He wrapped me in a tight hug. Over my shoulder, he spoke to Abner. 'You're here too?' He chuckled, then released the embrace, his hazel eyes warming as he looked at me. 'Happy to hear you're with Mother. I don't like her being all alone down there, but I can barely get away. And she'd never dream of leaving our beloved farm.' He gave me a once-over, then took my hand, held it up and made me do a twirl. 'Simply gorgeous.'

'Mom's here?' I looked around the room.

His pleased expression didn't change. 'No, she's busy. As always.' He crossed his arms and looked at Abner. 'You've signed the pledge? Is that why you're here?'

Abner sighed. 'Of course not. You know me. Where do you fall on this topic?'

'Much to the chagrin of Marta and the president, I have not voiced my opinion. And I'd like to keep it that way. It's very controversial right now and I'm trying my best to stay out of it.'

Abner turned to my father. 'Now is the time to make our voices heard, John David. You can't be on board with what they're doing. Trying to push us into a virtual world? For what purpose?'

My father scanned the room, his gaze landing on Anton. 'They're clever rolling out VR like they did social media. Get all of the federal government, the institutions, the big companies to use say a Facebook or TikTok first, add in the celebrities and influencers to make it trendy, compel you to join the platform so you can interact with them there and then you're hooked because all your friends are there and it's just so fun, and oh yeah, if you want to pay your light bill or file your taxes you need to be in VR.' He chuckled. 'Right?'

'Wrong,' Abner said.

'They're already asking us representatives to create VR offices so our constituents can stop by and visit with our avatars.' Abner rolled his eyes, but my father only laughed. 'They'll want to train their AI on how we talk, move, process information, so the avatars can organically respond . . . It's interesting but with the potential for shenanigans with deep fakes, I think I prefer the old-fashioned ways.'

My father patted me on my arm. 'I see a senator I need to talk to. Don't leave before saying goodbye.' He gave me a lingering look. A proud look, then moved into the crowd.

'We need to do something about this administration. I can only see them abusing VR.' I saw Marta and Anton across the room, sipping champagne and schmoozing with journalists and politicians.

'Finally, you believe me.'

'I definitely think legislation needs to be crafted to put limits in place. Like yesterday.'

Abner cast an evil eye the way of Marta as he spoke. 'As with the appearance of most new technologies, government is slow to create legislation to curtail its use. And in this case it's coming from the government . . .'

'So they're going to get away with as much as they can before there's public outrage.'

He snagged a glass of champagne from a passing waiter. 'They're probably hoping by the time everyone is plugged in, it will be too late for outrage.' Abner scanned the crowd, then sipped his wine. 'Besides me, I don't see one person who hasn't signed the pledge. I'm very concerned.'

'But it's voluntary, yes?'

'So they say.'

There was a flurry of action in a corner of the room, and several men in dark suits and cropped haircuts began moving through the crowds in an overly important way.

'Someone big is about to arrive,' Abner predicted. 'Maybe the VP?'

Across the room a band began to play. I recognized the tune. 'Hail To The Chief'. I looked around the ballroom as were many others. A minute later, President Williamson entered the room. A tanned white man with a cloud of soft white hair, bright blue eyes and a warm countenance.

The crowd parted as he waved and shook hands. I had to smile. This kind of thing happened all the time if you lived and worked in DC and traveled in the right circles. This was probably why my father was here. Ever the politician, he never missed an opportunity to be seen with the president in social settings.

I glanced at Abner who had a look of disgust on his face. 'Fix your face, before the secret service target you for giving the president dirty looks.'

Abner blanked his expression. 'I'm not angry with him. It's the people behind him doing this, not him. I am disappointed he caved, though. I met him once when he was a governor, and he talked a lot about his family's tree business and how he loved being in nature. The smell of trees, the benefits of replanting to prevent deforestation . . . And he seemed interested in helping his state and our country.'

My father made his way back to me. 'I've heard he's making a big announcement tonight.'

I looked around. 'That explains the media.'

Marta appeared at the podium again, introducing the president with a flourish of her hands. Camera lights were popping and video cameras were rolling.

The president preened for the cameras, then looked out at the room. 'Today is a momentous day in not just American history. We will make world history with a new initiative I'm announcing to you all in this very room. And it's my hope that other countries in Europe, Asia, Africa and beyond will follow our courageous lead.'

'My God. Are we going to war again?' Abner wondered aloud.

'Much like the beloved Fifteen-Minute City initiative designed to ease traffic congestion, reduce community footprints and create an institutionalized work-life balance that prioritize life, make our communities more livable by ensuring that all essential services, like schools, doctors' offices and retail are all within the distance of a short enjoyable walk or bicycle ride. We have a new plan.' He paused. 'This initiative is a natural extension of my Foundational Acts for Digital Reality Integration which –' he pointed to the ceiling – 'God willing, will be completed this year. Which paves the way for me to push through congress the Digital Reality Access Act.'

'When that happens nothing will be voluntary,' Abner said in a low voice.

'My hope is that this non-partisan bill will breeze through both houses without opposition by the end of the year so we can get started on what I hope will be my legacy. The most important thing I'm known for: The Virtual Metropolis 2050.' He paused so the media could go wild.

They did.

A hundred hands went up, with questions being flung at the president.

'Oh shit,' Abner muttered. 'It's about to hit the fan.'

Just then, a young man appeared on stage. 'No questions today, please. We're just announcing.'

A disappointed hiss floated over the press, but they settled down. The president nodded at the staff member. 'I don't want to take up too much of your time tonight. This is a lovely event, and I add my voice to Dr De Verona's when I say thank you from the bottom of my heart for supporting me in this cause by adapting early to the future.

'The Virtual Metropolis 2050 initiative is a visionary government program aimed at transforming ten major cities into fully immersive virtual environments by the year 2050.' The president paused to look at his notes. 'State-of-the-art VR and AR technologies will be seamlessly integrated into urban planning, enabling citizens to access virtual experiences, services, and even workplaces without leaving their homes.'

There was a ripple of noise in the crowd and the president looked up. His security details scanned the crowds.

'Virtual clinics will provide citizens with efficient healthcare services, enabling remote consultations, diagnoses, and treatments. Our children . . .' He paused to make eye contact with many of the women in the crowd. 'Our best resources, our future . . . will have access to the best virtualized education platforms offering personalized, interactive learning experiences, making education accessible to all and fostering innovation.'

He looked up, eyes bright. 'Think of it. No poverty divide. No education deserts . . . And lastly, a block chain-based virtual currency will facilitate secure transactions within the virtual ecosystem, promoting financial stability and inclusivity.'

He set his note cards down. 'These ten cities will be transformed. And the governor and the mayors of each city will receive generous grants for the city as well as bonuses and incentives to encourage business owners and residents to agree to becoming a Virtual Metropolis. There will be a referendum, a vote.' He laughed. 'This is America. Of course, each city will be selected democratically.'

'If the elections aren't rigged or the officials paid off,' Abner said, a dark expression on his face. 'Don't look now but the president

is coming this way.' His voice was flat, his expression grim as the
president flanked by his security detail approached them.

'Abner Robbins, so good of you to show up here tonight.' He
reached for Abner's hand, they both froze and smiled for the waiting
cameras. 'I hear you're one of the last holdouts for our voluntary
pledge.'

'If it's truly voluntary, it should be OK that I haven't signed.'

The president chuckled. 'It's OK, Abner,' he said, his voice firm.
'It's just better for everyone if you volunteer. That way you get the
incentives and bonuses. When it's law and you have to comply,
there'll only be penalties. Because then you'll be breaking the law
if you don't.'

'Then I'll wait for the law.'

'Hmm . . .' The president glanced at one of his staff members
nearby before focusing on Abner again. 'There's nothing I can say
or do or offer you to urge you to join voluntarily?'

Abner didn't even think about it. 'No.'

As odd as Abner could be at times, I was proud of him in that
moment. He was sticking to his guns even though the president
literally said he'd offer him anything if he'd just sign.

'Even though another colonial museum we both know and love
that is bigger than yours and much more popular than yours has
joined . . . still not moved?'

Sweat beads had begun to form on Abner's head. Poor guy.

He mopped his brow with his handkerchief. 'No. Respectfully.
Sir.'

A secret service agent standing to the left of the president stared
Abner dead in his face. His expression was so hard and mean I
had to wonder if his face was made of stone. But Abner stood his
ground.

'Well, all right,' President Williamson said with a surprised look
on his face. 'Gotta love a man with backbone.' He glanced at his
group of staff who all nodded like bobbleheads.

'Yes, sir,' Abner responded. 'And that's what our country needs.
A president with backbone. Vice President Witcover comes to mind.
Sir.'

The president paused, regarded Abner with a squint.

Because of his tone and the smile pasted on his face, it was hard
to tell how Abner meant it.

The president blinked, the only anomaly in his expression. And then he nodded, very curt, and walked away. He put an arm around my father's shoulder and asked him to come with.

My father gave me a peck on the cheek. 'It was good seeing you, Sidney. Tell mother I send my love.'

I watched my father taken away in a cloud of politics and politicians.

I decided to visit the ladies room and bumped into Marta, who was accepting a heated towel from an attendant in the corner.

'Sidney, isn't it?' she said.

I nodded.

She handed the used towel to the attendant. 'Your name was flagged to me as being related to Speaker Taylor. He's one of the few representatives who has not publicly voiced his support for the initiative. I hope he's not going against us and throwing his support in with the VP?' She raised an eyebrow.

I glanced at the next room which held the bathroom closets, hoping she'd take a hint. 'Mind if I . . .'

'Of course.'

When I left the bathroom, to my surprise she was waiting for me in the powder room.

'May I walk with?' she asked, as she stepped into line beside me.

'Sure. I was just getting a drink.' I needed one.

'I could do with some wine,' she said, like we were girlfriends from way back. 'Let's do it.'

I cringed inwardly wondering what she wanted but moved towards the open bar. Once we were in line she turned to me. 'I could use someone like you in my administration. Smart. Experienced. Connected. What do you think?'

I laughed nervously. 'That is an amazing offer, but VR is not really my thing.'

'Oh, honey,' she said, and couldn't have been more condescending. 'Pretty soon, VR is going to be everyone's thing.'

We moved up into the line.

'Obviously, DC is going to be one of the Virtual Metropolises. I can't imagine Washingtonians wanting to be left behind in the coming Virtual Revolution. And one of the projects will be to recreate the history of the district so that users can visit any area of the city at any time and see anything happen. Just imagine. You could watch Abraham Lincoln being shot.'

I couldn't help myself. I frowned. I'd much prefer seeing President Lincoln as he lived.

'Or the White House being burned down during the war of 1812? Just a fly on the wall.'

'I could watch the formerly enslaved Paul Jennings save the Gilbert Stuart portrait of George Washington,' I pointed out.

'Doesn't it just? And you can be a part of it, re-envisioning history as—' She stopped when she saw my expression. 'What did I say?'

I frowned. 'Re-envisioning?'

Marta paused, then laughed. '*Envisioning*,' she stressed. 'Obviously. As Chief Historical Virtual Experience Curator for the district.' She lifted a shoulder. 'Or maybe the country? I'm open.'

We reached the bar as all sorts of warning bells sounded in my mind. I requested a white wine. So did Marta.

'Sounds tempting,' I lied. 'But for now I'm going to keep my current post in Robbinsville.'

She chuckled. 'Ah, Robbinsville. Small-town America. Home of the infamous Madison letter.' Her lips quirked up. 'Do I have that right?'

I couldn't hide my surprise. She knew about the letter too?

'Yes, I was born in Robbinsville,' she said, misunderstanding the reason for my expression. 'Hard to believe someone as worldly and accomplished as me could be from a small town like that, right?'

I frowned. My father was from there. Many good people came from small towns. But I didn't say any of that to her. I was much more intrigued that she knew about President Madison. 'You've heard about the letter and what it leads to?' I clarified.

Marta shrugged. 'Supposedly leads to. It's a mythological object like the Arthurian sword in the stone. He's wasting time. And so are you.' She gave a doubtful look. 'I know both your mother and your father. Can't find two more ambitious people. Don't tell me their success gene skipped you?' she teased, her voice louder than it needed to be. Or at least I thought so.

I took her card. No need to make an enemy of this woman. 'Thank you, Dr De Verona. I better get back to my friends.'

Her expression changed. Slightly. 'Like Abner Robbins?'

'Yes . . .' I took a sip of wine, feeling like I needed it. 'What about him?'

'In the future, you may want to make sure you're friends with the right kinds of people.' Her smile was brittle. 'Eventually we'll be establishing a social credit system, and users – Americans – will be penalized for poor judgement calls. That includes friendships with the wrong sort.'

I swallowed the lump in my throat.

'That's all.'

I tried very hard to pretend she wasn't predicting a horrifying future for Americans – people she'd just called users for a system she wanted to run. I forced my lips in a thin smile. 'Abner's been very decent to me.'

Her face fell, clearly something of what I was feeling seeped through my polite response. 'Wait, I don't want to end things on a sour note.' She laughed, waving a hand. 'Come by my office tomorrow and we'll grab a coffee. Talk about how we can help Abner help his museum.'

I felt rude saying no again, but . . . 'I'm sorry, I have an early flight.'

Her thin eyebrows rose. 'Oh. So, it's like that, is it?' She looked at me as if she felt sorry for me. 'Have it your way.'

Her phone rang, and she looked at the screen, annoyance on her face. All bonhomie gone. 'I have to take this.'

SIXTEEN

Abner and I drove away from the gala in a chauffeured car. He glanced at the driver before turning to me. 'Do you see now? Do you see why it's so important we find the artifact? The people who opposed the founding of America during Madison's time are secretly in charge, making us think we're independent when we're still beholden to the very people we fought the revolutionary war against. And now they're purposely running our country into the ground. That's not why this country was founded. Our people deserve more.'

'You think Madison's letter leads to an artifact that can specifically stop the Virtual Metropolis 2050 from happening?'

'I know it sounds impossible, but it has to. I don't know how it's going to prevent this virtual revolution, but it will. I have faith.'

I grunted. 'I'm glad one of us does.'

'Do you think the goal is to stop at ten cities? It's a rollout. A test. Ten cities. Then twenty. Thirty. And then the whole world. Where does it end?'

I tried to envision the initiative stopping with ten cities. With Virtual Metropolises being cool, fun places to go like a tourist destination . . . And couldn't. I believed that this VR revolution could steamroll into something that evolved into a restrictive police state for our country. I just wasn't sure how President Madison foresaw this. It wasn't like he could see the future.

But Abner was right. I saw the gleam in President Williamson's eyes. Heard the determination in Marta's voice. This wouldn't stop with ten cities. It was only the beginning.

'Marta seems to have taken a liking to me.'

Abner scowled. 'Really?'

'She offered me a job.'

He barked a laugh. 'I hope you told her where to shove it.'

'I declined. But she knew about the letter.'

'You're serious. My letter?'

'Yeah.'

He stared ahead, eyes unfixed.

I broke the silence. 'She wanted me to meet her for coffee tomorrow. I said no.'

'What? You have to go. Find out what she knows. Why she brought the letter up. Snoop around her office, see what you can find.'

'Seriously?'

'Yes,' he said, vehemence roughening his voice. 'Yes.'

She'd given me her card. I pulled it out and sent her a text, telling her that I'd had a change of plans and could meet her after all.

The next morning, I found myself sitting in the DRIA headquarters. A sleek chromatic building of glass and mirrors with minimalistic furniture. I signed in with facial recognition, matched to my driver's license I was told. Then sent up an elevator to the top floor where I sat in another smaller waiting area with a DRIA employee working on a holographic screen at a sleek standing desk.

After only a few minutes, she brought me to Marta's penthouse office. It was surprising to say the least. It was empty save for two chairs – comfortable and expensive looking but quite lonely in the huge space.

Marta was standing at a window, her back to us, when I entered.

She turned and blinked when she saw me. 'You made it. Wonderful.'

I looked around her office. 'Moving?'

She laughed. 'Jane?'

Her assistant handed me a small box lined with a soft silk-like material. A VR headset lay inside. It was a thin rose-gold copper circlet, like a tiara or crown, with three small round crystals that seemed to hover just above it like magnets.

I looked around the office again. 'I get it. Your office is in VR.'

'How can I sell it to the American people if I'm not living and breathing it?'

'Makes sense.'

'Thanks, Jane.' She watched her employee leave, then turned to my set. 'Here, let me help you.' She placed the device on my head, murmuring, 'All that fabulous hair. The set could get lost in all those curls and waves.'

I actually smiled. Her admiration was palpable.

She positioned the first two crystals on my temples, then held up the third. 'I've got the latest prototype.' She firmly pressed it between my eyebrows and up half an inch. Right in front of my pineal gland.

'Being director has its perks.' She stepped back and looked at me. 'Anton really hooked me up with this one. The third crystal provides extra sensory input. You'll see.'

I put the set on. Heard a buzzing sound. Felt a moment of disorientation, then looked down at my hands. In the VR, Marta appeared before me looking the exact same, and like an actual person. Not an avatar.

'Scary, right?' Marta's avatar laughed. 'You look real too. We scanned you last night as you entered the building, and again when you looked at yourself in the bathroom mirrors, so if you were to look in a mirror here, you'd think you were actually seeing your true reflection.'

I looked around the space, and realized I was in the same room, except now it was fitted with furniture, art, plants, carpet. It was beautiful. I looked out the window. It was a view of London.

'The DC skyline gets boring.' She stood beside me. 'Have a seat. Coffee's coming.'

Did she say coffee? I sat in a chair, feeling the cushions under my legs. I could feel the carpet underfoot. Hear the whir of the air conditioner. Maybe President Williamson would be able to smell the trees.

'My set has advancements DARPA's been playing around with, nothing that will be on the market for at least five years.'

I knew the US Department of Defense's Defense Advanced Research Projects Agency developed some cutting-edge technology, but this was beyond anything I could have imagined.

We chatted about nothing for a few minutes, and then her assistant's avatar came in with coffee service on a cart. The smell of dark roast permeated the room.

Marta grinned. 'We have a neural ink that approximates smell. But watch this.'

The assistant handed me a cup of coffee. I felt the weight in my hand, the heat through the ceramic of the cup. 'How is this possible?'

'Technology. Ain't it grand?'

My avatar sipped the coffee and enjoyed the taste and feel of the warm beverage going down my throat. 'I can see how interacting in this environment could be addictive.'

'And this isn't even the fun stuff. You could go to the movies, a night club, see a concert, your favorite comedian, even a book signing. But I didn't ask you here for the bells and whistles. Let's get down to brass tacks. What's Abner Robbins' problem?'

'Why does he matter? He's just one man.'

'There are two hundred and fifty-seven museums that we want on board this year. And it's just him and a few others like him that are refusing to sign up. If everyone doesn't join the initiative it looks like there's something wrong with what we're doing.'

'*Is* there anything wrong with what you're doing?'

She stared at me. I mean her avatar did, and it was unnerving. But I stared back.

Her avatar's lips moved into a grin. 'See, this is why I need you to work for me. I need people not afraid to ask the tough questions. I'm doing this for our people. For our future.'

'Sell me on the initiative.'

'Happy to. There are many, many reasons Virtual Metropolises 2050 or VM 2050 is a good idea, but let's start with saving the planet, shall we? I think that's something we can all get behind, yes?'

'Of course.'

'VR provides a sustainable alternative to physical travel, reducing carbon emissions. It will also help us to conserve energy, water, and raw materials that would otherwise be used in physical infrastructure and activities. And overpopulation? Don't get me started on that problem. We're going to have people fall into the ocean because of a lack of land and resources.' She laughed. 'Do you want that?'

I'd never quite bought the overpopulation theory. If you traveled, you knew there was so much open land, undeveloped land in America alone. Canada . . . So much space to grow. Places to grow food. Sun and wind could be harvested for energy . . . I shrugged. 'How are we conserving energy with a massive worldwide VR matrix? Sounds like the opposite of saving energy.'

'We'll have all the energy we need to make sure the government's facilities and the VR environment runs properly. It's a matter of allocating the energy we have where it's most needed.'

'And the people, American citizens – you can't expect them to be plugged in twenty-four seven. There will be many who see it as a game but will want to leave and be in the real world. Go shopping, travel, see people.'

She laughed. 'Give it time. We've done the studies. People will develop patterns. Having their groceries, dinner and goods delivered. Virtual vacations will be the norm. The need for all the junk people fill their homes with will be replaced with something similar to in-app purchases. Why buy a fancy new chair when you can just buy one for your VR home and have your avatar sit on that?'

My smile felt wooden and pasted into place. The future this woman saw was scary. And she was in a position of power?

She watched me for a moment. 'I don't get you, Sidney Taylor. You seem so . . . ambivalent? Apathetic? Oh, right . . . you're a trust fund kid. Your money and privilege insulate you from the woes of society.'

'I care.' The words were confident, but my tone was hesitant. I was stunned by her assessment of me. But hadn't Professor Philippi said something similar? Were these two women both accusing me of being as superficial and frivolous as I thought my mother was?

'Regardless of how you feel, the law is the law. Or will be the law. Our goal is to have all federal, state and city level government offices, all schools, medical facilities, museums, amusement parks and theaters and retail stores in the virtual space by 2030. Abner will have to comply now or later.'

'Many Americans won't be interested in leaving the real world for all of this, as interesting as it is. You'd be better off starting just with entertainment and bringing in users that way.'

'We thought of that, and if we had more time . . . It's important that we have all the infrastructure in place.'

'What aren't you telling me?'

She stood. 'Come, let me show you something.'

I joined her beside her desk. She made a few wiping movements in the air and a holographic screen displayed weather radar images, photographs from NASA and various charts. 'What am I looking at?'

'You've heard about the solar flares, yes?'

I nodded.

'It started with that, about five years ago we received word from NASA that instances of solar flares might increase. And if they did, it would be a warning of sorts of a larger incident. One that could potentially destroy our power grid and all accompanying infrastructure.

'If you've been paying attention, the incidents of intermittent power failure are increasing. The media's working with us to cover up the true origins of the blackouts. I believe they've been saying it's home-grown terrorism.' She waved her hand dismissively. 'At any rate, we've been working on solutions ever since.'

'Going virtual is your solution?'

'After much research, debate and self-examination, we at the Global Virtualization Conference determined this was the best course of action to preserve as much of our world as possible before a solar flare decimated the power grids and caused our world to be changed forever. This way we're in charge of our own destiny and can do things on our own terms.'

I must've still looked skeptical. How would VR work if the power grids were decimated? Something here didn't add up.

'Look. We've always been planning a VR integration. This is just the perfect time, the best time to do it.'

'Making lemonade from lemons?'

'Sure.'

'You're predicting a catastrophic event but not sharing the news with the world?'

'The people who need to know, the decision makers are aware. Plus, the mother of all solar flares is supposed to come in a few years, with mini ones coming before. In order to sustain a high quality of life consistent with current levels, we'll need to severely ration our resources before the big event happens. Can you imagine your beloved Robbinsville in absolute chaos? Main Street won't be so charming with throngs of rioters looking for food.

'The best way to maintain our world as we know it, is if everyone stays home. If everyone does everything in virtual reality. That way we can route energy where it needs to go instead of wasting it on the random places users – Americans – may decide to go. Let me give you an example. Do you have an idea how much electricity and water all of the Targets in America use up? If we're rationing energy, instead of keeping say two thousand Targets open in America, there could be one amazing virtual Target where anyone can shop at any time and they're never out of stock. In terms of saving energy, it's almost incalculable.'

'Clearly, you've spent many, many years thinking about this.'

'It's my life's work. And no matter how fun and exciting it may all be, we can't forget this is about preserving the American way of life. If Abner had read our material, taken our calls or attended our information sessions, he would know why this is necessary. Why most of his peers are on board.'

A phone rang, and she moved to her desk. 'I'll be just a moment. Please help yourself to more coffee.'

She went to her window, looking out at her view of Paris – it had changed again while she took her call. My eyes slid to her desk, and I scanned the documents and folders lying there. Nothing caught my eye. Just paperwork from VirchWorld, contracts, licensing deals and other legal documents. I saw bills of purchase from QLabs. Surprising to see here but not unexpected since it was known that the DRIA funded them. I returned to my seat and finished my virtual coffee.

Marta ended her call, glanced at the papers on her desk, shuffled them together and slid them into a folder. 'My apologies, but I had to take that. And now, I also need to run,' she chuckled. 'In real life. One day soon, I can just stay here and have my avatar travel to my appointments. But that will only happen if everyone and everything is in VR. You will share with Abner what we've discussed today?'

'Of course.'

I removed the set. And was back in an empty room. I blinked, feeling like my body was swaying on a body of water.

'You'll be fine. It just takes a moment.'

* * *

I met Abner at the airport. We boarded the plane and got settled in our seats.

The pilot came back, introduced himself before going to the cockpit. Abner was all smiles until he left.

Then he turned to me, face grim. 'So what did she say?'

I buckled my seatbelt and thanked the stewardess for my blanket. When she moved away, I looked at him. 'She was compelling, I have to say.'

He rolled his eyes. 'Let me guess she's predicted a natural disaster and the government wants everyone to shelter inside, plug into the matrix for the safety of everyone and the planet.'

I laughed. 'Something like that, yes. How'd you know?'

'When you've been around as long as I have, you begin to see patterns of behavior in our politicians and leaders.'

I told him what she actually said.

He scoffed. 'And you believed her?'

'Solar flares are pretty convincing.'

He rolled his eyes. 'The world is not going to explode because of solar flares.'

'But it's already happening. Have you been watching the news?'

'You mean the propaganda machine.'

I sighed, rested against the seat and closed my eyes. Sometimes, not always but often, talking to someone who disbelieved everything he read and saw in the media was exhausting.

The pilot began his takeoff spiel.

'Just keep up your search. I'm convinced more than ever that if we don't stop this administration, nobody will.'

A balloon of anxiety began to form in the hollow of my chest. But I tried to ignore it, as I stretched out my legs, pulled out my phone and found the photograph I'd taken of the Madison letter in the library.

. . . *and spoke at length with a friend on the subject of moral philosophy. I even gifted his daughter with a trinket.*

I stared at the words. *Daughter.* That took on a new meaning now. Daughter was a member of the Hathor society. Madison understood who and what the women were, and he'd given the trinket to a Daughter of Hathor. But he said *his* daughter, so the female member had to be a part of his friend Knox's famlily. Only he didn't have a daughter. Professor Philippi said many of the daughters hid their true identities among the servant and salve classes . . . Knox probably had female servant and they would've been considered property at the time.

SEVENTEEN

A fter our driver dropped Abner off at his house, I pondered the clues in the Madison letter.

The Daughters were committed to protecting something. And under fear of prosecution and death they always stayed in proximity to it. So why didn't they know where it had been hidden?

Abner had me searching for an artifact President Madison had overheard servants say had magical powers and the ability to save our country.

What were the odds that there were two different objects? I pressed my head against the leather seats of the town car and pressed my eyes closed. Zero. It had to be zero.

I was looking for whatever the Daughters of Hathor vowed to protect. I just had to figure out what that was.

My phone rang. It was a researcher at the New Bern archives hopefully following up on my request for more information about the Knox family.

'The family line died out. A couple generations ago. I'm sorry.'

'So it's a dead end?'

'The family papers were donated to the New Bern Historical Society. Could be something of use there, but maybe not. You're a historian, you know how these things go.'

If there were papers, there was information, and I couldn't wait to get my fingers in the cardboard crates I'm sure the duplicated information probably resided in. 'As soon as I have a free moment in my schedule, I'll head down there. There has to be something I can use.'

I arrived home, dropped off my bag, took a quick shower and changed into a pair of shorts and a T-shirt. I searched the grounds until I found my grandmother. She was in the backyard wearing a flowing sundress, a big floppy hat and sandals. She was on her knees, hands deep in the abundant leaves of a bushy green plant plucking blackberries from the branches. She looked so serene. Not like she was the keeper of ancient secrets. Was anything as it seemed?

'Need some help?'

She looked up, smiling when she saw me. 'Hello, dear. Of course.' She pointed to a pail nearby. 'Fill it up with berries, I'll be making jam with these.'

'And cobbler?'

'If you like.'

'I saw Dad. He sends his love.'

'I know. He called me. Said you were stunning.'

She turned back to the berries, and we worked in comfortable quiet. When her own pail was full, she turned to me. 'So, how's the car running?'

'She's perfect. I can't keep her, but I'll certainly give her some road time while Gabe tries to salvage the bike.'

'Don't be silly. The paperwork has already been done. You'll receive the title in a few weeks. It's a family heirloom. Your father wanted that car, but I think you'll appreciate it more.'

I laughed, thinking of my father's collection of vintage cars. 'You're right. It would only be one of many nice cars he has, one of three Jaguars, come to think of it.'

'But you'll give it the TLC she deserves.' She gave me a knowing look. 'Gabe's a nice young man.'

I blushed. 'Yes, he is.' And left it at that.

I finished one pail even though I was probably eating one out of every three berries I picked. It was hard not to eat them, they were so fat and juicy and naturally sweet. I grabbed another to fill. I'd filled it halfway when I felt my grandmother looking at me.

'How's your search coming along?'

I stared at my hands. My fingers were stained purple. 'The search led me to DC. I've just returned from visiting Professor Philippi at the Smithsonian.'

'How is Gwen?'

I nodded. 'That's right. You know each other . . . How'd that happen?'

'We met at museum fundraisers. She's visited here several times.'

If she'd been keeping an eye on me, did that mean she'd contrived meetings with my grandmother to keep an eye on her as well? But to what end? What had my grandmother ever done besides live in a small town, be decent to folk and live her life?

'I don't think I knew that. I thought I'd met her in grad school . . . organically.'

Sighing, she hauled herself up. 'Come on.' She squinted skyward. 'The sun's at its peak.'

I followed her through the back door and into the kitchen. She peeled off her gloves and hung her hat on a nail on the wall. We both washed our hands with a rosemary and thyme soap she'd made herself.

'You wash the berries and I'll make us something cool and refreshing to drink.'

I went to the sink, turned on the cold water and let it flow over the berries, gently combing my finger through the fruit. When I was done, I joined my grandmother at the table.

My grandmother drank half her glass of icy peppermint water before she spoke.

'She's known about you for a while. Was interested in your progress.'

'So, she came down here to check up on me when I was in college?'

'Yes.'

'Why?'

'You're special, Sidney. Always have been.'

I looked up from my glass. 'Meaning?' Had I ignored the one person who could help me with my search? 'What do you know, Grams?'

She sighed. 'Only that certain people wanted to keep an eye . . . first on your father. And then you. In high school, he was on the radar for special scholarships, mentorships and programs. Later, he was directed into leadership curriculums and then politics.'

'But by whom?'

She shrugged. 'A counselor, a teacher . . . There was always someone around telling me how special he was. How he was meant for great things. Eventually we all believed it, including your father. And now he's the Speaker of the House. Third in line to be president, can you believe it?'

I could believe it. My father'd been a politician for most of my life. 'And this happened for me as well?'

She nodded. 'Not quite the same, but I know your parents were told the same types of things.'

'I never felt any pressure to study anything in particular.'

'You were on the radar of a few people . . . you received a partial academic scholarship to go to Hopkins, didn't you?'

I nodded. 'Professor Philippi was associated with that scholarship. It's how she became my mentor.'

My grandmother nodded.

I stared at my hands, then met her eyes. 'This is all because of your biological mother,' I began.

She shrugged. 'I come from a woman who didn't want to be a mother.' Her expression was frank. 'So, a lot was lost. Things I should've known . . . I didn't. When I went to college, I met your grandfather. We fell in love, got married after he graduated. I left school my sophomore year and we moved into this house. And after we'd been happily married for about a year, he told me who I was.'

'He knew something?'

She nodded. 'Only that his parents told him he could only marry certain women from certain families. And he knew I was one of them.'

'But how?'

'He was in a fraternity, and they only dated women from a certain sorority.'

'So he singled you out? How did you end up at this particular college in this particular sorority?'

'After I graduated from high school, my parents told me the church had raised money to send me to college. They told me which school to apply to, I did and was accepted. Once I was there, I was asked to join a sorority. Turns out most girls in the sorority were Daughters. That is what we're talking about? Daughters of Hathor?'

I leaned forward. 'So, you have heard of them? Why have you never mentioned them to me?'

'It's a name. No more.'

'This is all because of your biological mother – who and what she was. Don't you want to know more about her?'

The lines of my grandmother's face sharpened into angry planes. 'She didn't want me. It's all I need to know.'

'So Granddad was like predatory. He—'

'No. It wasn't like that at all. He said that he had several women to choose from and he thought I was the prettiest and the sweetest, so he chose me. And I chose him back. We loved each other and were happy for forty years.'

'What does my father know?'

'I'm not sure. Nothing from me and your grandfather. If he's been told more since being elected that first time, he's never mentioned it. As far as I know, he's just an intelligent, ambitious politician that many people support and would like to see as president. And he's accepted his role as champion for the people.'

'What does this mean for me?'

'You can live your life. Possibly marry a Son of Horus and have children that may or may not grow up to become important leaders in our world.'

'Like Aislin? She knows?'

My grandmother shook her head. 'She doesn't know. But she's always been a bit of a people pleaser. Your mother set her up with several eligible bachelors, all Sons of Horus, and she married one. I believe your mother tried to set you up with a few Sons of Horus as well?'

'As a member of this group, that's what I'm supposed to do? Just marry the right guy and have babies? And maybe one of them will grow up to rule the world? That's my fate?'

I thought of the numerous men my mother had paraded in front of me during my time at Hopkins. I'd rejected them all, and then I'd met my ex – Magnus. But that hadn't worked out either.

My grandmother laughed. 'Unless you're called to do more.'

Was I called to do more? 'What does my mother know? She has to be a Daughter of Hathor too, right?'

'Your mother has always reminded me of the girls in my sorority. Pretty, charismatic, privileged young women. She had children and a career. She should be applauded for doing both.'

'She knew she was a Daughter of Hathor and told me nothing?'

My grandmother shrugged. 'Call her.' She rose from her seat.

I clenched my teeth, as I watched her disappear upstairs.

I changed into a fresh pair of shorts and a T-shirt, settled onto my bed, sat in the full lotus position, mentally preparing myself to call my mother. Out of habit, I'd done my makeup for the webcam call. My mother was like that, she expected perfection at all times, and I didn't want to hear her say how unpolished I looked, because she would, irrationally, believe I looked that way all the time. So, I'd brushed my hair and pulled it back into a ponytail, added a light sprinkling of oil-reducing powder to my face and a hint of gloss. Natural. Understated. Just enough, hopefully to appease my mother.

I connected the call, holding my breath. And then the camera screen opened, and my mother was looking at me.

'Sidney, is that you? Is that really and truly you?'

My mother, beautiful as always, gazed at me with her big brown doe eyes expertly rimmed in blackest kohl. 'Yes, Mother. It's me.'

Her lips, covered in a matte merlot-colored lipstick spread

into a grateful smile. 'I have been dying to hear from you, *mon chéri*.'

My mother, who spent a few years in Paris after journalism school, occasionally lapsed into French. It was pretentious, yes. But that was just my mother.

'Why have you run away to that godforsaken little town, darling? When are you coming back?'

'I was just in DC. But you weren't there.'

'I know. I've been chasing the sun, as it were.' Her laugh was bell-like. 'Have you been watching me?'

'You know I don't watch the news.' I sighed. 'And what's this about chasing the sun?'

'The solar flares. It's all anyone can talk about. You have had your head in the sand.'

I bit the inside of my jaw. Deep breath, and one . . . two . . . three . . . 'What about them?'

'The recent flares have damaged power grids in LA and San Francisco. No one had power for up to two weeks in some areas. There were mini riots, schools were shut down, the film industry stopped filming . . . You really haven't heard about this? The West Coast is literally imploding and you're clueless. Darling, for once get your head out of your beloved history books.'

'OK, Mom. You're right. I should check the news occasionally. And watch you,' I added for good measure since I knew that's what she wanted to hear.

She tossed her long, thick, black hair over her shoulders. She still wore it the same. Center part, softly winged backwards a la Farah Fawcett with soft curls falling to her shoulder blades. Her lips formed a pout. 'I miss my *chéri*.'

Sighing, I looked away from the screen, away from my mother's flawless golden-honey complexion and haughty demeanor and took several deep breaths. Everything about my mother upset me. Even so, I always tried to stay calm on our calls. 'Is there something you want to tell me? Something you need to tell me?'

She cocked an eyebrow. 'Yes. I'm heading to Miami. The solar flares are predicted to hit there next.'

I knew my mother was a hardcore sorority girl in college. The two-toned monogrammed stuff all over her bedroom attested to that, but I found it hard to believe my mother was the member of a secret society. She was successful, smart and driven. But she was also very . . . self-centered. No big deal. She'd been that way my entire life. But even now, she couldn't tell me what I needed to know? I ignored the aching feeling in my chest.

She examined me for a moment. 'Eyeliner and mascara, darling. You know they make your eyes pop. Why aren't you wearing makeup?'

I sighed in response, and she shook her head. Apparently deeply disappointed. No matter. I was used to it. 'Tell me about your time in college. You were in a sorority? Same one as Grams?'

She paused, her brows furrowing ever so slightly. 'Yes. Why do you ask?'

'This is the same one you tried to get me and Aislin to join?'

'Aislin did join. You were the renegade, darling.'

It was all making sense now. 'What was the perk of being in this group? Why did you join?'

'Family tradition for one. Friendship . . . Networking . . .' A shoulder lifting. 'Mostly it was just fun. We were known as the prettiest girls on campus.'

Not surprising. But I realized something. 'You're doing your part with your job, aren't you?'

Her eyelashes fluttered, and then her lips spread into a slow smile. 'Yes. In my own way, I'm doing very, very important work. Sometimes, I'm called upon to shine a light on certain stories. Or perhaps to quash one. I do what I can for my Sisters . . . and Brothers.'

I was silent, rethinking my entire life and my view of my mother.

'I have to go, darling.' She blew me a kiss.

Perhaps she wasn't as superficial as I'd thought. I blew her a kiss back and ended the call.

After the call, I was returning to the living room when someone knocked on the door. I opened the front door and saw Gabe through the screen door.

'Sorry to stop by unannounced, but I wanted to bring you your bike.' He jerked a thumb over his shoulder. 'It's good as new.'

A flutter of happiness filled my chest. 'Hey you.' I unlocked the screen door and stepped onto the porch. 'Thank you so much. How much do I owe you?'

'Honestly?' He tilted his head in thought. 'A ride to the waterfront.'

I laughed. 'Right now?'

'Right now.'

'I'm not dressed—'

'You're wearing a T-shirt and shorts, same as me. Just put some shoes on. Be spontaneous. You don't even need money. I'll buy you ice cream.'

'OK. But I will bring my purse.' My shoes were by the front door, and I stepped into a pair of leather thongs and grabbed my bag.

Minutes later, I was inside his big, shiny pickup truck. Windows down and we were heading downtown and towards the Riverwalk. A lovely part of town that I didn't visit nearly enough. I told him this, and he shook his head.

'I try to visit the water a couple times a week. One because it relaxes me, but more importantly because Josiah used to own all of this land before he sold it to Elias for a nice profit.'

We parked in a gravel parking lot and jumped out of the truck. The boardwalk was right in front of us, and beside it the river, wide and a calm blue-gray. I stopped to read a sign. 'And Elias donated it to the city after Josiah died, and created a park.'

He reached for my hand. Feeling like a teenager, I allowed him to take it and we began walking. The breeze was soft and salty smelling since the river ran into the sea. It was dusk, so the sun was an orange-pink streak across the sky. The boardwalk was busy with couples strolling like us – not that we were a couple.

Vendors sold lemonade slushes, large pretzels, cotton candy and ice cream. 'What's your flavor?' Gabe asked when we were in front of the ice cream cart.

I studied the list and decided on strawberry cobbler. One scoop on a waffle cone. He got a double scoop of chocolate mint chip on a sugar cone.

After we received our ice cream, we walked a few more minutes until we veered off the walkway onto a tree-covered grassy area filled with benches and metallic structures. Flowering bushes and exotic stalky plants filled the empty spaces. A cobblestone path curved around the park. And a life-sized pewter statue on a large white limestone pedestal centered the park.

We found a bench, and Gabe pointed to the statue of Josiah Willoughby with his cone. 'Elias Robbins saved this acre from the parcel of land Josiah sold him.'

'Out of sentimentality?' I guessed.

'No.' He laughed. 'It was in Josiah's will that this land never be developed with new real estate or commercial ventures. It was Elias' idea to turn it into a park.'

I studied the area, seeing it with new eyes. I saw bits of a brick foundation covered by grass and bushes in one corner. A crumbling chimney nearby . . . 'He lived here. His house was right here under these trees and facing the river.'

'Yeah. He owned a few properties in Robbinsville and New Bern, but the original home place was right here. I like to sit here and pretend like I'm inside the house.' He pointed to an area nearby. 'It would've stood right there. His workshop was over there.' He pointed in another direction. 'And the remains of his cellar were there.'

I followed his gaze to a large metallic piece of art.

'And the statue would've been smack dab in the middle of the great room.'

'Wonderful you can still come here.'

'Yeah.' He leaned against the bench, and casually threw his arm behind me.

I relaxed against him.

We sat there in silence eating our ice cream and watching the river flow by until the sun set and the park was filled with fireflies. A large yellow moon floated in the distance, and I closed my eyes, tilting my head to the sky. A smile played on my lips as I imagined I could feel the icy fingers of the moon massaging my face.

Then I opened my eyes and found Gabe watching me. 'The moonlight becomes you.' Then he looked past me; I followed his gaze. 'You know that guy?'

I turned to see the silhouette of a man watching us. He stepped into the lamplight and waved. It was Matty holding the leash to a small dog. I waved back and he continued his walk.

'Well,' he began as he stood. 'I guess your debt is paid.'

Laughing, I held out my hand and he pulled me up.

'Ready to head back?'

I breathed in the fresh air. 'Yes, thank you. This has been lovely.'

He looked down at me, his face serious. 'You're lovely.'

And before I could respond, he kissed me on my cheek.

I closed my eyes and leaned into it, even if it was just a few seconds.

And then we went home.

*　*　*

The next morning, I cranked my new car up and drove to New Bern. I was determined to find out who the Daughter of Hathor was in the Knox family, and I knew I'd find her on the rolls of the house staff.

I arrived in New Bern, and found the Historical Society. Parked on the street and entered the building. I was directed to a back room full of archives. As I followed the staff woman down the hall, I passed several historical oil paintings on the wall. Prim and sober-looking men and women staring back from another time and place. I always liked old paintings, especially of people. Just interesting to look at people who lived hundreds of years before me.

The woman paused in front of a closed door. 'The records you want to see are in the queue to be digitized, but just not yet.' She opened the door and showed me shelves of crates upon crates. The room smelled dusty, but I smiled. I was in my happy place. She pointed to a section of the shelves. 'You'll find the documents you're after over there.'

I thanked her and waited for her to leave before I went to the shelves. I opened up a crate of documents and began filtering through them. When I finally found a folder on the family, I shuffled through the pages until I found what I was looking for. The Witherspoon registry. They owned slaves and indentured servants of all races. One name stood out. A woman. Marked 'F' for freedwoman. Described as 'stout, short, coffee brown in color, smart eyes, pleasant countenance'. She was the family's cook. I wrote down her name. *Bathsheba Montgomery.*

Why did that name seem familiar?

Then I remembered. She was one of the three women accused of stealing . . . the ones Professor Llew called the Witches of Robbinsville. Did this mean the Daughters of Hathor practiced witchcraft? Or was it just a coincidence? Did Llew know the witches were part of a secret group? What else had he discovered in his research?

I cleaned up my area and put everything back to rights. As I walked down the hall, I stopped to look at one of the paintings. It was a middle-aged woman with hazel eyes, dark blonde hair combed up into a mass of ringlets. She wore a conservative navy-blue dress and held a small book in her hand.

I returned her smile. It was small and secretive, and something about it niggled at me. *What was it?* I searched the painting. Dark swathes of velvet curtain were behind her. A wooden desk to her right with a vase full of white blooms.

The front-desk attendant came to stand beside me. 'It's a beautiful painting, isn't it?'

I nodded, wondering why it had caught my attention. It reminded me of something. 'She was one of the first founders of our archives. She donated papers from her personal library along with other women in the community. Apparently, they went around asking for family documents and important government papers to place here.'

'Her name?'

'Ironically, lost to time. Unfortunately. One of those great floods in the past.'

I thanked the front-desk attendant and found the address for my next location. The public library.

I applied for a library card, since I needed one to use their computers and access their genealogical databases. Once I was settled, I searched for the living descendant of Witherspoon's servant, of the woman who was probably the Daughter of Hathor in his house. The woman who would've passed down any pertinent information to the women in her family.

And then . . . I found it.

I found her.

The descendant of Bathsheba Montgomery.

EIGHTEEN

I stood on the porch of her house. And knocked.

A screened door opened, and Bess appeared. She looked surprised as all get out. 'Hey, Sidney. What are you doing here?' She looked at Bess' grandmother's house exterior. It was small and rundown, though beautiful flowers filled the front yard.

'I thought I'd stop by for a chat. Got some time?'

'Of course.' She blushed. 'You've never been here . . . In school, we had our dorms. And then you'd invite me to your grandmother's house.'

We stepped inside. The house was modern with beautiful furniture, elegant decorations and fresh flowers in strategic locations. Why were people always embarrassed to show me their homes? Yes, my parents were famous. Yes, they were rich. But that was my parent's wealth. I was basically homeless, driving around in my grandmother's car.

'Your house is adorable. It's giving cozy cottage vibes.'

Thin lines appeared on her forehead as she studied me. 'You want to grab a bite to eat? Maybe go back to The Patriot for a little line dancing?' She wiggled her bottom and laughed.

Wow, she was good. What was real? The Bess I knew in college, or the new and improved – her characterization not mine – Bess Montgomery of today.

I looked at her. Didn't hesitate. 'The cow jumped over the moon.'

Her eyes widened. Her mouth fell open. 'Sidney,' she said, her voice a high-pitched squeak.

Her grandmother entered the room then, wearing an apron covered in cute purple and white cows. 'And the dish,' she countered, 'ran away with the spoon.'

'Holy cow,' Bess said. 'It's real.' She turned to look at her grandmother. 'It's real?'

Her grandmother smiled at me. 'Come on in the kitchen. I just brought in a big ol' jar of sun tea. I'm Thea, by the way.'

I stood rooted to the spot letting it all sink in.

Bess gestured with her hand to follow.

I did.

I moved through the swinging door and sat down in the small kitchen. All brand-new appliances but very small. And decorated in cows. Cows everywhere and on every surface. Salt and pepper shaker cows. A cow clock on the wall. Cute cows saying funny things. Cow magnets on a huge, shiny silver three compartment refrigerator with a television screen.

When Bess' grandmother opened the door, it spoke to her telling her she needed to order more eggs.

Bess chatted nervously while her grandmother prepared tall glasses of iced tea.

'I can't believe it. It's real. She told me the story after college, and I was like, I don't believe you, but she was all, one day someone will come and say the phrase and I'll . . . well . . .' She looked at her grandmother who frowned at her. She set down our glasses and settled into a chair beside us. 'Of course it would be you. You're beautiful. Rich. And a member of a secret society. Nice to meet you . . . Sister.'

I swallowed, shooting her a strange look. 'Thank you. Nice to meet you as well.'

Bess waved a hand around the room. 'We actually have a lot of money. We just live like this to throw off any suspicion.' She blushed. 'I was always horribly embarrassed by . . . well. Once she told me. It made things a little better . . .'

'Your makeover?'

'I just got confident. When I found out I was part of something so huge. So amazing. I looked at myself in the mirror one day and was like: I definitely need to be a blonde. And then I upgraded my wardrobe. I mean, I'm a member of a secret organization.' A gleeful peel of laughter erupted from her glossy lips. 'What do I have to be shy about?' She shrugged. 'I'm amazing even if no one knows why.'

I reached out and touched her hand. 'You were always amazing.'

Her grandmother sighed. 'I tried to tell her that since she was a little girl.'

'Well, when your daddy runs off, and your mama drinks herself to death you just feel like you're cursed . . .'

I focused on my glass of tea, noting the two inches of sugar settling at the bottom. Ah, sweet tea . . . And waited for the awkward moment to pass.

It did. Thankfully.

'How did you find us?' Bess' grandmother asked.

'Bathsheba Montgomery.' I took a sip of the tea and closed my eyes. So good. And with just a hint of lemon. Perfection.

'Of course.' She smiled.

Bess' grandmother had fair skin, blue eyes, dirty blonde hair that curled around her face. She was short and stocky with a square angular face.

'Bathsheba was my great-great-grandmother. She was a free black woman of Scottish descent. And she married a white Scot, an indentured cabinetmaker. They had children. One of her daughters had a daughter with another Scot – lots of Scots around here in those days,' she laughed. 'And that daughter was light enough to pass for white. So she moved to Robbinsville and did. We've been white ever since.'

'Not so strange. Many white families have this story in their history. People of color and Native American ones too. They just might not know it.'

She drank her tea. 'I suppose you've come for it then.'

I swallowed. *The trinket gifted to a daughter.* 'Yes, that's why I'm here.'

She jerked her head. 'Bess, get the box.'

Bess jumped up. 'Yes, ma'am,' she said, and soon returned with a small object wrapped in a velvet pouch.

I carefully took the object from Bess, set it on the table and opened it. What looked like a fourteen carat gold coin rolled onto my palm. It was shiny and heavy, with a lotus engraved on one side and an owl on the other. But without it being minted by a governing body, and having a currency amount on it, I suppose it was technically . . . 'It's a medallion.'

She scowled. 'What of it?'

'The letter Abner told me to decode said President Madison visited the Witherspoon family, gave the daughter a trinket . . . I suppose I was expecting . . . Well, I'm not sure.'

'There's a lot of smoke and mirrors involved in this life.' Thea looked around her house. 'You'd never know I was a woman of means by the look of it, would you?'

'No, ma'am.'

'And that's the point. To throw anyone of interest off the scent. Because make no mistake. They're looking for us – the Daughters. They want to take us out.'

'Grandma, I've never heard you speak this way.' Bess bit her bottom lip. 'Sounds so serious when you—'

'It is serious. I've told you that.' Thea frowned at Bess, and I recalled Bess saying how mean her grandmother had been to her. I hadn't quite believed her, but now, here I was starting to think it was true. Poor Bess.

I thought of my class with Professor Sharp – Llew. 'Reminds me of the witch hunts of old.'

'Exactly. They've never ended. Not really.'

My throat tightened. A tendril of fear curled around my chest. It was true then. The Daughters were seen as witches. 'Do you think this is what the witch hunts were actually about? Finding the Daughters of Hathor?'

Her jaw hardened. 'I know it is. I've heard the stories. When Edward the First came swooping into Scotland and stole the Stone of Scone, he heard the stories about the sisterhood of women vowed to protect it. Scared the dickens out of him but not enough for him to not try and steal it.'

Vowed to protect? It sounded like this was the artifact I was looking for. 'What is the Stone of Scone?'

Bess and her grandmother exchanged glances. Bess cocked her head. 'You don't know?'

I rolled my eyes. 'I know I'm a historian. But I've never taken a class on . . . You said Edward the First, so . . . English history? I know the parts related to colonial and American history but even I know Edward the First was from, what . . . the second or third century?'

'You know the Bible, don't you?' Thea raised an eyebrow.

I frowned. 'Kind of.' We'd gone to a Southern Baptist church as a family when I was little but hadn't been back since.

'You heard of Jacob's Pillow?'

I shook my head. 'Sorry.'

'I'll have to get after your grandmama about your religious education. Seems it's been sorely lacking.' Then she cracked a smile. 'It's fine. I can tell you all you need to know. We Montgomerys are right proud of our Scottish heritage, ain't we, Bess?'

'Yes, ma'am. I'm a veritable encyclopedia of all things Scone.'

I stared at Bess, amazed at how confident she sounded. 'I'm all ears.'

Thea sniffed. 'I'll start. The Stone of Scone is also called the Stone of Destiny. It's an ancient rectangular block of red sandstone, supposedly, believed to be the same stone known as Jacob's Pillow in the Bible. See what you miss when you don't go to church?'

I nodded, quite aware that she was only half-kidding.

'The Stone of Scone was traditionally used in the coronation ceremonies of Scottish and British monarchs, symbolizing their rightful authority. It was originally housed in Scone, a royal residence in Scotland, but the stone was taken by Edward the First of England in 12 . . .' She paused trying to recall.

'96.' Bess piped up. '1296. During the Scottish Wars Of Independence.'

Thea pursed her lips, not seeming to like being interrupted. 'And placed beneath the Coronation Chair in Westminster Abbey.' She paused to sip her tea.

I raised my hand halfway like a shy student in class, loath to interrupt the woman. 'I love learning about history, obviously, but I don't see what this has to do with the Daughters of Hathor. Nor can I remotely fathom how you can link this to Robbinsville.'

'You've heard of Queen Scota?'

'Yes, but only recently . . . I discovered I-I guess all of us are distantly related to her? Still wrapping my head around that one.'

'The Stone of Scone came to Scotland when Scota and her court traveled from Egypt. This was all around 350 BE, and they were escaping political unrest.

'There along with her husband she established a lineage that would eventually lead to the Scottish people. And among those people were her direct descendants, men and women who carried her royal bloodline meant to rule the land. And women who vowed to protect the Stone of Scone from those who would use it for bad.'

This was it then. What I was looking for. What the Daughters were vowed to protect . . .

'Is it lost? Is this what Madison's letter is leading to?'

Bess frowned. 'Can't be. It's not lost. It's in Edinburgh Castle along with the Scottish Crown Jewels.'

'Oh,' I said, completely deflated.

'But it has an interesting history. In the early 1900s, the Women's Social and Political Union planted a bomb loaded with nuts and bolts to act as shrapnel next to the Coronation Chair and Stone; nobody was hurt but the Stone was damaged. No one knew though, until the 1950s when four college students stole it and brought it back to Scotland. Over seventy years later, King Charles the Third borrowed it for his coronation.'

'Why such an elaborate history for a boulder?'

Bess and her grandmother exchanged glances. 'It's not just a rock. Kings have used this stone as part of their coronation for thousands of years.'

'It's magic,' Bess said. 'It just is.'

'Magic how? What's it supposed to do?'

'Well,' Thea began, 'for one, it provides a divine blessing, it confers the divine right to rule to one crowned on it. It offers protection to the ruler and his people or nation, it creates an unbreakable bond, a covenant between the ruler and his people ensuring that his well-being is connected to the welfare of his subjects. And most importantly, the stone channels wisdom and guidance of past rulers to the newly crowned, providing insight and counsel when needed.'

'All that from one rock? I guess I can understand why a king would try to steal it. He must've had imposter syndrome and needed the stone to legitimize his position. It definitely seems like the type of artifact the Madison letter should lead to. But it can't be since it's public knowledge where it is . . .' And I was back to square one. I rubbed my temples feeling very, very tired.

Thea studied me. 'Why are you taking this so personally?'

I sat up. I couldn't tell them. 'I'm just tired . . .' But something bothered me. I was looking for an artifact the Daughters of Hathor protected. They didn't seem to be doing much protecting if the stone had been taken from them and wasn't resident in Scotland.

'How were the women meant to protect it?' I asked, trying to understand the layers of the story.

'Well, they say . . . Way back when, the daughters from the line of David would press both their palms on the stone and it . . . sort of activated latent abilities in them.'

'I've never heard this story, Grandma. What kinds of abilities?'

'The ability to protect the stone from those who would seek to steal it from its rightful owners. The ability to protect the rightful heir. To protect the people of their ruler's lands. And they'd received the combined guidance of all the Daughters who came before them.'

'But not to cast spells and hex people,' Bess said. 'Like they say.'

'Well . . .' Thea began. 'There might be a bit more.'

We both looked at her, but she didn't finish. 'With all those powers to protect seems like it turned these women into superheroes not witches. How do you think it works?' I asked.

Thea shrugged. 'Something about the right DNA plus the stone activated something in these women. But it's not evil, it comes from God. It's in the Bible. Jacob's Pillow. So any magic these women possess, has come from the good, sweet Lord above.' She pointed to a picture of Jesus on her wall for good measure.

I stared at Thea and then Bess. 'Do you have . . . powers?'

They both laughed. 'No,' Bess said. But her grandmother hesitated. She looked at her. 'Grandma?'

'Not really powers as such. I get dreams is all. Touched with a bit of the prophecy. Many people have that. Sometimes I look at people and I imagine I know what they're thinking.' For the first time her face went soft. 'But I'm probably just making things up.'

Bess studied her grandmother. 'Is that why you're so ornery? You know what people are thinking?'

She cocked an eyebrow. 'Possibly.'

Bess gulped. 'That include me?'

Thea sucked her teeth, a sour look on her face. 'Definitely includes you.'

Bess blanched, skin pale and she sucked in a breath. Then she smiled. 'Maybe I should try reading people's thoughts. It's probably like a superhero movie. First you get your powers, accept them and then practice until you're good. We just need to practice.'

'You're not practicing anything, Elizabeth. You stay the exact same as you are. You got a good job. You ain't got no babies out of wedlock and you ain't shacking up with no man. You keep to yourself and don't try to practice nothing. Not until you get married and settled down.' Her face relaxed into a smile. 'Then if you want to come out as a witch, so be it.'

Bess looked horrified. 'Grandma . . . OK. I won't, I mean – I don't need . . .' She gave up trying and gave me a helpless look.

Thea pointed to the coin. 'Does it mean anything to you?'

I stared at the medallion, trying to understand its importance. It was a beautiful piece of work to be sure, but what did it mean? 'No, unfortunately it doesn't.' I turned the medallion over and scrutinized the raised image of the owl.

'I always wondered who would be the one to come get that thing. Makes sense I guess that Fiona's kin would be the one.'

I looked up from the object. 'What do you mean?'

'You never thought your grandma was witchy with her herbs and potions?'

'Not potions,' I said. 'Teas. Tinctures . . .' A lifetime of my grandmother making soothing balms and lotions and homemade honey-based medicines washed over me. Crafty and clever, yes. But witchy? No. Never.

'Green witch. Hedge witch. Root worker. Whatever you want to call it.'

'My grandmother is not a witch.'

'Sure, honey.' Thea laughed. 'Fiona's a healer. You probably are too . . . I bet she's got an old book of spells, doesn't she?'

I thought of the leatherbound collection of recipes. 'Not spells, no . . .'

She gave me a knowing look. 'And a wild man don't live in the woods. But just so you know, they called us women witches since the olden days. But we were just women carrying a legacy, a lineage. You're a historian, you'll be familiar with King James and his *Daemonologie*?'

That again? 'Yes, I'm familiar with it. He's infamous for his witch hunts, especially in Scotland . . .'

She eyed me expectantly. 'Why do you think that was?'

'Scotland had more witches?' I thought of everything I'd learned. 'They were Daughters of Hathor, and he . . . was not. No. His mother was not.'

'Certainly not. He's descended from Edward, the one who stole the Stone of Scone in Scotland. The one who invaded Scotland when they had internal strife, were at their weakest. He took advantage and stole the right to heir. He and his heirs have been on the throne illegitimately for hundreds of years. All related. All pretenders to the throne.'

I let that sink in for a moment.

'The witch hunt was about stamping out the line . . .' She continued. 'Like they did with the Princes in the Tower, or the poisoning of Henry the Eighth's son Prince Edward. Destroying any chance for other royal contenders.'

'Searching for and killing our Sisters was about making sure the royal line of Queen Scota dies out,' I said aloud, finally understanding just as a heaviness filled my chest.

'Not just that,' Thea added with a scowl. 'They tortured our Sisters, forcing them to out other Sisters, and tried to find out where the true Stone of Scone was hidden.'

'So they knew—'

'They suspected the Stone was hidden but they could never be sure. So they terrorized our Sisters trying to find the true location. The Sisters had vowed to stay with the Stone no matter what. Only death could make them leave the area of the Stone. Or fear – fear for their loved ones. But with the witch hunts, Sisters were forced to leave their homelands, the few people who knew where the Stone was stopped sharing the information to save lives and protect the locations . . . The witch hunts were terroristic as we know it now.

'You can see that, right? How horrifying it must've been for these women whose only responsibility was to be near the Stone and protect it with their magic?'

I nodded. 'I get it. It was about making sure the women who vowed to protect the Stone with their abilities endowed by the Stone were no longer alive to do so. Or so far away from the Stone that their powers were useless.'

And the final result was that the women vowed to protect the Stone no longer knew where it was.

'It had nothing to do with them practicing witchcraft or being evil or working magic. They just said that so they had a reason to demonize them. Vanquish them from their societies. In some cases, kill them. We hold the legacy in our DNA. Our bodies are the vessel. Our memory holds the legacy. We have the ability to birth a king.'

'Or queen,' Bess interrupted.

'Or president,' I finished.

'And this? It's lovely. Exquisite, obviously made by a craftsman.' I turned it over, my finger running over the ridges of the medallion. 'It has the letters *SOH* inscribed under the bird. See here?' I showed it to both of them. 'Indicating membership in the Sons of Horus. Is there a story about how your ancestor received it?'

'Of course. My great-great-grandfather was a fiddler. A dance caller.'

'Was he at the Robbins' house, at the dinner that President Madison and Abner's ancestors and others were at?'

Her gaze slipped to Bess for just a moment. 'Yes. It was a big occasion. The president was coming . . .' She faltered. 'I can't do it. Not to another Sister.'

Eyes wide, Bess turned to her grandmother. 'Are you sure? But I thought . . .?'

'Yes, I'm sure.' Her voice was sharp. 'She's one of our own.'

One of our own. Where had I heard that before?

'She can know the truth.' She faced me. 'It's a lie. It's all a lie.'

'What's a lie?'

'Madison never came to Robbinsville.'

'What? I don't . . . What do you mean? This entire story that Abner tells rests on President Madison visiting here and working with Josiah and leaving this letter for Zadie to find. That's the story.'

'And I'm telling you, it's not the truth. I don't know why or how that story developed. Or if Abner knows it's true or not. But I know it's a lie.' She sat against her couch, arms crossed over her chest, looking at me like she dared me to call her a liar.

I was definitely not going to do that. Instead, I took a breath and tried to look open to her suggestion. 'So, what happened?'

She relaxed just a smidge, and I heard Bess exhale. 'Everyone who was anyone was invited to a ball at the Robbins' house. Dinner was fancy. Dresses were beautiful. There's a painting from that night somewhere . . .'

'At the Robbins'?'

'No. The Willoughby Estate. Josiah was a very important man during this time period, and he had his own servants and retinue. His own special guests. I believe he had a painter with him as well. Joshua Johnson. Heard of him?'

I thought of the art exhibits my mother had taken me and Aislin to as children. Johnson's included. 'He's considered the first painter of color. His oil paintings are in the National Gallery, the Met and others.'

'So, he painted a picture of the dinner. The story goes my ancestor played the music so fine, that President Madison said that even the Egyptian goddess of music, Hathor, would be pleased.' She gave me a plaintive look. 'Then gave him a coin as payment and told him that as long as he kept it with him it would bring him luck. My great-great-great-grandfather is in the picture holding his fiddle.' She smiled, allowing a moment of pride to shine through her otherwise stern features. 'Proud as punch.'

'But Madison didn't give him the coin.'

'No. This story is told in my family – the real story – that a Son of Horus gave him the coin. I'm not sure who that was but it happened. Madison came to New Bern but he didn't come here.'

'Then who wrote the letter that leads to the artifact Abner is looking for?'

Thea gave a deep shrug.

I looked at Bess. 'The other night at The Patriot . . . This is why you didn't believe the letter was real?'

She nodded. 'Yes. But at the time I didn't know you were . . . one of us. Our kind of people.' A sheepish grin appeared on her face. 'Sorry.'

'It's fine.' Abner didn't know the letter wasn't written by Madison. That was the only reasonable explanation. But that begged the question: who did write it? Josiah Willoughby had worked with someone – who was it? I gestured towards the coin. 'May I take it then?'

'Please do. We've had it for generations. Such a small thing but with a heavy price. It was an honor but also a burden to keep it safe and in pristine condition.'

Thea packed up the medallion and handed it to me.

Bess and her grandmother walked me to the door. 'Obviously, we can't talk about this at work.'

'Obviously.'

'But you know what this means, right?'

'What?'

'We're sisters. Not just friends or besties, but actually sisters in a secret society.'

'Yes, I suppose it does.'

'Miss Thea, if you don't mind me asking. Where does the money come from?'

She shrugged. 'It's just part of the inheritance. Always arrives in our bank. Has been for generations.'

Interesting. 'Which bank?'

'The only bank in town.' She laughed. 'Robbins Bank and Trust.'

I looked both ways as I stepped off the porch, wondering if anyone was watching me.

I slid inside my new car. Tucked the case under a seat and headed for the Robbins House. There was a safe there that no one used. I'd hide the medallion in my office safe.

I needed to talk to Llew. With his research into the Robbinsville witches, he may know something that could help me. But first, I needed to visit the Willoughby Museum.

I stood on Main Street, just outside the Josiah Willoughby Museum. From my vantage point, I could see several patrons inside reviewing exhibits, and reading placards. A young woman worked the front desk, and I wondered if Gabe was even here.

I looked up and down the street and saw someone leave the QLabs building. A man in a blue baseball cap, polo and jeans with a laptop bag in hand. I watched him curiously, as he walked down the street then crossed to the next block.

I wondered what they did at QLabs.

But then the door to the museum opened, and the last of the patrons spilled out. More Beethoven floated my way, and I entered the open door.

I searched the walls for paintings with Johnson's signature style of narrow pinched faces, blank eyes and unsmiling expressions, and found a trio of oils. The first one was of Josiah in fancy dress, hand flat on a desk. The second one was of Josiah and a woman, presumably his wife, seated while he stood behind her. The last was a ballroom scene filled with men and women dancing. I identified Thea's ancestor with the violin in the corner. Women were dressed in gowns with men standing stiffly beside them.

As Johnson typically painted portraits, this party scene may have been out of his element. The figures were posed rigidly, their faces not showing much joy, though the clothes were drawn with loving care. There was a diversity of skin tones present with two men of color standing to the side, heads close in discussion.

'You're a fan of Johnson's work?'

I turned around and saw Gabe.

'Not his usual commission.'

'No. My ancestor requested the painting especially. He wanted to commemorate the night.'

'Such an auspicious occasion.' I searched the painting. 'Where's President Madison?'

He chuckled. 'You noticed, huh?'

I noticed he didn't answer my question.

'Joshua was asked to paint him in, but he refused, stating he couldn't do the president justice without actually seeing him in the scene.'

I stared at the painting, recalling the story Thea had shared. 'By whom? Who made the request?'

Gabe inclined his head. 'No one seems to know. It's just the story told about the night.'

'Thank you for sharing that with me. As a historian, I find this type of insider knowledge fascinating.'

'I thought you might.'

I gave him a sideways glance, wondering if he knew about the secret societies in town. About what his ancestor had done.

Gabe was clearing his throat, and it was obvious I'd missed something he'd said. I smiled at him. 'Sorry. Lost in thought.'

'I asked you if you'd like to get a bite sometime.'

'Yes, that would be nice. Later this week?'

His eyebrows lifted. 'OK.' He handed me his card. 'Call me.'

I took his card and slid it into my purse.

'One more thing. President Madison didn't happen to . . . leave anything with Josiah?'

Gabe rubbed his chin, regarding me with curiosity. 'There is. But how would you know that?'

In the letter, Madison mentioned visiting Josiah and leaving him with good thoughts and cheer. But now I thought it was a tangible item. I couldn't share this with Gabe, though. 'I'm helping Abner with a project.'

'Ah.' He considered me for a moment. 'You're the first to ask about it.'

'Really?' I couldn't hide my surprise. I was onto something.

'Come with me.' He moved through the exhibits, and I followed him to a back room. 'It's a document. Never been on display.'

'Why not?'

'Because the story surrounding it is a lie, as you say. Supposedly President Madison left it for Josiah Willoughby, but since I know that didn't happen . . . We're not sure what context to provide in a display so it's been in the back.'

'Where did the story come from?'

His shrug was almost Gallic in its expansiveness. 'The Robbins Museum. They seem to be the origin of the entire story.'

He sat at a desk, opened a cabinet and pulled out a sheath of papers in a dust jacket. 'He left instructions for Josiah,' he began, as he pulled a pair of gloves on before handling the delicate yellowed papers.

I took a deep breath, trying to calm the fast tattoo of my heart. Would I find another clue to the artifact?

'Here we are.' He held the document out to me for review. 'Instructions for making a pie safe.'

I blinked. 'Pie safe?' I recalled the letter. *I've commissioned him to build you a new pie safe. Cook will be most delighted. It shall be ready and arrive home by the next full moon.* I hadn't actually thought I'd find one . . .

'Yes,' Gabe laughed. 'Apparently pie thieves were rampant back then. Most homes had a locked cabinet for pies.'

'I would love to see an antique pie safe.' I glanced at him. 'Any idea if Josiah ever made the safe?'

'He did. He was friendly with Robert Hay, a Scottish craftsman who lived in New Bern. He built a house for a member of the Stanly family, and then procured a commission to create additional pieces, so the pie safe was a gift for Senator John Stanly. I would assume, with it being a Josiah Willoughby piece, that it holds a place of honor in whatever museum has that estate's pieces. Or perhaps it's still in the home. It's a bed and breakfast now.'

I inspected the paper. It was indeed handwritten instructions for making a locked cabinet, complete with detailed drawings. I waited for him to return the papers to their spot. 'Would it be possible for me to take a look at the pie safe?'

'May I ask why? Pie safes are usually of little interest.' His eyebrows knitted together. 'You're working from the Madison letter.'

I playfully pressed a finger to my lips. 'You can't tell anyone.' I was taking a chance here that I could trust him. I felt that I could . . .

'Abner has sent you on his wild goose chase?' His lips teased, his voice low. 'Of course. I love a good mystery. How can I help?'

I looked at him anew. Perhaps he could help me. 'Find out where the pie safe is. I'd like to take a look at it.'

He laughed. 'You think Josiah hid something in a pie safe?'

'I'll find out where it is, and we'll make it part of our date. Dinner and then pie . . . safe.'

He grinned. 'It's a date?'

'It's a date.'

I left his museum with butterflies in my stomach. Whether because I was that close to finding the artifact or because of Gabe, well, that remained to be seen.

When I returned to my grandmother's house, the first thing I noticed was that the lights were out. Yes, it was almost eight o'clock and my grams was surely getting ready for bed, but the porch light was out and so were the spotlights that illuminated the darkness on the sides and back of the farmhouse.

As I walked down the worn path in the grass towards the porch, a strange feeling vibrated on my skin. And the hair on the back of my neck raised. Of course, I was being ridiculous. Grams had probably just forgotten to turn the lights on for the night . . . though I thought they were on a nightly timer.

I stepped onto the porch and touched the doorknob. The door was unlocked.

Open.

I pushed and called out softly, 'Grams, you awake?'

I heard a low keening noise and quickly rushed forward, scrambling for the light switch as I went. My grandmother was sitting in the middle of the living room, duct-taped to a kitchen table chair. She wore a long nightgown and her hair had been braided up for the night. Tendrils of hair escaped her braids and clung to her sweaty face. Her eyes were frightened.

I ran to her, ripping the gag off first. 'Grams, who did this to you!' I began to pull at the tape.

'Behind you!' she wheezed out.

I whirled around to see a black-clad figure wrapped in military-grade gear standing behind me. A man, several inches taller than me with a fit build had a balaclava covering his face and his hands were gloved. He wore a sleek black shirt and black pants made of a shiny metallic material. No way I could identify him.

'Where is it?' he asked, his voice transformed somehow to sound computerized.

'Where is what?' I repeated dumbly.

Ignoring the man, I turned to my grandmother and kneeled beside her. 'Are you OK? Did he hurt you?'

She took a deep breath, glaring at the man. 'I'm fine,' she said in a steely tone. 'Just a bit roughed up, is all.'

I lowered my voice, even though I knew he could hear me. 'How long has he been here? How long have you been . . . like this?'

'You can catch up later,' the voice seethed. 'Is it with your friend? What did you figure out?'

I stood up slowly, stepping between him and my grandmother. My body was shaking. Fear and anger buzzed through me. Fear for my grandmother. Anger this man had invaded my grandmother's home. Put his hands on her. *Manhandled* her. I wanted to throttle him. But first I needed to get him out of the house.

I finally managed to speak. 'I don't know what you're talking about.' My voice was surprisingly calm.

He shook his head slowly, taking a step towards me and my grandmother. 'Don't lie. This won't go well for you or your grandmother if you do. You went to the Montgomery house. I've been watching them for months.'

I struggled to keep my face free of expression. *Was Bess safe? Her grandmother?* I needed to call her. I still had my purse on my shoulder. And my cell phone was in my purse. I needed space and time to act. 'My grandmother needs water. She doesn't look well.'

On cue, my clever grandmother's face went slack, her eyes rolled back in her head and her mouth lolled open. I would've laughed at her dramatics if the situation hadn't been so dire. 'I'm not telling you anything if you don't give her a cup of water.'

He pulled a gun from behind his back and showed it to me. 'No water.'

My grandmother faked a wheeze, and he exhaled a huff of frustration. 'Only because I'm not here to kill you both.'

My grandmother and I exchanged worried glances as he returned the gun to its holster and stalked out of the room. When I heard a cabinet open, I slid my hand into my purse, found my phone, logged in my passcode and found Bess's contact. I was able to type: **are you OK? 911** and hit send before he returned.

He saw my hand move from my purse. I was not quick enough. He threw the glass of water against the nearest wall and swore. Striding towards me, he forcefully grabbed my purse, then shoved me away. I fell to my knees while he rifled through my purse, dumping all of the contents on the floor. He found my phone and stared at it. 'What did you do?'

'Nothing,' I said, through clenched jaws. 'She's my friend. It was just a visit.'

'You're telling me you didn't take anything from their house? That you didn't find something to lead you to the artifact?'

My heart raced with fear. He was after the artifact too. It was all real. Every single thing Abner told me. I could feel my grandmother's eyes on me. I turned to look at her and she gave me a disapproving shake of her head. I know she was telling me not to say a word.

I crossed my arms, jutting my chin forward defiantly. 'Yep, that's what I'm saying.'

He took a step towards me, raised the phone in the air like he wanted to hit me with it, but I didn't flinch. He paused, taking several deep breaths, then threw my phone to the ground.

The glass, of course, cracked. But that was the least of my worries.

He came towards me. Placed his hands on my shoulders and proceeded to pat me down in a very efficient and professional way. He'd obviously done this before. When he was done frisking me, he pushed me away, frustrated.

He trained his gun on my grandmother, but his eyes were on me. 'Stop asking questions. Stop trying to figure things out.' He chuckled and it was a hard bitter sound with a metallic edge. 'You don't have the clearance for this. If I have to come back, your grandmother gets it first. Then your pretty blonde friend, then you. Understood?'

Taking a deep breath, I nodded.

'I've tried to help you, remember? I told you to stop your search. Or leave.'

My mouth dropped open. He was the texter? My throat constricted. I felt nauseous.

He slid his gun back into its holster and backed up towards the door. 'No more questions. Got it?'

Anger warred with the sick feeling swirling in the base of my stomach. I glared back at him. 'I got it.'

And then he was gone.

NINETEEN

My grandmother stared at me as I removed the tape from her body. I was afraid to speak to her. I knew she was angry. I could tell by the cold glint in her eyes and how her jaw was set, her lips pursed in a thin angry line.

'I'm sorry, Grams,' I finally said.

Arms free, she stretched them in front of her, shaking the blood back into them. 'He pulled me from my bed. I'd just fallen asleep.' Her voice was clipped. 'He didn't say a word to me. Just forced me downstairs, pushed me into a chair and tied me up. And that's how we sat, him and I in the dark, waiting for you to return. I had no idea what he'd do to you when you got here, and I had no way to warn you.' She stood slowly.

I wrapped her in my arms tightly, breathing in her scent of cold cream and lavender. 'I'm so sorry, Grams. So sorry.'

She sighed. 'Call your friend and make sure she's OK.'

Bess.

'And then call the police. The regular number. Emergency's over. I'm going to bed.'

I ran to my phone. The screen was cracked but it still worked. I dialed Bess's number and waited impatiently for her to pick up.

'Hey! I just saw your message. Nine one one?' She laughed. 'Seriously? What's going on?'

I quickly explained to her all that had transpired.

She squealed into the phone. 'Oh my God. Nine one one meant you really needed help. I am so sorry. Are you OK? Is your grandma OK?'

I told her yes, we were all fine, but how was she? Where was she?

'Oh, I'm fine. After you left. Me and my grandmother went to the night market for ice cream. I—'

'Ice cream? At this hour?' But I also breathed a huge sigh of relief. 'You were both in a public place. Bess, I'm so glad you're both OK.'

Next, I called 911, told the dispatch what happened and waited for the police.

After the police had arrived and taken my statement, I was spent. Emotionally wrung out.

I went to bed.

TWENTY

The next morning, I woke up to an empty house and the smell of baked bread. I found a strong thermos of coffee on the table for me, plus a basket of biscuits covered with a red gingham cloth. My grandmother had already gone. The house was sparkling clean, and you'd never have known there'd been police inside. I wouldn't have been surprised if my grandmother was still in her bed, resting. But then she was made of sterner stuff. No lollygagging in the house feeling sorry for herself because of an intruder.

I went to work, and kept myself distracted. Except for a small break when I went to find Reba. She was at her post by the front door, pretending to keep the parlor clean while a family walked through it. The skirts of her bright yellow dress belled around her legs as she swung a broom.

She looked up when I entered. 'Good morning.'

'Morning.' I paused, not sure how to begin. When I'd first met her, Reba responded by saying, 'It's always nice to see one of our own doing well.' She winked and elbowed me like we shared a secret. I'd assumed she meant another woman of color, but now, I wanted to know . . . *did* we share a secret?

Thea had used the same language. *One of our own.* Was Reba a Sister?

'You need something?' she asked, coming to stand by my side when the patrons were gone.

I cleared my throat. 'The cow jumped over the moon.'

She stared at me for a moment, then burst out laughing. 'Girl, you crazy.'

So, I was wrong. But I'd—

She stopped laughing then, and her expression sobered. 'And the dish ran away with the spoon.'

I gasped. 'You're . . .'

She nodded. 'Yes. And I just knew you were too.'

'How could you know?'

'I'm not sure. It's like a witchdar.' She laughed. 'You can just sense your own. It's a feeling. Like, you get a nice, warm and cozy sensation that wraps around your body, making you feel safe and comfortable – I don't know exactly how to describe it.' She thought for a moment. 'Like a cousin you always played with growing up? You might have lost touch as an adult, but when you reconnect it's like no time or space has occurred? Like that.'

I nodded, understanding. It was how I'd felt when I'd first met Bess and we'd become roommates at college. Instabestfriends. And, come to think of it, I had felt something when I'd met Reba but had just considered it good vibes, I guess.

I patted her arm, not sure what else to do. 'OK, thanks for confirming . . .' I suddenly felt super awkward. 'I'll see you around.'

She waved her fingers at me as I returned to my office. 'Bye, sis.'

I'd ended up working longer than usual today, it was after five and all of the admin staff were gone except for me. I decided to do a little internet search. Professor Philippi had mentioned Special Projects, a division of the Smithsonian I'd never heard of.

A cursory search of the website described the division briefly as the research arm of the Smithsonian that provided support for internal documentation.

Apart from the brief mention on the Smithsonian website, only a few hits came up. I read through the list, a frown growing as I continued. 'A highly secretive division of the museum established by the Columbian Institute for the Promotion of Arts and Sciences. Not supposed to exist.'

I knew from my research on President Madison, that he was an honorary member of the Columbian Institute, considered to be a precursor to the Smithsonian Institute. Two years after British troops invaded DC, the scholarly society included former presidents, civic and military leaders and the leading scientists and educators for the time . . . more conspiracy theories about the founding fathers.

I kept clicking through the search results. Most of the items were YouTube videos. I selected one with the most views. It was a face-less video showing images of old artifacts. The creepy robotic voice told a story about a secret organization within the Smithsonian established possibly in the nineteenth century for the purpose of destroying historical sites and taking artifacts that did not support the official narrative of our country's founding.

I stopped there. Obviously, this was trash. Sighing, I closed out the browser and shut down my computer for the day. Having worked at the Smithsonian, I knew it was full of intelligent, rational people with a passion for history just like me. No one would be on board with destroying history or stealing artifacts with the purpose of hiding the truth.

I grabbed my purse, turned off the light in my office and was just closing the door when I heard a voice. Male. Deep, hard and angry. There were sounds of shoving, chairs scraping and knocking against walls.

Was somebody fighting? I thought the sound was coming from the breakroom. I walked softly so my heels wouldn't clack against the hardwood floors of the hall and peeked into the room. I stifled a gasp in my throat. It was Abner and Llewellyn. Abner had his forearm pressed against Llewellyn's throat, and he was up against the wall, almost off the ground on his tiptoes. A chair beside him was overturned and the journal and pencil he carried with him were on the floor a few yards away. Abner hissed something in his ear and stormed out of the room, nearly knocking me over.

He whirled around with his fist raised, and I shrunk back. 'It's me! Sidney.'

Eyes wide, he jerked his arm down. 'Sorry, I thought . . .'

He looked different. His face was haggard and drawn, he looked old and tired, and there was a streak of white in his beard. I blinked, and suddenly he looked fine. Angry as hell but not fatigued. No white in his beard. I rubbed my eyes. I must've been seeing things. 'What happened? Is everything OK?'

He took a deep shuddering breath. His anger was rolling off him in waves, though I could tell he was trying to calm himself down. His usually perfect hair mussed, his dark green cravat loosed and his perfectly pressed crisp shirt partially untucked from his velvet black breeches.

'I asked him if he was going to publish his book about the witches after all. And he just grinned at me and said yeah. And other things too. Things he knows I'd rather he keep to himself.' He ran a shaky hand through his hair. He looked down at his frilly white blouse and tucked it in. Tightened his cravat. 'Sorry. None of this is your concern.' His eyes narrowed as if I'd tricked the information out of him. 'Or your business.'

'I was just worried is all.' I forced a smile. 'You seemed so angry. But I'm glad you're OK.'

'Sure,' he said bitterly. 'Well, thanks for your concern,' he added politely, as if he just remembered his manners. 'I have to go.' Then he orchestrated a bow and tilt of his head.

I watched him stalk down the stairs and leave out the front door. The sound of the front door locking behind him. The museum closed at five p.m. on weekdays. Admin staff managers had keys if we needed to stay longer.

Llewellyn was still here – was he OK? I turned back to the entrance of the breakroom. He'd picked up the chair, his book and pencil and was seated again, a fresh cup of tea beside him. He looked calm and unbothered. Strange considering what had just happened.

I stepped inside the room. 'Llew, you OK?'

He looked startled and dropped his pencil. 'Sidney. I was just about to leave.'

'I heard the commotion from my office.'

'Oh, that? Abner's on edge.'

'You don't say.' I glanced at his shirt, lingered on a rip for a moment. 'What happened?'

'Same old same.'

'I didn't know Abner was capable of such anger . . . and violence.'

'Years of keeping secrets can do that to a man.'

'Right,' I agreed, not really understanding what he meant, but turning to leave. He followed me downstairs and I unlocked the front door. 'I actually hoped to find you. I wanted to talk more about your research. It may correspond with . . . some research of my own.'

'I'd be happy to talk with you. What are you researching?'

I paused. 'The Daughters of Hathor.'

A strange expression crossed his face, then he blinked it away. 'You know about them, then.'

'I do.'

'Interesting subject.'

'I agree. What can you tell me about them?'

'You have to ask yourself why they came here to Robbinsville. And who was responsible for outing them as witches once they arrived. I've discovered so much more since I wrote my draft of *The Witches of Robbinsville*. Some of it is truly explosive.'

'What have you discovered?'

He exhaled a shaky breath. 'I'm afraid my altercation with Abner has rattled me more than I care to admit.' He held his hand out for me to see the tremors. Sighing, he glanced at his watch. 'The bed and breakfast has an evening wine reception in the dining area in about an hour. I need a little time to . . . process what just happened. It's not every day you get attacked . . . I'm going to take a shower, grab a bite to eat. Have several glasses of wine. But then why don't you join me and we can chat?'

'Sounds like a plan.' I turned back to the front door. 'I'll just go back to the office and get some work done and then I'll pop by.'

I watched him cross the street and head for the Corrie Inn. When he saw that I was still watching, he threw up a hand.

I waved back, then returned to the office.

TWENTY-ONE

Lew had a good point. Why had Isla, Bathsheba and Zadie come to Robbinsville?

Instead of going to my office, I decided to return to the archives. But first, I'd stop by Daphne's office at the library to see if she knew of any research on historical witch hunts – maybe North Carolina folklore too – that may be helpful.

The library was closed but I knew that she'd still be there, as I'd often seen the darkened library with only a light on in her office as I walked to my bike at the end of the day. My badge worked to enter the back of the library through the employee's entrance. The library was quiet, a thick eeriness settled over the old building.

The air was still icy cold as I moved through the hallway. Her office door was ajar, and I could hear her moving around, but I stopped short when I stepped through. There was someone in her office, but it wasn't her.

An elderly woman with a petite, thin frame, stooped shoulders wearing a cardigan and skirt stood in the room. Her back was to me, and she was looking down at papers in her hand.

Sensing my presence, she looked up flinching with surprise, her hazel eyes widening behind her glasses.

'Excuse me, I was looking for Daphne . . .'

A cautious hand went to her cheek. 'You just missed her.'

I stared back, feeling strange. Almost as if I'd met this woman before. Certainly her face was familiar . . . 'Have we met?'

Her smile was slow. 'I don't think so. I'm Daphne's mother, just in town for a short visit.'

'Right . . .' And my confusion cleared. The woman did look like Daphne, just older. 'Sorry to bother you. I'll come back. Just let Daphne know I was here?'

'Of course.' She nodded.

'I'm going to head to the archives. I know the library's closed, but I don't think she'll mind.'

Another smile. 'I don't think she'll mind either.'

I left the office and went to the archives room, soon striking gold with a ship manifest from Perth, Scotland to Wilmington, North Carolina. Bathsheba's grandmother, an indentured servant, had been on board, described as 'aged 22, tawny colored with a clear complexion, brown eyes, dark curly hair; short in stature, skilling with sewing'.

I wasn't surprised that Dinah, a woman of color, had come from Scotland. Being a student of history, I knew that there were people of color indigenous to Scotland at this time.

What *was* surprising, though, was that Zadie and Isla had sailed on the same ship. I checked my watch. I didn't have time right now to follow up on this, but I felt sure these three women must have known each other. Traveled together. Which meant they were probably all Daughters of Hathor.

But why North Carolina? And why did they end up in Robbinsville?

I packed up my things, turned off the light and left the archive room.

The sound of crickets and croaking frogs accompanied me as I crossed the village, and a few minutes later, I stood in the dining room of the bed and breakfast.

There was a couple in a corner drinking wine and chatting. And a woman at a table drinking wine and flipping through a magazine. But no Llew.

I checked with the innkeeper – Harriet as her nametag read – a petite elderly woman who manned the front desk, but she said she hadn't seen him since he returned over an hour ago. At my request, she called his room, but he didn't answer.

For some reason, a nervous feeling crept into my stomach. I reached inside my purse, found the Hathor coin and rubbed it between my two fingers until it warmed. 'Mind if I go up and see if he's there?'

She looked me up and down with interest. 'You a special friend of his?' Her eyebrow arched.

'God, no,' I laughed. 'Nothing like that. We're . . . working on a research project for the museum.'

Satisfied with my answer, she paged through her guest book, looking for his room number then shared it with me. I went to the third floor where his room was located at the end of a hallway, and knocked on the door. There was no movement from behind the door, and I knocked again. Louder.

This time I heard a noise coming from the room. Something creaking, maybe a window opening? My breath caught in my throat. Was someone leaving by the window? The house was three stories, and I was on the third floor. I jiggled on the doorknob and was surprised when it opened. I called out Llew's name and heard a low moan in response.

Suddenly wishing I had some sort of weapon, I grabbed my keys from my purse and held them the way I'd learned in a long-ago self-defense class. Our father had made both me and my sister take the class when we left for college. And it was all coming back to me. Hold the key like a knife. A key to the eye or soft part of the throat was a suitable defensive move when necessary.

Blood thrummed in my ears and my body screamed at me that I should be afraid. *Very afraid.* But Llew could be hurt. I couldn't *not* do anything. I entered the room and saw that a window was open, the curtains flapping in a slight breeze. If an attacker was here, they were probably long gone. But that thought didn't ease the anxiety gripping my chest, and I clutched my keys even tighter.

I went to the window and looked outside. I could see a small backyard with wrought-iron fixtures among abundant flower beds, and the lush woods that edged the property. The perpetrator could be anywhere.

I turned away from the window and inspected the room. Nothing was amiss, but there was another room behind a closed door. It had to be the bedroom. I called out to Llew again and I heard another moan. I went for the door then, jerking it open. And I saw him. He was sprawled on a chair, his arms hung limply at his side, his head lolling backwards. In front of him was a small round table and an empty wine glass.

With my free hand, I felt his cheek and forehead. He was ice-cold, though beads of sweat covered his forehead. His lips were tinged with blue, and his eyes rolled in the back of his head. I felt for a pulse. It was there but so faint, that I couldn't be sure I was imagining it.

'I'm going to get you help, Llew. Don't worry, just breathe. Who did this to you? Tell me,' I said as panic almost choked me. He looked bad and I was afraid I would lose him before help could arrive. Before he could tell me who *did* this – whatever 'this' was. I ran my hands over his face and head looking for an injury. He was hurt. But how?

'The wine . . .' he finally got out, his tongue thick and heavy in his mouth. 'Can't move . . .'

The wine? How could his condition be caused by wine? Unless . . . 'Poison? Someone poisoned you with the wine?' I sniffed the glass but could only smell the earthy sweetness of a red grapes. I set my keys down on the floor beside me, dug into my purse for my phone. And called 911. I could tell Llew was getting worse, but he was mumbling, rasping for air trying to say something. Desperate it seemed to communicate something to me.

Phone still at my ear, I went to him and pressed my ear to his lips. 'Say it again,' I urged.

He repeated his message. Three words. 'I'm onto you.'

I almost dropped my phone but tightened my fingers around it, staring at him. What did that mean? He knew I was searching for the artifact?

Before I could think more on it or question him, a uniformed officer appeared at the door, quickly scanning the area. 'Ma'am, are you OK?'

Tearing my gaze from Llew's pale face, I exhaled slowly. 'Yes.

Thank you.' Then I watched as the officer went to Llew, dragged him to the ground and began performing CPR.

TWENTY-TWO

L
lew was pronounced dead at the hospital.
     I'm onto you.
     I couldn't understand it, couldn't make sense of anything. The words knocked around my brain as I drove to work in silence the following morning. And once in my office, I stayed there all morning with my head down.

A man was killed. And I still needed to know if his research connected with mine in any way. I thought I understood why the Daughters of Hathor had traveled from Scotland to North Carolina. To escape prosecution. But they were also supposed to protect the Stone of Scone, something they couldn't do with it being in Westminster Abbey and them in America.

Llew.

I couldn't stop thinking about what happened to him. Nor what he'd said to me with his dying breath. Couldn't stop feeling like it was my fault either. Did someone know I wanted to talk to him? Is that why he'd been targeted? Or was it his research? His death had to be connected to me, didn't it? Only Abner seemed concerned about him though . . . but surely Abner wouldn't want him dead.

I wondered if Llew's research was still in his room. I looked out my window toward the B & B. Maybe the innkeeper would let me in . . .

A few minutes later after a brisk walk across the museum grounds and across the street, I was back at the Corrie Inn.

'It's a shame, isn't it?' Harriet said when she saw me walk through the door. 'He seemed like a nice man. Quiet and nosy, but nice none the less.'

I considered the woman. 'Nosy how?'

'Oh, you know. Asking questions about Abner mostly.'

'Not . . . fairy doors and witches?'

'That too, a bit.' She paused, fixing me with an interested gaze.

'But mostly he wanted information on Abner's past. His relation-ships, stuff like that.'

I noticed she'd said mostly. *Twice.* 'But he asked about other things?' I prompted, getting the feeling this woman liked to gossip.

She leaned over her desk. 'Well, since you asked . . . He had a few questions about you too.'

'Me?' There was a fluttery feeling in my stomach. 'That's weird. He's my former college professor . . . What did he want to know?'

'Just how well you knew Abner. Last time you'd visited.' She moved her glasses up the bridge of her nose. 'Mean something to you?'

I shook my head. 'Not at all. But thanks for letting me know . . . Anyway, I'm here because I think I left an earring in his room last night. With all the commotion . . . and it's a family heirloom. Do you think you could let me into his room so I could try and find it?'

A doubtful look crossed her face. 'I've already cleaned that room. It was the first thing I did when the police gave me the all clear. I didn't—'

'I'll be fast,' I interrupted. 'Promise. And I'll make sure to keep you updated if I hear anything.'

'I suppose if you're quick. The police are coming back to take my statement this morning.' She leaned across the desk, lowering her voice. 'What did you tell them?'

I shared, and a satisfied expression settled across her features. She looked up the stairs. 'If they don't know you're up there.' She reached for a key hanging on the wall behind her. 'Come on. And let's be quick.'

I followed her up the two flights of stairs, watched her maneuver her arm under the yellow tape blocking the door, unlock the door and push it open.

She jerked her head at me. 'Hurry.'

'Thank you,' I whispered, as I ducked under the tape and slid into the room. I grabbed a linen handkerchief still folded with crisp lines and embroidered with flowers and opened the drawers first. A Bible in one. Tourism brochures in another.

I looked under the bed. Under the mattress. In the closet and his suitcases. I stopped in the middle of the room, my chest filled with fluttery heartbeats. Where was his research?

'Found it yet?' the innkeeper called from the hallway.

'Not yet.'

His leather satchel was tossed in a corner. I'd seen him carrying it on the museum grounds. He'd stuck his journal inside it after the altercation with Abner. I went to it and opened it. Empty. The intruder must've taken it.

I'd searched everywhere. Everywhere except . . . my gaze landed on the mini fridge in the kitchenette corner. I kneeled on the floor, opened the appliance and saw a greasy takeout bag from a food truck that made the rounds on the museum's busiest days. Cheesy McCheesy's.

'Yoohoo,' Harriet sang out in a nervous pitch. 'The cops just arrived. I can hear their vehicles humming in the parking lot,' she rambled on, as her voice timber went higher. 'You've got to skootch.'

I should've just closed the refrigerator then, but something told me to check out the bag. I grabbed it and shoved it in my purse. I rose, gave the room a final scan then hotfooted it back to the hallway.

A second later, there was the sound of heavy boots in the foyer, then bodies were moving up the stairs. The innkeeper stretched her face into a comic *eek* expression, then scurried to greet them, while I turned my face in the opposite direction, placed my phone to my ear and pretended to be in a conversation.

Two officers brushed by, their strides purposeful. And I took a deep breath and pushed out the front door.

Back in my office with the door closed, I opened up the white bag slippery with grease, riffled through a Styrofoam carton that held French fries, judging by the smell and crumbs. A silver aluminum foil wrapper, packets of ketchup . . . and a memory stick.

I knew it.

I held up the small square, wondering if this was the reason Llew had been attacked, when my desk phone rang. I slid it into my laptop USB port and answered on the third ring.

It was Gabe.

I immediately smiled. 'Hi stranger.'

He chuckled, 'Hi . . .' Then paused. 'I heard about what happened. With the writer? He was a friend?'

I eased into my chair, relaxing against the back. 'Not exactly. But I did know him.'

'Well hopefully my news will cheer you up. The pie safe is at the Stanly house like I thought. I made us a reservation at a restaurant in New Bern if you'd like to leave in thirty?'

'Right now?' I looked at my desk. It was a mess of papers.

'Or maybe you'd rather not? Walking into that scene last night was difficult, I'm sure.'

'No, it's not that . . .' I glanced at the USB stick, emailed the contents to my email for safekeeping, then removed it from the computer. It could wait a few more hours, I guess.

I slid it into my purse along with the Hathor coin and medallion, which I hoped were all safe and sound in a hidden false bottom.

'Sure. Lunch in New Bern sounds great.'

We drove to New Bern and reached the Stanly house, a large, three-story, white house.

'The proprietors are New York transplants. Moved down here five years ago, purchased the home from the previous inn owners. They haven't made many changes.'

'And you explained . . . what exactly?'

'The truth, mostly. I'm Josiah's descendant, wanted to check out the pie safe to possibly loan out to the museum. And you're a representative of the Robbins Museum.'

'We sound legit.'

'We are legit. Zero lies have been told.' He laughed. 'Ready?'

We walked up the stairs, entered the foyer.

Josiah spoke with the innkeeper, who led us down a flight of stairs into a dim basement. I was getting flashbacks from the secret room and took a deep breath. Gabe noticed and touched my arm.

'You OK?'

I nodded, my hand tight on a rail as we descended the stairs.

'We use the basement as storage,' she said, switching on a bare bulb. 'No owner has ever thrown anything out it would seem.' She pointed to furniture covered in dust cloths. Moths flew from corners, and I coughed as we moved through a dust cloud.

The scent of mold permeated the dank space as we walked towards a back wall.

'This is it.'

The pie safe was about three feet tall, made of wood, with tin panels across the doors. Lotus flowers embellished the tin.

'It certainly looks like one of his pieces.' Gabe touched the safe gently.

The innkeeper's cell phone chimed. 'I need to take this. I'll be right back.'

I looked at the front of the cabinet. It held a rectangular metal box with a slot in it. 'If I didn't know better, I'd think this was a very old vending machine? Put in a coin, get a pie?'

'That's exactly what it is.'

'Not possible. Vending machines weren't invented until . . .' I stopped, because actually I didn't know. 'The fifties? Maybe the forties?'

'Heron of Alexandria invented the first vending machine.'

'But that would've been the first century.'

He shrugged. 'Sometimes it seems like our world was advanced first, lost everything and is still being found.'

I touched the slot, wondering. 'It's too big for a conventional coin. What do you think your ancestor intended?'

'Only someone with the exact coin, size and weight could open this cabinet. If I'm correct, there's a scale inside that will only open the door if a coin of the correct weight is used.'

I retrieved the Hathor coin from my purse, held it up to the dim light. 'Like this?'

His eyes widened. 'Where'd that come from?'

'Long story.' I glanced over my shoulder. 'Shall I try before she returns?'

He nodded and I pushed the coin into the slot. We could hear it rolling down a shaft, then it hit something with a clink. A moment later we heard the sound of rusty gears and a rectangular-shaped tray on the side slid out from a hidden compartment.

We both stared at it. 'Did Heron of Alexandria also invent a CD player because . . .' I laughed. The tray appeared to hold space for a small circular object. The outline of a feather was burned onto the bottom of the plate.

Gabe leaned closer, touching the imprint of the feather. 'You wouldn't happen to have another snazzy coin on you, would you?'

The feather had to refer to . . . I reached into my purse and unzipped the false bottom. I felt for the case Thea had given me and retrieved the medallion. It was heavier than the coin, larger and embossed with an owl. 'Will this do?'

A slow shake of his head, and Gabe couldn't take his eyes off me. 'You're full of surprises, Sidney Taylor.' He held out his hand. 'May I see it?'

'Of course.'

He took a moment to inspect the medallion, rubbing his finger over the owl's feathers before returning it to me.

I pressed the medallion into the tray. It fit perfectly, but nothing happened. We looked at each other. And then I leaned forward, grasping the raised edges of the pendant, and turned it first clockwise then counterclockwise until I heard a clicking sound.

The tray retracted back into the cabinet and the doors swung open.

I peered inside holding my breath, and then exhaled in frustration. 'It's empty.'

Gabe laughed. 'You were expecting a pie?'

'Of course not.' I sighed. I began moving my hands along the floor of the safe. And then the walls. It was solid. I glanced towards the stairs. 'She'll be back soon.'

He squinted at the cabinet. Then moved his hands inside pressing his palms against the walls. He dragged his finger across a series of seams that seemed to form a letter.

'It's the letter "J", isn't it?' I said.

'Yeah. And I've seen this before. On a writing instrument case Josiah made for a member of the Culper ring.'

Culper? I marveled at his name drop of George Washington's spy ring.

He winked. 'Watch this.'

I leaned in over his shoulder, so close I could feel the heat emanating from his broad shoulders and back.

He knocked once on a portion of the floor, then twice on another and three times on a wall. He waited a few seconds then knocked four times on the opposite wall. And a cabinet under the main section slid out.

'How in the world . . .?'

Gabe chuckled and reached into the drawer, and very much to my surprise, he retrieved a packet wrapped in linen.

He stood, looking quite satisfied with himself. 'Craftsmen have been using this type of secret lock method since Ancient Egypt. I've seen examples in Medieval, Renaissance and Victorian furniture.'

I grabbed it, slid it into my tote and then began closing the safe. 'And the combination?'

'He left notes in his journals for the writing box. I took a chance it was the same. And it was.'

The door to the basement opened, and I'd just finished up when the innkeeper returned.

We stood side by side, hopefully looking innocent. Not like two people who'd disassembled an antique and taken a historical document from inside.

'Seen enough?'

Gabe grinned back. 'It's definitely a Josiah Willoughby, and we'd love to show it at the museum.' He handed her a card. 'We offer a generous loan fee if you're interested. Give me a call when you've had time to talk it over with your husband.'

When we were safely in the car, we both sighed in relief. Then looked at each other and burst into laughter.

'Well, that was exciting.'

I looked at the packet. 'Shall we?'

Gabe nodded, and I looked around wondering if we'd been followed. If anyone was watching us. I didn't see anyone and for the moment felt safe to inspect the packet.

I carefully unrolled the linen to reveal a handwritten book. The cramped curled writing was a doozy to read, and the author was anonymous. But the title was clear: *The Carolina Housewife's Key to Cookery.*

'A cookbook?'

He shrugged. 'Unless it's a code.'

He drove slowly towards our restaurant. 'Anything stand out to you?'

'Not really. We've got . . . a recipe for haggis, and then a page on the Loch Ness monster with a sketch.' I turned the page. 'And then we've got a recipe for shortbread and a story about mischievous brownies. Cute drawing of a hobgoblin . . . I think it's safe to assume the author was Scottish. Next, porridge and fairies. Bannocks and banshees . . .' An odd mix for sure.

'So a recipe and a story for the kids?' He laughed. 'Truly a complete guide for the busy wife and mother.'

'Indeed.'

We turned into the parking lot.

'Do you think this is what we're looking for? James Madison's – I mean *not* James Madison's letter leads us to a . . . cookbook?'

'I'm starving. And I think better on a full stomach. Let's eat and then we can discuss.'

We entered Hot Grease, a trendy soul food restaurant with a couple of James Beard awards under its belt. The building, a wooden storefront with a red-and-white striped awning, shared the historic charm of the rest of the downtown district. The plate-glass windows on either side of the door featured displays of homemade cakes and pies, one of their specialties.

We were seated at a cherrywood table in the long, narrow dining room, and a waitress appeared to take our orders. I requested the soul food side – a trio of vegetarian dishes with a wedge of lemon-blueberry cornbread – and Gabe ordered the fried chicken with biscuit and farmer's market salad.

Once the waitress vanished, Gabe leaned in, his expression serious. 'So. First the truck. And then your grandmother.'

I shrugged, noncommittally. 'It's nothing.'

'Some guy *threatened* you. I know we just met, but if this is about the letter, perhaps you should stop searching for it.'

I tried to laugh it off. 'We haven't even figured out the mystery of the cookbook.'

He lifted his eyebrows in concern.

My smile slipped away. 'I'm sorry, I can't promise I'll stop. At first it was a professional interest, but then I learned something that makes it personal. And . . . well, my grandmother was threatened. And now Llew? It's the same person. And my instinct tells me that if I keep searching, not only will I find what I seek, but I'll find out who's behind this. I'll get answers.'

'I get it. I spend a lot of time tracking down artifacts myself when I'm not at the museum. Sometimes you're changing history when you find these relics. It's a thrill. It can be addictive.' He lowered his voice. 'But your life and the life of your loved ones have been threatened.' His eyes simmered with intensity. 'You're not scared?'

'I'm not *not* scared, if that makes sense. I'm just more curious, determined, I guess.' I thought of the Daughters of Hathor. It was my legacy. My responsibility. I would not let some guy hiding behind a mask deter me. But I wasn't sure how to articulate this to Gabe without telling him about the secret society. 'I have a responsibility to do this.'

Sighing, he nodded, like I'd disappointed him . . . But then . . . oddly, he smiled, like I'd pleased him after all.

Our food came, but I wasn't ready to let the conversation drop. 'You want me to stop. You're worried about me?'

He pulled his plate close. 'Let's just enjoy our meal.'

I crossed my arms. Leaving my food untouched. 'It's almost as if you've brought me to this lovely restaurant to deter me from looking further.' I considered him for a moment. 'Have you brought me to New Bern under a ruse?' I smiled, but my words had weight. 'Someone put you up to this? My grandmother?'

He held up a hand. 'Beautiful woman. Good food. May I please enjoy the moment?'

'Of course.' But he didn't answer the question.

As we ate, we made small talk. Discussed the weather. Authors. Favorite vacation spots and the like. I didn't want to get too personal. One, I didn't want to lead him on. And two, I was afraid if I learned more about him, I'd like him more than I already did. I was busy trying to track down an artifact, and I'd be returning to DC very soon. No time to start a relationship.

Gabe pushed his empty plate away. 'We've been talking for thirty minutes, and I still don't know anything about you.'

I shrugged. 'I could say the same.'

'That's because you haven't asked. What do you want to know? I'm an open book.'

A waiter came and took our dishes. Refilled our glasses.

I ignored his invite to get to know him better, and he thankfully let it slide.

He sipped his tea, eyeing me thoughtfully. 'You left town?'

'I went to DC on business.'

'And you found something?'

I nodded, not sure how much to tell him. I decided the least amount of information was for the best.

'But you're not going to tell me?' He cleared his throat. 'Got it. No problem. But you needed me today, right?'

I winced. 'I appreciate your help, Gabe. I do.' I moved my empty plate to the edge of the table, brought out the cookbook and we went over the pages. 'There *has* to be a pattern. In the secret room, drawings on Benjamin Banneker's almanac were a code.' When I'd told Gabe about the almanac his mouth had literally dropped open, and he made me promise to show it to him later. 'Could be the same for these drawings?' I tapped the drawing of a fairy. 'However, it might be too simplistic to do the same thing twice.'

'Agreed. I don't think he would.'

I skimmed the pages again. Then looked at the title. *The Carolina Housewife's Key to Cookery.* 'The *key*?' My eyes rose to meet Gabe's.

'Hiding in plain sight?'

'Who would think to look in a cookbook?' First we had the key to heaven, which led to the church. Was the cookbook the key? Literally? I turned to the index. It was simply titled: The Key. I read through the recipes, and then it hit me. I laughed, it was so simple.

'You figured it out?'

'Maybe.' I showed him a picture of the Madison letter. 'Having viewed the cookbook . . .'

He nodded. 'The dinner menu.'

I wrote down the entrees Madison mentioned in his letter to his wife: *peanut soup, dandelion salad, country ham, crab cakes, oysters, corn pudding, sautéed celery. Peas Francoise, apple pie.* I flipped to the index, to the key, and found each item and wrote down the very next word beside it, for it was capitalized in a way other first words were not. Put together, they formed a sentence: Search For Tryon's Cook You'll Find The Hidden Nook.

'What does that mean?' he wondered.

'Tryon's Palace? One of the kitchens.'

'Shall we see this through?'

I stared at him. 'What? Go to Tryon Palace right now and mess around in one of their kitchens and hope no one notices?'

'I'm game if you are.'

I returned to the cookbook and turned to the last page. There was a small image drawn in the bottom right corner of the otherwise blank page. I studied it, surprised that I knew what it meant. 'Daphne has this in her office,' I explained. 'She said it was the Egyptian hieroglyph for scribe.'

'OK. So we're looking for something related to writing in the kitchen at Tryon Palace. I'd say we're on a proper treasure hunt.'

I couldn't help but blush under his gaze.

Gabe flagged the waitress. 'Check.'

I watched him sign for the bill, all the while my mind running rampant with hypothesis and supposition.

TWENTY-THREE

We walked through the tall wrought-iron gates, and towards the large Federal style home.

'How many times have you been here?' I asked.

He guided me around the circular path to the house. 'Probably twelve or so times. I have a season pass.'

'I think I've met my match. You love history as much as I do.'

We shared a moment, before I stepped onto the white steps and entered the building, joining a long line of patrons. Tryon Palace was grand, and I felt right at home with the costumed attendants and tour guides.

'Do you know what you're looking for?' Gabe asked.

'No.'

He chuckled. 'OK. This just got interesting.'

'But I think it's related to rulership in America. Something about all of the presidents being related.'

He looked thoughtful but didn't comment.

'Isn't it weird that they're all related? Like, what does that mean for democracy?' We continued walking, joining the long line of patrons waiting to get in. 'I mean, if for example both Hilary Clinton and President Trump are distantly related, are we really voting for different people with different platforms?' I continued.

'I know your dad's a politician, but are you interested in politics as well?'

'No.' At least, that used to be true . . .

'The interesting thing about those two,' Gabe said, 'Is that they're both related to John of Gaunt, also known as the Earl of Richmond or the Duc d'Aquitaine. He was an English prince, the son of Edward III and Philippa of Hainaut.'

I couldn't believe my ears. 'Edward III was the grandson of the man who stole the Stone of Scone.'

'That concerns you?' He chuckled. 'This happened a long time ago.'

'I know. But . . . I guess I didn't believe the story about how our presidents are related. And now to hear that the ancestors of the man who stole the right to rule hundreds of years ago are still running our country. It's kind of mind-blowing.'

'The majority of American presidents are descended from Edward I and III of England. A few are related to James I of Scotland. But both Edward I and James I are distantly related to Edward III, so . . .'

'That's surprising Are there any who aren't related to British royalty?'

'Just Lincoln, JFK, Lyndon B. Johnson, Reagan and Clinton. And the funny thing is that both JFK and Clinton, while not genetically related to royalty, married women who were.' He looked around, then grabbed my hand and peeled away from our group. 'Come on.' We ran-walked in the opposite direction, stopping short when we reached the kitchen. A short elderly black man in period dress sat on a stool. He nodded at me. 'Welcome to the Kitchen Office.' Then launched into his spiel.

When he said this wasn't the original building, I stopped him, exchanging glances with Gabe. 'What do you mean?'

'It survived the fire of 1798 but was torn down by developers when houses were built on the grounds.' He waved a hand around. 'This is all new. A replica. Not near as nice, to hear my grandfather tell it.'

I lowered my voice and turned to Gabe. 'It can't be here then.'

'What can't be here?' the man said. He cackled. 'I'm old but ain't nothing wrong with my ears.'

I cringed and looked around. We were alone in the kitchen though there were patrons near the entrance. 'I'm . . . we're doing a treasure hunt.' I grabbed Gabe's arm and hugged him to me. 'Right, hon?'

He wrapped his other arm around me, easily slipping into the role of lover. And I had to admit, it felt nice. Despite myself, I gave him a sideways glance.

He grinned down at me. 'Anything to keep her happy.'

'What are you looking for? Maybe I can help.'

I snuggled into the crook of Gabe's arm – just to make the act more believable, of course. 'Something related to writing or a book?'

The man cocked his head, lost in thought. 'Can't say I know of anything like that.' His gaze bounced around the room, still searching. Then he punched the air with his forefinger. 'How about a poem? Will that do?'

Gabe and I exchanged hopeful looks. 'Maybe. What do you have?'

'The poet George Horton was famously sweet on a young woman that worked here.' He raised an eyebrow. 'You've heard of him?'

Heard of him? Of course I had. Known as the Slave Poet, he was born in North Carolina and was considered the first African-American author to be published in the United States.

'Horton was a friend to Josiah,' Gabe murmured in my ear.

'Yes, I know who he is,' I answered the man, anxious for the rest of the story.

'He wrote poems for her and left them on scraps of paper in the kitchen for her.' He moved around the room. 'Several survived, and we keep them here in the kitchen in this portfolio.' The man removed a leather case from a shelf and opened it up to reveal pages of poems protected by plastic.

I carefully turned the pages until I found a poem with the same little drawing on the bottom. I inhaled sharply. This had to be it.

Gabe nodded encouragingly as I began to read.

"'In a garden, serene and fair. Where lilac blooms scent the air, I sat beneath the verdant tree, To sip the nectar, lilac tea. Its fragrance danced upon the breeze, A symphony of floral keys, With every sip, a soothing grace, A sweet elixir, to embrace.'"

'Pretty good, right?' the man said. 'Smooth operator that one.' He chuckled. 'This one's called "Garden Tea With My Lover".'

Gabe turned to me. 'The gardens?'

Excitement fluttered in my chest. 'Last one there's a rotten egg.'

We made our way to the kitchen garden, and when we arrived I turned around in a circle, taking in the landscape. 'I'm trying to remember everything in the poem. There was a key, that's for sure.'

'Lilac trees. Lilac tea,' Gabe added.

'And he mentioned sitting under the tree. Josiah was friends with everyone, it seemed. What was his relationship to George?'

'They'd have dinner whenever he was in town, and George would recite his latest works. It was a popular amusement back then.'

The gardens were full of colorful blooms. I let my nose lead me to the lilac, a favorite scent. I pointed. 'There's the lilac trees.'

He followed my gaze to a bench underneath the tree. 'Shall we sit as George and his lady friend must've?'

We went to the bench and inspected the seat and the area around it. Nothing seemed out of the ordinary.

We sat. Took a breath and enjoyed the view. The sky was blue. Fluffy white clouds floated by, and the sun was high in the sky and shone a brilliantly clear yellow. Butterflies and bees hovered in the air, and flowers scented the air around us.

'Kind of perfect.'

He looked at me. 'Certainly my company is.'

I blushed. Directly across from us at a statue poised about fifty feet away. It was Apollo, holding a cup from which water flowed out of his hand to a basin below. At his foot was a lyre.

"'A symphony of floral keys." That's what he wrote,' I reminded. 'And there's the god of music.'

'Let's check it out.'

We went to the statue. It was about three feet tall. 'A symphony of floral keys makes me think of a piano made of flowers.' I kneeled down, inspecting the base of the statue. Flowers were carved around the feet of Apollo. Gabe stood behind me guarding me from view while I touched and tugged at each one, hoping one would unlock something as the daisies had on the mantle.

'Anything?' he whispered.

'Not yet.' I moved my hands around the base of the statue, though my gaze lingered on one of the flowers that was a darker shade of white, with an ash tint. I returned to it, and instead of pushing and twisting it . . . I pressed down on it. It popped back up and I pulled it out of its sheath of dirt.

A rust-incrusted key lay inside. I flipped it over and saw the image of a mortar and pestle engraved on it. A common sign for an apothecary.

'He wrote something about an elixir,' Gabe said.

'Is there an apothecary in the grounds?'

Gabe began searching on his phone. Frowned. 'No.'

'Was there one here during Josiah's time?'

Gabe scrolled his screen. 'Yes, there was. Downtown New Bern . . . Well, at least the building is still there. It ceased being an apothecary at least a hundred years ago. It's a bar now.'

I held up the key. 'Maybe we can find what this opens.'

We began walking towards the gate, when I noticed a man watching us. Blue baseball cap, sunglasses. Jeans and running shoes. I hesitated, touched Gabe's arm. 'To your right. Is it me or is that guy following us?'

'I was just about to ask you about the guy over there.' He nodded his head to my left. I cut my eyes towards a wall of rose bushes, and saw a man in a red baseball cap, athletic shoes and jeans.

We walked slowly, and Gabe curled his arm around my waist.

'Just go with it,' he murmured into my ear. 'Check out Red, and I'll do the same for Blue.'

He pulled me into a hug, which I can't say I didn't enjoy. He was muscular and comforting and smelled of cedar and sandalwood.

'Blue is pretending to be on his phone, but he's definitely watching us.'

Something about Red was familiar. 'He's not looking over here, but he's talking. Like he has an earbud in.'

'OK.' He pulled back and took my hand. 'Let's walk slowly but with purpose to the car. I'll see if they're following us.'

We began to walk.

'And if they are?'

His jaw firmed. 'I'll lose them.'

TWENTY-FOUR

G abe drove out of the parking lot at normal speed. Both men also left, in two different vehicles. One had a small sports car, and the other . . . a black pickup truck.

I gasped. 'That's the truck!' I said, my heart racing.

'What?' Gabe's voice was tight, his hands gripped around the wheel.

I wanted to turn around in my seat and stare out the back window for a better look. But that would be too obvious. Instead, I adjusted my side mirror. Blue was driving the truck. 'The truck that drove me off the road.'

He glanced into his rearview mirror again before making a turn on George Street. 'These guys are serious. It's about time you told me what this is all about.'

I heaved a sigh. 'I could tell you, but—'

He rolled his eyes good-naturedly. 'You'll have to kill me?'

'No, I was going to say . . .' I bit my lip. 'But you won't believe me.'

He fixed me with a long look. 'Try me.'

'I'm sorry . . . I can't.'

Slight frown lines appeared on his forehead. But he only nodded. 'OK.' He turned south on Front Street, and we began driving parallel to the Trent River.

I pushed away my guilt, looked into my mirror, my hand gripping the door handle. 'They're still following us.'

'I know.' He looked into oncoming traffic. 'Hold on.' Then quickly did a U-turn with a screech of tires. Both vehicles sped by us in the opposite direction.

'Where'd you learn that?'

His lips quirked upwards. 'I didn't always run a museum. We

need to get to that bar before they can find us.' He increased the speed and zoomed down the street swerving in between cars. 'I'm going to slow down when we get to the park. When I do, jump out, run down Middle Street. The bar should be two blocks up.' He glanced into his rearview mirror. 'I'll try and buy you some time.'

Minutes later, we pulled up to Union Point Park. 'Go.'

I opened the door and took off running. Good thing I was wearing sneakers.

TWENTY-FIVE

I ran all the way to the bar.

When I got there, I placed one hand on the brick exterior and bent at the waist to catch my breath. My face was sweaty, and my hair was probably a mess. I pushed it back from my face as best I could.

Customers spilled out of the bar, and a Chris Stapleton tune flowed onto the street when the doors swung open. I read the sign over the glass door. Potions And Prose. Half-bar, half-bookstore. It was definitely the kind of place I'd like to spend more time at when I wasn't being chased. I glanced down the street hoping Gabe was doing OK.

I pushed open the door and saw the owners had kept the apothecary shelves and tools as part of the theme. Drink specials had herbal remedy names like Absinthe Dreams, Lavender Fizz and Chamomile Cure scrawled in multi-colored chalk on a blackboard above a mirrored backboard. The staff wore black T-shirts and jeans, and books lined two of the walls.

'Get you a drink, hon?' an older blonde woman asked me with a smoker's voice. Lines pinched her lip like she had a three-pack a day habit. But her blue eyes were warm as she looked at me.

Water, actually, was what I needed after that sprint. 'Just a glass of water until I can make a decision.'

She gave me a cautious look. 'You gotta buy a drink, hon. No drink. No seat.'

I didn't need alcohol right now; I'd probably throw up. I handed her a twenty-dollar bill. 'We good?'

She cocked her head in surprise. Then waved a hand. 'Wherever you like, missy.'

I checked my pocket, making sure the key was still there. Grabbed my icy glass of water and then moved around the room looking for something that could take the key. Nothing stood out.

'You looking for something, hon?'

I turned around. It was her, the bartender. She grinned. 'You wantin' to buy a knickknack or a book?'

'Possibly,' I hedged.

'Upstairs.' She yanked her head towards a staircase I hadn't noticed before. 'That's the museum and gift shop.'

'Museum?'

'Sure, honey. This was an apothecary back when Ol' Governor Tryon was building his mansion. It's changed hands a few times. By the time it came to our family, it was a museum, but when I inherited the place from my grandmother it wasn't making no money. So, I added the bar, and my daughter came up with the books considering the clause that came with purchase. Nice, right?' She looked around the bar, pride gleaming in her eyes.

'Very nice.' I saw a small painting on the wall and went to it. *Well, well . . . I was definitely in the right place.*

The owner followed me. 'Wanna hear some local history?' I nodded, and she continued. 'This place was once owned by Josiah Willoughby. Most people don't know that.'

I leaned close to the painting, staring into his eyes. I could imagine a mischievous twinkle in them. *I'm going to find this artifact, Josiah.*

I turned to look at her, her last words returning to me. 'What clause, if you don't mind me asking?'

She rolled her eyes. 'The building came with a book. Oddest thing. We can never sell it. It just has to stay on the premises. Josiah here put that in the contract. Obviously he wanted this place to become a bookstore, but it's not books that bring in the money.' She smirked. 'It's the booze.'

The story was interesting, but books didn't come with locks so it couldn't be what I was looking for. 'I'll take a look at the museum then. Thanks.'

I left her on the landing and made my way up the rickety flight of stairs. The museum was a wide open space. Counters lined the walls, with shelves full of glass jars of dried herbs. Large, framed pictures showed downtown New Bern in the 1800s with horses and carriages on dirt roads, the river glistening in the background.

I pulled the key from my pocket and stared at it. What could it open? I roved around the room looking for anything with a keyhole, and started to feel a little panicky. Gabe was driving around with two men on his trail, and I couldn't find anything.

After a moment, the owner followed me up. 'I'm Vera, by the way. You looking for something special?'

'Sidney,' I introduced myself. 'I'm trying to find a gift for someone who loves . . . old things that require . . . keys. You know, the trend for lock and key antiques?' I swallowed hoping she'd believe the lie.

She stared at me, her blue eyes glinting in the neon light on the wall. For a moment, I wondered if she was a Daughter too.

I cleared my throat ceremoniously. 'The cow jumped over the moon,' I said, feeling a bit silly. But also a bit hopeful.

She barked a laugh. Paused. Then, 'Hickory, dickory dock. The mouse ran up the clock.'

OK, not her.

'We through with the nursery rhymes, hon? I do have a bar to run, though my nephew's out there trying his best to screw things up.' She rolled her eyes good-naturedly. 'You want to see the book I'm not allowed to sell?'

I glanced towards the door. 'Show me.'

She led me to her office and closed the door. Unlocked a cabinet and retrieved a large leather book covered in intricate designs and inlaid with gold. The pages were gilded in gold as well. It was so large and so heavy she needed two hands to heft it from its resting place. She set it down with a thunk. The pages were enclosed with a leather strap joined by a gold lock. 'I've never been able to open it. No one has. It didn't come with a key.'

I squinted at her. This seemed too easy. 'No locksmith?'

'It looks important, don't it? Worth a lot of money? No one wanted to rip the thing open and destroy its value.'

'And yet, you never had it appraised?'

'I can't open it. Not supposed to sell it.' She shrugged. 'It's just a piece of beautiful but useless junk as far as I'm concerned.'

'What happens if you sell it?'

'I have no idea. I guess the building will fall down around me.' She laughed. 'It was an apothecary. Herbs and such? Maybe Josiah purchased it from a witch who cursed the place. I'm not exactly superstitious but I'm not courting trouble either.'

I inspected the cover, realizing the flowers on the cover were lotuses.

'My grandmother did have it looked at once by an artist specialist at Tryon. He said he thought this was the work of Joshua Johnson. You've heard of him, right?'

I nodded. He was the same artist who'd painted the dinner and ball for Josiah. That couldn't be a coincidence.

There was a knock at the door, and someone stuck his head in the office. 'Aunt V, we just got a tourist bus come from Nashville and they're thirstier than a camel in the desert.'

'I'll be right there, Zeke.' She turned to me. 'Give it a look. Then look around. I got other stuff for sale.'

When she was gone, I took the key and inserted it into the book's lock. I didn't realize I was holding my breath until the lock turned and the straps released. I gently opened the cover and saw the book was not a book at all. A rectangular well had been carved inside. And on a square piece of fabric, gold and satiny, soft to the touch, was a silhouette of a cow, and a message embroidered in purple thread: *Where destiny lies, a daughter lays her head.*

I stared at the cloth, wondering who had embroidered the beautiful line. And then I heard footsteps by the door, and hurriedly placed it in my purse, then closed the book and locked it. I was just slipping the key back into my pocket when Vera reappeared.

'Well, anything caught your eye?'

I affected an apologetic expression. 'No, sorry. But I appreciate the hospitality.'

We had just reached the bar floor, when the front door opened. Red and Blue stepped inside. Took off their hats respectful like and I got a good look at their faces. They looked like older versions of the Marines I used to see hanging out on H Street in DC.

I took a step back into the hallway.

'Those guys friends of yours?'

'Definitely not.'

She grunted, crossing her arms. 'That one on the right looks mean, don't he?'

'It's the scar,' I said, trying to keep things light. But I think my voice quivered. The one on the right was the one who'd tried to run me off the road. I recognized him from the truck. 'I met him once online and it didn't work out,' I lied. Again. 'Now, every time I go out, he and his friend show up.'

'Oh no, honey. We're ending that today.' She put her fingers to her mouth and let out a whistle that only a dog, and apparently her bouncer, could hear. A tall, shaggy-haired, bearded white man built like a tree moved out of the shadows, he made eye contact with her and went for the men.

'Out the back, by the bathrooms. Down the alley and you'll be at Bear Plaza. Cut across it and you can get lost on Craven Street.'

I thanked her and tried to move unseen towards the back entrance, when I heard a man shout, 'There she is.'

Tables and chairs scraped against the floor and people screamed as they were shoved out of the way while both Red and Blue scrambled towards me. The bouncer rushed them like he was trying out for the Carolina Panthers and knocked them both down like bowling pins.

In the chaos of the moment, a blue baseball cap landed at my feet. I stared at the monogram on the hat. The image of a cute robot. From QLabs, I realized. And I remembered now. Blue was the man I'd seen walking into the tech company on Main Street. How was QLabs involved with this?

But no time to think about that now.

I hurried to the doors, looking past my shoulder to see punches being thrown and legs flailing on the ground. I pushed open the door, holding my breath as I dodged past piles of garbage and began running towards the plaza, attracting a few strange looks from the tourists in the square. I stopped when I reached the opposite side and pressed against a wall to catch my breath and wonder where Gabe was.

I checked my phone and saw I'd missed a text from him. He would meet me at the corner of Pollock and Craven in ten minutes. I just had to stay hidden until then.

I slipped inside a clothing boutique, just as Red trotted by the window. I caught a glimpse of a busted lip and a torn T-shirt. I shrunk back, then peered out and saw Blue without his baseball cap about a hundred yards away scanning the area with a focused gaze. He was going to have one heck of a shiner in the morning.

Who were they? Was one of them the texter? The man who'd broken into my grandmother's house? The one who'd attacked and killed Llew? Or was there a third helping them? How many were there? Who was behind QLabs and why were they out to get me?

Frantic thoughts zipped through my mind, and I tried to calm myself with deep breathing. These men were dangerous. They had to work for The Opposition, didn't they?

I looked around the boutique, realizing I could disguise my appearance. I greeted the clerk, a teenager in a hot pink mini dress with eyes glued to her cell phone screen, then searched for a new look.

When I stepped out of the shop, I was brand new. I had on a chartreuse sun dress, chunky high-heeled sandals, large white Jackie-O sunglasses and a dark brown bob from a mannequin. I looked like a Southern belle heading for an ice cream social. The wig had cost me a fifty-dollar tip since it wasn't for sale, but the teenager was open to telling her manager it was misplaced if I paid her. The only thing I'd kept was my purse.

I took my sweet time walking to the meeting point, pretending to talk on my phone to add to the charade. I was fake talking to my sister about her kids when I saw Gabe's car. He did a double take when I got close, then pushed the door open from the inside. 'Get in.'

I did.

And we sped down the road.

TWENTY-SIX

'How did you know it was me?' I asked Gabe as I pulled the wig off, undid my hastily braided hair and fluffed it up. His lips moved into a lopsided grin, as he turned into my grandmother's driveway. 'Can't hide those freckles.'

I blushed, and he placed the truck in park, and turned to me. 'You good?'

I nodded, shoving the wig into my purse, knowing I owed him a big explanation but unwilling to share my secret. 'Thank you. For everything.'

'Is this our thing?' His tone was teasing, but seriousness darkened his eyes. 'I see you, weird things happen, I'm kept in the dark, days pass without hearing anything and then . . . repeat?'

'I'm sorry,' I said for what felt like the millionth time. 'I do like spending time with you. Maybe when I'm done, we can . . .' I sighed. Wasn't sure what I could promise. 'Maybe we can have dinner again.' But not tell him the truth? Pretty sure I could never, ever tell him about any of this.

'Maybe.' He mimicked my word, then gave me a curious look. 'When I first saw you, you told me you had my ancestor's writing box here at your grandmother's. Would you mind if I borrowed it?'

'No, of course not.' I unbuckled my seat. 'Just give me a sec and I'll go get it. I'm sure my grandmother won't mind.'

I returned in a jiff, presenting him the box with a questioning look.

He held it up, examining it from all angles. 'It's been missing from our inventory for so long, I'd like to update our records. Take pictures, create a description . . . That sort of thing.'

We stood there for an awkward moment more while I wondered if I should let him kiss me on the cheek, and he looked like he wanted to kiss me on the lips.

He broke the moment with a self-conscious shrug of his shoulders. 'I better get out of here. Let me know if you have any problems with the car.'

I stood on the porch and watched him back his truck up the dirt driveway, then drive off in a cloud of red dust.

Once inside, I took a shower. After my day, I not only needed to clean myself, I needed to relax under streams of hot water and my grandmother's handmade lemongrass soap.

The heat and lemongrass oil did the trick. Then I got comfortable in a T-shirt and a pair of running shorts. My grandmother wasn't home. Probably at church or her knitting group. I made sure the doors were locked and settled into a chair to do a little internet sleuthing.

I began with QLabs. Their website was a sleek minimalistic space of gray and blue full of high-tech gobbledygook. There were stock photos of office workers, but no names of real people, just an address and a contact page.

I went back to the search engine and finally found a profile of the company on an obscure database of quantum computing companies. I skimmed the page, stopping to read a few paragraphs that stuck out to me:

> QLabs is actively involved in high-energy physics experiments, exploring phenomena such as quantum entanglement, dark matter, and neutrino oscillations. Their experiments often take place in remote locations, ensuring minimal interference from external factors . . .
>
> The company has initiated investigations into the manipulation of time-related phenomena. Their work in experimental temporal mechanics holds potential applications in precision timekeeping and synchronization systems.

Clearly, the writer of the profile was a fan of quantum science and thought the folks at QLabs were doing cutting-edge research. But I was just confused. Why was this company in Robbinsville of all places? And why would they have someone connected to them trying to harm me?

After more research, I still had no idea who worked for them or what they did. I mean, did they provide services or products? I rose from my computer and rubbed my temples until inspiration hit.

I went back to my computer and searched for any patents related to the company. If they had a product, they'd have to have a patent for it. I found the website and began my search and after only a few moments found one entry for QLabs. For a Quantum Temporal Synchronizer.

The patent explained that the highly-advanced machine used

principles from quantum mechanics and special materials to do precise things with time. That was about all I could understand. I skimmed the technical details and scrolled to a diagram that was full of symbols, equations and notations. So far, unhelpful. Was it just an ultra-precise clock?

I went over the page again, hoping to find a contact. A name of an actual person associated with the company. But the patent was submitted by and assigned to QLabs.

There was a second patent. But by this time, I'd hit the wall for scientific writing, and I gave it an even quicker look. It was for a device called the Enhanced Electromagnetic Resonance Inducer. I read the description twice and still didn't understand what it did.

I bookmarked each patent page in case I decided to return to it, then I loaded Llew's memory stick into my laptop. There were several folders. I clicked on the first one and saw an image of Abner. Several, actually, through the years. Him in the seventies with long sideburns and bell bottoms at a museum function. Him in the eighties wearing his colonial costume and pointing to the museum behind him. And several more in more contemporary times in a mix of menswear and his museum costume. He looked the same in all of them. Only the style of his hair changed, and even then he always kept it longish.

The next document was a profile of him and his accomplishments in town. Then there were old articles from the 1800s. One explaining how Elias and Susannah had taken a trip by boat, when heavy winds hit and Susannah perished in the storm leaving Elias a widow. And another, from three months later, describing how Elias died in a mining accident when a tunnel collapsed on him. The last document in the folder showed the schematics for what used to be the coffee shop in town . . . the QLabs building. Now why was that there?

I clicked on the next folder. Inside were several PDFs. One was filled with schematics for various technologies, some from the Victorian era, some sleek and futuristic. One contained old news articles on Indian mounds and old indigenous sites. Nothing relevant to my search.

The next PDF had several articles relating to a man named Lucius Abernathy, born in London, England, and his ancestors. I skimmed, learning that Lucius was a member of King James' court, and one of several religious advisers who stepped up to support the king in his anti-witch beliefs. Lucius had written several anti-occult pamphlets that were used in court hearings and became canon for the cause. His ancestors eventually moved to America and settled in Virginia, where they established churches and presided over several witch trials.

I went to the next document. It was several old news clippings about Matthias Toliver, the preacher at Robbins Village. This was the character Matty re-enacted. His ancestor. A sick feeling roiled in my stomach. The newspaper publicized several anti-witch sermons he'd preached, including one on how red-haired women were the mistress of the devil. I recalled how he'd seemed fixated on my hair for a moment.

I sat back in my chair, frowning at the screen. Then I clicked on the next document – a family tree that connected Matthias Toliver to a witch-hunter named Matthew Hopkins through a daughter who married and took the surname of Toliver. It would seem the Tolivers' family business was witch-hunting. I wondered what Matty thought about his ancestors' work.

Thea's words came to me then. *The witch hunt was about stamping out the line . . . Destroying any chance for other royal contenders. Searching for and killing our Sisters was about making sure the royal line of Queen Scota dies out. It was about making sure the women vowed to protect the stone with their abilities endowed by the stone were no longer alive to do so.*

If Matthew Hopkins was hunting and killing Daughters of Hathor for the king in England, did his descendants move to America, to North Carolina, to do the same thing when the Daughters fled for safety?

The key to heaven.

The name of Matthias Toliver's famous sermon came to mind then. He'd preached it as a response to the theft of Susannah Robbins' mirror. The one that hadn't really been stolen. The one that was a prompt to accuse three women of witchcraft. I did a search on my phone, and cross-referenced the dates. He'd given the sermon two months before the women were accused of theft. But if the accusations weren't about a stolen item, what had prompted the sermon?

I logged into oldnewspapers.com and searched for articles during the appropriate time period and location. The first article discussed an outbreak of cholera in Robbinsville that made many people sick. Susannah Robbins herself, with the help of several servants, had tended to the sick.

The second page was from Toliver's handwritten journal. Toliver claimed four women had called on the devil to save the villagers, and their wicked calls were heard. 'But now I know who the Daughters of Hathor are,' he concluded, 'they will not be able to save themselves from me.'

I blinked.

He knew about the Daughters of Hathor? And they had outed themselves by healing the sick. He'd mentioned four women, but only three had been charged.

I kept reading, feeling a voracious need to know everything that Llew knew. Some of the details I recognized from his short unpublished book, but what he'd written had barely scratched the surface, it seemed. The next article was a court document, a complaint to the registrar detailing how four women had been seen by the river at night holding hands and chanting with dark shadows forming over the water and dancing in the night sky.

The complaint had been dismissed.

The next page showed another journal entry from Matthias. He complained that he'd gone to Elias and told him about the women, their healing abilities and the dark magic they'd practiced by the water. But Elias had quoted England's Witchcraft Act of 1735 which made it illegal to accuse anyone of making magic or being a witch.

The next page was a court document accusing three women of stealing.

I huffed in frustration. He'd set them up. This so-called man of God had falsely accused these women of theft because he couldn't get them accused of witchcraft.

I reread the document. This time it said three women had been accused. But Matty's ancestor had claimed *four* women were practicing witchcraft. Who was the fourth woman, and what had happened to her?

I wondered if Matty knew this about his ancestor. And if he did, would he be so eager to enact his character playing the godly man about church for all to see?

The next article was an editorial written stating it would be a mistake to kill the women since they may punish the entire town. Another article offered a solution. Kill one of the women and banish the others, only don't let the women know who was to die until the last moment so they wouldn't have time to cast a complex spell.

This seemed to have been the option taken, since it was only on the day of the hanging that the paper announced the name of the woman to be hanged to death on the old oak tree.

I looked up from the screen, disturbed by what I was reading. Llew had been targeted because of this research. But who wouldn't want this published in a book? Of course, there was Abner, but I couldn't believe he was behind the attack. Who else?

My mind was a blank. There was one more file to review, but I needed to learn more about these women.

I stopped by Daphne's office at the library and poked my head inside her open door. She smiled when she saw me.

'Hey, I know it's late and you're probably about to close up. But would it be possible for me to spend about an hour in the archives room?'

She rose from her seat. 'Of course. This is related to the Madison letter?'

I stepped inside her office. 'I'm not sure,' I hedged, unsure of how much to tell her. Yes, she knew about my search but what did she know about the witchy past of the museum?

'Tell me. Maybe I can help.' She crossed her arms, waiting for me to elaborate.

'I've discovered an intrigue of witches here at the museum.'

Her eyes widened just a smidge. 'Oh?'

'And Matty's ancestor was deeply involved in their prosecution. Are you familiar with this at all?'

'I've come across some documents . . .' Faint lines appeared on her forehead. 'Disturbing, yes?'

I noticed her shoulders seemed to tense a bit. 'Matty seems like a nice guy. Do you think he's aware of what his ancestor did?'

'He knows his history, but Abner doesn't allow him to share that part as a historical interpreter so it's never come up. Not in all the time I've been here.' She shrugged. 'We can't choose our family, and neither can Matty.' She laughed lightly. 'The archives?'

'Right. Yes.'

'Go ahead. I don't mind.'

Fortunately, everything had been digitized so I could search on one of their computers. The first document I read was the old newspaper article that advertised the hanging of one Isla McIntosh, an indentured servant. Her fellow witches were Bathsheba Montgomery and Zadie Jefferson. They were freed when they agreed to leave the community. The fourth woman was never identified.

I cross-referenced the names and discovered that Isla worked as a cook in the kitchen, and Zadie was paid weekly as a seamstress. There was very little about the women prior to the accusations, just a mention that Zadie received silks from Paris and was sewing a dress for Susannah, and Isla was pregnant.

The last document was a post-mortem as it were of the hanging, which was attended by throngs of crowds seeking justice for wrongs. This from the journalist who appeared to consider himself something of a wordsmith. The most interesting part of the story was the description of Isla: beautiful of face, elegant in bearing. She'd worn a beautiful purple gown of silk for her hanging. Maintaining a noble persona until the end, she had died with her dignity intact.

Her body had been removed from the tree, and it was assumed her female friends had spirited the remains away.

There was a noise behind me, and I jumped.

'I didn't mean to startle you.' Abner slid into the room. 'Daphne told me you were here.'

I glanced at the computer screen. 'Just doing a little research.'

'How was your trip to New Bern? Find anything?' He closed the door and leaned on the edge of the table.

I noticed the white streak in his beard was back. 'First of all, you should know that two men were tracking me. One was the driver of the truck that ran me off the road.'

Abner's eyes widened. 'Were you hurt?'

'No. I got away. But . . . they seemed intent on doing me harm.'

His expression darkened but he didn't say anything.

'I learned about the Stone of Scone. It would fit the artifact I'm searching for, only it's not lost.'

'No, it's not. King Charles was famously crowned on it and returned it back to Scotland, the rightful owner.'

'So you know about Queen Scota . . . and the Daughters?' I tried.

He nodded. 'I do. It was a story my father used to tell me and my brother before bed. A pretty fairytale about a beautiful Egyptian queen and her court of maidens . . .' He smiled at the memory. 'And he learned it from his mother.'

'Do you understand how the Stone works because I'm still having trouble understanding.'

Abner moved from his perch on the table like he was restless and began prowling the room. 'When someone is crowned on it and they are not of the bloodline . . . not with a selfless, humble heart and mind to rule . . . you get bad rulers. Money-hungry, narcissistic, not caring about their people, leading their country to ruin . . .'

'Sounds horrible.'

'America was always meant to be ruled by certain families, but democratically elected. That choice was taken from us when men not fit to rule stole the Stone and the office.'

I kept my expression unchanged but not for the first time I was surprised by the intensity of his emotion.

'And now we have to fight those who would oppose the divinely ordered to rule. The Opposition,' he said firmly.

'The Opposition is in power now?'

'Yes. Here in America, Great Britain, China . . . it's not the heirs of the House of David . . . It's The Opposition. They are the descendants of the group responsible for taking the Stone in the first place and bullying themselves into places of position and power.'

'The Opposition . . . Can't we find a better name for them?' I halfway joked, trying to lighten the mood.

He shrugged. 'They have a name. We just don't like to say it.'

'What is it?'

'The Order of Apophis.'

'The snake that eats Ra eternally. Nice.'

'Yeah.' His lips twisted.

'This order . . . They're the reason why it seems like our world is falling apart?'

He nodded. 'That's by design. Chaos is kind of their brand. They create it and then monetize the fallout. It's been happening for a long time. All the wars, the financial depressions, so-called natural disasters . . .'

I think I understood where he was going with this. 'Like blowing up a building, then getting the contract for rebuilding it. Or creating a disease, then selling the treatment.'

'Or forcing Americans to plug into a virtual reality so they'll be easier to control and monetize.' He gave me a hard look. 'Like setting off solar flares. Like burning down a museum so they have no choice but to stay exclusively in the VR.'

'But how? How could they replicate a solar flare? Have the audacity to burn down an entire museum of priceless artifacts hundreds of years old?'

'Because they can. And because it supports the Opposition's goal of one hundred percent compliance to the upcoming VR laws. You see why this is so urgent, then?'

'The two men chasing me today are in this order. And at least one of them works at QLabs. I don't understand how that company could be related.' I hesitated when I saw Abner's expression change. 'Do you know anything about them?'

'I don't know anything about the leadership of the company except that they are headquartered in northern Virginia. All of their paperwork was done through a registered agent connected to an LLC based in the Caribbean. As you probably heard, QLabs came to town throwing a lot of government grants around. We were able to restore a few old buildings on the back side of Main Street, restore a pier damaged in the last hurricane and beautify several parks. The employees are mostly remote, or at least that's what Matty says.'

'Matty?'

'Yeah. He works there. But even he says he has no idea who his boss is.'

I thought of his Star Trek lunchbox. 'What does he do there?'

'No idea. He tried to explain it to me once and I almost fell asleep. If I can't make it with a hammer and nails, I don't need to know about it.'

I needed to talk to Matty next. Maybe he could help me connect the dots or knew of a co-worker with an odd hobby of trying to cause me harm. I'd have to check his schedule and see when he worked next. 'What do you think of him?'

'Matty?' He shrugged. 'He's reliable, knows his history and does a great job inventorying the museum's artifacts and maintaining the church. It's a boon to us that we have an actual ancestor of a real person who lived here.' He gave me a concerned look. 'Our visitors eat it up – his tours are very popular.'

'OK.'

'Well,' Abner said, his tone impatient. 'Are you going to tell me what you found?'

I looked around the enclosed room like spies were hiding in the stacks. 'A piece of fabric with a sentence knitted on it.' I repeated the phrase for him. '"Where destiny lies, a daughter lays her head."'

He stared at me, his expression unchanged, and for some reason, I hesitated.

'What do you think it means?' he asked.

'I don't know. Daughter has to mean a Daughter of Hathor. A daughter lays her head . . . A bed. A bedroom. We search a bedroom?'

He rubbed his mustache thoughtfully. 'Unless it refers to the eternal sleep.'

I stared at him. 'A *dead* Daughter?'

'Just a possibility.'

'I have no idea where to go with that. Many Daughters would have passed away if from nothing else but old age. How could I possibly know which—' I stopped. 'Could it be Isla McIntosh? She was the only Daughter to famously die in Robbinsville.' My mind raced. 'Was she buried on the grounds?'

Deep frown lines creased Abner's forehead. 'No. Someone stole her body the night she was hanged. She never had a proper funeral.'

'How horrible.'

Abner looked uncomfortable.

And I realized something. He was very aware of the Isla McIntosh case. Did he know she'd been set up? 'I thought you told me you didn't know much about the case.'

He squinted his eyes, staring into the distance behind me.

What was he hiding?

'Abner, why were you so upset with Llew? What was he looking into that you didn't want revealed?'

He suddenly stood. 'This has nothing to do with the Madison letter. He's trying to publicize stories about the museum unrelated to American history. And he wants to drag my family members through the mud. Why are we talking about him?'

'Because it could be related. I think that Llew's research had everything to do with my search for the artifact. He was looking into witches, and those witches are Daughters of Hathor. So, I'd appreciate some transparency from you.'

'I don't know anything that could help you. Not about dead Daughters.'

'Have you known about the Daughters of Hathor all this time?'

He didn't answer, and I watched him leave the room in a hurry.

TWENTY-SEVEN

Something was up with Abner, and I had to figure out what it was.

I packed up my tote, locked my office door and headed down the stairs. The museum was mostly empty, so I began my nightly ritual of saying goodnight to the paintings on the wall as I passed them on my way to the front door.

I passed by the portrait of Elias' mother and father. 'Goodnight, Hannah and Martin.' I chuckled to myself, knowing how silly my little habit was. I passed a painting of a rakish young man leaning on a rifle. Elias' younger brother, Isaac, a handsome young man with dark hair, strong features and a pointed chin. Clearly, Abner had inherited the family features since he looked very similar to Isaac.

I passed by the empty space for Elias' painting. 'Goodnight, Elias.' Then there was Susannah. 'Goodnight, Susannah.' I moved on to . . . *Wait*. I stopped, took a step back returning to the painting of Elias' wife. Her dress. I *recognized* it. Or rather, I recognized the color. The fabric. It was a gorgeous dark gold. Sumptuous and shiny looking. Just like the square of silk I'd found in the illuminated book.

I reached for the fabric, kept wrapped up in a leather pouch in my purse's false bottom, and studied it. Compared it to the painting. Yes, this fabric was the same fabric Susannah wore. Then something else came to me. A brief line in a newspaper article. Zadie Jefferson received silks from Paris . . . Was making Susannah a dress. She'd probably made the beautiful purple silk gown Isla had worn as well.

Had Zadie knitted the sentence on the fabric? She'd been accused of being a witch, even though the accusation hadn't stuck, and I knew Toliver thought all witches were Daughters of Hathor. What was Zadie trying to tell me?

Where destiny lies, a daughter lays her head.

She must've been distraught, beside herself with worry and pain and anger. Accounts had the three women together. Possibly a fourth . . .

Zadie had just been accused herself. Had she thought she was close to being hanged, only to find it wasn't her but her friend, Isla?

Her *sister*. In that moment, in that time, what else could she mean when she embroidered that extract except where her sister, a Daughter rested, where her body remained. But which sister?

And how sad. My chest ached for her. What must she and the other women have felt?

I blinked, surprised to feel my eyes filling with water. I wiped at the tears and moved from the painting then stopped, thinking I'd heard something.

I closed my eyes and listened but could only hear the sounds of an old house settling down for the night.

I opened my eyes and Matty Toliver was standing before me.

TWENTY-EIGHT

I jumped.

I think I made a little squeaky noise too. 'Matty, what are you doing here?'

He chuckled, holding both his hands out. 'Hey, sorry. Didn't mean to startle you. You surprised me too standing here in the hall all by your lonesome.' He looked past me, then up at the painting of Susannah. 'Everything OK? It's pretty late.'

'Yes. I'm fine. Thank you.' I tightened my fist around the fabric then casually slid my hand into my pants pocket. For some reason, I was nervous, and I wasn't sure why.

'She was a beauty.' He pointed to the painting. 'Elias was so in love with her that some thought she enchanted him.'

I stared at the painting. 'Enchanted? Really?'

'Oh yes.' His laugh was light. 'She was from New Orleans, you probably know. Voodoo and all that sort of thing. Even girls from the best families with a convent education like she had, might be tempted to dabble in magic for fun.' His smile twisted. 'Though playing mistress to Satan can never end well.'

I side-eyed him then. Serious side-eye. It may have been me, but I thought his tone took on a nasty edge.

'That's why Abner doesn't like to bring her up. She's an embarrassment to the legacy of the museum.'

I looked at the beautiful painting. 'Really?'

'Oh yeah. Can you imagine how the thousands of visitors would feel if they knew they were visiting the home of a Satan worshipper?' He laughed.

But I frowned. *Satan worshipper?* Susannah Robbins?

Matty kept his gaze on the painting. 'Abner has tried very hard to suppress that knowledge and maintain the integrity of the museum. No easy feat when that writer was snooping around again, ripping open nasty old wounds.'

Llew.

'I have a lot of respect for Abner and his family. As you can probably imagine the Robbins and Tolivers have been long intertwined. We grew up learning stories about them.'

'We?'

His face cleared, and he turned to look at me. 'I have a sister.' He grinned. 'Very proud of her.'

'And you both learned about the witches of Robbinsville, like bedtime stories?'

One of his eyebrows rose. 'You know the stories too?' An odd expression filtered across his face. 'Of course you do.'

'Oh, no,' I countered, suddenly feeling like I'd said the wrong thing. 'I've only recently heard about them. Very interesting history. You think about witches in America and Salem, Massachusetts comes to mind, but I guess the prosecution of women was widespread.'

He chuckled. 'The prosecution of women? I think my ancestor saw it as the punishment of witches. There were many God-fearing women who raised families, loved their husbands and participated in the community. Women like Susannah were a blight on the community.'

Women like Susannah.

I'd thought Matthias was preaching to Isla and Zadie and the other women. That he'd set them up for theft because he couldn't punish them for their witchcraft. But his ancestor had preached a whole sermon just for Susannah when he saw her being less than humble with her pretty shiny new things from France.

I observed Matty's expression, noticed how his upper lip had moved into a snarl as he gazed at the painting. Almost if he hated her.

In that moment, I knew without a doubt that Susannah was the witch Matthias had wanted to punish. And since he was only after a certain type of witch, she must be a Daughter of Hathor too. He'd taken the mirror away from her, possibly to stop what he thought was narcissistic behavior. And then saw an opportunity to accuse her sisters, still finding a way to punish her and rid the community of a witch.

How mean and spiteful and petty and evil Matthias must've been. Poor Susannah. Like Zadie and the other women, she must've been horrified to watch her sister die and be unable to do anything about it.

I turned to look at Matty. His face was covered in sweat, and he had a sly look in his eyes. He reached under his shirt and pulled out a silver necklace heavy with a large silver cross on it. It looked old and worn, and was carved with symbols I didn't recognize.

He held it in his fingers and pressed it in the air towards me.

'You're one of them, aren't you?' His voice was low and husky. 'Those harlots of Hathor. Those witches.' He licked his lips. 'Those evil *bitches*.'

I swallowed, my throat suddenly dry. 'I don't know what you're talking about.'

'All that red hair.' He shook his head. 'I knew the moment I laid eyes on you, you were trouble.' He pushed the cross closer to me, muttering under his breath.

I caught a few words. He was praying, banishing demons. I took a step back. 'I have no idea what you're talking about.' And another step. 'I'm a Baptist. A Southern Baptist.'

'Your kind can't hide from me. You couldn't hide from my father. Or his father. Or his fathers before.' He lunged for me then, wrapping a hank of my hair around his fist and pulling me close. 'You think I didn't know what you were doing nosing around the church basement?'

I grabbed for his wrist, but he swung his arm out of my reach and my head with it. I flailed, my hands trying to connect with his face, his head, anything, but he only laughed as my fingers grazed him.

'You're looking for that stone, aren't you? So you can conjure up all kinds of evil.' He began dragging me down the hallway, his hand slipping from my hair to a chokehold around my neck.

He knew the Daughters protected the Stone? I clawed at his forearm, surprisingly thick and muscular. Then he must know the Stone was in Edinburgh Castle, in Scotland. 'Where are you taking me?'

'You need Jesus,' he snickered. We reached the back exit and he kicked it open. 'I'm taking you to church.'

I elbowed him then. Did a mule kick aiming for his knee. I screamed.

He laughed. 'I watched Daphne and Abner leave. No one's here.'

I did all the things I'd learned in self-defense class. And while he swayed out of the way of my jabs, and grunted when I made contact, nothing made him lose his hold on me. Until I remembered a move from a how-to-fight-dirty seminar my ex had taken me to as a weird but oddly enjoyable kind of date. Eye pokes and martinis later. Fun times.

I reared my head back and head-butted him, hoping I'd break his nose. I hit something, and I did it again. He moaned in pain and let go of me. I turned around and saw blood spurting from his nose as he grabbed his face, bent over at the torso.

'You bitch. I'm going to kill you.'

I pushed through the door and began running across the grounds. Past the gardens, the coffee shop, the tavern, trying to make it to the parking lot. Jesus, where was everybody? And it was so dark. Except for colonial-era street lighting that burned a low orange, only the full moon overhead illuminated the museum grounds.

I heard him running after me. I looked behind me and saw something in his hand. Something glinting in the moonlight.

A gun? My heart almost leaped out my throat. *No. It was a knife.*

I kept running, and then I saw a shadow to my right. I squinted my eyes. What was that? Who was that? 'Help,' I screamed to the shape as I ran closer to it. To him. It was a man. Thank God.

No.

No. No. I knew that face. *It was Blue.* The scar on the face. Tweedle Dee without the Dum. No hat this time. Just a smug expression and a high and tight.

I tried to double back but Matty was there. Bent over, panting. Pissed. His preacher's blouse white and billowing in the breeze and covered with blood from his nose. 'Get her,' he called out.

I turned back and Blue was there, his mouth a twisted dark shadow. A tight grip on my upper arm. And then there was a handkerchief in his hand, coming straight for my face. I smelled something sweet and fruity. I tried to scream.

And then blackness.

TWENTY-NINE

When I woke up, I was in the dark. A musty smell mixed with earthiness surrounded me.

And I was dizzy.

I blinked my eyes trying to get used to the darkness. I recognized the smell first. I was in the church basement. Cold ground seeped through my pants. Not a floor. Dirt.

A lower level then. A cellar maybe. Something below the basement. Or maybe a secret room?

I tried to scramble to my knees and discovered both my wrists and ankles were tied.

I rested my head against a wall, allowing gentle waves of nausea to pass over me. I wondered where my phone was . . .

There was a click, and a light came on.

I looked around and saw that yes, I was in a cellar with a dirt floor and brick walls. The light was just a bare bulb that threw shadows over three-quarters of the room that was about a thousand square feet.

Matty stepped forward holding an old-fashioned lantern. 'I've been keeping an eye on you, Sidney. Or rather my men have.'

I shook my head trying to clear the cobwebs. 'You have men?' I asked, wanting to laugh. But my head hurt too much to do much more than sound like I was teasing. 'For what purpose?'

'We're an order of men older than time itself. The first sons of first sons of first sons vowed to rid the earth of you harlots, vowed to guarantee the line of David doesn't continue . . .'

I looked up then. Abner's oddly detailed history lesson returning to me. 'Apophis?'

'You've heard of us?' Skepticism tinged his words. But then he grinned. Pulled up the sleeve of his puffy white sleeve and showed me a red and green tattoo of a dragon. 'There's a ring, but I can't wear it. Doesn't go with the preacher costume.'

'Why have you been following me? Why have you been trying to stop me?' No need to be discreet now. He was from the Order of Apophis – the Opposition – and he knew about the Daughters of Hathor. He knew about the Stone of Scone. What he didn't know about though was the artifact I was looking for.

'Because I know what you and your kind have been up to,' he hissed, taking a step closer. 'You need the stone so you can stop us from going through with our plan.'

'What are you talking about?'

He stepped even closer, and this time I could see the knife he held in his other hand. Long and thin, with a serrated edge, the hilt glistened with beautiful black crystals. 'It's beautiful, no? Tourmaline, jet and smoky quartz. Crystals that repel negative energies like yourself.'

I stared at him. 'You hunt witches because you hate them and the magic they practice, but somehow magical crystals are OK?'

He laughed. 'You think it's magic? It's science. Crystals are known to exhibit unique vibrational frequencies, which can interact with the energy fields around them. This interaction, is called quantum entanglement, and it forms the basis for the crystals' effects.' He twisted the hilt around so I could see the tourmaline.

For all the wrong reasons, I was reminded of the virtual reality headsets. Of a future I didn't care to see.

'But you *believe* in magic, though,' I asked, not understanding. 'You believe it's real but want to punish the women that practice it?'

His smile was barely noticeable. 'That's where the world went wrong, making the decision to stop believing in magic. What do you think the Age of Enlightenment was about?'

I squinted at him, as dizziness made his image shimmy in front of me.

'Secrets are often hidden in words. It's called spelling. For example, naming an island Iceland, so no other countries will travel to it and try to claim the land because they think it's covered in ice and inhospitable, while another island covered in ice is named Greenland to attract people to its shores.'

He took a step closer to me, bending down to get a good look at me in the lamplight. 'Philosophers and thinkers promoted reason, science, and empirical evidence over superstition and dogma. This emphasis on rationalism led to a questioning of traditional beliefs in magic and witchcraft. For the first time ever, humans wondered if maybe magic was a figment of their deluded ignorant minds.'

I gagged, then choked back bile. 'What did that guy do to me?'
I finally asked when I could speak.

'Chloroform,' he said in a tone like I was complaining about a
paper cut. 'You're fine.'

'You're a witch-hunter, right?'

His nod was curt.

'Then why are you so bothered by the Age of Enlightenment and
the . . .' I searched for the words through my foggy brain. 'Cultural
shift. You sound annoyed. Angry.'

'Because, you stupid witch, it made my people, my family's job
harder. Before, witch-hunters were considered heroes, welcomed
into communities as saviors. But when the so-called Scientific
Revolution happened, suddenly no one wanted or needed supernatural explanations for things their little minds couldn't
understand.'

I pushed back against the wall, trying to get further away from
him. His anger, his vitriol, his condescension for the average man
and woman verged on hatred. I had to remember, he wasn't really
a man of God. He worked for a technology company.

My head began to ache then, and I moaned against the pain.

'And then churches got into the act with Deism. They lectured
to their idiot flocks that God would never allow a world where
witches and magic existed. But our order was literally made to fight
magic. To rid the world of magic-doers. Do you know how difficult
that became when almost everyone stopped believing? It made us
look ridiculous.'

Even though the light from the lantern was changing colors and
dancing before my eyes, I understood the problem. I understood the
root of his anger. 'That's why your ancestor set up the women for
stealing. That's why Susannah couldn't be punished.'

He nodded. 'Exactly. Susannah, lovely spoiled bitch Susannah,
who lorded over the house like a queen, was untouchable.' He spat
the words out. 'It had to be theft. It was the only way Matthias could
get one of them to hang. But that was just the beginning. Our legal
systems began to adopt more rational and evidence-based approaches
to justice. Laws started protecting witches instead of killing them.'
His eyes hardened. 'You bitches have run amok ever since.'

I could do nothing but stare at him. He was clearly . . . not OK.
I needed a plan. A way to get out of this cellar. I also needed the
effects of this chloroform to wear off so I had my wits about me.

I felt helpless with my hands and ankles tied. Afraid because Matty was obviously not thinking clearly and had a horribly ancient vendetta against witches . . . and red hair.

'This world is going to hell in a handbasket because of your kind. But that will soon all change.' His grin returned. 'The work for our order will not be in vain. See this blade? It's infused with the quantum vibrations of smoky quartz. It has the ability to anchor your energy, limiting your ability to practice your craft.'

'Not my craft,' I fumed, some of my fear churning into anger as my head finally began to clear. I slowly twisted at the ties on my wrists hidden from view behind my back.

'And this jet, with its gorgeous black color, is thought to absorb and transmute negative energies.' He gazed at the crystal for a moment, admiring its shape and luster. 'From a quantum physics perspective, jet's atomic structure resonates in a way that can neutralize harmful vibrations. Dark energy. Black magic,' he clarified, as if I was a student not paying attention. I looked away from him then, tired of his ranting, tired of his stupid red shiny face.

'Look at me, witch.' He pointed the knife at me like a teacher with a pointer stick.

I looked at him.

He shook his head. 'So willful. Don't give me that evil eye.' He laughed. 'I know you're afraid. Your magic doesn't work, does it?'

'It doesn't work because I don't practice witchcraft. I have no so-called magical abilities. Are you listening to anything I'm saying?'

'You're evil. You expect me to believe anything that comes out of your mouth?'

I glared at him. 'I'm evil? I'm the one tied up and being held captive in a dark, dank cellar. And you wonder why you aren't viewed as the good guy?' I laughed, my head clearing and the heaviness leaving my limbs. His ramblings, his odd rant on the quantum properties of crystals, broke through the cobwebs of my brain. I stared at him in the dim light. 'You seem to know a lot about the quantum properties of crystals for a witch-hunting museum re-enactor.'

He laughed again.

I scowled at him.

'My work here at the museum is part-time. I'm here as a representative of the Order of Apophis, to make sure you witches don't appear in town or at the museum. We haven't been able to create an act of deterrence since Isla McIntosh but that's all about to change with you.'

Anger, fear and nerves swirled in the pit of my stomach, and I tried to ignore the blatant threat on my life. I needed answers. So when I made it out of here I could explain his madness . . . If I got out of here. If . . . I shook my head, trying to push away the doubts. 'But why? Why does your order care so much about this town? This museum?'

He squinted at me, cocked his head and studied me. 'My father taught me about you witches starting when I was ten years old. Me and my sister, actually. I know in order for you girls to recapture your powers you need to touch the stone. To be near it. To draw from its power.'

I shook my head, negating every single ridiculous thing he was saying.

'Do your rituals. Dance your dance. Sing your chants. Like Isla, Zadie, Bathsheba, and Susannah did that night by the water.'

I closed my eyes, sighing. 'I'm not a witch. I don't know anything about witches. And you have no idea who or what Susannah was.'

His laugh was sharp. 'Are you kidding me? She was their leader.'

Even as my heart raced, i tried to keep my face expressionless, even in the dim light. If Susannah was a Daughter and their leader . . . the artifact was probably buried where *she* was laid to rest, not Isla.

Where had she been buried? I wasn't sure. But there was the Susannah Garden, her living memorial, filled with flowers from where she was born. The same garden where my grandmother had been found abandoned by her mother.

Was it really that simple? I just needed to go to the garden and start digging and I'd find the artifact?

I was still working on my wrist ties, even though I was beginning to rub the skin raw, when something occurred to me. Something weird and far-fetched and couldn't possibly be true. Something that made my stomach flip-flop and quiver.

Earlier, the way he spoke about magic, the science foundation of it . . . his language reminded me of the patent I'd found for QLabs. Now I wondered if that device wasn't somehow related to . . . all of this.

I looked at Matty. 'I know you work at QLabs. What do you do there?'

He held the lantern up so close to his face, that I could see the light dance off the blue of his eyes. 'I'm a quantum physicist.' He couldn't stop the smile that spread across his face. 'Like my sister? I believe you've met. Marta. Marta De Verona.'

THIRTY

'**M**arta is your sister?'
'My twin sister actually.'
I stared at him trying to see the resemblance. There was none. Where she was tall and lithe, he was short and stocky. Her face was narrow and angular, his wide and child-like.

'I know. We don't look alike, but we are alike in the most important ways. She and I both hate witches. And the best way forward is to rid our world of the whole lot of you.'

Nausea washed over me anew and I almost threw up. Marta was a member of the Order of Apophis? The Global Virtualization Conference was a front for witch-hunters? Which meant so was QLabs? But no, it couldn't be possible.

Then something he'd said . . . *This world is going to hell in a handbasket because of your kind. But that will soon all change.*

I looked at him, a feeling of panic fluttering in my chest. 'The Virtual Revolution, the Order of Apophis is behind that?' Abner was right.

'We all have our parts to play. Me here in Robbinsville and my sister in DC with the president and the reporters . . .'

'Your sister funded QLabs. Brought them to town. And you're building a device? The QTS-2020?'

He cocked his head, looking impressed. 'You've been busy.'

'What I don't understand, is why Robbinsville. Why are you here? Why does Marta care about this town?'

'You really don't get it.' He chuckled. 'You should talk to Isla, ask her why.'

He began to move away, the light with him.

Talk to a woman who's been dead for hundreds of years? 'What are you talking about?'

'Ask her why tens of thousands of Scots came to North Carolina in the eighteenth and nineteenth century. Anson, Cumberland,

Scotland, Montgomery, just a handful of the numerous counties
named for Scots. Edinburg, Aberdeen, Caledonia? Just a few of the
cities with Scottish roots.'

He read the confusion correctly on my face.

'You're ranting, you realize?'

But he only laughed. 'Can't you talk to the dead? Or maybe raise
the dead?' He stopped, lifting his lantern and pointed to a slice of
wall in the corner. 'She's over there. Just hanging around.' He moved
to the corner and shone his light on the wall. A skeleton hung there,
a stake running through its ribs into a wood plank on the wall.

I screamed.

He laughed. 'Talk to your Sister, see if she'll explain things to
you.'

I recalled reading the article stating her body had been taken, no
one knew where. It had been here all along.

Matty moved away from the wall, and I watched the light bounce
up the stairs as he ascended the stairs. A door opened and closed. A
lock was bolted. And then I was alone. In the dark. With a skeleton.

I took deep breaths. Tried not to think of the skeleton in the room
with me.

Deep breaths. De-e-e-p breaths.

OK, so if Isla was in here, and Bathsheba and Zadie had been
banished out of town, then Susannah was definitely the Daughter
at rest. The square of yellow fabric all but confirmed that. Thank
you Zadie for that.

The tie on my wrist finally popped loose, and I brought my hands
forward, rubbing the bruised skin. Matty may have been a quantum
physicist, but he sucked at tying knots, I thought with a laugh, then
burst into tears.

Stupid tears. No time for crying. But I was scared. I willed myself
to stop crying. No. I wasn't scared. I was angry. I had so much to
do and this stupid knot on my ankles – I jerked at it, but it wouldn't
budge. I swallowed a sob and tried to focus. Matty and Marta were
family. They were both in the Order of Apophis. Them both working
to virtualize the world – as it turned out – was a diabolical plan to
subjugate the population. Abner hadn't been the delusional one.
That was me, for not seeing the red flags in the news and in the
laws being made.

Both Professor Philippi and Marta, oddly enough, were right. My
mother too. I'd had my head in the sand.

I tugged at the knots on my ankles again.

The artifact had to be buried with Susannah.

I had to get out of here.

I tugged again, all the anger focused on that yank.

It released.

I exhaled slowly. Rose from my seated position and tried my legs. Wobbly at first, better once the blood began to flow. I moved around the room remembering the layout. It was empty, so nothing to trip me up.

I paused. Isla's skeleton still hung on the wall. Macabre. Sad. She'd have to have a proper burial. I closed my eyes. 'Isla,' I whispered into the dark, 'I'll be back for you. We'll give you a proper burial. Promise.'

I may have imagined it, but I thought I felt a whisper of a soft breeze whip around the room, the scent of something sweet and gentle blended with bright grass, almost like a field of daisies.

I knew what I needed to do but I didn't know *how* to do it. First things first, I needed to get out of the room. I went up the long, narrow flight of stairs, and gently worked the doorknob in case anyone was standing guard outside. It was locked, as I knew it would be.

I studied the movements of the shadows underneath the door. They never moved, indicating as I hoped that the coast was clear, so I tried the door again. All futile, I know, but I had to try something.

I also needed a weapon. What if Matty or Blue came back? I went back down the stairs trying to find a rock, a loose brick, anything to defend myself against.

There was nothing.

I heard someone whistling, and I rushed back to my sitting position, head against the wall, hands behind my back and ankles tucked underneath me.

The door opened and an obtuse triangle of yellow light spilled into the room. It was Blue. He stood in the light, his shadow looming large at the head of the stairs. He didn't say anything. Just stood there.

Sweat appeared on my forehead, and I swallowed. Loudly. Sure he could hear me even from a distance. I pressed myself against the wall and closed my eyes. A minute later the door closed and he was gone.

THIRTY-ONE

I must've passed out because I came to with the sense that time had passed but not sure how much. There were no windows, so I couldn't see outside, but my eyes had adjusted to the darkness. Not that there was anything to see besides a skeleton.

Surely, my grandmother would call the police? I hadn't come home. I hadn't called and wasn't answering my phone. Abner, Bess . . . someone would wonder where I was and start looking.

The door opened, and my body jerked at the sound. Matty appeared with his lantern. I could see that he'd cleaned himself up and changed into a fresh preacher's costume.

'How long have I been here?' I called out to him as he descended the stairs.

'Long enough for me to make some plans.' He stood in front of me, the lantern swinging in his hand. 'Thanks to you and your efforts, we've been able to identify other witches in the area. Your grandmother. The Montgomerys. Bess is a descendant of Bathsheba herself and I never knew it. Here we were looking for a black woman.' He chuckled. 'So here's what's going to happen. My two helpers – who, by the way hate witches almost as much as I do – are going to round up your coven-mates, and we're going to have a little bonfire.' He paused. 'But not the kind with marshmallows.'

My mind raced as he got his jollies threatening people I cared about. What could I do? How could I overpower him?

'Are you listening to me, Sidney? I'm going to put an end to the line of Robbinsville witches for good. I'm going to do what my forefathers weren't able to do because the Robbins men have always had an affection for witches. It would seem Abner cares for you.'

'Abner is my boss. That's it.'

'But you think he doesn't know who you are? What you are?'

That got me to thinking. Abner invited me here knowing my history. Said he decided to contact me because he wanted someone with a connection to the artifact to find it. What did that mean?

'Still pretending like you don't know?' he asked.

'Does Abner have any idea what you're up to?'

'That guy?' He snorted. 'Clueless. But you'll be interested to know I called my sister. Thankfully DC is only a very short flight. She'll be here soon to see that it's over.'

While he talked, I planned. He was all alone now. Just me and him. I thought of my self-defense classes. What could I do? He had about three inches of height on me and at least fifty pounds. And he was extraordinarily strong. Was that normal male strength or witch-hunter strength?

'Do witch-hunters have powers?' I asked him.

'What?' He stared at me, a frown spreading across his face.

'Earlier you said you believed in magic, that you knew it still existed. If your job is to hunt down witches, do you have any special powers?'

His frown twitched into a weird grin. 'You've been thinking, I see.'

I just wanted to know if I could take him. I didn't believe in magic. I had no proof it existed, but if he and his family had spent thousands of years hunting witches, maybe magic was real. And maybe he had some sort of superpower. Whatever it was I needed to know before I decided to poke him in his eyes or punch him in the throat . . . My dirty fighting moves were limited. I was really wishing I'd taken a refresher course right about now.

'You don't believe magic exists?'

I shook my head.

'That it resides in our ethereal plane?' He shook his head. 'You want me to believe you grew up without knowing your history?' He regarded me in the dim light. 'Even if that was true, it doesn't change what you are. Why you're here or what you could begin if left to your own devices.' He kneeled on one knee. 'Magic is real, Sidney.' He chuckled. 'The Order of Apophis are sorcerers. Historically speaking.'

'You're a sorcerer?' I was pretty sure my voice dripped with both skepticism and sarcasm.

'You doubt me?' He laughed. 'I didn't say I disliked magic. I said I hate witches. And a particular kind of witch at that. The kind that think their bloodline should be in power. The kind that think they have a monopoly on practicing magic. The kind that think they should police practitioners of magic. It's the age-old story of good versus bad, isn't it? Only your kind thinks you're good. While we *know* we're the good ones and our world will be better off without you.'

'How does your sister factor into all of this?'

'We are a large, diverse group. Our order has its goal, but there are others with different objectives. Some manipulate politics, others society. Some media . . . We're rational. Organized. Monetized. While you and your kind? You're a bunch of small groups scattered around, hiding, cowering . . . that's why we've been able to accomplish so much in just a couple hundred years. While you witches are busy hiding from us, we're creating policies at the federal level. And getting rich while we manipulate and herd the masses.'

'And Marta?'

'Has plans to control the entire population.' He shook his head. 'I know, I sound terribly villainous and pretentious when I say that . . . but it's true. And the masses will allow it because they'll see their subjugation as fun and convenient.'

And there it was again, that complete disregard for mankind. A condescension, a disgust for humanity.

'They'll plug in, and they'll stay there. From morning to night. Eventually even sleeping in VR with diapers on. We'll manipulate them by day and in their dreams. And all those in-VR purchases they'll be making? Think spontaneous purchases on autopilot. Amazon is already priming – pun intended – humans to purchase on a rhythm in alignment with virtual living. There's so much money to be made.'

'You talk about humans like you're not one.'

'I guess we do consider ourselves better.' He stood. 'Superior.'

'You're power mad, not magic.'

'Don't you get it? Sorcerers manipulate the source code. We understand how the world works . . . at a quantum level and use it to our advantage. We make money with the financial systems because we can manipulate the algorithms, we control the masses with media because we've mastered the concepts of illusion and manifestation. We cast spells with our lies and deceit. Words have power beyond what most people can conceive. We spell it, and you people believe it.' He laughed. 'We create and change historical narratives at will, and in real time like changing shoes.

'We're not pulling rabbits out of hats, we're telling humans the sky is green and making them believe it.' He laughed. 'Because that's what we do, and that's how awesome we are. That's our magic. World-building. Socio-engineering. Chaos creation.'

And now I fully understood why Abner was frantic to stop these maniacs. Only, I still couldn't comprehend how an artifact could stop it. Or why I was involved, even if I was of the bloodline . . .

Then it came to me. 'The Daughters of Hathor protect the Stone of Scone. The Stone isn't magic, it's . . . capable of quantum manipulations?'

He nodded. 'Now you're getting it, witch.' He crossed his arms, thinking. 'I suppose I can tell you . . . We have a working theory called the Unified Energy Matrix Theory in which we postulate that the Stone accesses a field of energy that connects it to past leaders and influences Earth's natural energy patterns, and electromagnetic phenomena. This energy matrix holds the collective knowledge, experiences, and energies of everyone who's ever wielded the artifact.'

I wasn't stupid but I wasn't a quantum physicist either. I tried to understand the concept. 'So, there's like a Wi-Fi field that contains the psychic energy of past leaders crowned on the Stone, because energy never dies it just transmutes to another form . . .' Thank you fifth-grade science teacher. 'And the Stone works like a router?'

'That's very good and quite accurate. The Stone of Scone is composed of a unique crystalline structure that exhibits quantum entanglement on a macroscopic scale. This entanglement connects the artifact to an ethereal energy matrix, allowing it to access the thoughts, intentions, and energies of past leaders who held the artifact.'

'I did some research on the Stone and its red sandstone. That mineral is capable of doing all that?'

He chuckled. 'The real Stone of Scone is not red, and it's not made of sandstone.'

The real? 'But the Stone that King Charles was crowned on . . .' I stopped. 'Are you saying the Stone of Scone in Scotland, the one King Edward the First stole, the one that sat in Westminster Abbey for hundreds of years is not the real thing?'

'That's exactly what I'm saying.'

THIRTY-TWO

'How do you know this?' I asked, stalling for time.

His sneer deepened. 'My ancestors placed spies among the witches when we realized their leadership stopped telling them the location of the Stone.' An amused expression warped his features. 'You think my ancestors didn't know the Stone was being moved around?'

'I actually have no idea since, one: I wasn't there, and two: still not a witch.'

'We knew, even if the royal class didn't.'

'If your ancestors knew the witches didn't know the location, why did the hunts continue?'

He laughed. 'Didn't really need a reason to get rid of your kind.'

Your kind. That's what the texter meant. Witches, not . . . I shook my head. And then it all made sense.

The Daughters of Hathor moving to North Carolina. The droves of Scottish immigrants following suit. Abner asking me to find an artifact associated with the Daughters. And they have only ever been associated with one. The Stone of Scone.

It was here.

What was the other name for the Stone of Scone? The Stone of Destiny?

Where Destiny lies, a daughter lays her head.

Zadie had sewn the location of the real, true Stone of Scone on to a scrap of Susannah's dress. It had to be buried in the Susannah Garden. It was here on the grounds of the museum all this time.

And that's why Marta was singling out Abner. That's why Matty worked here. They knew it was here in Robbinsville somewhere, they just didn't know where exactly.

But I did.

I stared at Matty. He knew I knew where it was. I almost laughed. *Oh shit.* And *that's* why I was here.

He nodded. 'Yeah, that's right.' His grin turned into a leer. 'Before I burn you and your coven alive, you're going to tell me where I can find that Stone of Scone.'

My throat was dry, my heart pounded against my chest and my head swam but I tried to calm myself. Tried to focus. Literally, the fate of the world rested on my shoulders. If I could get past him and out of this godforsaken dungeon.

But first, I had to find out what his plans for the Stone were.

'Let's say I take you to the Stone. What are you going to do with it?'

'Up until now, we've ruled the world with our wits, intelligence and . . . sorcery. The Stone would take us to the next level. A level of divinity. Back to ruling the earth like the gods we are.'

I didn't want to encourage him, but I wanted to understand their plans in case – no, when I definitely escaped from here. 'The Stone can't possibly be capable of all that?'

'You have no idea what that Stone is capable of. When we connect it to our Virtual Reality Network, we'll be able to control the whole world's minds in a way we couldn't do with technology alone. We will literally run the world like the gods we are.

'There was a time when serpent-worshipping cultures covered the Earth. The Sumerians, the Hopi tribe, the Mayans, just to name a few. We'll bring that back. Everyone will worship us.' He pulled his shirtsleeve up and bared the tattoo of a red snake on his arms, like a badge of honor. 'We are the serpent gods of the past.'

'I think you've watched too many cartoons. All you need is a curling black mustache and a cape, Matty.' I forced myself to laugh, because honestly? I was scared. If Matty with his high intellect mixed with condescension and scorn for the average person was an example of the people behind this VR agenda, we were all screwed.

His phone chimed with a notification, and he retrieved it from a pocket and looked at the screen. The blue light shone on his face, and I could see him smile. 'My sister has arrived.'

A few minutes later, the door opened, and Marta stood under a pool of light, one of Matty's henchmen behind her. She wore a gray pantsuit, white Converse sneakers and a red DC Capital's baseball cap over her hair.

'Matty,' she called out in greeting. 'It's been too long.' Blue handed her a lantern and she descended the stairs, while Matty waited for her at the base. She wrapped her arms around him in a tight hug. 'Been holding down the fort?'

'You know it, sis.'

She peered into the darkness. 'And our special guest?'

He held up his lantern, a beam of yellow light scattering the darkness. 'Over there by the wall.'

I tensed as they both approached me.

Marta kneeled to my level, holding the lantern to my face. 'I wish you'd taken me up on my job offer. At least that way I could've kept an eye on you, and you wouldn't have had to die.'

I noticed a delicate gold chain with a small snake pendant around her neck. As she stood, she turned to her brother and asked, 'Did she tell you where the Stone is?'

'She claims not to know anything about it or her history.'

Marta turned to look at me, eyebrows lifted. 'Really?' She drew the words out. 'How is that possible? The history is passed down by the women. Surely your mother—'

'Told me nothing. And she's just a news anchor herself.'

Marta laughed. 'She's one of the top news anchors on the planet. No one gets to that level without a dash of ye old magic. I know who your mother is. Fredericka Taylor. Her beauty. Her communication skills. The way she shines on the camera. Even the way the viewers see her . . . you may think it's talent or skill or charisma or simple beauty. It's a type of magic – one of many.' She paused, thoughtful for a moment. 'Some people have it and some don't.' Then she shrugged. 'It's true some people aren't aware of their abilities, but trust me, they know how to use them regardless of what they know. And your mother? Oh, she knows how to work it.'

'*If* I had some magic power, I'd make you both disappear right now.'

Brother and sister looked at each other and laughed.

'Why are you here? What do you plan on doing with me?'

She looked at her brother. 'You didn't tell her?'

'I told her.'

Marta turned to me. 'He kills witches. It's literally his purpose in life. I mean, it's inherent in the job title, right?'

Matty nodded. 'Witch. Hunter.' He pronounced each word carefully in case I wasn't aware.

'He's been trained for it, and it's been a while, so I know he's very excited.'

He nodded. 'Particularly because I'll be able to say that I've rooted out and destroyed this elusive coven forever.'

'It's been what? Over a hundred years?' Marta asked.

'Yeah.' He nodded, turning to me. 'We have a list of covens to destroy and the Robbinsville one has remained in limbo for over a century because we could never find the descendants of the Robbinsville witches.'

'And that's important. Following the family tree and making sure we stamp out every single branch,' Marta added helpfully.

'Bathsheba was an enslaved woman of color, and her descendants were especially hard to track down with the census-takers classifying them as white, colored, mulatto and Indian as they saw fit. Sometimes we'd lose a witch simply because her race changed on paper. When entire tribes of indigenous people were reclassified as colored or black, we literally lost whole covens. We may never find them.' Matty winked. 'Unless we get lucky.'

And that's why they'd lost track of Bathsheba. While her descendants had passed for white, they were looking for descendants classified as African-American.

'We knew Isla had a child, but it died during the cholera outbreak,' Matty said.

'And Zadie Jefferson has been lost to history as well.'

Zadie. Reba played her character. But was she an actual descendant of Zadie or just an interpreter? She was a Daughter. But her last name was Jeffries. Was Zadie's last name written down incorrectly, as they often were back then, thereby hiding her descendants in plain sight? If so, good for her.

'And Susannah and Elias had no children.'

I didn't want to put a target on Abner's back, but I was confused. 'I thought Abner was a direct descendant of Susannah and Elias?'

They both turned to look at me as if I wasn't particularly bright. 'Abner is related to a brother of Elias. The magic descends from Susannah's side of the family. She died in a shipwreck that apparently even her magic couldn't prevent. But Elias was no one to us. Just a wealthy landowner,' Matty said.

I glared at him, trying to figure out how a witch-hunter became a quantum scientist. 'If witch-hunting keeps you so busy, when do you have time for your mad experiments at QLabs?'

He looked at me, with no hint of a smile. 'What I'm doing at QLabs is none of your damn business.'

'Language,' Marta said with a frown. 'It's a top-secret project that we're working on – the kind that if you know about it, we have to kill you?' She chuckled. 'DARPA is funding the research.'

Llew. Had he stumbled upon their work? 'What kind of research?'

'See,' she began with a cock of her head, 'that's exactly the type of question that got that writer killed.'

My mouth dropped open. I was right.

'Curiosity killed the cat,' Matty chimed in.

Marta threw her hands up. 'Poking around the town's history somehow led to us and our work. He had to go.'

'What could you possibly be working on that you had to take Llew's life?' I asked, angry, sad and only partially relieved his death was not because of me.

'Robbinsville is home to some naturally occurring temporal fluc-tuations that we're studying. And we've . . .' She regarded me for a moment, and Matty shook his head. 'And that's all you get to know. But you –' she crossed her arms – 'have been a bit of an enigma for us. You weren't on our radar until you arrived in town, and then –' her nose wrinkled – 'you were all we could see.'

I tried not to squirm under her intense gaze.

'I don't know how you're related to these Hathor witches. We know you have descent through your mother's family by way of covens based in the Virginia mountains. But your father's mother was adopted, and we can't find any records on who her biological mother could have been.'

Only the fairies know, I thought with a smirk.

'When I overheard you talking to Daphne about the letter, I became suspicious.' Matty glared at me. 'And when you came into the church asking questions, I began to wonder if you were a Hathor witch. And then I caught you worshipping the moon. At the Riverwalk.'

Was he referencing the night Gabe and I shared ice cream by the river? I scoffed. 'I wasn't *worshipping* the moon, you lunatic.'

'Enough.' Marta stared at me, her expression hard before turning to her brother. 'Is everything in place for our party?'

'Oh yeah, all of the guests have been invited.' He lifted his chin, like a child proud of an accomplishment. 'The cake is ready. All we need is the guest of honor and we can blow out the candles.'

I looked from one to the other. Did they think I didn't know they were talking in code? I rolled my eyes.

'Excellent.' Her teeth gleamed in the lantern light. 'Our big day will be here before we know it, Matty. Everything we've worked for . . .' She wrapped an arm around him and pressed her cheek to his, then tapped her watch. 'I have meetings with the VR office in China. They'll want to know Paul's party is happening soon. You got this?'

'Yeah. Take your meeting. She'll be dead by the time it's through.'

'Good. Then we can get on with finding the Stone and imple-menting our plan to get the world online.' She fixed me with an interested look. 'I'd say take care, but you know . . . you're dying soon. So . . .'

She gave her brother another hug. 'Lunch tomorrow?'

He nodded and watched her go, with Blue opening and closing the door behind her.

When she was gone, Matty turned back to me. 'You sure you don't know where the Stone is? It would save us a lot of time and trouble.'

I laughed. 'You think I'm helping you?'

He shrugged. 'It's your funeral. Literally.' His phone chimed with a notification, and he read the screen. 'My man is about to detain your friend Bess and her grandmother as we speak.'

'By man you mean your henchman? Since you're a cartoon villain you need a henchman.'

His smile twisted into a scowl. 'I've had enough of your mouth, witch. Let's go.'

It was dark, and I was hoping he couldn't see that my limbs were free. I pretended like I was still bound with my hands behind me, and shuffled like my ankles were tied.

'Where are we going?'

He ignored me, and we moved slowly while I formulated a plan.

He stepped behind me, pushing me in the back to move faster. I stiffened at his touch. When I was halfway up the stairs, I mule-kicked backward aiming for his right knee.

I made contact and he grunted, crashing to both knees. The lantern fell down the stairs rolling with a clang back to the floor. I began running, but he reached for my ankle. I yanked my leg away from him, but his grip was tight and he jerked me backwards. I almost fell but grabbed onto a bannister and pulled myself back up.

I kicked again. And again. And again. His face. His jaw. His head.

I don't know what I was kicking but I was hitting something. He was making all sorts of sounds, so I know he was hurt.

He rolled backwards down the stairs heavily, like a boulder crashing into the wall that ran the length of the stairs, splintering part of the railing. Panting, I watched him land near the lantern which had cracked open, small flames spilling out with the oil.

I watched in horror as the oil flowed towards him, the orange licking at his hair, then bursting into larger flames. My hand went to my mouth, and I took a step backwards. One. Two . . . and then I began to run. Screaming up the flight upstairs to the basement of the church and finally up to the main floor.

When I reached the windows, I could see the morning was just dawning, the sky streaked with orange and purple light. I'd guess it was about five or five thirty in the morning. The grounds were still empty, the village quiet.

I had to get help. The fire department. The police. My nerves were tight springs, but my mind was clear. As I ran to the main house, I saw Blue run into the burning building.

I kept running, made it to the back door and swiped the back door keypad with my key card. I ran up to the front desk where I knew there was a landline and called 911.

THIRTY-THREE

I sat on a bench across from the wrought-iron, gated entrance to the Susannah Garden.

Even though it was a warm morning, an EMT had still placed a weighted blanket around my shoulders to reduce the chances I'd go into shock. The grounds were filled with emergency crews. Even a news reporter team from New Bern was flitting around trying to get the story.

I stared into the distance, watching black smoke float above the historic church. The cellar was completely destroyed. Would they still be able to find Isla's skeleton? Or had I just imagined that? The whole experience was beginning to feel like a nightmare, and I wondered if I'd actually gone through it.

The basement full of priceless artifacts had sustained serious water damage. The first floor of the church had smoke damage and some destruction from having firemen running through it with heavy equipment.

And me? I'd been abducted by a psychopath who thought he was a witch-hunting sorcerer. He'd threaten to burn me alive after I led him to a magical stone. When Abner had arrived and instructed me not to tell anyone anything, it seemed like sensible advice.

I'd been checked out, and physically I was fine. But I only felt better when I was able to find my phone in my office and check on my grandmother, who was perfectly fine, and on Bess and her grandmother . . . who'd staved off a burglar at the back door with a warning shot through an open kitchen window.

Thank goodness for grannies with shotguns.

That newspaper reporter and her cameraman were marching towards me. Again. A pretty woman with fluffy black curls and

glossy red lips, she waved at me with long French-manicured nails.
'Please, Miss Taylor, just a word. I understand you were the one
that made the frantic nine one one call? I'm Amy Sanchez. From
New Bern Twenty-four Seven?'

The cameraman hoisted his equipment onto his shoulder and a
blinking red light appeared on the camera.

I glanced around for Abner but couldn't find him. I'd much prefer
they speak to him as the official representative of the museum.
Sighing, I turned to her. 'Not much to say. I was working late, saw
smoke as I was about to leave and called nine one one.'

She turned to look as a stretcher with a covered body rolled past
her.

'Matthias Toliver, a historical interpreter.' She looked into the camera
with widely stretched, maple syrup brown eyes. 'You knew him?'

'Not really. I'm new to the museum and met him only a few
times.'

Just then another body was pushed past us. That must be Blue.
And then a third. Uh oh, that had to be Isla's skeleton.

Amy turned to me, slight frown lines appearing on her forehead.
'Who else was down there?'

I shrugged.

'It's a mystery then, folks.' She faced the camera. 'One I personally vow to get to the bottom of.' She gestured for her cameraman
to stop taping. 'Thanks, Sidney.' She handed me her card. 'If you
want to do an interview, please call me. I'm a big fan of your
mother's work. She's my she-ro.'

I acknowledged her compliment with a curt smile. 'Has Marta
De Verona made a comment?'

'Funny you should ask. She just happened to be in town checking
on QLabs for the DRIA.'

I nodded.

'She posted a statement on her Instagram account saying that she
was saddened by what happened, shared that the historical interpreter
was her brother.' She stopped to pull an affected surprised face.
'Who knew? And that she'd discuss the situation more at a future
press conference. You know I'll be there.'

'Thanks, Amy.'

The journalist then ran-walked in heels in the grass after the
EMTs. No easy feat.

I turned to look at the gardens. I needed to check them out. But not with fifty people on the grounds milling around to witness me digging up a grave for a magical stone. That would have to wait. I also had to figure out what to do with Marta. But for now, I was going home to take a shower and get some sleep.

THIRTY-FOUR

I slept the entire day.

Fitfully at first, until my grandmother came into the room with a calming herbal tea. Then I slept like a baby. When I woke, it was dinner time. I shuffled into the living room in a fuzzy pink robe, my hair in a messy top knot and white knee-high slouchy socks covered in pink hearts.

I'd put the yellow square in my robe pocket to show my grandmother. But we had company.

Abner sat at the dinner table, with Bess, her grandmother and Reba. I noticed he no longer had a white streak in his beard. I blinked, still feeling out of sorts. 'The white in your beard is gone again.'

He froze, then touched his beard. 'Ah. Yes, that.' He chuckled. 'Just needed a little touch-up.'

My grandmother's face wrinkled in concern. 'Sidney?'

I looked down at my robe and hesitated.

'Come on in. You're among family here. No one begrudges you a comfortable robe, not after the day you've had.'

I smiled weakly at everyone who watched me with apprehension. Then Bess rushed to me, wrapping me in a tight hug. 'You're OK?'

I nodded.

'Who knew Matty was a psychopath? A little socially awkward maybe. But a witch-hunter?' She shook her heard. 'I'm so sorry.'

My grandmother handed me a mug of coffee. 'Here you go, hon.'

I fell into a chair, everyone's eyes on me.

Grams pointed to Reba. 'Zadie's descendant.'

'We've met. And I figured.' We were all Daughters of Hathor. All descended from the Robbinsville witches. I'd read so much about them, I felt as if I knew them.

'And of course, you know about the Montgomerys,' my grandmother continued.

I nodded. 'And I know why Abner is here. Susannah.'

He sighed, bowing his head.

'Why keep it a secret?'

He shook his head. 'We're not a Halloween attraction.'

'And your family's history with the mines?' I raised an eyebrow. 'Another subject you don't want to discuss.'

His brows dipped down, and he scowled at me. 'Where did you hear about that?'

Bess waved a hand. 'I told her. I also told her you didn't want to explore a family tragedy for profit.'

'Right,' I added. 'But you've got this habit of . . . I don't know . . . keeping secrets?' I shrugged. 'Not trying to start anything. I just wondered.'

'It's OK, Abner.' Her smile was reassuring. 'Susannah's reputation remains intact.'

'Is she a Daughter of Hathor?' I asked.

He nodded, seemingly mollified by the return to safer subjects. 'Elias was a member of the Sons of Horus, and he went all the way to New Orleans to find him a wife of the blood. That was Susannah.'

Matty hadn't known about Elias' own magical heritage. 'So you're . . .'

'A member of the brotherhood. The Sons of Horus. Sorry I kept it from you, but I planned to share with you when the time was right.'

'You learn anything?' Thea asked me, mouth a grim line.

I held up a finger still trying to process everything. 'Let me just . . .' I wrapped my arms around the coffee and drank several sips, allowing the warmth to envelop me, the caffeine to perk me up.

After a moment, I looked around the table. And then I told them everything.

When I was done, it was so quiet you could've heard the proverbial pin drop in the room.

'The artifact is the real Stone of Scone.' Abner dragged a palm across his face. 'All this time, and the answer was staring me right in my face. May I see the yellow square of fabric?'

I removed it from my robe pocket and handed it to Abner.

He studied it for a moment. Held it up to the light, a look of surprise on his face. Then handed it back to me with raised eyebrows.

'What they want to do,' Reba began, 'with the virtual reality?

It's evil. Pure evil. And the president is on board with this? I voted for him.'

Thea rolled her eyes. 'Me too. He was supposed to be the people's president.'

My grandmother looked at me, eyes flinty. 'You know what we have to do.'

Everyone nodded.

I stood. 'But first . . .' I smiled for the first time. 'I need to get out of this robe.'

Thirty minutes later, we'd carpooled to the museum in two cars. I kept checking the rearview mirrors for Red, since Blue died in the fire, but I never saw anyone.

Once we were on the grounds, Abner led the way, providing shovels from the garden shed.

'Together, we should get this done in no time,' Reba observed, her grip tight around the handle of her shovel.

It was after six, so the museum was closed with no one left on the grounds. We followed Abner to the garden, stepped over the brick border and followed a cobblestone path that wound through the tall purple blooms. Placards highlighted the different flowers and explained their significance to Susannah.

It was so beautiful there, and any other day I would've taken in the way the setting sun streamed light onto the water. Or how vibrant the orange, pink and purple flower petals were against the perfectly laid lush grass.

But not today. The darkness of the cellar, the evil glint in Matty's eyes . . . it stayed with me, hovered just out of reach where I couldn't push it away. But I couldn't fully grasp it either – if that made sense . . . I wasn't sure I *was* making sense. A part of me was still processing how close I'd come to being a victim of a modern-day witch-hunter.

I told them about Isla's skeleton.

Thea gasped. 'Horrible. They did that on purpose.'

'What do you mean?' I asked, taking in the stricken faces of the rest of the group.

'Sisters have a special homegoing ceremony so their souls can be free to return to the other sisters in the spiritual realm. Matthias' elder probably knew that and kept her remains so it couldn't happen. Just another kick in the ribs.'

My grandmother sighed. 'We'll have to make it right. Once this is all done. She must be at the coroner's office.'

We began walking again, and this time a heavy silence floated with us.

Abner finally came to a stop in the middle of the garden, and we gathered around him in a semi-circle.

'This is a lot of ground to cover for guesswork,' Reba said.

'I'm afraid we have one last puzzle to solve,' Abner said.

'What do you mean?'

'The fabric square holds a second clue. When you held it up to the light, I could see a series of symbols. I have no idea what they mean but there has to be a reason they're there.'

I held the fabric to the waning light and saw it. Four geometric shapes stamped on the fabric in a goldish brown stain barely discernible unless you held it up to a bright light.

'Josiah's last hurrah,' my grandmother observed.

I looked around the garden. 'What could the triangle represent?'

We wandered around the garden until I came upon a trio of benches made of marble and accented with lions' heads on each side. A tombstone for Susannah was nearby. Abner kneeled before it, his eyes closed and took a moment.

We all watched in silence until he rose, swiped at his eyes and joined us.

I went to my grandmother who was a few paces behind me. I pointed to the benches. 'They're set in a triangle of sorts, aren't they?'

'I'd say so.' My grandmother went to the first bench, touching the marble, and I read the bronze placard attached to the back of one of the benches.

'This is a memorial to Elias' parents and a younger brother that died. Each bench represents a family member.'

My grandmother moved to the second bench. 'Do you see any sort of clues?'

I was kneeling on the ground beside the third bench when I saw something. A Roman numeral inscribed on the inside of the bench. I ran my fingers over the inscription: VII.

'Yes, I do.' I showed her the number seven. Then went to the other benches and looked in the same location. None of them had an inscription.

We returned to the group who had been doing their own searching and told them about the number.

'OK. Number seven,' Reba said. 'Maybe it will come in handy.'

Bess had walked away from the group, moving to an area of rose bushes. She returned, a hesitant look on her face. 'I think I found the oval. Come.'

We followed her through the rose bushes and found a beautiful white wooden gazebo with a brick foundation that matched the main house. Shaped in an oval with kudzu and roses climbing up and down it, the gazebo was a romantic memorial to Elias' love for his wife.

Abner stared at it. 'Elias had this built for Susannah. She'd come out here with a blanket and a picnic basket and read letters from her family and friends in New Orleans. She was homesick quite often.'

Thea went to the structure touching a post. 'It's definitely oval.'

We descended on the gazebo like children at an Easter egg hunt.

After almost an hour of finding nothing, Abner laughed out loud. 'I found it.'

He pushed on a brick that was loose. He wiggled it and it slid out easily. He turned the brick over and it was stamped with the number four. 'This has to be it.'

'Seven. Four,' I reminded everyone.

We walked around the gardens some more, until Bess pointed at a bed of bright red Cardinal flower. 'Those flowers are planted in the shape of a rectangle. See the way the cobblestone walkway surrounds it? The negative space is a rectangle.'

We all looked at the large section of fuchsia Carolina Roses. 'You're right,' Abner agreed. 'Let's take a look.'

'Should we study the flower bed or the path?' Bess asked.

'Both,' Abner said.

'I'll take the path,' I said, and moved to the cobblestones. Irregular stones in varying colors of beige, tan and rust-colored stone ran along the perimeter of the flower bed. I walked along each stone, testing with my foot. Searching for an inscription or a symbol etched on each one.

I walked up one path then turned right, looking back from where I came. Then I walked the second length, slowly and methodically, seeing nothing amiss. I walked the third stretch. And the fourth. There was nothing.

Bess approached me after inspecting the flowers. 'I didn't see anything amid the flowers.'

'Nothing to report here either.'

She gave me a long look. 'I'm worried about you.' She took my arm and looped hers through mine. 'Let's check again. Two heads are better than one.'

I allowed her to rest her head on my shoulder for a moment while she gave me a compassionate squeeze. And then we walked the paths again. This time when we were on the third stretch, we both stepped on a stone at the exact same time and it sunk in, then popped back up. We both stepped backward. I sank to the ground and lifted up the stone. Four vertical lines with a horizontal line through them, with three additional vertical marks beside it, were on the bottom. I showed it to her. 'Seven. Four. Eight,' I said, and she nodded, her eyes bright with tears.

'We're almost done.'

THIRTY-FIVE

'What's the last shape?' I asked the group.

'A circle within a circle. What does it mean?' Reba said.

Bess had her phone out. 'I'm googling it now.' She stopped and took a photograph of the symbol. 'Reverse searching.' A moment later, she looked up from her screen, confusion on her face. 'It says it's an Egyptian hieroglyph . . . for the sun.'

Abner looked across the garden, his gaze unfixed. And then he blinked, turning back to us. 'I know what it is. Let's go.'

We walked almost the length of the garden, passing a water fountain, until we came to stand in front of a sundial. It appeared to be made of bronze upon a cement foundation. Its perimeter was covered in an alphabet similar to English, but slightly different. The letters were faced upside down, right side up and to the right and left.

'I've never noticed this before,' my grandmother admitted. 'The significance?' She turned to Abner.

'I used to play with it when I was little, and my father liked to explain how it worked.' An innocent smile played on his lips as if he could see himself at the device as a child.

He touched the large circular disk. 'This is called the dial plate.' His hand went to the triangle on top of it. 'And this is the gnomon. It casts a shadow as the Earth rotates.' He walked around the sundial, his fingers touching every raised symbol that framed the disk.

'How old were you?' Reba asked.

'Four or five. And then my father died . . . The memories of him and coming here to play . . . are foggy.'

'If the fourth symbol represents the sundial,' I asked, 'is there a way for us to input the numbers?'

Abner scratched his head. 'I'm not sure.' He dragged his fingers around the perimeter of the clock. 'There's nothing loose. Nothing to press.' He frowned then bent over the dial, bracing his hands on the edges of the disk at the ten and three o'clock positions. 'I can remember my father turning this.' He moved the frame an inch to the right and it clicked. 'Yes, like this, and him saying he didn't understand why it moved. Most sundials don't move in this way.'

'It must mean something,' my grandmother said, moving closer to Abner. 'Try to remember.'

Hands still in place, he shook his head like a stubborn child. 'I can't.'

A slow, patient smile spread across my grandmother's face, and she leaned forward, placing fingertips on either side of his head at the temple and moving her fingers in a circular pattern. She took a deep breath and closed her eyes. 'Now try,' she said, removing her fingers.

Surprise registered on his face. 'He thought it was a code. A puzzle. He spent hours and hours trying to figure it out.' He turned to look at us. 'I'd completely forgotten. I told my father, right before he died that I'd figure it out for him.' He swallowed. 'And he patted me on my arm. And said, "Don't worry about it, son. You won't remember any of this". And then he leaned in front of me and touched my temples.' His gaze floated back to my grandmother. 'Like you just did. And I forgot. Until now.'

Something fluttered in my chest. 'What's going on?'

My grandmother smiled. 'Just a little thing I do. A massage of the temples, a suggestion to remember . . .'

'Like magic?'

My grams laughed. 'I don't think so. A little reflexology of the temples kickstarts the memories. And then I visualized Abner remembering. And so he did.'

Bess looked at her grandmother. 'Can you do that?'

Thea rolled her eyes in response, but I moved closer to my grandmother. 'What else can you do?'

Irritation tightened her features. 'We have more important things to focus on right now. Abner?'

He returned to the dial. 'The numbers?'

'Seven,' I called out.

He moved the dial's frame to the seven o'clock position.

It clicked into place, and the fountain nearby stopped gushing water upwards into the sky.

He twisted the frame to the four o'clock position.

We looked back at the fountain. The cement foundation sank into the ground, leaving only two round basins left.

'Eight,' I said, excitement filling my chest.

He moved the frame slightly to the left and it clicked again.

The entire fountain, all seven feet of sculpted flowers, leaves and mermaids, sank into the ground.

A round of gasps floated over our small group. And then we rushed over to peer downward, to see where the fountain had gone.

In its place was a brick-lined cylinder similar to a water well. Only this one had a difference.

A hidden staircase.

THIRTY-SIX

My grandmother touched my shoulder. 'As much as I'd like to see what's down there, I'm afraid I'll have to sit this little adventure out.' She held out a leg. 'My knees can't take it.'

'Me too,' Thea agreed. 'I don't do stairs anymore.'

Bess and I looked at each other. She nodded.

Reba grinned. 'I'm game.'

'I'll lead,' Abner added, eyes wide with awe. He grabbed the rim of the well and lowered himself down onto the brick steps, which were sturdy and in good condition. I went next, then Bess and Reba.

I turned to the closest wall and saw a three-dimensional replica of the sundial protruding from the wall. 'Look at this,' I called out, touching the dial. I pushed on it, and there was a loud creaking noise.

We all turned and saw the stairs disappear and the fountain rise back up to the surface. I heard my grandmother call my name right before the entrance was sealed off and we were in complete darkness.

'Sorry,' I said. 'I'm sure it will re-open if I press it again.'

We all pulled out our phones and turned the lights on, even though as we progressed through the tunnels, dapples of sunlight appeared from some unknown source. Fresh air flowed freely through the tunnels. Whomever had created the tunnels had built them well.

I reached the lowest level and looked around. We stood in an open space about a thousand square feet surrounded by polished walls that appeared to be made of marble. Colored images were drawn on the walls. Dark-brown and tan-skinned men and women dressed in Native American style clothes worshipping, sowing crops, having ceremonies and warring, among other activities. One image in particular caught my attention. A group of men and women, surrounded by luminescent flecks of light.

Bess turned around in a circle taking it all in, before getting a closer look at a wall. She stood shoulder to shoulder with me, and we both studied the drawing.

'Lightning bugs?' I suggested.

'No,' she said, her voice wistful. 'Those are fairies.'

I called over to Abner to join us. 'What do you think?'

'I don't know.' His voice was flat.

'Did you have any idea this was under your property?'

Abner's face tensed, as he looked about. He shook his head. 'No, I didn't. I don't think anyone knew this place was here.'

I turned to look at him, there was something in his voice. And I wondered if keeping the tunnels secret was tied to his disinterest in discussing the family's mining past. I could understand that because of the death it would be a painful subject, but hundreds of years later it seemed like the topic could be explored.

But I didn't want to ask him in front of everyone, especially if it made him uncomfortable. I'd ask him later.

I wanted to explore the tunnels that branched off the main room in four different directions, but I was drawn to the ancient-looking device in the middle of the chamber. Its body was crafted from a mix of polished wood and aged bronze. Similar to the pipes of a cathedral organ, it featured an array of elongated tubes arranged in various heights and sizes. The pipes' openings were covered with ornate grilles, adding to the machine's majestic appearance.

Reba stared at the device. 'Looks like a steampunk version of an organ at my grandmother's church in Charleston. It played melodies so low you could feel the vibrations in the wooden pews.'

There was a metallic control panel covered in symbols and dials. And there was a brass plate with four sentences etched on it. I touched the symbols but hesitated to touch the dials. I looked at the group. 'Who knows what to do?'

Everyone shrugged, so I turned back to examine the machine. It had a row of keys like a piano. I touched one. The sound was deafening, and it shook the entire earthen chamber.

Bess covered her ears until the sound subsided.

'I'm guessing we need to play the right chords.' Abner loosened his cravat. 'We need letters. Musical notes to play.'

I glanced around us. 'We have the numbers. Seven. Four. Eight. And this list of four random sentences that have no relation to anything or each other.'

Bess held up her phone. 'Remember, I took a picture of the sundial. Maybe there's something there we missed.'

We studied the image. There were four symbols at the twelve, three, six and nine o'clock positions. An ankh, which I knew represented life and vitality. Cow horns, which represented the goddess Hathor. A sistrum, a musical instrument associated with Hathor. And an eye, which I could guess symbolized Hathor's all-knowing nature.

The small brass plate on the machine read:

A cat has nine lives.
The cow jumped over the moon.
Music makes the world go round.
And eyes are the windows to the soul.

We studied the keys which replicated a traditional piano keyboard, trying to figure out what letters we were supposed to play. 'Songs about cats? Cows?' I thought of an idea and played the chord. We heard a grating noise and watched in horror as a door to the only entrance slid closed a few inches.

'Uhm,' Reba hummed, as her eyes tracked the door's movements. 'That's not good.'

I stared at the keys. 'Who wants to try something else?'

Abner shook his head. 'It has to be that the numbers represent letters . . .' Looking resolute, he positioned his hands in front of the keyboard and paused.

I remembered the classical music playing in the Willoughby museum. The piece of sheet music in a frame. 'Try Moonlight Sonata. Josiah played it.'

'You're right. He did. And fortunately, so can I.' He played the first four notes.

We stared at the door. A groaning noise and it inched forward.

'What if we get locked in here?' Reba posed.

And then a thought occurred to me. 'What if the keys are a red herring – just something here to throw us off track?'

The door opened wider.

'But it worked,' Reba observed.

'True. But maybe the numbers no longer serve a purpose.' I stared at the brass plate, with its four-line poem.

Bess shrugged. 'My brain is swimming. Not sure I can figure out one more thing.'

'"A cat has nine lives",' I said. 'Life. Ankh. Press the ankh nine times?'

Abner bent down and inspected the symbol. It was on a raised square, about four by four by four inches. 'I'm not sure the symbol can be pressed.'

'I don't want to find out we're wrong,' Bess hedged. 'But we've discovered that everything has its purpose . . .'

'Try it,' Reba urged. 'We have one more chance. If the door closes another inch, we need to leave.'

'Without the Stone of Scone?' I asked. 'We've come too far to leave empty-handed.'

'Better empty-handed than trapped in an underground cavern,' Bess said.

'Our grams would send for help,' I added. 'Even though it may take the police some time to find us . . .' I looked at the symbols. 'The ankh nine times?' I asked the group again.

Reba shook her head. Bess shrugged, looking horrified while Abner nodded.

I hovered my finger over the ankh. 'Ready?'

Bess grabbed Reba's hand for support. Reba frowned at her, then relented and squeezed her hand. She reached over and grabbed Abner's. He chuckled, turning to me. 'I think I'm supposed to hold your hand.'

I offered him my free hand, took a breath and pressed the symbol nine times. A sound emitted from the device, high-pitched.

Silence. And then the door inched back open.

A collective breath swept the room, and I exhaled. 'Next. "The cow jumped over the moon . . ." One cow. One jump. One moon. One.'

'Obviously Hathor's horns,' Bess said. 'Go for it.'

I didn't hesitate. Pressed it once. A lower pitch this time. Nothing happened. Kind of.

Reba looked around the room. 'Did you see that?'

'See what?' Abner asked, squinting as he turned in a circle.

'I'm not sure. Like a . . . a glimmer of light? Like a glimpse of a rainbow.'

'From what light source?' Bess asked, skepticism making her look like her grandmother.

'I don't know. Forget it.' She gestured for me to continue.

'"Music makes the world go round",' I read.

'Music is referenced once. Going around once,' Reba said. 'The sistrum. Once.'

I looked at the group for agreement. I had it. I pressed the musical instrument. A low growly pitch. Then a glimmer of light in the room with us, like the way the sun distorts the pavement on a hot day and you think you see a mirage. 'Reba, I saw it too.'

'Me too,' Abner murmured staring at the spot.

There was nothing there and yet the air had almost rippled with a luminescent sheen of color for just a moment.

'Maybe we don't realize we're losing air down here or something, and it's hard to breathe and we're beginning to hallucinate,' Bess said doubtfully.

'Must be a group hallucination then,' Reba said, with a puzzled look on her face. 'Because I saw it too.'

Bess looked at us. 'Do you think because we held hands, like, we did something? Created energy or synergy?'

I looked at Abner's hand. 'Maybe. There was a story in an old newspaper about the witches holding hands at the water and chanting.'

'Keep holding hands?' Bess asked, her cheeks flushing pink with excitement.

I nodded, then read the last sentence. '"And eyes are the windows to the soul." Two eyes. Has to be two windows . . . One soul. Is it two for the references to the eyes and windows, or one for the soul?'

Reba moved closer to the device. 'It's an eye. So let's go with two.'

'OK.' I pressed the eye symbol twice. And then . . . something happened.

THIRTY-SEVEN

First, a jolt of something . . . like electricity but not as strong. Not painful.

Happy. Joyful. It ran through my hands and into Abner's and the others. We all looked at each other, our hands and let go. And then the shimmer thing happened again.

Only this time it was . . . bigger, like a huge portion of the room shimmered and quivered then evaporated. When the translucent light dissipated, we were standing in front of a very old rectangular block of stone.

'Is that what I think it is?' Bess asked, her voice shaking.

I nodded, not believing my eyes. An object had just appeared in the room. But from where? It was like on *Star Trek* when Scotty beamed somebody up and they were just there.

Abner went to it first, knelt in front of it and placed both hands on it. 'It's real. It's the Stone of Scone. Here. All this time. On my family's property.'

'How did it get here?' Bess asked.

He shrugged. 'It's a mystery.'

As I gazed at the stone, I felt . . . almost a calling to press my palms on it and feel the cold stone under my hand. 'Is the stone doing something to us?' I asked, as I walked to the stone.

'Not . . . us,' Bess replied.

'I think it's just you,' Reba observed. 'You OK?'

I nodded. 'I feel wonderful.' And I did. High on something natural and wonderful that filled my heart, mind and soul. I felt fulfilled. Unified. One with nature and everyone around me.

I knelt beside the stone and pressed my palms to it. I can't say for sure what happened, but I felt a buzzing inside of me, and I suddenly couldn't keep my eyes open.

Eyes closed, the buzzing increased. In my head, or in the room around us, I couldn't tell. And then there was silence. And I was in darkness, almost like floating in space. Black with bursts of stars on the horizon. But I could see Abner and Bess and Reba floating too. We were in a circle, legs folded in lotus position, smiling at each other.

Words murmured in my ears. Information, knowledge, images flooded my brain. I saw ancient kings crowned. Lush green mountainscapes with sheep grazing in the distance. Crumbling castles. Armies classing, holding banners and shields with old heraldry. Women, young and old, floated by in my mind's eye. White skin. Brown skin. Tan skin. Long hair. Short hair. Straight. Curly. Dark. Light. Eyes blue, green. Brown.

The voices increased. And I began to feel lightheaded, as if my head was swimming. But I couldn't open my eyes. I felt frozen in place, rooted to the spot.

No images. No sounds. No buzzing.

I was back in the room.

I opened my eyes. 'What just happened?'

Abner reached for my arm and steadied me. 'I don't know. You just stood there with a smile on your face swaying back and forth. You looked peaceful, that's for sure.'

The rest of the group crowded around me. 'Do you feel OK?' Bess asked.

'I think so.'

I saw Reba observe the metal rings on either side of the stone. *Could we lift it?*

I shook my head. 'Reba, no. It stays here. This is its home.'

Reba's head jerked my way. 'I didn't say anything.'

'But I heard your question.' I blinked. 'You didn't say it aloud?'

She shook her head, and I stared at the artifact. 'The stone wants to stay here.' I paused, thinking about what I'd just said. Implying the stone was sentient? Had a mind of its own, could make decisions. Had a will. 'OK, this is weird. It's like I can read the stone's thoughts.'

'It can't be a stone if it has thoughts,' Abner said. 'A crystal maybe. Crystals can retain memories, that's why we use them in technology. So maybe it's not talking to you. You're accessing the recorded memories.'

I'd heard Matty talk about crystalline structures. 'Sounds about right.' And then I told them about Dr. Philippi, my name on the scroll, the purple star and what it meant.

Bess' eyes widened. "Direct descendent?'

Throat dry, I nodded.

Reba stepped forwards. 'If you're the chosen one, then we're its keepers. Its protectors.' She looked around the room. 'That's the story, right? You're the direct descendant of Queen Scota and the rest are like her crew?'

Bess laughed. 'Yeah, we're Sidney's crew.'

'I don't know how long we've been down here, but we should probably head back up before the grandmothers begin to worry.' Abner held out his pocket watch. 'It's stopped working for some reason.' His forehead creased. 'And that's never happened before.' He looked at the stone. 'We need to hide it again, just in case someone else is able to find this place.'

I hurried to the device, trying to remember the chords I played. 'I'll play them in reverse. Hopefully that works.' I pressed the symbols, there was a shimmer in the air and the stone was gone.

'It worked.' Bess gawked at the area where the stone used to be.

We moved to the hallway, and I pressed the sundial, hoping it would work in reverse. When it began to move, we all let out a collective sigh. The staircase descended and we rushed back to the surface.

My grandmother hurried towards me. 'What happened down there? We waited and waited, and you never returned. I wanted to call the police much earlier, but Thea told me no. That you'd all be OK . . .' She searched my face. 'Are you OK?'

I nodded, tears filling my eyes. 'We found it, Grams. We found it.'

'What did you find?'

'The Stone of Scone. The real one. And it . . . it called to me. And I touched it.' I blinked in the sunlight, while Abner rushed to the sundial to close the entrance. 'We were just—'

Thea wrapped her arms around Bess, her face tight with worry. 'When we saw the fountain moving, I lied and told the officers I thought I saw you across the village and sent them running, but—'

I spun around. 'What officers?'

And then there were the sound of boots pounding on dirt and the police chief was there with several officers and EMTs.

'You're OK?' he said in surprise, studying our group. 'Your grandmother called us when you didn't return.' His eyes narrowed as he searched our faces. 'We've been searching every inch of the village. In fact, we were just here in this very spot and there was no sign of you.'

'It's only been . . . what, thirty minutes? An hour at the most?' I shrugged. 'We're fine.'

Chief Warren exchanged glances with an EMT then nodded. 'We're going to need to check you out, ma'am.'

Abner stepped forward. 'We're all fine. Got turned around in the . . . forest but we're here now.'

'Mr Robbins, you've been gone for almost three days.' His eyebrows floated upwards. 'I just don't understand why Mrs Taylor waited so long to call us.' A suspicious squint transformed his expression. 'What were you all doing in the woods anyway?'

Three days had passed in the tunnels? I exchanged stunned glances with the rest of the group.

'What were we doing in the woods?' Bess repeated slowly. She cleared her throat. 'It's a social media thing.' She pulled out her phone and waved it in the air. 'Colonial-era camping. We're doing a new exhibit and were trying to find a new site for an outdoor exhibit.'

The chief scratched his head. 'Where's your camping gear?'

Abner spun some lie while I wondered about his timepiece. It had stopped working when we were down there. What was going on with those tunnels?

'I'm surprised you'd go camping at a time like this,' the chief was saying.

Abner returned the chief's suspicious expression. 'What do you mean?'

The chief paused. 'Oh, that's right. You've been gone for three days so you probably don't know . . . With the fire, and then you all missing – it was in the local news . . . They're calling it Mayhem At The Museum.' He chuckled. 'Pretty sensational. Especially with the skeleton found . . .' He grimaced. 'A group of museum staff go missing? Can't make this stuff up.'

'We weren't missing,' I insisted. 'My grandmother was just . . .' I grimaced. 'Worrying for nothing.'

The chief rocked back on his heels. 'The president of the United States is coming here for a visit. Don't you need to . . . I don't know, cut the grass. Decorate?'

Bess ran two hands through her hair. 'The actual president? Why is he coming here?'

'Well, when there's a fire at one of the, and I quote, "Most beloved historical institutions in the country", it's kind of a big deal. At least that's what he said in his press conference.'

A press conference? Great. 'I don't understand why he needs to come down here.'

'The head of the virtual reality initiative is already here, what with her brother passing. She's been staying in the family home, but she'll be here with the president.'

Marta De Verona? I felt sick to my stomach. That couldn't be good.

'This is the biggest thing to happen to Robbinsville since . . . Well, forever.'

I stopped listening to him then. Marta wasn't coming to show her support for her brother, she wanted me and the rest of the Daughters. And she was coming for revenge. Did she know I was the one who'd caused her brother's death? She had to.

Bess touched my arm. 'Did you hear what he said?'

I shook my head. 'Sorry?'

The chief fixed me with a concerned look. 'I said, the DRIA is going to use the fire as an example of why all museums need to go virtual. That's what she said in the press conference. Now, I can't say I'm in agreement with this push to VR, but in this case they may have a point. She talked about how this museum is one of the only museums not to have a VR version and this is exactly why it's needed.'

An EMT approached the chief. 'Except for a loss of time, those two seem fine, sir.'

The chief nodded. 'Abner. Sidney, you're next. And then? Let's get out of here.'

THIRTY-EIGHT

The next morning, I woke up before my alarm went off, showered, and was downstairs frying eggs and making toast when my grandmother came down.

'You beat me down this morning,' she said, yawning, looking out the kitchen window. It was still dark out, the sky a dark streak of navy blue and purple. 'I was going to make you coffee.' She sniffed the air appreciatively. 'But you beat me to that as well.'

I prepared her plate and sat it on the table. 'I just woke up with a lot of energy. Feeling rested and really, really good.' So good in fact, I wondered if the stone had done something to me.

She settled into her seat. 'That's wonderful. I was worried about you. About all of you being down there so long.'

I poured her a cup of coffee, then joined her with my own plate.

'So what happened down there?'

I told her everything. 'Grams, you're descended from a Daughter of Hathor.'

Her jaw tightened. 'That's news to me.'

'But you have to be. Because I am . . . I thought it was through my mother. But that little thing you did with your mind, and the herbs . . . You never suspected?'

'Suspected what?' She laughed. 'That I come from a long line of women who . . .' She shrugged. 'Who what?' She sipped her coffee. 'I come from a woman who shirked her responsibility to be a mother.'

I forked eggs into my mouth. 'But not you.'

'Not me.'

'And look what happened. You have a son who is a US Representative. The Speaker of the House. Daughters of Hathor birth kings and presidents.'

'Speaking of which, your father is coming for a visit.'

'Of course he is. The president will be here.'

'And your mother.'

I almost choked on my coffee.

My grandmother smiled. 'You'll probably want to buy a new dress.'

Probably.

'What happens next? Now that we've found the real Stone of Scone?'

'I suspect someone will come for it.'

There was a knock at the door. My grandmother and I exchanged glances. 'Early for a visitor,' I said.

She smoothed down her blouse. 'I'll get it.'

I followed my grandmother to the door, and we were both surprised to see Daphne. Her eyes were bright behind her glasses. 'Good morning.'

We both responded in kind. A little hesitant. Very curious. To my knowledge Daphne had never paid my grandmother a visit, and outside of seeing her at the library I could count on one hand the times we'd spoken.

'May I come in? We need to talk.'

I stepped forward, alarm bells clanging. 'Has something happened at the museum?'

She hesitated. 'The cow jumped over the moon.'

Jesus Christ. Her too? 'And the dish ran away with the spoon,' I said automatically.

My grandmother chuckled slightly. 'This means something to you?'

I nodded and stepped aside. 'Come in.'

My grandmother closed the door behind her. 'Coffee?'

'Yes, please.'

More coffee was served, this time in the living room. Daphne looked uncomfortable, pulling her soft cardigan, this time a mustard yellow, close to her waist. I looked at her expectantly.

She smiled as if it pained her. 'I'm a Baruch,' she finally said.

I glanced at my grandmother, then back at her. Dr Philippi had mentioned that name but still . . . 'I don't understand.'

She pressed her lips together. 'Baruch. As in the scribe to the prophet Jeremiah?'

'We're talking about the Bible again?'

'Yes. I believe the stories can also be found in the *Septuagint* and Ethiopian Orthodox Bible, but Baruch was part of a priestly caste, of royal lineage actually. He was the brother of the king, uncle to Queen Scota . . . and the recorder of very important events.'

'But you say the name as if it's a noun.'

'It is. Now. It became the term for the scribes in the Daughters of Hathor.' She paused to drink her coffee. 'Traditionally, the scribes were men but with the members of King Zedekiah's court being hunted down . . . even though Baruch was allowed to live, a decision was made to hide the later scribes by training women to do it.' She laughed. 'It was the perfect disguise. No one would have ever thought a young woman would have such an important position.'

'The scrolls,' I said. 'You and your order maintain the scrolls I saw at the Smithsonian.'

She nodded. 'And I specifically maintain information related to the direct descendants of Scota.' She paused, her gaze settling on me.

'You knew the Stone of Scone was here?'

'I suspected. Everything I'd learned said it was put on the *Seonaidh* and sailed over here.

'That's the ship that crashed off the coast of Morehead City.'

'And when those Scots were coming in droves in small boats with their belongings . . .'

'Someone secreted the stone to Robbinsville.'

She nodded.

'But why Robbinsville?'

'Susannah. She was descendant from a line of women who were

the Lady-In-Waiting for Scota's direct descendant. Sometimes the two were confused for each other, they were that close . . . And it helped to keep the descendant safe when no one was sure who she was.'

'Matty thought she was the leader of the witches . . .' I shook my head. "But he was wrong? He was confusing her for another?'

"Yes.' Daphne's fingers tightened around her cup handle. 'She was working on behalf of the *true* leader who asked her to find a new hiding spot, one that would be safe from witch-hunters. At first Susannah planned on having it hid in New Orleans, but it was such a busy, populace city even then . . . She paused to sip her coffee.

'She met and married Elias and moved to Robbinsville. Once she got here, she probably realized a small town in the middle of nowhere would be a good hiding place . . . For the Stone, the Daughters and Scota's heir. So she put out the call for the heir and the Daughters to come to Robbinsville, at the same time plans were being made to remove the stone from Scotland.'

'And then the witch-hunters followed.'

She nodded, her face darkening. 'It's all written down by my predecessors. It was an ugly time and Matthias Toliver was an important part of the hunt. He tried his best to turn Elias against Susannah, not knowing he was a Son of Horus himself. And he desperately tried to find the other Daughters . . .'

'And now you're here,' I said, my brow creasing. 'Why?'

'The time has come for us to crown our true heir, imprint the stone with its true leader.'

'Imprint,' I chuckled. 'Sounds like some sort of technology.'

She shrugged. 'I don't understand it, but in a way maybe it is. When a Daughter presses her palm to the stone, it somehow recognizes her DNA, and she receives a . . . download, you might say, of information and sometimes abilities.'

'I think . . .' I began slowly, 'That has already happened to me.'

My grandmother shook her head slowly. 'I'm not following.'

I explained what I did, how I could hear a frequency buzzing in my ear that seemed to be attracting me to the stone in a way that I could not reject it. The laying of hands on the stone, the information download. All of it.

'But most importantly,' Daphne was saying, 'you locked onto the frequency of the stone which allows the Daughters to access it through you, almost like Bluetooth.' Her laugh was light. 'And can work with it to protect it.'

'In what ways?'

'It can emit different frequencies, much like some sea creatures can shock predators for protection? Cause numbness. Brain fog . . .'

'It's a weapon?'

'It could definitely be weaponized in the wrong hands. Oh, and it can block anything with electricity, just fry everything.'

'Dangerous,' my grandmother said.

'How do you know this?' I asked.

'We have the journals of Daughters who once worked with the stone, trying to understand its powers, the scope of its abilities. Because of its abilities, many of the Sisters work and complete research in STEM.'

'Now I understand why Matty wanted it. They must have a lot of evil plans for the stone.'

'And we have plans as well. The time has come for the Daughters and Sons to come out of hiding, connect with each other and take our world back.'

'What are *your* plans, Daphne?' my grandmother asked, eyes narrowing in concern. 'What brings you to our house this early in the morning?'

'It's time you understood who you are, Fiona.' Her words were heavy with emotion.

My grandmother's eyes hardened. 'I don't know much about my family, and I'm fine with that. I've lived over seventy years not knowing anything about where I came from, and—'

Daphne held her hand up. 'You may be fine with it, respectfully. But Sidney needs to know.' Her expression was kind. 'And honestly, it's time you did too.'

My grandmother squinted in confusion. 'You've done my family tree?' Her shoulders stiffened. 'Let's hear it then. I suppose you're going to tell me I'm a Daughter of Hathor.' Her tone dipped dismissively. 'However that happened.'

I reached for my grandmother's hand and squeezed it gently.

'I *know* how it happened.' Daphne reached into her purse and retrieved a manila envelope. She opened it and pulled out a full-color sketch. She showed it to my grandmother, who leaned forward, placing the glasses that hung around her neck on a chain onto the bridge of her nose.

I inspected the drawing too. It was a very old image of a beautiful woman. A black woman with a noble bone structure. High cheekbones, with a burst of freckles. A broad, haughty nose, wide full lips, and red textured curls teased into a complicated coiffeur held together by pins decorated with enamel flowers. Her green eyes were defiant, brave almost, as she gazed at the artist with her pointed chin dipped upward. Haughty came to mind.

'Pretty dress,' my grandmother said in a hushed, awestruck tone.

I studied the dress, which was a simple frock of midnight color with a deep décolletage, fitted waist and voluminous skirts that belled around her. 'You recognize her?'

She shook her head. 'I've never seen this drawing before, but she looks like I did when I was younger.' She went to a cabinet and found a black and white, framed photo of a young girl in a starched dress with crinoline, and shiny black patent shoes. She faced the camera with a tentative expression as if she wanted to smile but not sure she should.

I studied the drawing and then the photograph. The similarity was unmistakable. And since I looked like my grandmother, I also shared a resemblance to this woman. I turned to Daphne, but it was my grandmother who spoke first. 'Who is she?'

Daphne's gaze softened as she watched my grandmother. 'Fiona, she's your mother.'

I stared at the image. And my grandmother. But then I realized what she was saying. 'That's not possible. According to the style of dress, this had to have been drawn in the . . . early nineteenth century.'

She turned the drawing over, and we saw a date written on the back. *1820.* The script looked familiar. The slant, the whirls, the way the 'i' was dotted . . .

'The same year she died. Or rather, was killed.'

A hand went to my grandmother's mouth. 'What happened to her?'

'She was hanged. This is a picture of Isla McIntosh.' She looked at my grandmother. 'The Witch of Robbinsville.'

THIRTY-NINE

'Daphne, I've heard of this woman. She was from Scotland.' My grandmother rolled her eyes, her face taut with annoyance. 'You may have noticed I'm a black woman?'

The librarian folded her hands in her lap. 'And so was your mother. It may not be widely known or even widely accepted in today's society, but there was a time when brown and black people were indigenous to Europe. You have only to look at historical art, tapestries and heraldry to see that America was not the first melting pot.

'Queen Scota traveled from Egypt to Spain to Ireland. Her descendants married others from European royal bloodlines, including Moorish royals from North Africa, Spain, Portugal and Germany, who were what we would consider black today. Brown skin. Curly hair. African or African-American in appearance. Surely, you've seen the tapestry, "Wild Men And Moors", held at the Museum of Fine Art in Boston?'

I held up a tentative hand. 'I've seen it.'

'One of the finest examples of a Moorish king and queen in Germany.' She reached for Fiona's hand. 'You have the most elite of bloodlines, my dear.' She smiled at me. 'The same as Queen Charlotte, I might add.'

'Dr Philippi mentioned her as well.'

Daphne practically swooned. 'We're just very proud of Charlotte. She's the last time one of our bloodline reached the level of Queen.'

But my grandmother was not charmed by her story. 'What are you playing at, Daphne? Do you know how old I'd have to be if that woman was actually my mother?' She picked up the picture of her younger self and returned it to the shelf.

Daphne's gold-flecked hazel eyes followed her. 'During the time your mother – Isla – lived, Matthias had created a toxic environment for women who were healers, or too pretty or too outspoken. He'd stoked the anger of many in the community, saying certain women had caused plagues, or problems with farm animals dying or children getting sick . . . It didn't matter. He turned the community against women he thought were Daughters, so he could hide his pursuit of them.'

'And Elias?'

'While he did what he could do to protect the women, in the end he could only protect his wife. He had money and owned land, yes, but Matthias supposedly had God on his side. So when Isla knew her life was forfeit . . .' She sighed, 'She began to put her affairs in order, hiding important papers and family relics, and most importantly . . .' She looked at my grandmother. 'Made arrangements to protect her daughter, who would be a target for Matthias if he could find her.'

'Go on,' my grandmother said, forehead creased with deep lines.

'She and her Sisters put out a lie that her daughter died in the last sickness to sweep the community, and then – and here's where you'll have to just believe me – she used the Stone of Scone's powers to create a portal one hundred and thirty some years into the future . . . where she hoped you'd be safe.'

The room was quiet. And then my grandmother waved her hand. 'This is all utter nonsense. Daphne, I expected more from you. You've always seemed like such a reasonable woman.'

'And I promise you I am.'

My grandmother gently removed her hand from my own and walked across the room, like she needed to put space between herself and Daphne's words.

'You arrived in the year of your birth, were placed with a family of the brotherhood that had not been outed. They vowed to protect you and keep the secret of your heritage hidden.'

'The secret being?' I prompted as my heart pounded against my ribs.

'That Fiona was the last living descendant of the royal House of David.'

I blinked. Looked at my grandmother, whose jaw had gone slack.

'The true heir of the prophecy Jeremiah foretold, the Egyptian princess, landing in Scotland, the stone . . . No. It could not all be related to us. To me.'

My grandmother's legs buckled, and I went to her then. Wrapped her in my arms. 'You OK, Grams?'

She nodded, though I could feel her body trembling.

'Isla was your mother, and . . . Elias Robbins was your father.'

'Elias?' My grandmother's hand flew to her mouth. 'I don't understand.'

'Elias was obsessed with finding the direct descendant of Queen Scota. He thought it might be Susannah, but while she was related to the House of David, and very powerful and prominent in the sisterhood, she was not a direct descendant. He wanted his son or daughter to be the heir. Obsessed with the idea, really. I don't know why, but power can do that for some.' She shrugged.

'When Susannah died, Elias mourned, of course. But eventually he took Isla as his mistress, and she became pregnant . . . with you. And your hair, which historically has been a sign of both royalty and witches, was so red. It didn't seem possible to keep you in the main house, as Elias had hoped to do, with Matthias around. Even though everyone thought Isla's daughter had died, he still searched for anyone with red hair. Or women who behaved strangely. Or worked with herbs and could heal . . . I couldn't allow you to grow up in that environment, and neither would Elias. Not to mention that the fate of our kind rested on your tiny little shoulders . . .' She sighed, her face pained as if she were reliving the experience.

'Getting rid of Matthias wasn't an option, as his people would only send another in his place. No, it was best to give the impression that there was nothing amiss at Robbinsville, as difficult as that seems. The devil you know, and all that.'

'Abner is my cousin,' my grandmother ventured, her voice dry and hoarse.

'Despite your likeness to Isla – and trust me, they knew what she looked like – the Apophis witch-hunters of today were not looking for any descendants of Isla's, though families from the House of David still exist. So, you were safe, for a while. Free to marry, have children of your own, have a lovely life.'

'How can I believe this?'

'The cookbook I gave you. Do you have it?'

My grandmother's eyes brightened. 'Of course, yes, I still have it.'

'Get it, please.'

My grandmother retrieved the thick leather-bound book full of yellowed pages. 'You said this was a gift, what . . . forty years ago?'

Daphne nodded then produced a yellowed envelope from her tote. 'Your mother wrote this letter and gave it to the Baruch in her time for safekeeping. For this very moment.' She handed her the envelope. 'It's been kept in our secret archives for over a hundred years. Read it.'

Tears moistened my grandmother's eyes as she took the letter. Her hands trembled, and she gently opened the envelope and pulled out the letter. The script was beautiful and elegant with pronounced lines sloping to the right and bulbous loops.

My dearest Fiona,
    I hope that if you're reading this letter you now know the truth about who I am, and what you are. You are my prized

possession, my beautiful Fiona, who I shall protect by sending you forth to another time.

I hope my plan is brilliant, and you may hide in plain sight for all your days and have the life I am destined not to. I pray your family will be kind and living and will shield you from the monsters who prey upon us.

All my love, Your máthair.

Beside her name was the drawing of a simple flower and her initials I.M.

'*Máthair* is Gaelic for mother,' Daphne explained.

My grandmother looked up from the paper, her hand shaking and tears dripping onto the page.

'Now compare the handwriting to the back of the drawing, and then to the writing in the book.'

We both leaned forward studying the script. After a long moment, I spoke. 'Looks very similar.' I looked at my grandmother. 'What do you think?'

She nodded, her forehead creased with lines. She touched the loop of a 't', and the slant of a letter 'l'. 'Hard to say . . . But yes, possibly.'

'How about this?' She pointed to the emblem of the flower, and then leaned forward and turned to one of the last pages in the book. The same flower was drawn there as a border. A lotus flower. Just like the ones on the writing box I'd given to Gabe.

'Same?'

I couldn't deny it, and neither could my grandmother. 'Yes. It's the same.'

'But how?' my grandmother finally asked.

'The Stone of Scone is a miraculous artifact.' Daphne lifted a shoulder. 'Its capabilities are beyond understanding, and yet we have people trying.'

'What have you understood so far?'

'Well, without the actual stone for study it's been a challenge. But we have some of the greatest minds in our brother- and sister-hoods working on the project, creating studies and case reports based on what we know the stone has done. We think the stone can act as a temporal resonance device, creating a bridge between different points in time. We're not sure how it works, or what your mother did to send you forward, though.'

'There are stories in the Bible about time travel,' my grandmother said. 'Did you know?'

I shook my head, but Daphne smiled. 'There is a Deuterocanonical book of the Bible, the Book of Baruch. In the first couple chapters of the book, Jeremiah is told by Jehovah that the Chaldeans will destroy Jerusalem and that he should bury the sacred vessels from the temple. After that he is to go into the Babylonian captivity. Before the destruction of Jerusalem, Jeremiah sends Abimelech, a eunuch, to obtain figs from the orchard of Agrippa. The eunuch falls asleep in the orchard and awakes sixty-six years later as an old man. It is an old man who informs him what has transpired while he was sleep.'

'Kind of like Rip Van Winkle,' I added.

'Many people interpret that story as symbolic. But others . . . me included, think he unknowingly stepped into a space where the boundaries of time were altered by divine intervention. The veil between past and present thinned, and Abimelech experienced a temporal displacement, effectively falling asleep in one era and awakening many decades later.'

'Strange that it was in the Book of Baruch . . .'

'Not so strange. Baruchs can do more than just write.' A dimple appeared on her cheek.

'What do you mean?'

'We can . . . find weaknesses in the time-space continuum, places where time travel is possible.'

'What are you talking about?'

'Surely you've heard of certain places known to be paranormal or magical? Usually there's some truth to that even if the locals don't know exactly what that is.'

Exactly what Llew was researching. And yet . . . 'Time travel isn't a thing . . . is it?'

She shrugged. 'The military and our government, and China and Russia are all experimenting with it. For us it's an ancient technology—'

'That you—'

'That I . . . and others like me oversee. Coordinate. Administrate over . . . whatever you want to call it. Who better to record history than a time-traveling writer?' Her laugh was light, belying the heaviness of her words. 'There are certain places in our world and certain objects that facilitate the travel. Baruchs manage the experience.'

'So who was with . . . me, I guess, when I traveled?' my grand-mother asked.

Daphne sighed, her eyes suddenly moist.

I gazed at her. And I knew.

She nodded her head slowly.

Alarmed, my grandmother made eye contact with me, then slowly turned to look at Daphne. 'You?'

Daphne dipped her head. 'You were so small. I couldn't just put you in a basket and hope someone kind and decent found you. Or that we could connect with a Baruch in your time. Our mission was too great.' She pulled a handkerchief from her purse and dabbed the corners of her eyes.

'I mean you *were* found in a basket, but I was the one to *find* you.' She made air quotes with her fingers around the word find. 'And I brought you to the local leaders . . . Once I had you settled with the right family, I was supposed to go back to my own timeline, but I found that . . . well, I wanted to make sure you were OK. I made a promise to your mother . . .'

'*That's* why you were so uncomfortable around Matty.'

Daphne nodded. 'I knew his ancestor, and he was an evil man. I found it very difficult to separate the two, especially when Matty wore his ancestor's costume.'

'How were you to return to your own time?'

'The tunnels lead to certain underground areas of temporal fluc-tuations. However, without a Daughter's assistance in guiding the travel, it wasn't certain when and where I'd go back to. I could've gone back to the 1940s or the 1600s, for example. But it was just a chance I had to take.'

'Temporal fluctuations,' I repeated. 'Under the old coffee shop?' I guessed. 'There's a tunnel entrance there?'

'How did you know? Yes, that was exactly where I was supposed to go. Back then it wasn't a coffee shop . . . A feed store, I think.'

'QLabs is over that tunnel entrance now.'

'That could just be a coincidence,' Daphne suggested.

I stood. 'I'll be right back.' I went upstairs to my room and returned with my laptop. I opened up the browser and showed her the image.

Her eyes widened.

I nodded. 'Right?'

She nodded in agreement.

My grandmother leaned forward. 'What are we looking at?'

It was one of the patents from QLabs.

Daphne sat back. 'They're building a time machine.'

'Or pretending to,' I said. 'If their office is over a real time portal. But what would the Order of Apophis need with a time machine? And how does it relate to the VR initiatives?'

'I'm not sure,' Daphne began. 'Perhaps it was a plan B if they couldn't get their hands on the stone? But for what purpose? Maybe they wanted to establish VR environments in different time periods, allowing anyone with a connection to virtually time travel.'

'That would be worth a lot of money indeed,' I said, trying to imagine.

My grandmother raised a finger. 'If I may? Time machines are quite interesting, of course. I read H.G. Wells in my day . . . but I have another important question.' She faced Daphne. 'If you traveled from the eighteenth century to bring me forward, that means you must've been an adult when I was a baby . . .'

'You haven't aged,' I said, my eyes on her firm jawline and baby smooth skin.

'I have,' Daphne admitted. She touched her face lightly and the gesture reminded me of the elderly woman I saw in her office. When she'd seen me, she'd touched her cheek in just the same manner. Wait . . .

'It's what you might call . . . a glamour.' She glanced at me. 'A spell for keeping up appearances.'

'That day in your office when I saw an elderly lady wearing a cardigan like yours. She said she was your mother.'

'*I* said I was my mother,' she corrected. 'My mother is long gone. That was me you saw. The real me. Sometimes when I'm tired and alone, I let the glamour slip. It requires quite a lot of energy to maintain for extended periods of time. It's why I'm so thin. And my bones are a bit fragile. Something about the process leaches vitamin D and potassium . . . And my palms are always sweaty.' She laughed, embarrassed. 'Just one of the side effects. At any rate, you caught me off guard.'

'I would've never guessed there were side effects to beauty spells. That is the definition of a glamour?'

She nodded. 'People respond to extended glamour spells in different ways. It's terribly wearing on the body for long periods of time. Dangerously high metabolism systems, nervous tics, profuse sweating, organ failure as the worst example.'

'My goodness,' I laughed. 'It's like one of those pharmaceutical company advertisements.'

Her face was grim. 'Anyone who agrees to use glamours in this way will understand the risks, and like me, determine it's worth the risk.'

'So you can really practice . . . magic?'

'It's just something I can do. I visualize . . . well. I call upon the ether around us to . . .' She chuckled. 'It's actually very hard to explain. But that's it. I'm a scribe and I can make myself appear younger as needed in the execution of my duties. There are others much more accomplished than me.'

'I'd say you were pretty darn impressive.'

An image came to me then. 'I saw a picture of a woman . . .' I gazed at her features. 'A painting at the archives in New Bern . . .'

'That was me. A year before I traveled to the future with your grandmother.' She nodded. 'Before Robbinsville, I'd lived in New Bern. I've always worked with books and papers. No matter the time.'

A heavy silence hung between us, and I glanced at my grand-mother who had a tentative expression on her face.

'What about the fairies?' she asked, her voice soft. 'I rather liked the idea of being left in a garden by fairies. It gave a soft, whimsical launch to my life that I thought was an otherwise cold and rude abandonment.'

Daphne cocked her head, her eyes gentle as they met my grand-mother's. 'I'm sorry to say, there are no fairies. At least not that I'm aware of.'

'But the stories? People have seen little flecks of light like light-ning bugs around these places we know – or thought to be magical, mystical . . .' She shook her head. 'What of that?'

'You said lightning bugs?' I told them about the drawing in the cave. The cluster of lights like lightning bugs, the Native Americans around them.

'Sounds like a drawing of a time portal known in pre-colonial times.' Daphne's eyes lit up with interest. 'This would be the second one in the area.'

'Maybe they were fairies,' my grandmother insisted, hope bright-ening her tone.

'No.' Daphne's voice was firm. 'It was Quantum Entanglement Residue. When someone travels through a time portal, quantum particles entangled with the traveler emit minuscule bursts of photons, creating the appearance of pinpricks of light.'

'That doesn't sound fairytale–like at all,' I observed, glancing at my grandmother whose face had fallen. I bit my lip, worried Daphne was overloading my grandmother with too much information. 'Grams? You OK?'

'I will be.' She soldiered an optimistic expression as she eyed a fairy garden in a glass bowl nearby. 'But I think I like my version better.'

At that, Daphne stood, clapping her hands together. All business. 'It's a burden off my chest to finally tell you, Fiona, about your mother.'

'You were friends?'

She nodded. 'The heir is always assigned a scribe. And I was hers, to record her activities and thoughts for posterity. Once she decided to send you forward, and she couldn't be persuaded to explore other options, it was my idea for her to write down her recipes and bits of wisdom.'

My grandmother picked up the book, dragged her finger along the cover. 'I've been making my mother's recipes?'

Daphne nodded.

'Reading her words . . . it's like she's been with me all this time.' She gazed at the book until her eyes unfocused.

'I thought it would be nice for you to have. A piece of your mother. Well, that and the writing box.'

I perked up at her words. 'The writing box?'

She nodded. 'Your mother commissioned Josiah Willoughby to create it. You probably noticed the flowers on it – the lotus? Same as the ones on her letter and the cookbook. They are a symbol of the House of David, of Isla's royal lineage. Of your royal lineage.'

My grandmother chuckled. 'You're telling me I'm a princess?' A whimsical expression softened her face. 'I'm the Lotus Princess?'

'In another time? Absolutely. In New Orleans, you'd be the Fleur De Lis Princess, there's an ancient link there. Elias used to call Susannah that, his fleur de lis. That case is part of your family. Part of the family's royal honors and regalia, similar to a crown and scepter a king might have.'

My grandmother glanced upstairs. 'That writing box is here somewhere . . .'

I winced. Now was probably not the best time to tell them I'd given the case to Gabe. But surely he'd take good care of it and return it in due time.

'When I traveled forward, I had Fiona, the book and the case. The case got lost somehow and I spent a lot of time searching for it, but it never turned up. I assumed it went to another spot in the space-time continuum – or underground, as we've called it for centuries.'

'OK ladies. There's work to be done. The president will be here tomorrow, along with your father, Sidney, and the director of DRIA, who we now know is a card-carrying member of the Order of Apophis. There will be press and crowds. And we have to get Fiona crowned and imprinted.'

'Me?' she stuttered. 'No, I can't.'

'But why not?' Daphne countered. 'You're Isla's daughter. I know this is coming later in life, but there are things you need to do.'

'My son,' Fiona said. 'He can do it. He's a leader. He's a—'

'A man. This legacy is a matrilineal inheritance. From mother to daughter.'

My grandmother turned to look at me, her eyes hopeful. 'Then Sidney can do it. Be it. Whatever it is you need.'

'Grams, I don't want to take this from you.'

'Child, please. I'm old. It's enough for me to go to church and knitting club. You really think I want to take on another responsibility at my age?'

Daphne's forehead folded into a deep V as she turned to me. 'You're the eldest daughter of the eldest daughter. Because Fiona had a boy, the legacy goes to the first girl. That would be you.'

I let that sink in. 'My father's always talked about running for president. If he were to do that . . . and win, he'd be in position to—'

'Help *you*.' Daphne's resolve was clear. 'That's all he can do as a male heir of Scota.'

'I don't know if—'

'You have to.' A weariness swept across Daphne's face. 'This has been a long time coming. So many people working together for this very moment. Hundreds of years of hoping and waiting . . .' She pressed her lips together, and a tear slid down her cheek. 'For you.'

She reached forward and pressed a hand to my arm. 'You will save the world.'

FORTY

The next day was a whirlwind of events. The press was en force, not just regional and state but national at the museum. Any other time this would've been a dream for both Abner and Bess, but with us trying to keep so many secrets, it was a nightmare, to say the least.

The grounds were darkened with men in black suits and earpieces. Crowds were held back by policemen and artificial barriers, while the costumed interpreters scurried around the museum.

The entire DC delegation, the president, Marta and my parents were staying at the Corrie Inn, which had been commandeered for the purpose and had strict security protocols in place.

I was sitting in the kitchen while my grandmother messed about making finger sandwiches and lemonade should my father stop by with a friend – you know, the president?

'Grams, you don't have to prepare snacks. I hardly think my dad would—'

'You never know.' She turned to face me. 'How do I look?'

She wore a yellow dress with a gathered waist, calf-length skirt and sheer sleeves that ballooned around her thin arms. 'Like a sunflower. Lovely, Grams.'

She'd pulled her hair back into a twist then bound into a bun with a jeweled hair pin, her face still glossy with face cream. Her lips pressed into a smile, and she nodded.

'I've met the president a few times,' I said, 'it's nothing to—'

'It's not that,' she said, her tone sharp. 'I've been thinking . . .' Her voice relaxed when she saw my startled expression. 'About my life. I was trying to go back and find pieces of me that belong to this ancient royal lineage, these women that can make magic . . .' Her face crumpled as she tried to make sense of it all. 'I can heal people.' Her unexpected words floated between us, soft and fuzzy with mysticism.

'What?'

She didn't speak, and I reached for something that made sense. 'Your teas? Your creams?'

'No.' Her headshake was firm. 'Those are just teas and creams
. . . When I was little, maybe three? Four? My mother – the woman
who raised me,' she clarified, 'had a bad headache. She had a history
of migraines, I recall her saying when I was older. And I remember
crawling onto her lap and placing my hands on either side of her
face for just a moment. And then I told her, she'd be fine now. Her
head would never hurt again.'

My grandmother looked at me. 'And it never did. That's when
she changed. She was always kind and loving, but she was also a
little afraid of me. One day, my father fell at work and hurt his
knee, and I went to him to lay my hand on his leg, and she yelled
at me. I was six then. She rushed across the room and pushed me
away from her husband. I fell to the floor and started crying.'

She balled up her hand, pressing her knuckles against her lips.
'And then she started crying and picked me up and held me. We
blubbered together. She told me she loved me, and that I was special,
and she was sorry she didn't mean to hurt me. But that I couldn't
do that again. That someone would see. Someone would tell. And
someone would come for me. Now I understand her fear.'

Her hand fell to her side. 'And I never did – heal anyone. Even
when I had the compulsion to do something. To help someone. To
alleviate their pain. I just taught myself to ignore it. And then I
grew up and I met Daphne and she gave me the book. And I started
making the recipes for family and friends. That's when I discovered
I enjoyed working with flowers and plants. A lavender tea to calm.
Or a peppermint tincture to soothe a scratchy throat. Not enchanted,
mind you. Just herbal remedies.'

'So, you *are* magic, Grandma.'

'I suppose so. But I've had a lifetime of pretending to be something I'm not. Suppressing a very important part of me.' She took
a calming breath. 'And I'll be facing my son for the first time
knowing the truth about who I am. Despite being adopted, I've
always had a strong sense of self. My parents gave that to me but
now . . .' She shook her head. 'I just don't know anymore.'

I went to her, reached for her hand. 'You're his mother. And my
grandmother.'

'And my mother's daughter,' she added softly. 'Not abandoned.
Not birthed by a woman who didn't love me and want me. I'm the
daughter of a woman who gave up everything to keep me safe. And
I never even knew it.'

'That's how she wanted it, Grams.'

She pressed her eyes closed, and a tear seeped out.

There was a knock at the door. I took a step and looked out the kitchen window. 'The car's here.'

She wiped her tears and forced her lips into a smile. 'I'm ready.'

My father had sent a chauffeured car for us, which helped us navigate the security lines and deposited us at VIP seating for family and friends of the speakers.

A podium was located in the center of the grassy quad with two sections divided by a walkway of ten rows of five white folding chairs for special guests, the museum staff, the town mayor and his staff and select media. The majority of the crowds were about two hundred yards away but would be able to hear what the president said through speakers.

I saw my mother first. Tall and willowy, a sparkling bronze dream of flat-ironed, silky, black hair, glossy nude lips and a sleek dress of burgundy silk I recognized as a Diane von Furstenberg. I settled beside her, whispering a greeting. 'Hi, Mom.'

Her grin was wide. 'Darling, you made it.' She air-kissed my cheek, then gave me a once-over, taking in my hair pulled into a high, braided ponytail, the olive green dress with thick straps, boat neck and skirt that skimmed my knees. I'd lined my eyes with kohl and mascara, dusted my cheek with bronzing powder and finished the look with bright red lip gloss. No way she could disapprove of a fiery red lip.

She tilted her head. 'You look nice.' My mother leaned forward and touched my grandmother's hand. 'Miss Fiona, nice to see you.'

My grandmother's expression was pained but she grimaced her way into a smile.

I looked around the crowded area. 'Where's Dad?'

'With President Williamson and the VR czar.'

'My, my . . .' My mother surveyed the crowd with a cool eye. 'Only the top media is represented.' She waved at various news anchors and TV magazine hosts. 'The gang's all here.'

I leaned in towards her ear. 'Were you never going to tell me about who we really are? About what we're capable of?'

'Darling, black girl magic has always been a thing. I was just waiting for you to discover it for yourself. It's better that way.'

'Your mother didn't tell you?'

'I figured it out when I was sixteen, and able to make boys and men do whatever I wanted.' She grinned, and I couldn't help but return the gesture.

I was settling into my seat when my mother made an exasperated noise.

'What's wrong?'

She scowled at her phone, then looked towards the perimeter of the grounds. 'My camera crew has arrived. Said they got wind of something big happening here.' She saw her two-man team lounging under a tree and waved. They two-finger saluted her back.

Her phone chimed again, and this time a sharp gasp escaped her lips. 'My God . . .' She showed me the screen. It was copy for her to use in an upcoming broadcast, presumably the one her camera crew were here to shoot.

It read: President Declares A State Of Emergency.

'What in the world?' I shared a questioning look with my mother, but then the president's band marched by playing 'Hail To The Chief'. We stood for the entrance of the president.

'I wouldn't worry about it,' my mother said. 'It's probably a mistake, the way famous people's obituaries are written in advance and occasionally shared before the death? Someone will get fired, I'm certain.' She quickly shoved her phone into her purse. 'I can't be seen texting while the president walks past, but as soon as he does, I'll contact my people.'

The president appeared flanked by his security detail, with Marta behind him and then my father. My mother stood taller, tossing her hair over her shoulders. My father saw me and winked while butter-flies were doing flybys in my stomach.

Abner appeared at the podium and introduced the president. I looked around and saw Bess on the periphery of the stage, with her grandmother and Reba a few rows behind me.

The president spoke about the tragedy of the fire, the importance of preserving our history and the uniqueness of Robbinsville in the American historical and cultural landscape. There was a round of applause, and then he introduced Marta, who he personally had appointed to the position of head of the VR initiative for the federal government.

I leaned in towards my mother as she retrieved her phone. 'Will you be able to speak with the president?'

'Yes,' she said, with a determined lift of her chin. 'He's agreed

to sit down with me at a local biscuit spot for an interview. Show
how "of the people" he is.'

I turned to my mother. 'I know you're well-connected but how
did you score an interview with the president that fast? You couldn't
have known that the fire would happen.'

'Of course not.' She began scanning her text messages. 'He and
Marta were always planning to come here to discuss their VR initiatives for small towns. Our interview was planned months ago.'

Months ago?

There was a round of applause for Marta. I tensed, wondering
what she would say. She surprised me by speaking about her brother
first.

'Most of you know my brother, Matthias Toliver, worked at this
museum. I grew up with him in this very town for the first three
years of our lives.'

I heard my mother murmur, 'What in the world?' Then the area
exploded with the sound of chiming phone notifications. Several
people made embarrassed motions and turned their phones off.

I was distracted by several men in black, no doubt Secret Service,
moving to the right of me. One spoke into an earpiece. 'Paul Bunyan
is moving in fifteen minutes. Cadillac One is in the west parking
lot. I repeat, Paul Bunyan moves in fifteen.'

Obviously, Paul Bunyan was the Secret Service code name for
the president, like Biden's was Celtic, Obama's was Renegade and
Trump's was Mogul. And I got it, he grew up in Alaska with a
family that worked in the logging industry. Ha ha, very cute but
something was going on.

The air crackled with tension, and people were whispering to
each other. 'Mom?'

'One sec, honey.' She didn't look up, instead her fingers flew
furiously over her screen. 'There may be a . . . situation.' She looked
up then and gave me a reassuring smile. Only I didn't feel comforted.

'We grew up in a house full of books and maps,' Marta was
saying. 'A love for history and science. Matty loved history, and he
loved Robbinsville. I am horrified to know he died in a fire, but
gratified to hear he died trying to save precious relics of our history.'

I found Bess's gaze and nodded, knowing she'd made up that
story for the press. Doubting that Marta believed it for a second.

'Our family is steeped in public service and civic duty,' she
continued.

If you could call witch-hunting a civic duty, I thought to myself.

'And while we both had a love for history, we both had an eye for the future, which is why we both went into the field of quantum science. Our parents divorced at a young age, and he lived with our father here, while I moved up north with my mother. But that didn't keep Matty and I from developing a strong bond.'

More phone notifications chimed. Not mine because I'd already had the foresight to turn it off, but something was happening around me as more and more people stared at their phones. I turned to my mother. 'What's going on?'

A Secret Service operative walked briskly by me talking into his watch, a detour from the normal earpiece they typically used. 'The cake is ready,' I heard him say as his words lifted on the wind and floated by me.

I picked up my phone and saw numerous news outlet alerts covering my screen. Someone gasped behind me. With nervous fingers, I unlocked my phone and clicked on the first message. 'Mom,' I hissed, my voice shaking. 'This says the vice president's helicopter crashed. A solar flare over California. No word on his condition.'

Frowning, she pressed the phone to her ear. 'Something major is going on right now.'

Would this be the cause of the state of emergency? Was this planned then, and someone had sent it too early? As horrible as the VP's helicopter crashing was it couldn't be the cause of a state of emergency. So what else was it?

Marta was still talking, her voice smooth and silky. '. . . Made more so by our shared interest in virtual reality. I was first exposed to the idea of a so-called dream reality when I spent time in the Yucatan and learned about the dream world of the Maya. It spurred me to delve into quantum science, and the rest as they say is history.' Her laugh bounced on the wind as a wave of nausea rolled over me.

Something else was bothering me. *The cake is ready.* That's what the man walking by me had just said. Sure, there could be cake at an event like this. But that wasn't the Secret Service's job. I twisted in my chair, scanned past the worried faces reading their phones, looking for catering trucks or waiters. But no, there was no food being served at this event. And no signs of a special presentation of cake at the end of the speeches.

'It was my brother's express desire to create a VR environment for this museum, and to also make Robbinsville a part of our Virtual City initiative. We are also starting a pilot program for small towns like Robbinsville. And with the support of the president, and in my brother's memory, I hope we can make that happen.'

'The cake is ready,' is what Matty had said when he was speaking to his sister in code. But what was it code for?

There was thunderous applause, and the press went wild with questions. I saw an aid rush to the president and whisper something in his ear. Surely, he was telling him about his vice president. His face fell, shadows crossed his solemn features and he nodded, gesturing for the aid to speak with Marta.

The aid scurried off, while the president waited a moment before looking at the audience.

The pool of media was larger than usual and at least fifty hands shot up while light bulbs went off. All of the top national media and some international were represented. A first for Robbinsville. 'The gang's all here,' my mother had said. *All of the guests have been invited.* Code for the media? My chest tightened.

'A party for Paul,' Marta had said. I inhaled sharply. Paul as in Paul Bunyan? Of course it was. The party for Paul was this pre-arranged speaking engagement. And now the cake was ready. What was the cake? A bomb? Or something else?

Without trying to alarm anyone, I searched the crowd looking for anything out of place.

My grandmother touched my arm. 'What's wrong?' she whispered.

'I'm not sure. I think something is planned to . . .' I searched for a word that didn't sound like screaming fire in a movie theater. 'Disrupt this event.' I scanned the area again, and this time I saw something. It was Red, dressed as a waiter. And he was pushing a cart with an actual large six-tier cake on it close to the podium where the president had returned, a solemn look on his face.

He cleared his throat and leaned into the microphone. 'My fellow Americans,' he began. 'It is with a deep sadness . . .'

I heard words whispered in my mind. *What's wrong? Are you OK? What can I do?*

I stilled, trying to clear my mind, but the words came again. I looked across the grounds and saw Bess staring at me. It was her talking to me but in my mind. Telepathically.

Bess, can you hear me?

I heard her laugh. Saw her eyes grow wide.

Oh my God. We are so witches. We're telepathic.

I wished we could kee-kee about this but there was no time. *We have a problem.*

I explained everything as quickly as possible and saw her searching the crowd from her place on the podium.

My grandmother touched my arm. *I can hear you too.*

Alarmed, I jerked my head her way. *You too?*

The president shared his news about the vice president and a buzz filled the area. He continued talking, giving a premature eulogy since none of the media had reported the VP as dead, only in a crash.

And me. That was my mother. Her eyes were on the stage, but she was all in my conversation. *The VP is assumed dead. Obviously, we have to stop this attack on the president,* she telepathed. *When you connected to the stone,* my mother explained, *you must've unlocked new abilities and then shared them with the rest of your Sisters in your immediate friends and family circle.*

My mother was as cool as a cucumber. Even telepathing. *A state of emergency is coming,* she continued. *Someone is planning some sort of catastrophe.*

I need to do something. What can I do? My breath was short, and I felt like my chest might explode from the pressure.

My grandmother reached for my hand. My mother took my other. Something strong and pure and comforting flowed through me at their touch. I calmed down and my breathing slowed.

Use your mental powers to see what's inside the cake, my grandmother suggested.

I have mental powers?

My grandmother smiled beside me. *Something tells me you do. We all do.*

I'm not sure how to do that, I countered.

Just use your imagination and see what happens. My grandmother's thoughts were so calming and encouraging, I lost all fear.

In my mind's eye, I imagined myself standing up, walking to the cart. I knew immediately the device was not hidden in the cake, rather, it was under the cake on a second floor of the cart and covered with a white tablecloth.

I could see under the cloth that there was a sleek metallic cylinder, about eighteen inches in length and six inches in diameter. High-frequency antennae encircled its upper portion.

Anxiety gripped my chest like a vise. *What am I looking at?*

Connected to the cylinder was a transparent chamber made of reinforced glass. A complex array of cables, coils, and superconducting materials were intricately connected to the ionization chamber. The modulator was shielded within a metallic casing to protect sensitive components. Multiple dials, digital displays, and controls were affixed to the casing.

How did I know all this? *I can't do it,* I telepathed in a panic.

Focus, I heard my grandmother say.

I took a deep breath and tuned into the device. Next to the cylinder was a high-tech control panel, and the device was powered by a network of thick cables and high-capacity transformers. I could also see something I somehow knew was a liquid cooling system, with radiators and coolant tanks to dissipate excess heat generated during experiments.

I can see it, I told them. *And it's activated.*

Is it a bomb? my mother asked.

I turned back to the device. It wasn't a bomb. What was it?

The abstract from the patent I'd read online and hadn't understood manifested for me, and I suddenly knew exactly what the device was and how it worked. And what would happen if I didn't stop it. It wasn't a bomb – but just as devastating.

Phones went off again. Notifications chiming like fairy bells all around us. This time I was afraid to look.

'The media,' my mother began, her voice full of dread, 'is reporting that the president has placed the country under a state of emergency.'

'It's a lie,' my grandmother whispered. 'We can see him in front of us and he's done no such thing.'

It was the device. It was going to *create* the state of emergency.

You have to focus, my grandmother urged me again.

I was trembling with nerves. The device operated on principles akin to a supercharged microwave oven. It would emit invisible waves of energy that were so potent that, upon contact with the atmosphere, they would induce a substantial increase in temperature.

As these effects intensified, like a powerful, invisible tempest, the conditions would become so extreme that it would be like a tiny sun manifested briefly on Earth.

'It's going to create a solar flare,' I whispered to my mother.

She looked confused. 'Like the one that caused the VP's crash?' She showed me her phone. 'They're saying he's confirmed dead.'

My grandmother heard me too. 'Can we stop it?'

My mother's face hardened. 'I've been covering the devastation these solar flares have been causing across the nation,' she began, her voice low. Incredulous. 'They're man-made? This destruction is purposeful? Someone just murdered our VP.'

I recalled what Marta had told me in her office. That NASA predicted a massive solar flare would disrupt our electronic systems and power grids forcing everyone to go online to conserve energy. Making her virtual reality initiative a necessity. The prediction was fake. But DRIA was going to create enough devastation with smaller flares that people would believe it – and dive into VR of their own free will.

I had to stop this. But how? And how much time did I have?

The Secret Service agent said the president was leaving in fifteen minutes, which meant the event would probably take place before he left for the most impact. Otherwise why stage a party for Paul at all, as Marta and Matty had discussed?

No, he'd be here, which meant I had less than ten minutes to figure this out. I sensed that I had power and abilities, but without knowing exactly what I could do and how to do it, I was stumped as to the best and fastest way to deactivate the device. Now was a horrible time to try and test newfound talents.

Something caught my eye to the left of me. I glanced over and saw Gabe standing under a tree. He was watching me, eyes crinkled at the corners in concern. I conjured a smile and waved at him, and tried to pretend like I wasn't trying to figure out my superpowers before a device that used quantum science destroyed our electrical grid.

He waved back, just as a large dark cloud moved over the grounds blocking out the sun and casting shadows on the crowd. I saw him glance at the sky, a questioning look on his face.

And I took a breath. That was it. I'd used quantum science. What had Matty said? He was a sorcerer because he knew how to manipulate the source code, the building blocks of the universe?

I suddenly felt a strange, subtle vibration, like the resonance of an otherworldly hum in my body. Bess was suddenly in my mind, her energy panicky and nervous. *Can you feel that?*

Yes.

I turned to the cart, closed my eyes, imagining I could see the device underneath. And then I *could* see the device once again. The text and images of the patent came back to me, as if it was imprinted on my brain. I'd only scanned it very quickly but the knowledge was there. All I had to do was access it. I could see and identify each part. *The resonance emitter. The ionization chamber. The electromagnetic field modulator. The control interface. The power supply and cooling system.* I could see them. And I understood how they worked.

The air swirling around appeared to thicken, like a heavy fog had settled over the crowd. It was cloying and moist . . . like stepping into a steam room. And the temperature was rising.

Beads of sweat appeared on my face and began rolling into my eyes. I could hear murmuring in the crowd about the unexpected heat.

With my hands outstretched, palms up, I tuned my awareness to the essence of the device. Despite it being made of minerals and metals, it was there. I could sense it. All things even machines had something we might call a soul or spirit that vibrated and hummed with energy.

The faint traces of quantum energy became more vivid, like a symphony of colors and sensations playing out before me. The energy, the essence, the life force of the device manifested itself as a yellowy-green light illuminating around the device like a ghostly aura.

The wind around us began to pick up, making a howling noise as gusts of air moved through the seating. Cries erupted from the audience as hats were lost and programs were ripped off laps and out of hands.

As I connected with the machine, I sensed the gazillion vibrating nano parts of the device, so tiny there was space between them. And it was in that space that I was able to fill it with my own ethereal energy. My own life force.

My . . . magic.

But then I began to hear something. Something that distracted me. It was phone notifications. Beginning to go off all around me. My mother's phone. My grandmother's phone. My own.

I didn't want to lose my connection to the device. I was so close to stopping it from creating a—

My mother gasped beside me.

What is it?

The crowd began to buzz with noise and Marta had stopped talking.

'It's the media again, sending out more alerts.' My mother spoke aloud.

My eyes were still closed, palms out, and I was taking deep breaths trying to maintain the connection. It was still there, I was still joined to the device, and it had stopped its work, stopped amassing energy, but I wasn't sure how much longer I could hold on . . .

'It's happening,' my mother cried out, her voice full of alarm. 'NASA just sent out alerts. A massive solar flare is about to hit.'

From far off, a siren loud and lingering wailed its warning of impending doom.

'They're recommending everyone to shelter in place,' my mother continued over the siren. 'Unplug all electrical devices and turn off all cell phones and smart devices.'

It's not happening, Mom. Not if I can stop it.

But I could hear people moving around, standing up, media running to take calls, send messages just as the wind increased. My hair came undone, its pins flying into the gathering storm and my curls floated upward, raging with the violent currents of the wind.

A Secret Service agent ran past me. 'Paul Bunyan is on the move. Let's go. Let's go. Let's *go*.'

I have to get your grandmother out of this heat. It's over a hundred degrees.

No, we need to stay with her, my grandmother responded. *Stay with her. Hold her hand. We'll keep her strong when her energy wanes.*

I stood and felt my chair fly away on the wind. My mother and grandmother stood with me, both wrapping an arm around me while I kept my palms out. And I did feel their energy coursing into me, making me stronger, urging me on.

I returned to the inner workings of my mind, the universe within, the place where I could manipulate the building blocks of the universe, and filled in the spaces between the vibrating minuscule parts of the device, then covered it, like I was casting a net of my own magical making.

I felt like a conductor, spinning and weaving with ethereal energy spun from my own fingertips, the nano parts of the machine, so small you couldn't see them with the naked eye, but I could see them in my mind's eye. And they were like tiny, synchronized dancers, following a rhythm known only to the quantum universe.

I felt their vibrations, their movements, and their resonance in my fingers, my hands, my arms spiraling and moving into the rest of my body. I focused my intent on the device's parts. I visualized their quantum vibrations, initially distinct from my own, gradually shifting to match my frequency. It was so subtle as to be imperceptible, but I could feel it, sense it. Like two instruments tuning to the same pitch.

I was becoming one with the machine. I could do this. I could turn the device off.

The sensation was incredible. As I inhaled, I felt the device inhale with me. As I exhaled, it mirrored my breath. We were in perfect harmony, like a conductor leading an orchestra through a magnificent crescendo. I had the source code at my fingertips, and it did as I commanded.

Finally, with a sense of mastery over the quantum symphony unfolding within the device, I began to issue commands. In my mind's eye, I could see the particles respond, shifting and rearranging themselves according to my will. They were no longer individual entities but extensions of my intent.

But the heat was intense, I felt like I was on fire. Tears ran from my eyes. But I focused. I could send the threads of energy attached to my fingers connected to the dancing particles of the machine. And then the particles hovered in a state of suspended animation, awaiting my directive. With a calm but resolute mind, I issued the final command.

I bid it to stop.

And it did.

The wind died down.

The heat lifted.

The heavy, wet air floated away.

And the dark clouds dissipated, revealing a perfect blue sky with a bright yellow sun glowing above us.

My mother and grandmother were unharmed. They hugged each other and then me. Bess ran over to check on us. My father was walking around with purpose, doing whatever politicians do in a crisis. When he saw me watching him, he waved. Abner was barking orders to a clean-up crew, and the Secret Service and the president were long gone.

It looked like the worst was over. But where was Marta? She was the head of DRIA. This was her plan. The Order of Apophis' plan.

The grounds were a mess, and I stepped over paper, broken chairs and other debris. Audience members that were still here looked windblown and sweaty. Not to mention confused and scared. I went to the cart. The device was still there but it was damaged with smoke curling around from its parts.

I scanned the area, and then I saw her. Marta was run-walking to the parking lot. I began to run after her, jumping over broken chairs, trying not to knock anyone over. I reached the parking lot just as she jumped into a car and careened towards the exit.

I ran to my car, jumped inside and followed her. I wasn't sure what I'd do when I found her. If I found her. But she had to answer for what she'd done. What she'd hoped to do.

She could not be allowed to go free.

FORTY-ONE

She was headed downtown.

I followed, weaving in and out of the slow-moving traffic ignoring the honks of other vehicles and hoping a local police officer didn't try to stop me. Because today would be the day I ran from the cops.

She had to be going at least seventy in a thirty-five. *Where did she think she was going?*

My phone rang, and I saw Gabe's number on the screen. I debated for half a second, then answered through my car's Bluetooth system.

'Hey,' I answered, trying not to sound like I was in a high-speed chase.

'Hey yourself,' he greeted. 'Just checking in on you. I tried to find you after that . . . solar flare, I guess? But you were gone. You OK?'

My eyes were on Marta's car, and she'd turned onto Main Street, almost turning her car on two wheels to make the fast turn. I followed suit, thankfully keeping all my wheels on the road. The Jag drove like a dream.

'Yeah, I'm good. Thanks.'

Marta was parking on the street, and I found a spot across the street and a few cars down.

'You sound busy . . .' He trailed off. 'Distracted. You weren't hurt, were you?'

'No, but I am in the middle of something, so . . .' I watched as Marta jumped out of her car with a small leather bag clutched in her hands. 'Call you back?'

'Yeah, sure.' His voice was hesitant, like he didn't want to end the call.

So I did. 'Bye, Gabe.' Hopefully he wouldn't take offense.

I jumped out of my car and ran after Marta. She was headed to QLabs, I realized. Why would she go there?

She looked over her shoulders at me and badged into the entrance. She grinned at me before stepping inside, the thick steel door slamming behind her.

I reached the door and stared at it. I took a breath and looked at the keyless entrance. I touched it and felt a spark as something in me spread into the lock. There was a buzzing sound, a flashing light like the device wasn't functioning properly. An error code showed on the screen and the door opened.

I stared at the open door and then my fingertips before entering the building.

I remembered it from when it was a coffee shop, but the layout was totally different now. What used to be the café area was now a reception area. I heard a noise and looked past the reception desk. Marta had to be back there.

Quietly, I moved forward past several offices filled with sleek, minimalistic furniture, digital devices, computers and other tech I couldn't recognize. I heard another noise, saw the door to the maintenance closet swinging.

I followed, finding a staircase behind a shelf of cleaning supplies left open. Marta didn't seem to care that I was following her. A sense of urgency filled my chest, and I ran down the stairs holding my cell phone as a light in the dark space.

And then I saw her. Almost like a shadow in the dark, she stood at the mouth of a tunnel with endless darkness stretching behind her. It looked just like the ones under the museum. I scanned the area with the flashlight on my phone and saw drawings on the walls.

She was breathing heavily, her bag under her arm. 'You can't follow me.' She spoke into the silence. 'Not where I'm going.'

'You're not going anywhere.' I pressed nine one one on my phone, then noticed the lack of bars. No service. I groaned in disbelief, as my anger flared. 'You're a coward. Afraid to face what you've done. You had the vice president killed? Were planning solar flares so your VR plan could be implemented? What is wrong with you?'

She turned to look into the darkness of the tunnel before facing me. 'It was a good plan. Still is. And just because I'm gone doesn't mean someone else with vision won't come along and implement it.'

'I won't let that happen.' My chest tightened as I made the vow. 'I'm going to track down the members of Apophis and make sure you and your kind can't destroy our world.'

A brittle laugh echoed in the cavernous area. 'Good luck with that, witch.' She took a deep breath. 'If you follow me, you lose everything,' she warned. 'But me? I can find my brother.'

What? Was she crazy?

'I can start over,' she continued. 'I'm no longer a threat to you . . . Just let me go.'

'Where do you think—'

She stepped inside the tunnel, disappeared into the inky black.

I ran after her and grabbed her wrist. She shrieked for me to let go but I held tight. No way I was going to—

But then I saw a shimmer in the air, heard a sucking sound like pulling an object out of a bowl of jelly as a strong force pulled her inside the tunnel . . . and me along with her if I didn't release her.

A million voices inside my head screamed for me to let go. I listened, and allowed her fingers to slide through my grasp.

'Marta,' I called out, my voice extra loud to my ears and bouncing off the walls of the cavern. 'Where are you?'

The silence that followed was eerie.

Where the hell had she gone that fast? I peered into the dark but could see nothing.

And then I saw it. Something like a group of fireflies . . . or maybe fairies . . . floated into the air, flickering like bioluminescent worms in an undersea cave. I took several steps back until I was well away from the tunnel opening.

I held up a hand, watching the fairy-like particles float around me, settle at my feet and then disappear into the black.

My God, she'd escaped through a time portal.

FORTY-TWO

I didn't tell anyone about Marta, except for my grandmother and Daphne. Someone in DC would have to spin her disappearance, but that wasn't my problem. Today was a new day, and I had bigger fish to fry. Literally, the biggest fish.

My mother sat across from the president.

We were all crammed into a tiny biscuit shop filled with card tables and folding chairs. Fifty kinds of biscuits, from liver pudding, fried bologna to chicken fried steak scrawled on a blackboard menu.

Townsfolk were strategically placed behind the president in various states of casualness. One man was reading the local paper. A family shared a stack of biscuits, while two women gossiped over jam biscuits.

My mother's camera crew, with all their hot lights and white backdrops and shiny foil reflectors, crowded around her, while she sat unbothered, beautiful and calm in a teal pantsuit with a necklace of chunky aquamarine and teak nuggets. I had to give it to her, she was good at her job.

I sat at a counter on a stool out of view of the cameras, listening to my mother question the president about why the media had received false news of a state of emergency. I picked up my phone, making sure the recording app was open and ready to record.

He fumbled the question but ultimately blamed it on a junior press secretary who'd been immediately fired.

She pressed him on why he eulogized the vice president before knowing he was actually dead. He blamed that on an aid who gave him bad intel. She'd been fired too.

And when asked point-blank about the device built by QLabs

and placed at the museum, he said it was a new weather manipulation device designed to ensure a beautiful sunny day when rain had been predicted. It had simply gone haywire, and with a chuckle, he'd added, it was back to the drawing board for that design. While many news watchers would believe him, I knew the conspiracy theorists would have a field day with that revelation. Fake or not.

When the interview was over, my mother slid out of her seat, and I slid in it before the Secret Service detail could stop me.

The president recognized me and gave his agents a friendly wave. 'She's fine. This is the Speaker's daughter.'

They stepped back but not too far away, while I searched the president's face for signs of culpability. Remorse. Regret.

When the townsfolk and extra camera crew were hustled out, I began recording on my cell phone with the case closed so he couldn't see anything. I asked him if he knew about the Order of Apophis.

His eyes stretched wide, and he scanned the area around us. He leaned in, the fluffy white hair on top of his head almost touching mine. 'You're playing a dangerous game, young lady,' he said, his voice deep and sonorous. 'These people are not to be played with.'

Taking a deep breath, I settled in my seat. 'Neither is a Daughter of Hathor.'

His eyebrows shot up, a look of concern on his face. 'I've had to do things I'm not proud of to get to where I am today. You couldn't possibly understand.'

'I understand you're complicit in killing your vice president.'

'No,' he hissed, his voice both panicky and guttural. 'Don't say that. *Don't* say that. I tried to get him to come around, told him what could happen if he didn't.' He splayed his palms wide. 'He refused to play ball.'

'That's how you rationalize the murder of a good man?' He flinched at my words, but I wasn't done. 'How many people would have died if that solar flare had been allowed to activate?'

He bowed his head and closed his eyes, giving a deep exhale before looking at me.

An agent stepped close, and he raised a hand and flicked him away.

'I had no choice. These people . . . are rotten. Devious. Brutal.' His voice had changed to whiny, begging. Unbecoming of a president. 'There are things in my past . . . they knew about them and told me if I didn't do what they wanted, they'd be leaked to the news.' His blue eyes were watery. 'My wife. My children . . . not to mention my constituents. I just couldn't.'

'No. You could. You just chose the easy way out.'

His voice lowered another octave. 'What do you want from me?'

I held up the cell phone, case opened. 'I just recorded this conversation.'

His eyes flashed. 'No.'

'Yes. And I'm going to give it to my mother to share with her news anchor friends, if you don't decide to do the right thing and step down from your position as POTUS.'

'Give it to me.' His voice was hoarse with emotion. He reached for my hand, held it tight.

I yanked my hand free of his, and the agents near us moved as a unit to crowd our table. He rounded on them. 'For the love of God, get back.' His face had turned red with anger and spittle flew from his lips. 'Give me space.'

The agents moved away a couple of yards, faces hard, lips thin looking at me like I was the bad guy. I scowled at them. 'Hey, I'm not the threat here.' But they only glared at me like they were robots with one program.

'You can't do this to me,' the president continued. 'I'll do better. I'll fix things. I'll begin by dismantling the VR—'

I stood. 'No. You'll walk outside this biscuit shop where the media is still waiting for you. And you'll tell them you have an announcement to make.'

Tears splashed down his face. Angry or sad, I couldn't tell. Also, didn't care.

'If I do this,' he called after me as I slowly made my way out of the diner, 'without a new vice president being elected . . .' He stopped, realization smacking him in the face like a wave of icy cold water. 'The Speaker of the House is next in line. Your father will become the president.'

I stopped at the front door and smiled at him. 'Yes, I know.'

FORTY-THREE

We waited until the cover of night.

Still dressed in our black dresses and suits from the funeral, me, my grandmother, father and mother, Abner, Bess and her grandmother, Reba and Daphne all walked in a line across the museum grounds.

Three days after what the media was still calling 'Mayhem at the Museum', we'd finally lain Isla, my great-grandmother to rest with words, songs and music from the Daughters of Hathor, a special ceremony that sent the Daughter on her way with love and gratitude, releasing her back into the ether from which she first came.

The sky was a bruised purple dotted with twinkling specks of light, and the moon was hidden behind darker amorphous shapes. A perfect night to crown a queen.

By conventional terms we were seven witches and two men traveling through secret gardens to get to hidden staircases to find underground tunnels. But we finally made it, with Daphne making a mysterious call right before we descended underground.

The way lit by lanterns, we found the device. I revealed the stone and we all stared at it. In the dark, it seemed to give off an ethereal glow, almost as if it shimmered from within.

My grandmother cleared her throat. 'The ceremony was lovely, Daphne. Thank you for arranging it all.'

Daphne dipped her head modestly. 'It was a long time coming. I'm glad we could finally send our sister on her way.'

There was a sound in the hall, and I turned to see the glow of a light approaching us. I tensed.

'Don't worry. He's invited,' Daphne said.

And Gabe appeared at the entrance. 'I'm not too late, am I?' He searched the room until his gaze landed on mine.

Well, well.

'You made it.' Abner extended a hand. 'Come on in, brother.'

'This is not the easiest place to find, but the map helped.' He found Daphne in the dimness. 'Thanks for that.'

I eyed at him, wondering why he was here. 'You're a . . .'

'Member of the Sons of Horus, yes. As was my father, and his father . . . it's the reason why Josiah—'

'I get it,' I interrupted, crossing my arms, wanting to be angry with him but instead only feeling a thrill of excitement. 'But all this time, you could've said something.'

He grinned down at me. 'Like what?'

Like what indeed.

'I wasn't sure what you knew,' he explained. 'You certainly weren't forthcoming with information.'

'Good,' Daphne said. 'She's not supposed to tell anyone without already knowing they are one of us.'

Gabe had a leather tote across his chest, and he pulled back the flap and brought out a wooden case.

'That looks like—'

'My writing box,' my grandmother finished for me, her voice lifting in surprise.

'But why—'

Gabe stepped forward, until he was right in front of me, and everyone circled around us, shining their light until a blaze of light luminated the area around me and Gabe. When I'd first met him and told him I had the box, he'd said Josiah designed it for a daughter. *A Daughter.*

He opened the box, displaying the velvet-lined tray inside, ran his hand across it to show me there was no way to move the lining. 'Now you try it.'

I looked at him. 'If you can't do it, why do you think I can?'

'Just try,' he urged.

I reached forward, my hand on top of the velvet lining. I felt a whoosh of cold air, and the velvet disappeared. And in its place was a thin circular band of gold studded with a series of jewels. 'I don't understand.'

'You're of the direct bloodline. You've been imprinted by the stone. Only you can retrieve the crown from the case.'

'It's one of the House of David Crown Jewels,' Daphne explained.

'And Gabe?' I eyed him with even more interest.

'Is a Regal Keeper, a member of Sons of Horus tasked with keeping the royal ceremonial objects together and in good condition.'

As if on cue, he held out his hands and Daphne gave him the case to hold. He took it, inspecting it from all angles.

I seriously wanted to make a joke right now, but the moment felt way too . . . momentous for that. Instead, I tamped down my sarcasm. 'You lost the crown?'

He looked up from the tiara. 'My ancestor misplaced the case,' he corrected. Then grinned. 'And I found it.'

'I'm afraid that's my fault,' Daphne said, tone apologetic. 'When I brought Fiona forward, I took it. The cookbook and the crown.'

I gazed down at the royal artifact. 'The crown I get. But a cookbook?'

She huffed, half in exasperation, half amusement. 'It's not *just* a cookbook. There's secret information encoded in the recipes. Information we'll need in coming days.'

My grandmother chuckled. 'So not just apple pies and the best times to plant sweet potatoes?'

'There's a bit more in there. Yes.'

'The case,' Gabe said, his eyes on the ancient relic.

'During our travel through time, the case was lost, and it ended up in Robbinsville but at the wrong period. I had feelers out for a case that fit the description, and after I'd been here about twenty-five years I found it at a thrift store. Someone'd found it on the riverbanks and brought it in. It was suggested to your husband,' she looked at my grandmother, 'that it might make a nice gift for you.'

'And it was,' my grandmother replied, her voice tender with memories. 'He gave it to me for our fifth anniversary.'

'Seems like it's found its way to you no matter what,' my mother observed.

'Sidney Grace Taylor, come forth,' Daphne said, her voice huskier than usual.

My mother kissed me on the cheek, and I stepped forward. I noticed Daphne's glamour had dropped and her real, much older face appeared in the darkness along with a voice change. If anyone else noticed, they didn't say a word.

'Normally, the role of crowning our queen would go to the eldest Sister, not a scribe, but in this instance –' her gaze landed on Abner for a moment – 'I am the eldest by far,' she chuckled. 'So, I will do the honors.' She held out her hand for the crown.

Gabe lifted the crown out of the case. It glowed in the lamplight, and the colored stones, blue, green, red, purple, white and yellow, shone like bright bursts of light in the darkness.

I sat on the stone and bowed my head. Daphne placed the crown with its jewels dangling down upon my head. One jewel between my eyebrows, one at either temple and three curling around the base of my neck. For a moment, I was reminded of the VR headset with its circlet and hanging crystals, the difficulty Marta had settling it around my mane of curls.

Daphne dragged her fingers softly over my lids, and I closed my eyes. She began to chant. Somehow I knew the words and began to chant them with her. They weren't English or any language I'd ever heard before, but the sounds were soft and melodic.

As we chanted, I sensed the light within the stone growing stronger. I opened my eyes, just as an orb of green light shot from under me.

Everyone in the room collectively took a step back and I was alone in the center of the room seated on the stone. Unbelievably, I felt myself rising off the stone, just an inch or so and hovering in the air with strong vibrations coursing through my body. Pinpricks of energy ran through my backside and thighs flowing up to the crown of my head.

A force like sleepiness closed my lids again, and images rose before my eyes, of kings and queens crowned before me. And then the stone began to vibrate, with an accompanying low vibration filling the room. There was a high-pitched squeal, and then the room went silent.

I slid back onto the stone.

Another moment of silence, and then Daphne cleared her throat. 'It is done.'

I tried to stand, but my legs were wobbly. My mother ran to my side.

'No,' Daphne said, her voice firm. 'Let her rise alone. She must do it herself.'

My mother sniffed, her response to what she thought of Daphne's command, but took a step back.

I felt a little queasy. 'I'm OK. Just a little shaky.' I lifted myself off the stone and stood, feeling the weight of the crown on my head. Everyone stared at me, and I lifted my chin higher, feeling spikes of something like energy coursing through my limbs.

Gabe faced me square, smiling down at me. He lifted the crown off my head, with my mother rushing forward to detangle my curls from the circlet. I laughed, embarrassed by Gabe's intense gaze and my mother's attention, and a tear slid down my grandmother's cheek.

Gabe carefully placed it back into the box. 'Wave your hand across it.'

This time, I didn't hesitate, confident in my ability. I did so, and the velvet lining reappeared.

He snapped the box shut.

My mother looked at Daphne. 'Now what?'

Daphne turned to look at my father. 'You're soon to become president. And your daughter will help you take back our world from the Order of Apophis.'

Gabe stood nearby. I somehow felt closer to him, a connection snaking between us and binding us together. I touched his hand. 'What's next for you?'

His gaze was warm and familiar. 'I told you I like to find old things, but not just cars. I'm on a quest to find the rest of the regalia. It's missing, and you'll need them.'

'Oh yeah? What's next on your list?'

'A wand. A silver-gilt wand.'

I couldn't help but giggle. 'I have a wand?'

'Yes. A silver wand was found with the Honours Of Scotland in 1817 by Sir Walter Scott but has since gone missing. It's our wand, that somehow found its way to the Scottish crown jewels. We need it back. Rather, you need it.'

'For what?'

He grinned. 'To take down the baddies.'

FORTY-FOUR

I walked through the hallway of the main house with a large empty cardboard box in hand. I was packing up.

I'd found the Stone of Scone, and much more in the bargain. But with my father stepping in as president, I felt like I was needed in DC. With payment for my services minus taxes deposited in my account – thank you, Abner – I planned on calling Dr Philippi. She had every reason to end my furlough now.

Glancing at the paintings of the Robbins family as I made my way to my office, I acknowledged the empty space for Elias, but stopped when I saw Susannah's. Her smile was enigmatic. Mona Lisa had nothing on her. She had secrets. A magical heritage. If it wasn't for her, my great-great grandmother Isla, and my father and I wouldn't be in the position to save our country, dare I say our world?

I found the painting of Isaac, Elias' younger brother. Abner was descended from his line, since Elias and Susannah had never had children. Wait, no, that wasn't true. My grandmother was descendant from Elias, which made me a Robbins. I looked around the big house, twirled around in a circle. This house was my legacy too.

I continued down the hallway until I reached my office. Then I stopped. Both Marta and Matty had said Elias and Susannah didn't have children. Abner was descended from Elias' brother, Isaac. But when we were searching the gardens and had come upon the family memorial, we'd found a bench for Elias' younger brother. He'd died in infancy with no name.

I went back to the Robbins' family painting. Studied the one of Isaac. This couldn't be the younger brother; he was in his late twenties.

I frowned. *Hold up.*

It also meant that Abner was not descended from Elias' brother— 'Isaac' Robbins was a fiction.

I returned to my office where I'd been packing up my things. Setting the box on my desk, I began putting desktop items in the box still thinking about Abner. *Who was he really? And what was he hiding?*

My pen holder. A paperweight . . .

I paused, seeing him mopping his brow. The handkerchiefs always white, with delicate stitching of a flower. No . . . a fleur de lis. It was a fleur de lis on his handkerchiefs. And the fleur de lis represented Susannah, didn't it? Hadn't Daphne said Elias had always called Susannah his fleur de lis? So why did Abner have Elias' handkerchiefs?

I returned to my packing. The handkerchiefs must be a family heirloom. I opened up my desk drawers, looking for more items to pack. Odd that Abner could keep up with handkerchiefs but somehow lose a large painting of the patriarch of the family.

I closed the drawer and went to the bookshelf, pulling off the few books I'd brought with me. When I'd asked Abner about the painting one time, he'd acted strange. Began sweating and mopping his brow, something I knew could be a tell for someone lying. Or maybe a medical condition.

Was Abner lying about what happened to the painting? But if he was, what could possibly be the reason?

And if Abner wasn't the son of Elias' brother, who was he really?

I set the box at my feet and turned on my laptop. Llew had a file on Abner, one that I'd looked at but hadn't given much attention to. Matty confessed to having him killed because he was close to sharing information they didn't want public. With his schematics of the coffee shop in his files, it made sense that he was killed because he'd learned about the time travel research QLabs was doing.

But with everything said and done, it didn't make sense that he'd be looking into Abner. Why did he have a dossier on him? Had he discovered something Abner'd rather keep quiet? Was that why they were really fighting?

I'd sent myself a copy of Llew's files for safekeeping, so I found it in my email account and opened the email. There was one folder I hadn't read. I'd start with that, and then re-read Abner's.

I selected the folder and waited for the contents to appear. I blinked. I was looking at a photograph of . . . me. They were *all* photographs of me. Walking into the church. The library. On Main Street . . . And there were others from my time in DC. Based on the coat I was wearing in one image, it was a year ago.

I sat back in my chair. Llew was stalking me? But *why*? There were close-ups of my face, longshots from across the street . . . I moved through the files, trying to find something for context. They were all JPEGs. But then I found a document. Taken from the Smithsonian.

Why would he have this? He'd left there over thirty years ago to become a professor. It was a report about my findings, the one I'd been told to hush up. Written by my supervisor, it contained the questions I'd asked about the artifact and described me as . . . *potentially problematic?*

I screwed my face up. What the hell? And why did Llew have this? The document was stamped in red block letters: Special Projects Division.

Was I the special project?

There were no other revelations in the folder, so I returned to Abner's file, skimming his biographical details. I read the second article and noticed Abner's graduation year was different. Off by a few years. Possibly a typo or just a mistake? I went to the museum website and read Abner's bio. Then read it again. His college graduation year was different still. Three different dates for his college graduation. Why the discrepancy?

I sat back in my chair, lost in thought. And then I went to the Robbins' College website, logged into my alumni account and

accessed the online yearbooks. I went to the first year mentioned
in an article and searched for Abner.

He wasn't there.

I searched for the second year.

He wasn't there either.

So obviously, the last year had to be the correct year. I began
the search and waited for the results to appear.

Huh.

No Abner Robbins. Did Abner never go to college, or did he just
not want anyone to know when he went? So many secrets . . .

I stood, feeling restless and antsy, like I was missing something. I'd
found the Stone of Scone. I could figure out who Abner really was.

I moved around my office, thinking of the times I'd spent with
Abner. Had he done or said anything I could use to find the painting?
Abner in his office. Abner on the plane. Abner in DC. Abner in
early American clothes. Abner looking oddly out of place when he
wore jeans and a polo.

I saw him after his fight with Llew. Angry. Distraught. I'd thought
I'd seen white streaked in his hair, his beard. But the next moment
it was black again. What had he said when I commented on the
color? He'd had a touch-up.

Touch-up.

Who else had used that same language? I closed my eyes and
saw Daphne sitting on my grandmother's couch. She'd said she had
to give her glamour touch-ups periodically . . .

But Abner would've meant touch-up his beard. With hair dye. Clearly,
he was dying his hair. The shiny jet-black color of his hair was a little
too perfect to be real. Like an actor. A matinee idol from the past.

From the past.

Images whizzed by my mind's eye. Daphne running forward in
time with a baby, searching for safety and security. Marta escaping
into the past hoping for a fresh start. Of Abner mopping his brow
with a handkerchief. Sweating. Always sweating. And then . . . Abner
dressed in colonial clothes. Giving a courtly bow here and there.

I returned to my chair and looked at Llew's article on Elias' death.

Elias who had made his fortune, not growing crops on a plantation but by discovering and mining limestone. Abner didn't want
to discuss that part of his family's history either. Why?

The article was dated to 1820, the year Isla was hanged. The
headline read: 'Local Landowner And Town Founder Elias

Robbins Reported Dead After Mining Tunnels Collapse'. I began to read.

First Elias went missing. It was known that he'd gone to the mines to oversee the site, but he'd gone before dusk alone just as his workers were returning to their homes. When he didn't come back that evening, his plantation manager sent a search party for him. The tunnel collapse was discovered, and a search and dig out continued throughout the next two days.

His body was never found, and he was assumed to be dead.

Where were these mining tunnels? I went to my internet browser and found a map of the now defunct mining tunnels the Robbins family owned. There couldn't be that many tunnels in the area. Why hadn't Abner mentioned that the tunnels we'd found could've been related to his family's limestone mining past?

I studied the underground passageways. They led away from the museum property going towards the river, not where I'd expect them to intersect with the ones hiding the Stone of Scone. But that didn't mean the tunnels on the museum grounds, and the ones that went under Main Street, didn't connect with the tunnels dedicated to mining.

Tunnels that led to at least one known time portal. The one under QLabs.

This I knew was all somehow related to the painting.

Bess told me Abner had been angry with her when she found documents about the family's mines. That any proof about the family's mining past was kept in a place that only he knew about. *Where was that place?*

And in all of the excitement of the last few days, I'd forgotten about the major bomb Thea had shared with me. She'd told me that President Madison *never* visited the museum. Never came to Robbinsville. Which meant he had nothing to do with the letter or the Daughters of Hathor. It was all a lie.

Then Gabe said Josiah and Elias had worked on the letter together. But who made up the lie?

Who'd written the Madison letter? And what did Abner know?

I finished packing up my office, locked up and headed down the hall. The museum was closed, and the parking lot was empty. I placed my box in the back of my car and drove towards the river-front and Willoughby Park.

Parking on the street this time, I went directly to the park Gabe and I had visited. It was late and only a few people were on the well-lit riverfront. No one was in the park. Just me and a cluster of lightning bugs that whimsically seemed to be lighting my way.

I walked the cobblestone path around the park, past the large metal sculptures, past the statue and the crumbling foundation of the old house. I stopped in front of one sculpture in particular. The one Gabe said stood on top of the old house's cellar.

I studied the piece of abstract art, wondering what it was. What it meant, and would Josiah even approve. To me, it seemed like he might appreciate classic lines and concrete expression, but surely the Willoughby family had input in the type of art installed in the park.

I walked around the art piece, casually glancing over my shoulder to make sure no one was watching me and then I laid my hand on it. It began to vibrate, and I used the frequency of the particles to find areas of the work that might unlock or fold or otherwise change shape to allow for movement.

I found it. One of the spikes on the sculpture retracted when I pushed it. Another spike folded upward and a third rotated in a circle. I stepped back and the sculpture glided to the side, revealing the entryway to the cellar.

Exactly where I thought it would be.

FORTY-FIVE

As I descended the stairs of the cellar, I thought I understood.

Elias and Josiah were in this subterfuge together. They'd written the letter together. Daphne had to be involved as well.

I reached out and found a railing to guide my descent. Using my phone's light I made my way to the base, ran my hands along the wall and found a modern-day light switch.

I turned it on, and saw a large room filled with artifacts. It wasn't just relics from the nineteenth century. There were statues that looked African and Asian, items made of solid gold reminiscent of the Mayans and Aztecs, tablets with Viking runes on them, and futuristic devices I didn't understand. An entire wall was covered in large-framed paintings of dark-skinned Native Americans with curly hair decorated with feathers, and black people styled as kings and queens in European castles.

What was this place? And how . . . why had Abner collected it?

I stopped in front of each painting until I caught my breath. I was staring at a large, gilded frame with gorgeous ornamental trim.

It looked like it would fit the empty space on the wall in the museum.

The painting was not of one man, rather it was a couple. A man and woman. The woman clearly was Susannah, beautiful and lushly drawn, this time in an exquisite gown of violet. Her lips were ruby red, her eyes flashing for the artist, and her hair fell in sensuous waves past her shoulders.

Beside her was a man. Short, and powerfully built like a bulldog but with proud, defiant features. Longish black hair pulled back into a ponytail at the nape of his neck, a beard covering his chin. He was dressed in royal blue breeches, a red overcoat, a white frilly blouse, and white stockings ending in black leather buckled shoes.

He was posed in profile, his eyes on the woman, his gaze one of adoration. One of his hands held hers in a courtly manner, while the other held a handkerchief with a fleur de lis stitched on it.

The man was Abner Robbins.

FORTY-SIX

I'd never been to Abner's home.

While the museum was his family's ancestral estate, he lived on the far edge of the property. You could barely find the driveway – a narrow dirt road – unless you knew where to look. I drove my car down the road, kicking up gravel and dust clouds along the way until I came to a large twelve-foot, black, wrought-iron gate with a security box. I rolled down my window and pressed the call button.

A moment later, Abner's voice crackled through. I identified myself and asked if I could visit him.

There was a pregnant pause. 'Sure, Sidney. Come on up.'

I rolled my window up, watched the tall gates slide open and drove through. It was another half mile before his house, a large imposing Romanesque villa with sweeping columns, came into view.

Abner was on the porch in his shirtsleeves and breeches. His suspenders hung down to his waist and he wore boots.

As I took in his visage, I wondered if I'd gone back in time when I'd passed through the gates. But no . . . I glanced at my cell phone which still had service. I hadn't traveled through time.

He carried a fishing pole in his hand with several large silvery fish hanging down from the line.

I got out of the car. Waved. 'That your dinner?'

He nodded. 'I have a pond out back.' He jerked a thumb. 'And a fire going if you don't mind. I was just about to fry these.'

Nodding, I followed him around the side of the house to a large backyard with a roaring fire pit and low-slung chairs made of soft leather and wood around it. A black cast iron pan lay in the grass, an open jar of lard glistening beside it.

'I see you keep with the old ways at home.'

He chuckled. 'In some ways, yes. But I do have electricity and running water. Wonderful inventions those.'

'I'll bet.' I sat in one of the chairs and he followed suit.

'I've got corn roasting over there.' He pointed to a bare patch of ground where I assumed he'd dug a pit full of coals for roasting. 'And I've got salad from my garden.' He pointed to a modest patch of greenery a few yards away. 'Nothing like your grandmother's but it's enough for me.'

He leaned over the fire, placing the fish in the pan and beginning to cook it while I tried to find the words to start the conversation. How did one accuse another of being a time traveler? I cleared my throat. 'Elias?'

There was a heavy silence, and Abner stared into the flames, his face frozen as the red and orange flames danced between us. I thought I'd made a mistake.

He finally looked up. 'Yes?'

My throat dried up in that moment. 'It's true? You're Elias, not Abner.'

He shook the pan in the flames, moving the fish around in the lard. 'How'd you figure it out?'

I found my voice. 'Your stash. In the park?'

He nodded, his grin rueful. 'I couldn't get rid of that painting. Not just because it showed me with the love of my life, but . . . it was the last remnant of who I used to be. A life that seems almost like a dream now.' His eyes met mine. 'Abner's not real. He never was. I made him up when I came forward. Through time.'

I exhaled sharply. 'You're my grandmother's father.'

His features melted into an expression of pure love. 'And I'm *your* great-grandfather.'

I couldn't stop looking at him. 'We have to tell Grams.' He nodded, and I continued. 'At the gala you said that I'd eventually see that everything you'd done was in the best interest of my family. You meant . . . our family.'

The smell of fried fish, delicious and tantalizing, rose in the air around us. 'I went through a lot to find Isla, to create an heir with her. Only to have her die, and our child lost to time.'

'You didn't know where Daphne took my grandmother?'

'No. I went into a deep depression after Isla was killed. And I'd heard the rumors that the baby had died as well. I traveled to western North Carolina, found a cabin and just stayed there, walking in the woods, fishing, spending time with the natives once they'd have me. It calmed my spirit and brought me back to life.

'By the time I'd returned home, I was unrecognizable with my beard and leather skins.' He chuckled, and removed the fish from the fire, poking it with a stick and lifting it sizzling into the air, inspecting it for doneness. Satisfied, he placed it back into the pan. 'One day, I was in my study, removed a favorite book and a letter from Isla fell out. She'd written it the night before she was to . . . be *punished*, and had Daphne slip it into a book she was sure I'd read soon. But I hadn't because of my malaise . . .'

He sat the pan down, a troubled look on his face. 'She explained the intrigue she and Daphne had plotted to save our daughter and preserve the line. I found out too late that Daphne tried to wait for me before going forward, but worried for the safety of your grandmother she left while I was gone.'

'What did you do?'

'I went after them. Only, the time portal in the tunnels seems to lead right back to Robbinsville. Just different time periods. An odd time loop.'

I thought of Marta then. She was stuck in that time loop, destined to end up in Robbinsville, whatever time period she tried to run to. A just punishment for someone who wanted to place everyone in a virtual reality environment.

'I went through many different time periods and timelines before I found them.'

'I don't understand. Periods *and* timelines? Like the metaverse theory?'

'Yes, exactly. I went to places where I was already there or I'd died . . . It was strange to be sure.'

'Why did you stay in *this* timeline and period?'

'I'd just arrived and was walking along the river when I found Isla's writing box.'

My heart jumped. 'The one that carried the crown?'

'Yes. It was like a sign for me. I plucked it out of the grass and carried it with me back to town. Once I was settled, my cover as Abner established, I gave it to a shopkeeper for safekeeping, and told Daphne where to find it when the time was right.'

He shifted in his seat, and I heard his knees pop.

'Before I landed here, I saw the Tolivers in other timelines where they were in power, places where magic was still known, witches were oppressed and witch hunters were treated like kings and rockstars . . . It was the reason I decided to keep Matty close. I needed to have an eye on him. And for a very long time he was no trouble. Just doing his job. I thought – rather, I hoped – he'd ended the witch-hunting business, but we both know he was only biding his time.

'In this timeline Elias really had died in a mining accident, so I just stepped in as a family member and took over the business and waited for my daughter – for Fiona – to grow up, have children . . .' His vision blurred. 'All so I could be here with you.'

'Because . . . only I could find the stone,' I said, still not under-standing why.

'Others may have been able to decode the clues, but only Isla's heir could reveal the final location of the stone.' He checked the fish for heat, then grabbed the stick and brought it to his mouth, biting into the tender flesh with an appreciative moan.

'So who hid the stone if not President Madison? And how did it get here in Robbinsville of all places?'

'That was your grandmother's plot. Isla was a brilliantly crafty woman. It was also her undoing. When the English came for the original stone, the Daughters protecting it did a simple switcheroo and the English took the fake to London while we kept the original in Scotland, moving it around to different locations every fifty years or so.

'As you can imagine it became tedious having to move the stone around the Scottish countryside. When your great-grandmother was of age, she decided the Stone would be moved to America. She disguised herself amongst the immigrants and traveled first to New Orleans with Susannah, and then, eventually landing in North Carolina.'

'The stone with her?'

'Yes.'

'And the clues? Hiding the stone?'

'All Isla. Her idea to hide the stone on the property. She went to Josiah knowing about his work with encrypting secrets, and he took it from there. The clues were created especially . . . for you.'

'For me?'

'She had the gift of prophecy.'

'Like Grams, with her dreams . . .' I realized. Just like she'd known I'd come for a visit.

'Isla knew you'd return to Robbinsville as an adult.' A lopsided grin appeared above his beard. 'Knew you'd look like her too.' He reached out and patted my arm. 'I got impatient and helped you along.' He dipped his head. 'I'm sorry about that, by the way. I know I can be a bit . . . presumptuous, but I knew you were my granddaughter. I knew you'd come eventually, and I knew you'd eventually understand. You do, don't you? Understand?'

I nodded, watching him finish eating his fish before going to the dirt and digging up the roasting corn.

He glanced over his shoulder at me. 'I've been out of the loop for a while. I was trying to get my agency back. First my beloved wife died. Then Isla who I also came to love had her life ended by Toliver. Then Daphne spirited my daughter away. Everything had been taken from me. I needed to get something back. And that began by bringing you here to Robbinsville. Back to me. Where you belong. Can you see that?'

I could feel his sadness and pain wafting off him in thick waves. He was being honest, his sincerity ugly and raw like a fresh bruise. 'I see.'

'Having you call me Elias a few minutes ago was the sweetest thing I've heard in decades. Just the sound of my name.' He retrieved a handful of corn wrapped in its silk and deposited it on a wooden tray.

'I suppose I should be calling you Great-grandpa,' I teased.

He almost smiled, but his pain was acute.

'And President Madison? How did he become involved?'

He shrugged, looking embarrassed. 'Your thesis.'

'My thesis?'

'On one of my travels forward, or rather sideways, I encountered a version of you.'

I laughed. 'I'm having a hard time believing this.'

'And yet . . .' He splayed his hands wide. 'I was in a different timeline, *so* like this one, but your father and mother were slightly different. You were different . . .' He searched my face, then shook his head as if it weren't a good memory. 'I asked you to help me find the stone. I explained everything to you. No subterfuge. The secret society. The artifact . . . nothing was held back. And you turned me down flat. Laughed in my face actually.'

I pressed a hand against my chest. 'Me?' Laughing, I shook my head. 'I would never.'

He wagged a finger at me. 'But you did. And nothing I could do would deter you. In that timeline, you were . . . Harder. More skeptical. No softness like you have now.'

Frowning, I considered his words. 'I'd call myself a skeptic now – well, before I knew magic existed – still exists,' I corrected.

'So, based on my interaction with you I came up with the idea of the letter. I knew you'd studied Madison, considered him a personal favorite . . .' He searched my face. 'You said you'd only do it for money . . . a lot of money, and you'd need to be out of a job on top of all that before you'd consider going on a wild goose chase for me.'

'Really? I said all of that?'

His lips moved into a lopsided smile, 'Yeah.'

I laughed. 'So you just made it all happen.'

He picked up a stalk of corn, weighed it in his hand and began peeling it. 'I guess I did.'

'And now?'

'And now . . .' He sighed, exhaling slowly and his shoulders slumped. 'You're here. You can carry the torch.'

'I wouldn't know where to start. I mean, supposedly I'm a witch? I'm a . . . princess from this ancient magical bloodline? I have no idea what any of this means or how I'm supposed to move forward.'

'You're none of those things,' he said, voice rough with emotion. He leaned forward and reached for my hand.

I stared at his large hand for a moment then took it.

"Don't you get it? The bloodline. The ceremony. The crown . . . Yes, it's all in secret. For now. But you're royalty in exile. Sidney . . . You're a queen."

I stared at him, his intensity searing me the core. I tried to speak but my voice came out in a whisper. I shook my head. 'It's just going to take some time . . .

He released my hand, a rueful grin on his face. 'I'm afraid you don't have time.'

'Why do you say that?'

'I'm tired.' He sighed, his expression somber. He waved a hand over his face. 'All of this? A glamour. And I don't know how much more I can take. I'm well over a hundred years.' He laughed. 'You don't want to know how old I am. What I really look like.'

I quickly did the math. Closer to two hundred was more like it. 'The sweats?' I recalled what Daphne said about side effects of long term glamours.

He nodded. 'I'm not well. The sweats are just a sign you can see. My bones and joints hurt. I require constant top-ups. Not just for my appearance but for my general health. Streaks of white show in my hair when I'm emotional or if I'm too tired—'

'Like after the fight with Llew.'

'My face is a patchwork of wrinkles. It ain't pretty, that's for sure. I feel a million years old.'

I moved closer to him, taking his free arm and snuggling it under my own, I pressed my face to his shoulder. This man was my great-grandfather. 'You know, for a while I was worried that you were involved with Llew's death. I'm really glad you weren't.'

'That guy had it coming. Can't say I'm sad to see the last of him. He seemed to really have it in for my family . . . That includes you.'

'I know.' I told him about the file he had on me. About the Special Projects Division.

'They may send someone else after you.'

'Then I guess I'll have to be ready.'

'Sounds like a plan.' He leaned into my hug. 'But one more thing I need from you . . . Run the museum for me.'

I gently pulled away from him so I could see him eye to eye. 'But—'

'No buts. You're family. You're beyond qualified. Let me step down, so you can become the director of the museum and the family trust.'

I considered his words.

'I'll still be around, help you however you need. Train you. But you taking over the museum will give me a chance to finally . . .' He laughed. 'Retire. Do you have any idea how long I've been working?'

I joined in his laughter. 'You must be exhausted.'

He stopped laughing, and his expression cleared. 'Managing the museum, taking over as the new director will be the perfect cover for your true purpose.'

My gaze met his. 'Which is?'

'Taking down the Order of Apophis.'

I told him about Marta.

He dragged a palm across his face. 'She could be anywhere. Without a scribe or witch for guidance, she could spend the next fifty years traveling to Robbinsville in every decade a hundred years in both ways.'

'I guess she'll be too busy to cause us any trouble. A girl can hope?'

'There will be others. And as soon as they know she's missing. They'll be coming for you and your father.'

'Then I better get ready.'

He wrapped his arm around me again, and I leaned into it. 'I'll help you. With my dying breath if necessary, don't you worry about that.' The silence, thick and heavy settled around us, the air sweet with magnolia, crickets chirping their night song and lightning bugs flickering in the distance.

He cleared his throat and began to walk to his chair. 'Hungry?'

I crossed my arms. Is that what we were doing now? Pretending like everything was normal? Like he wasn't a time-traveling grandpa from another century? Like he wasn't a member of a secret society? Like I wasn't descendant from an Egyptian princess?

'I know you're a vegetarian. I've got a baked potato and some roasted corn with your name on it.' He raised one eyebrow.

My stomach grumbled.

Yeah, that's exactly what we were doing.

And I guess . . . that's what I was doing too.

Author's Note

When I lived in Virginia several years ago, our family made numerous trips to Colonial Williamsburg and the homes of George Washington, Thomas Jefferson and James Madison. I lived in an area full of Colonial American history and Revolutionary War-era sites, and I knew I would one day write a story that somehow incorporated this time in America's history and most definitely include a history museum. More recently, I've spent time in Colonial Beach, a small cozy town on the Potomac with its own rich American heritage. Alexander Graham Bell, a Scotsman, had a summer home there, and both George Washington and James Monroe were born there. A house used in one of my favorite television shows, AMC's *Turn*, about George Washington's ring of spies is also located there.

I began this story in 2018, and over the years it has evolved to include a search for an artefact and women with paranormal abilities, two elements I didn't foresee in my original vision. But as I dove deeper into the story, both of these elements 'wrote' their way into my novel. However, what I always planned for this story was to incorporate real historical figures in a fun and interesting way.

An important character in the story is Josiah Willoughby. He is inspired by a real person – Thomas Day, a visionary cabinetmaker and entrepreneur, who defied the constraints of his time, achieving remarkable success during an era when most African-Americans faced enslavement, and free blacks confronted severe restrictions on their mobility and pursuits. To my knowledge he was not a cryptographer, nor did he hide secrets during the Revolutionary War. That's all me! I also tweaked the years when he was alive to match my story. But otherwise, much of Josiah's background is similar to Thomas Day's.

Born into a family with a legacy in cabinetry, Day established his workshop in 1827 in Milton, North Carolina. He meticulously crafted fine furniture and designed architectural interiors that catered to an elite clientele of presidents, governors and plantation owners. Fusing his unique motifs with popular designs, he fashioned a style unmistakably associated with his workshop. I learned about Thomas Day when I interned at a black-owned film studio in Yanceyville, North Carolina called Carolina Pinnacle Studios many years ago. Milton is right next door, and I discovered that Thomas lived and worked in the area. Fast forward a few years, and my mother brought home a chair from an estate sale Thomas Day created. Needless to say, I knew I'd write about him one day as well.

I also reference Benjamin Banneker, a self-taught African-American mathematician, astronomer and surveyor who was born a free man in Maryland in 1731; Joshua Johnson, a pioneering African-American portrait painter active during the late 18th and early 19th centuries; and George Horton, the first African-American in the South to publish a book (of poems), *The Hope of Liberty*, in 1829. My mother went to a high school named for him and I'd heard her mention Horton High, with no clue what the 'Horton' referenced until I researched African-American poets writing during this era. George Horton lived in North Carolina. He was known far and wide for his poetic genius and was even paid to write poems.

This story is set in a fictional town located near New Bern, North Carolina. New Bern residents Robert Hay, a Scottish immigrant who was a skilled woodworker, chair maker, wagon maker, carriage maker, and briefly a house carpenter in the early 19th century, and Senator John Stanly, who was born in 1774, and was a prominent Federalist congressman and legislator, are both referenced. Interestingly enough, Stanly had a half-brother named John C. Stanly, a man classified as African-American who was born a slave but freed, and went on to become a successful entrepreneur, land developer, and plantation owner who was the largest slave owner in Craven County. John C., as he was known, is not in the book, but I may have to write him into another.

So much interesting history . . . I love mysteries, especially those with a foundation in the past. I hope *An Intrigue Of Witches* encourages you to learn more about these interesting figures in North Carolina and American history. And of course, there is the myth of Scota, daughter of an Egyptian pharaoh and heir to the Davidic line who brought the Stone of Scone to a land that would eventually be named . . . Scotland. It's all true! At least, the myth is – yes, it's all myth and there are so many versions of the Scota origins story, I may have combined one or two versions for my novel. But then, I tried to be true to the legend and write it as authentically as possible. It was fun to speculate the ways in which the myth could be true, and how it would present itself in contemporary times.

I hope you have enjoyed the way in which I weave fantasy and history and mystery together. Thanks for reading,

Esme xxooxx